THE INITIATION

CHRIS BABU

PERMUTED
PRESS

A PERMUTED PRESS BOOK

The Initiation
© 2018 by Chris Babu
All Rights Reserved
First Permuted Press Hardcover Edition: February 2018

ISBN: 978-1-68261-848-6

Cover art by Ryan Truso
Interior Design and Composition by Greg Johnson/Textbook Perfect

PERMUTED
PRESS
Permuted Press, LLC
New York • Nashville
permutedpress.com
Published in the United States of America

For Lily

I hope this book always reminds you
it's never too late to follow your dreams.

New America

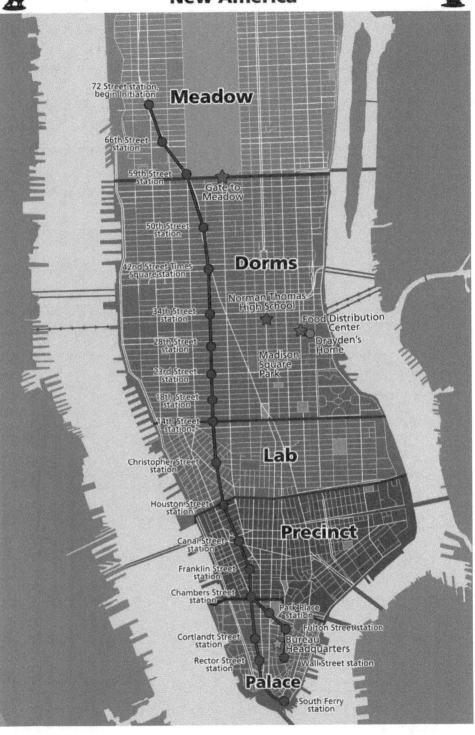

72 Street station,
begin Initiation

Meadow

66th Street
station

59th Street
station

Gate to
Meadow

50th Street
station

Dorms

42nd Street Times
Square station

Norman Thomas
High School

Food Distribution
Center

34th Street
station

Drayden's
Home

28th Street
station

Madison
Square
Park

23rd Street
station

18th Street
station

14th Street
station

Lab

Christopher Street
station

Houston Street
station

Precinct

Canal Street
station

Franklin Street
station

Chambers Street
station

Park Place
station

Fulton Street station

Cortlandt Street
station

Bureau
Headquarters

Rector Street
station

Wall Street station

Palace

South Ferry
station

CHAPTER 1

Drayden was lounging in bed, his physics textbook balanced on his gangly leg, when the front door exploded with a splintering crash.

He sat bolt upright.

Footsteps thundered through the apartment. Boots, by the sound of it, stomped past his closed bedroom door. Voices boomed through the walls.

Drayden leapt off the bed and tiptoed in bare feet across the cold hardwood floor. He pressed his ear against the door.

A high-pitched scream ripped through the air.

Mom?

Hands trembling, Drayden swung the door open to the dim living room, and froze.

The same room he'd always known stood before him: the floors dull, hardly a trace of the shine they once had; the shkatty burnt-orange couch, now too short for him to lie on without curling up his legs; the mahogany coffee table, missing one leg, with an old bottle of ack doing the job instead.

Guardians occupied the cramped space now, decked out in their black, military-like uniforms. With bulging eyes and clenched jaws, they brandished semi-automatic rifles. The typical Guardians

patrolled the streets half asleep, but these guys were muscular and heavily armed. Special Forces. Two Guardians gripped his petite Korean mother, one on each arm. She struggled against their grasp, her eyes wide and wild. She was breathing heavily, on the verge of tears. Her normally straight black hair was tangled into a wispy mess.

"Mom!" Drayden screamed.

His father cowered in the corner, his gaze fixed to a spot on the floor, his hands clasped in front of him.

Drayden's brother Wesley emerged from his bedroom, mouth open and brow furrowed. A Guardian faced him with his weapon drawn.

"Freeze, chotch."

Wesley obeyed, for the moment. His eyes met Drayden's. They showed fear and confusion, but something else too. Anger. No, rage.

Drayden turned left, only to find a gun in his own face.

The Guardian had menacing black eyes and wore his long black hair in a ponytail. "Same deal, string bean," he snarled. "Stay put, right there."

Drayden couldn't move even if he wished. Adrenaline coursed through his body, like when those flunks at school tried to pick a fight with him. His legs turned to rubber. He'd trained in jiu-jitsu a bit, but he'd never had a gun pointed at him before.

"Mom? Dad?" he pleaded.

His mother sniffled. "It's all right, Dray. I don't know why they're here. Everything's going to be fine, honey. Just do what they say."

"This isn't what I think it is. Is it?"

"Quiet!" a Guardian barked.

A Chancellor strode through the front door, now permanently open, thanks to the battering ram lying on the floor. She was an elderly woman with short gray hair, cut like a boy's. Her pale cheeks were reddened from the chilly April night, and her piercing blue

eyes bore holes in them. She wore Guardian black as well, in the form of a baggy suit—standard issue for Chancellors—rather than tight military fatigues. A red pin identifying her as a Bureau member stood out on her chest. Chancellors worked closely with the Guardians, acting as society's judges.

She faced Drayden's mother with her nose in the air. "Maya Coulson, you have been found guilty of conspiring against the Bureau of New America. You are hereby sentenced to exile. You have ten minutes to gather a few things and say goodbye to your family."

No, no, no!

This couldn't be happening. The room spun and spots clouded Drayden's field of vision. When tears welled up, he tried to blink them away.

Conspiring against the Bureau? Exiled?

His enraged mother battled to free herself from the Guardians' grip, but they were too strong. "How dare you!" she roared. "I haven't conspired against anyone! Where's the proof?" She was animalistic, seething. "This is my family. You can't take me away from them!"

The Chancellor sneered at his mother. "Mrs. Coulson," she said in a most patronizing tone, "as you well know, we have no mandate to show proof or provide an explanation. The Bureau handles these decisions with the utmost consideration and care. Once made, our decision is final. You have nine minutes left, so I suggest you use them wisely."

The Guardians lowered their weapons and released his mother. Drayden's father slouched, his eyes locked on the floor.

Say something! Drayden willed, his disgust welling up. What kind of man would let his wife be hauled away like this? He glanced at his brother.

At eighteen, Wesley was two years older than Drayden. While Drayden was taller at six feet, Wesley was a much bulkier kid, built up by lifting heavy crates of food all day. He even dwarfed some Guardians in the room. Wesley's eyes focused on the nearest Guardian's rifle, which hung down on his left side.

Uh-oh.

"Wes, no!" Drayden yelled at the exact moment his brother dove for the rifle.

Wesley punched the gun out of the Guardian's hand, jettisoning the weapon toward the center of the room. When he lunged for the fallen gun, another Guardian cracked him on the skull with the butt of his rifle. Wesley crumpled to the floor, a huge gash near his temple oozing blood down his face. He moaned in pain, his hand clasped over the cut.

What a flunk, Drayden thought. What did Wes think would happen? Still, part of him admired Wesley's fearlessness. Drayden could never do something like that.

Their father rushed to Wesley's aid and applied pressure to the wound with his shirt sleeve. "Hold still, Wes," he whispered.

The Guardians retreated to the edges of the living room.

Drayden tugged on his left earlobe, debating the few options. Taking on a room full of armed soldiers was dumb. There had to be another way. He shook out his hands and approached the Chancellor.

Two Guardians stormed over and blocked him.

With as firm a voice as he could muster, he addressed her from behind the men. "Chancellor, clearly there's been some sort of a mistake. My mother isn't part of any conspiracy." He racked his brain for anything left from mock debating at school last year. *Use logic, not personal attacks.* "I'm assuming you didn't do the investigating yourself. Someone else did it for you." No expression on the woman's face at all. *An alternative solution.* Maybe that. "What

harm would it do to detain her overnight in a cell while you verify it? I'm confident you'll find out this is all a mix-up. If you force her outside the walls right now and discover later you were wrong, she can't return."

The Chancellor cocked her head, a scornful expression flitted across her face. "Young man, there has been no mistake. The information has already been verified." She checked her watch. "Now, in eight minutes, you will never see your mother again. I recommend you make the most of it." She glared at him with those deadly blue eyes.

Drayden shrunk away from her, wishing he had Wesley's guts. How could someone be so unreasonable? This woman knew battering rams and power, not compassion.

The moment was surreal. His mom, the most important person in his life, would be unceremoniously cast off in minutes and he was powerless to stop it. He ran to his mother and clung to her. "Mom, no."

She hugged him back.

Drayden yearned to hold her forever. So many memories flooded his mind. At eleven, when he'd battled an infection from that damn rusty slide, she'd stayed by his side for weeks and they'd played cards nonstop. All he'd wanted for his eighth birthday was to climb the Empire State Building. They'd snuck in, and it took all day, but they did it together. Mom pointed out Brooklyn and Queens, and she brought an avocado to share, which was heaven.

Of course, nobody could forget the time she marched down to school when Wesley got in trouble. She caught him hanging out with the winoozes around the corner, drinking ack from a flask. Although he'd dwarfed her even at fourteen, that didn't stop her from yanking him up by his shirt and physically dragging him home, humiliating him in front of all his flunk friends. No, Drayden was going to stay right here, clutching her tight.

She eased back and wiped away her tears one eye at a time. "I need you to listen to me. You're going to be fine. The three of you have each other. Your father and Wesley need you now. You're so smart, baby, you'll always be fine." She smiled the unhappiest smile Drayden could imagine. "I'm not worried about you at all. You're a strong, strong boy."

No, I'm not, he thought.

Across the living room, Dad helped Wesley to his feet. Wesley's knees wobbled as he stood. The Guardians spoke in hushed tones around the edges of the living room. The stoic Chancellor hovered by the splintered door, observing the family.

"I'm sure you know this already," Mom said, "but this conspiracy stuff is complete hogwash. I have no clue why this happened."

Drayden hesitated. "Maybe I can figure out who did this," he said under his breath.

"No," she snapped, her whisper forceful. "I don't want you getting in trouble. Besides, you could never find that out, the Bureau would never reveal it."

"Not from here in the Dorms, but I could from the Palace."

"No!"

She knew exactly what he was thinking. He'd never been able to fool her, ever. Oh, how he'd tried! It had seemed like a game until now.

"I can enter the Initiation. Then I could get into the Palace."

"Absolutely not," his mother fired back. "Finding out won't matter anyway, I can't ever return. Do you understand me? *Promise* me you won't do that."

Drayden jutted his jaw and clenched his fists. "It's not right. They can't exile people for no reason."

She glanced around the room. "Dray, honey, I'm almost out of time. I have to say goodbye to your dad and brother now. Promise."

His mind raced. These might be his last words to his mother. The thought made him sick to his stomach. He lowered his eyes. "Okay."

"Good." She placed her hands on his cheeks. "Baby, I love you more than you'll ever know. You be strong for me."

His tears flowed. "What about you? You'll be *outside*. Nobody ever comes back from outside the walls. What's going to happen to you? Who's going to take care of you if you get sick?"

"Dray, you know me better than that." She forced that unhappy smile again.

Acid crept up the back of Drayden's throat.

"Your mother is strong, baby. I'll find a way to stay safe. Trust me. I bet others have survived. There's probably a community of people out there somewhere."

He looked at her hopefully through blurry eyes.

She nodded with authority. "Yeah. Yeah. It's been ages, hasn't it? The superbug might be ancient history."

Drayden was bawling now, barely able to hear her.

"Don't worry about me. Just take care of your father and brother." She kissed his forehead. "I love you so much."

"I love you too, Mom." He wasn't sure the words made any sense through his sobs.

His mother pulled away and crossed the room. His strong, brave mother. She hugged his dad, and stood on her tippy-toes to whisper in his ear. He towered over her, his baggy pajamas sagging on his lanky frame, yet he seemed small next to her. And wooden, in shock. He wouldn't look at her. She moved to Wesley and spent a few minutes with him as he struggled to fight back tears himself. He closed his eyes and pursed his lips.

Wesley finally said, "I will, Mama, I promise," and opened his eyes to look straight at Drayden.

The few feet between Drayden and his brother felt like a thousand miles. A whole country. A whole planet. His mom was his life. He hadn't realized it till that moment but now he knew it with every cell in his body. With her gone, he was alone.

While she left to change into warmer clothes, his father came to life once again. He stuffed a few essentials in a backpack for her: an extra set of clothes, a pair of shoes, two bottles of drinkable water, a box of matches, a knife, a banana, a cantaloupe, and three uncooked potatoes.

Drayden watched, uselessly cataloging each item, registering the futility of it. Because none of it mattered for shkat. No one lived outside the walls. Outside was death.

Dad stopped when nothing else fit. Mom returned in tan wool pants. Ironically, they'd been a rare gift from the Bureau for all her backbreaking work managing their local Food Distribution Center. She'd been with the FDC all Drayden's life. Exile was her reward.

Drayden's tears dried. Coldness settled into his gut.

Mom was also wearing her favorite sweatshirt, likely one of the last remaining pieces of cotton clothing in the entire city. The ripped blue New York Knicks hoodie now only read "N— Y—r— — cks." She flopped on the backpack and tugged the straps tight, as if she were going on a hike.

They all stood in silence. Time seemed to stop for the briefest of moments.

It was too much. Drayden broke the spell, ran up, and hugged his mother one last time. He kissed her cheek, and told her he loved her over and over.

She smiled, but her eyes radiated heartbreak. And for the first time, fear. The Guardians began stirring again, and without a word, the Chancellor marched out the door. As swiftly as the whole ordeal began, it ended. The Guardians escorted his mom out of their apartment, and out of their lives forever.

Drayden stared at the crack in the ceiling above his bed. Curved, shaped like an elephant, the paint hung down in a strip where the trunk would be. Sleep was out of the question. Cursing, he scrambled to his feet and tore off the elephant's trunk. The paint scrap lay limp in his hand, weightless. His anger felt just as hot, his sorrow just as wrenching.

He flopped down onto his back.

Was his mother still inside the city walls? Besides the Guardians and Chancellors, nobody had ever witnessed the conclusion of an exile, whatever happened after the Bureau snatched people from their homes. The Guardians weren't exactly a quiet bunch, particularly when drunk, and over the years the process became common knowledge. Exiles usually occurred at night. The Guardians drove the exiled in an electric bus to the top of the city in what used to be called Inwood. A Chancellor escorted them to guarantee the person wasn't abused.

So considerate. The Bureau ensured his mother's protection right before they pushed her to her probable death.

When they reached the old Henry Hudson Bridge and removed the exiled from the bus, the begging, pleading, and crying usually began. The Guardians opened a gate, and basically shoved the person out onto the bridge.

There were stories of people lingering so long the Guardians would threaten to shoot them if they didn't cross the bridge into the Bronx. Guardians manned the few gates in the walls surrounding New America around the clock. Supposedly some of the exiled would return and try to negotiate their re-entry, which of course never worked. For one thing, the law said that once you were out, you were out. Plus, letting people back in would expose everyone to deadly bacteria. No exiled person had ever been seen

again. Everyone assumed they died, most likely from sickness or starvation.

Unfortunately, the exiles happened up in the Bronx instead of toward Queens. His mother was tough, Drayden knew that, but she didn't know the Bronx. If they used the Fifty-Ninth Street Bridge on the east side of New America, at least she might know her way around. She grew up in Queens, Pre-Confluence—PreCon, people called it—before the Bureau erected walls around the city. Back when New America was still called Manhattan. Her family lived in a community of other Koreans in the Flushing neighborhood. Though Drayden wished he could have seen it, nobody born inside New America had ever been outside its walls. Hell, pretty much nobody had left their own zone.

Zone was everything here.

The Bureau drilled the zone system into kids' heads as soon as they could talk. Their first words might've been "mama" and "dada" but their third word was probably "zone." New America was divided by job type into four residential zones, Zones A through D. Because of the Bureau's stunning lack of naming creativity, nobody called the zones by their letters. Zone D, where Drayden's family and the rest of the working stiffs lived, was known as the Dorms. Nobody could leave the Dorms since everyone had to remain in their zone, with a few exceptions for work. In case someone blacked out drunk, or suffered a prolonged brain fart and forgot, physical walls separated the zones. They were the same twenty-five-foot-high concrete blockades encircling the entire city.

Drayden dragged himself out of bed. With the heat broken again, the frigid air attacked his skin within seconds. The Bureau outlawed lights after 10:00 p.m. to conserve power, but the moonlight glistened on the floor just enough to see. He pulled out a wooden box from beneath his bed and rifled through some dusty toys and clothes. He found his green New York Yankees baseball

cap. It was a gift from Mom for his ninth birthday, and he hadn't worn it in years. Drayden longed to have her near him, a piece of her with him at all times.

Shivering, he adjusted the band in the back, punched the inside a few times, rounded the brim, and pulled it on. Though barely visible in the darkness, he viewed himself in the full-length mirror beside his bed. He straightened the cap. Drayden never wished more that he looked like his mother, that he could recognize her when he saw himself. He'd only inherited her olive skin. Otherwise he was all Dad—tall, skinny, dark brown hair, and hazel eyes. Wesley, on the other hand, looked Korean and was the spitting image of their mother.

Drayden jumped back into his warm bed and pulled up the covers. Without Mom around, their rock, what would happen to them? They couldn't just carry on as if nothing had happened. Wesley might start hitting the ack again. Drayden couldn't imagine Dad withdrawing from life any further, though he supposed it was possible. How in the world would he take care of the family like Mom asked?

Maybe Dad would have some idea about the truth behind her exile. Nobody loved the Bureau, but Drayden had always respected it. They did save humanity, after all. The occasional exile was part of life in New America. Still, he'd never considered this moment, never imagined what it would be like, because you had to break the law to be exiled. Major or minor, some crime needed to be committed. He never would, and he was positive his mother wouldn't either.

Drayden fancied himself a budding scientist. Science was about order, and expected results. Cause and effect. This exile didn't make any sense in a scientific way. If people were exiled for committing crimes, but his mother would never commit one, how could she have been exiled? It was unusual and illogical. Something was different and frightening about it. Either the Bureau made a

mistake, or some other factor entirely was at play. There was only one way to figure it out. Research.

He had to get to the bottom of this. He might never get Mom back, but he could uncover what happened. Somebody screwed up. Drayden was going to find out who.

CHAPTER 2

The scent of frying butter wafted into the room.

Drayden woke up, his stomach growling. He rubbed his eyes and then it hit him. Mom was the one who cooked breakfast every day.

He flew out of bed and sprinted to the kitchen, forgetting about his baseball cap, now cocked unevenly to one side of his head.

It wasn't her. His father towered over the stove in his pajamas. He turned, brushing his graying hair away from his eyes. "Good morning, Drayden."

Drayden hesitated. "Hi."

Dad adjusted his glasses. "I thought today might be a good day to have these eggs."

Ah yes, the eggs.

Twice a year, each family received *two* eggs in their weekly food allocation. Not everyone at the same time, obviously. The 250 chickens could only lay so many eggs each day, so the Bureau distributed them on a rigid schedule.

It was total shkat, receiving two eggs for a family of four every six months. Why even bother? Yet nobody turned down those eggs. It was such a treat, in fact, no occasion seemed special enough to eat them. Drayden believed they should just sit around the eggs, watch

them, admire them, caress them. Though illegal, some people sold their eggs on the black market.

Heated debates erupted in their family about how to cook and divide them. One time Mom tried to make something called a frittata, which was supposed to be all fancy and special. She ruined both eggs, but they ate it anyway. Some of his and Wesley's biggest fights involved those eggs. Needless to say, egg day was kind of a big deal.

Drayden plopped down at the rickety table. He must have slept right through the wake-up siren.

His father had no clue how to cook eggs. He was a genius though, so perhaps he would employ some scientific technique to engineer the perfectly fried egg. He'd been a doctor PreCon, but now he worked as a lab tech in one of the Dorm hospitals.

Right after the Confluence, the fragmented city huddled in survival mode. The early Bureau divided the population by skills to deal with the crisis. They immediately directed the scientists to work on food and power production, doctors to care for the sick, bus drivers to transport people, utilizing everyone's abilities. For convenience and efficiency, the Bureau housed like-skilled people together. That initiative was the genesis of the zone system.

Way back at the beginning, the Bureau granted people one opportunity to declare their skills. Ultimately, in whichever zone you started, you remained. Too bad Dad never mentioned to anyone he was a doctor. Doctors, scientists, teachers, and anyone else with intellectual expertise lived in Zone C, known as the Lab. He claimed he'd been in shock or something, so the brilliant Dr. Adam Coulson was relegated to lab tech, and they were stuck in the Dorms.

The rest of the usual sad breakfast appeared smaller than normal. Drayden poured a tiny glass of milk, careful not to spill a drop. Wasn't Dad going to say anything about Mom?

"Not too much," his father cautioned. "Leave some for Wesley."

Drayden downed the miniscule glass in one gulp and slammed it onto the table. "Suddenly you care about how much milk I have?"

His dad eyed him for a moment and returned to the eggs. As with eggs, milk ran in short supply. Every family received one liter per month. In reality, it was solid work from the measly thirty cows of New America.

Drayden snagged an orange and a puny chunk of bread. After twenty consecutive days of oranges, the smell alone made him gag. Luckily next month they'd score strawberries and cherries. Although they occasionally received fish, their diet was vegetarian with limited dairy. Butter was an elective, not included in the weekly food allocation, but available for sale if desired. Eating eggs cooked in butter was akin to being the Premier of New America for a day.

His father scraped a paltry pile of burnt scrambled eggs onto his plate. "Uh, I'm sorry. They didn't turn out so great."

It looked like...well, a turd. "This looks delicious, Dad. Nice job."

"I was just trying to make this day a little better, Drayden." He grabbed an orange. "Is that a new hat?"

Drayden shook his head. So this was what they were going to do: Pretend everything was fine.

Wesley strolled into the kitchen and sat at the table. The right side of his forehead bulged, the bruise purple, the cut crusted with dark blood. "Nice hat, bro," he said without looking up. He poured himself a miniature glass of milk. "You want me to try and teach you how to play baseball again? If you're gonna wear a cap like that, you gotta be able to play ball. I promise this time you won't accidentally bash yourself in the head with the bat."

Drayden flung an orange peel at him. "Shut up." His brother was always a comedian, a nerf. Drayden knew his way of dealing with the exile would be to make light of it.

"What...who voted for scrambled eggs?" Wesley asked. "And why are they black?"

"Dad's continuing his multi-year losing streak," Drayden grumbled under his breath.

"That's enough, Drayden," Dad snapped.

Drayden threw his hands in the air. "So, what, we're just going to pretend like nothing happened last night?"

Dad sat between them, removed his glasses and rubbed his eyes. "I'm not sure what there is to say. We just need to, you know, continue on with our lives the best we can."

Drayden dropped his half-eaten orange on the table. "That's it? That's all you have to say?"

Wesley set his fork down. "Dray."

"Well, what do you suggest?" Dad's voice shook, his eyes darting back and forth between them. "What do you want to do? Storm the Palace? Shoot the Premier?"

"Yeah!" Wesley yelled, smirking. "Let's go in there guns blazin'!"

"Oh, for crying out loud." Dad rubbed his eyes again, the bags under them darker than usual, making him appear older than his fifty-five years.

"People are exiled for murder and drug dealing," Drayden said. "Because they committed a *crime*. There's no way Mom did."

Of course Mom wasn't plotting against the Bureau. That accusation was ludicrous. Still, it wasn't like anyone trusted the Bureau. Plenty believed the Bureau over-exiled as a means of population control. Even with a high death rate because of crappy medical care, the population grew since they lacked birth control. Jailing people was too much of a hassle, so the Bureau exiled for every crime except the most minor ones. It made Drayden physically ill. The Bureau usually tried to appear thoughtful about it. Like, if a child robbed someone at the direction of their parents, the parents would be exiled, not the kid. The kid would be pardoned. There was nothing considerate about this one, though. They'd exiled a mother,

a pillar of the community, who everyone knew would never do anything wrong.

Drayden shoved his plate away. "Even if it's just skipping work or school, people who are exiled always broke some law."

Dad picked up his glasses and fumbled with the red electrical wire holding them together. "I don't have any idea what happened," he said quietly. "But the Bureau doesn't exile people without a reason."

Drayden gawked at him in stunned silence. "I can't believe this. You think it's true? Mom conspired against the Bureau? Is that why you didn't do anything?"

"What could any of us do?" Dad asked.

Drayden pushed back from the table and stood up so fast his chair tipped over backward. He narrowed his eyes, burning with disdain, and stormed out.

"Drayden!"

Drayden slammed his bedroom door behind him, his father's words slipping through.

"There were some things you didn't know about your mother..."

When Drayden stomped out of their brownstone on East Thirtieth Street, the smell hit him like a sledgehammer. This ugly city smelled just like he felt. You got used to it, most times not noticing it at all. But every so often, particularly after being inside for a while, it assaulted your senses.

Sewage. The complex sewage system of the old Manhattan required constant maintenance and fed into a sewage treatment plant outside the city. Surprising no one, that broke down, or rather backed up, immediately after the Confluence. Now the entire population lived on the far east side of New America. The Bureau congregated people in specific apartment buildings. It outfitted those with

new sewage lines that simply employed gravity and a pipe to dump into the East River, turning it into a giant cesspool.

Drayden hustled west toward school, at Park Avenue and Thirty-Third Street. The foul smell dissipated further away from the river, and disappeared by Lexington Avenue.

Not only was breakfast unusually meager, a power outage had followed it, meaning no hot water. The power had been going out more often these days. He couldn't shower, and he felt sticky and gross. His legs kept sticking to his green imitation jeans, and his gray t-shirt smelled. Hopefully his wool sweater would mute his stench.

It was a sunny but chilly April morning. He prayed the serenity of the city would calm him down. It was deserted and silent. The Bureau had cleared the streets of cars decades ago, pushing them to their final resting place at the bottom of the East River. The rising sun illuminated the windows of the abandoned buildings, which glowed brilliant blues, oranges, and yellows, many of them missing or broken. The structures featured gaping cracks across their facades, showing the effects of time.

He crossed Third Avenue and still hadn't seen anyone else. The external peacefulness did little to quell the fire in his soul or the ice in his heart. Instead, the isolation made it more acute. *Mom.* How dare his father suggest they do their best to carry on? Like Drayden could go to school and pretend everything was normal. He couldn't do it. He couldn't face all the other kids laughing and messing around, as if everything in the world was grand. They wouldn't know or care about his pain.

Drayden turned up Lexington Avenue and ran straight up the middle of the street. Huge cracks streaked through the pavement like bolts of lightning. He didn't even know where he was going, just not school. He passed Thirty-Third Street, where he should have gone left, and kept running. He turned left on Thirty-Fourth Street. His eyes were drawn to the Empire State Building glistening in the

distance. On this block, a skinny brick tower soared above the other buildings. The old Dumont Hotel.

Hotels, like most buildings, were long abandoned. The Dumont Hotel was special, known to teenagers by another name: the hookup house. It was thirty-seven stories of decrepit bedrooms, but still. Teenagers didn't really "date" in the Dorms since there wasn't anywhere to go or much to do. Teens "hung out" sometimes, in a park, or in empty buildings like the hookup house, which afforded some privacy. There wouldn't be anyone inside right now.

Drayden pulled open the shattered front door, darted through the lobby to the staircase, and began climbing. Each landing contained a door with a small window, revealing a rundown hallway lined with rooms. He'd only been here once, and it was with his mom, not a girl. To be used according to its namesake, the hookup house required someone to hook up with, so he'd never had a reason to use it. He and Mom had come to check out the view from the roof deck. That's where he was headed now.

By the fifteenth floor Drayden was out of breath and walking slow. By the twentieth, he had to rest. After a few minutes, he resumed his ascent and reached the top, stepping onto the roof. Besides empty bottles of ack strewn about, and cigarette butts littering the tiled roof, it was empty. A black wrought iron fence enclosed the small space.

Cold wind blasted his face as he walked to the west side of the deck, beholding the majestic Empire State Building again, thinking of his mother. He gripped the bars of the fence and shook with all his strength. He peered down at the precipitous drop, and for a hot second considered jumping. No. He pushed the thought away. That wasn't the answer.

Drayden pulled his baseball hat down tighter to ensure it didn't blow off. He walked to the south side of the building. You could see all the zones from up here. The World Trade Center, way

down in the Palace, dominated the skyline. The stupid Bureau, the governing body, resided there, at the very southern tip of New America in the former Financial District. Technically it was Zone A. Only the Bureau and its workers were allowed inside. Even the Guardians couldn't enter the Palace. The Bureau supposedly had its own military police force, cleaning crews, doctors, and everything else needed to be self-sufficient. Bureau members could travel anywhere in the city unchallenged. Clearly, since they could do whatever they wanted.

Just north of there, in the former TriBeCa, SoHo, and Lower East Side, was Zone B, called the Precinct. The Guardians, New America's police force, lived there. It was now Drayden's second most-hated zone after the Palace. The Guardians could basically go everywhere except the Palace. His favorite zone, the one in which his family *should* live, was just north of there. He gazed longingly at the Lab, which comprised the former Greenwich Village and East Village, wishing he was a scientist there. Instead he was stuck here in the shkatty Dorms where most people lived. The Dorms were bigger than the other three residential zones combined, stretching from Fourteenth Street all the way up to Fifty-Ninth Street.

Drayden headed to the north side of the building to get a view of the windmills, but too many skyscrapers blocked the view. Besides the four residential zones, the one non-residential zone was Zone E, called the Meadow. It went from Fifty-Ninth Street at the bottom of Central Park to the top of the city. It housed the solar and windmill farms, the food production, the farm animals, the water purification, the technology development, the recycling plants, and other activities that sustained society. The Meadow was strictly off limits to most, except the few members of each zone who worked there, certain Guardians, and of course, the Bureau.

What the hell was he doing up here anyway? Maybe he needed to physically be alone, to match how he felt. He needed to dig into

Mom's exile, but didn't know where to start. He wanted to fulfill Mom's request to take care of Dad and Wes, but wasn't sure how to do that either. Job placements were a few days away, yet he had no clue what job to take. He hated all the Dorm jobs. Drayden was lost.

He stared at the empty streets below, absorbing the loneliness and coldness of the city. He felt like the only person in the world. Time might as well have stopped, and Drayden had no idea how long he languished there.

He couldn't go back to school. The life he'd known was over. He could head to the FDC to talk to Wesley, return home, or simply wander the streets. Whatever he did, he needed to be careful. He was cutting school, a crime for which the Bureau could exile him. With only two days of school left this year, the teachers wouldn't care, but the Bureau might.

Drayden headed downstairs. Flight after flight. It was monotonous and numbing, which fit his mood. Twenty-second floor. Thirteenth floor. Eighth floor. Going down sure was easier. He was almost out when he stopped abruptly.

Voices. Below him.

He tiptoed down the metal steps to the third-floor landing, keeping his head away from the window in the doorway.

A discussion in the hallway. Two men.

It was hard to make out what they were saying. Drayden couldn't resist a peek through the small window.

A Guardian and a worker in overalls, like a plumber. The Guardian was older, bald, and overweight. He looked sweaty. The plumber handed over cash and the Guardian gave him a baggie full of...some herb. *Hay.*

Drayden drew in a quick breath. He wasn't supposed to see this.

The Bureau grew marijuana in the Meadow, and other drugs too, strictly for its own use. They also produced alcohol and tobacco, as electives available for sale in the Retail Centers. Drugs were

illegal for ordinary citizens. The Guardians transported them from the Meadow to the Palace. Some seized the opportunity to score a little side money, smuggling drugs into the Dorms. Usually they sold them to drug dealers behind the scenes, although Drayden was unaware of a Guardian ever selling them himself.

The Guardian turned his head and saw Drayden. "Hey!"

Oh shkat. Drayden bolted down the stairs, jumping four or five at a time. In an instant, he was in the lobby and burst out the doors. He turned left and sprinted west down Thirty-Fourth Street. Thinking ahead, he pulled off his backpack as he ran and stuffed his green hat inside. He tugged off his sweater too and shoved it in. He didn't want to give the Guardian anything noteworthy to remember him by.

"Get back here! Freeze!" the Guardian screamed from way behind.

No way. Not only was he cutting school, he'd busted the Guardian selling drugs. That guy would need him gone. Where should he go? School! He could disappear in there. He turned left on Park, darting the one short block to Thirty-Third Street. The Guardian would hopefully only see a tall, skinny boy with brown hair. As he reached Thirty-Third and turned left, the Guardian was just turning down Park Avenue, a full block behind.

Move! Drayden flung open the school doors and dashed inside. School was already in session and nobody monitored the door or lobby. He took a hard right and bolted up the stairs, two flights, into a hallway, and then an empty classroom.

He was out of breath and shaking, but safe. For now.

CHAPTER 3

Drayden slumped at a desk in the back of Mr. Kale's class, which would start in a few minutes, cold sweat coating his skin.

He couldn't believe his luck. The first time in his whole life he broke a rule, he got caught. Maybe the Guardian hadn't gotten a good look at him. Hopefully the flunk would just forget about the whole incident.

This day sucked already. Drayden couldn't even look at his father earlier, but now that he'd settled into a dull misery his father's parting words resurfaced. What had Dad meant? Drayden knew his mom. Of course he did. Better than anyone. He—

An arm slinked underneath his neck to choke him from behind.

Drayden instinctively tucked his chin. He pulled the arm down with his right hand, away from his throat in a textbook jiu-jitsu defense. His eyes followed the twisted arm up to the smiling face of Timmius Zade, his best friend.

"Ohhhh, I totally had you there," Tim said, releasing the hold. "You were mine, kid, done."

Tim was a blue belt in jiu-jitsu at a martial arts club, while Drayden was self-taught from a book. Yet Drayden dwarfed Tim, who only stood five foot seven. Even though Tim was more

experienced, Drayden's size gave him a distinct advantage when they grappled.

"Knock it off, man," Drayden said, sounding a little more serious than he intended. He shoved his friend away, only half playing. "I'm not in the mood."

Tim sat at an adjacent desk, his expression turning serious. "Hey, bud...I'm so sorry about your mom. I bumped into Wes this morning, and he told me. Think it's gotten around the school now. That's nuts. Where you been anyway? I been looking all over for you. You doing all right?"

"Not really." Drayden didn't want to tell Tim about the Guardian, because he felt stupid. "Oh man, I don't want everyone talking about my mom. Would *you* be all right?"

"Probably not. Though your mom is way cooler than mine. That's some serious shkat. Gotta be more to the story."

Drayden turned away and yawned, his eyelids heavy.

Tim glanced around the room and cleared his throat. "Hey, uh, I know what'll cheer you up." He nodded in the direction of the door.

She sat at a desk in the corner wearing a simple gray dress, her face buried in a book. With a delicate hand tucked up into her sleeve, she brushed a strand of blonde hair behind her ear.

Catrice Zevery, Drayden's first and only love. Or at least his crush. Either way, she wasn't aware of it. Time was running short to mention it to her as well. Tomorrow was Friday, the last day of school, and graduation and job placements occurred on Monday. He needed to make a move right away, but he knew he wouldn't, especially given the circumstances. Girls were the last thing on his mind right now.

Though she wasn't popular, boys knew Catrice because of her ethereal beauty, like someone from a fairytale. She kept to herself and didn't seem to have many friends.

"Go talk to her," Tim implored.

Drayden appreciated his friend's attempt to take his mind off the exile. This just wasn't the time. "I can't. We didn't have power this morning and I smell."

"Dude, you do know if you didn't have power then nobody else did either, right? Everybody probably smells a little today. I know I do."

"I've talked to her before," Drayden said.

"Following her around in the hall isn't exactly talking. It's more like stalking. And when you yardsale the contents of your backpack all over the hallway floor, it's pretty ineffective stalking." Tim chuckled.

That one never got old for him. "It was one time. And I *have* talked to her. But she's shy."

"That's why you have to be the aggressive one. Give her something to talk about. You guys are both math nerds. Talk about—I don't know—geometry or something."

Drayden rolled his eyes. "Yeah. 'Hey, Catrice, I love the way the sun reflects off the angles of your head.'"

"C'mon, man. I'm trying to help you."

"Or how about, 'Catrice, you have nicer legs than an isosceles triangle?'"

Tim shook his head. "You're hopeless. You do want to actually kiss a girl at some point, right? Watch how easy this is. I'm gonna go chat up Clara."

"What about Michelle?"

"She dumped me," Tim said matter-of-factly. "Something about me flirting with other girls all the time. Apparently she didn't appreciate that. I don't think she was the one." He winked. "Now watch and learn."

Tim rose, straightened his white linen shirt, and strutted up the row of desks, glancing back at Drayden with a sly grin. He tapped Clara on the left shoulder and zipped behind her to the right. She

fell for it. She peeked over her left shoulder before looking right, smirking. Tim sat on the desk beside her and spouted his best rap.

Drayden had long grown tired of Tim's nonstop quest to prove how macho he was. Tim considered himself quite the ladies' man, even if most of society didn't. He was decent looking, a fairly athletic dude, with a shaggy mop of sandy brown hair and blue eyes. But a horrible four-inch scar arched down the left side of his face, from the corner of his eye to his mouth, like a sliver of the moon. Kids teased him about it years ago, which initially drove him to learn martial arts. A similar story to Drayden's. These days, Tim carried on as if the scar didn't exist.

Mr. Kale finally strode through the door looking quite sharp, sporting a brown wool sweater vest over a white linen shirt. He adjusted his glasses, reinforced with green electrical wire, and called the class to attention. A tall African American man, his graying temples gave him the dignified air of a professor. Given the shortage of qualified teachers, he taught both math and social studies. He was the best teacher in the school, and one of Drayden's only friends. Thankfully, *he* didn't think being smart made you uncool.

His classroom was a confused mishmash of education. Globes and half-torn posters of Egypt over here; signs of famous equations, like the Pythagorean Theorem, over there. What it didn't have were computers. No one in the Dorms had them, since there wasn't enough power. They didn't have calculators, lacking batteries, which had expired decades ago. Even pens and pencils had gone extinct. Drayden's generation used quills, made from empty ink cartridges from those dead pens. Ink came from raspberries and blackberries.

Drayden often fantasized about the days of computers and the internet. Everything was destroyed when cyberterrorists crashed the web, as well as communication systems, power grids, and satellites. Their unprecedented global attack was one of the four

major simultaneous events of the Confluence. That not only killed the internet; it ceased all phone communication, radio, television, and GPS.

Mr. Kale taught social studies today. "The Bureau believes it's essential that new generations of the population understand the Confluence. Today we'll be talking about the Inequality Riots of the 21st century, one of the four main elements of the Confluence. Who can tell me about some of the causes of inequality in the United States back then?"

Becky Jennings in the first row shot her arm up like she was trying to crush a bug on the ceiling.

She was so annoying. Usually the one dying to answer questions to which everyone knew the answers. The Bureau made them study the Confluence every year in school. Becky was simply a suck-up.

Mr. Kale pointed at her. "Yes, Becky?"

"Well, social and economic inequality was getting bad. Lots of people were out of work."

"And why were they out of work?" Mr. Kale asked.

"Well, globalization provided cheaper labor overseas. Because of all the technological advances, computers and robots took over peoples' jobs. Companies needed less workers, so labor costs dropped and profits skyrocketed." Becky beamed. She glanced around the classroom, seeking approval and admiration. Instead, other kids gave her the stink-eye or didn't pay attention at all.

Discussions of the Confluence always reminded Drayden of his mom, who was only thirteen when it happened. Three years younger than he was now. It wasn't just that she survived; it was *how* she survived.

"Thank you, Becky," Mr. Kale said. "Those lost jobs, particularly in manufacturing, would never return."

Mr. Kale droned on about the one percent and the ninety-nine percent, but Drayden didn't give a damn about any of it. For him,

it only mattered because his mother belonged to that ninety-nine percent. That was why her family lived in a humble apartment in Queens. She shouldn't have even survived the Confluence since she wasn't in Manhattan. She should have died along with everyone else.

Apparently, Mr. Kale had asked another question, because Becky couldn't contain herself. She practically jumped out of her seat, thrusting her arm so high it was hard to believe it was still in the socket.

Mr. Kale let out a long breath, with his eyes closed. He looked up at the ceiling. "Go ahead, Becky."

Stupid Becky. Yes, please tell us for the hundredth time why raising taxes on the wealthy and hiking the minimum wage didn't work in a recession. Drayden jabbed his quill into his palm just short of breaking the skin. He tried to tune Becky out, her words still passing through his ears in bursts.

"...unemployed...disincentivized even to look for work...heavily taxed businesses...employed less people...wealthy people and businesses...moved to other countries with lower taxes..."

Drayden eyed the desolate city out the window. *Moved.* People moved, or rather fled, Manhattan in droves during the Confluence to escape the chaos and the city's quarantine. Not Mom. She and her brother Dan decided to sneak *into* the city, despite being ridiculed. The quarantine was already in effect, the government having blown up some of the city's bridges and guarding the border. Under the cover of darkness, in a tiny rowboat, Mom and Uncle Dan paddled across the East River and landed in East Harlem, avoiding detection. That was years before the Bureau built walls. They started a new life, while everybody who stayed behind died.

Mr. Kale was still yammering. "The economy tanked. The government had no money to pay for the ever-increasing entitlements, leaving it no choice but to cut services. Support for education

and housing ended, programs for the mentally ill and elderly were shuttered. Becky, what happened next?"

Becky appeared overjoyed to be called upon again. "People had been aggressively protesting already, each protest more violent than the last. Eventually, an epic class war erupted. Like, an actual war. Mobs of angry people, many of them armed, stormed Wall Street. People trashed nice apartments. The defining moment of the war was Zak Hann's murder. You're going to ask me who Zak Hann was, so I'll just tell you!" Becky laughed to herself. "He was a billionaire software businessman, a self-made one, from Brooklyn I think. Rioters broke into his apartment and beat him to death."

"Literally anyone else besides Becky. What happened next?" Mr. Kale pleaded.

"Shkat went bad!" someone screamed from the back of the class. The whole room burst into laughter.

"Yes, indeed. Care to elaborate, Mr. Clark?" Mr. Kale called across the room.

"Not really, Mr. Kale."

"Fine," he said, giving the boy a sarcastic thumbs-up. "I don't want to spend much more time on this anyway, so I'll summarize. The one percent and the government finally had enough, resulting in a huge crackdown. The police arrested thousands and brought the National Guard in to restore order. But the city fell into disarray, and residents evacuated en masse. This coincided with the superbug showing up on U.S. soil in the Washington, D.C. area, our former nation's capital. That, in turn, led to the closure and quarantine of New York City. That's a whole other lesson, for another day."

Mr. Kale sat at his desk. "At the exact time of the quarantine, the National Guard presence was giant relative to the suddenly miniscule population of New York City. Many citizens had fled. It's the reason New America has such a disproportionately large police

force today. It's also why they're called the Guardians. Let's move on to something more interesting. The American Revolution."

Drayden couldn't do school today. His mother had made that gutsy decision when she was thirteen and saved her life, and the Bureau just threw it away. He peered out the window again. She was out there, somewhere past those buildings, over those walls. If she was still alive. The thought sent chills down his spine. Even if the superbug didn't kill her, there couldn't be any food or water. No way she could survive.

His dad was an idiot. Carry on with their lives? Mom had been *taken*. Thrown outside to die. Nothing made sense anymore. The thought of asking his father to explain himself made Drayden so angry. Dad would probably shut down anyway, the way he consistently did when life got tough. Perhaps Wesley knew something about Dad's last comment. He'd start with Wes.

The bell rang, snapping Drayden from his thoughts.

As he stood, Tim approached. "Hey, bro. You gonna be okay?"

Drayden rubbed his eyes. "I don't know."

"Why don't you come to jiu-jitsu this afternoon? We'll roll a bit. You can blow off some steam."

"I...maybe." Drayden shook his head. "I cut school this morning and got chased by a Guardian. I don't know if he'd recognize me, so I don't know if I'm in trouble. I gotta be kinda careful walking around for a while."

"Oh, shkat. Alright, man. I'm sure it's no big deal." Tim patted Drayden's shoulder. "Hang in there, Dray. I'll catch up with you later."

With the cafeteria three floors up, Drayden wished for the 586th time the elevators worked. No buildings in the Dorms had working elevators. He wasn't hungry anyway, and he needed to get out of there.

Drayden stepped outside the doors of Norman Thomas High School, scanning the streets for Guardians. Thankfully there were none in sight.

Despite being one of the few buildings actively maintained, the brick structure's dilapidated sign read "No—— T—— —— —c—ool." It supplied a dependable source of jokes at school. Why didn't someone just fix the sign? If someone pissed you off, the standard response was "not cool."

It was a classic April day where it was warm in the sun, but nippy in the shade, and the air was crisp. If his world weren't crashing down around him he probably would have called it refreshing. Drayden pulled his hat down tighter and walked down the steps to the sidewalk. Groups of kids chatted, played cards, and rode the school's few bicycles. Laughter saturated the air in bursts. With one day of school left, the upbeat mood electrified the whole building. For the seniors in the Dorms, even though menial job assignments awaited them on Monday, it still signified a major milestone. He plopped down on the steps.

"Drayden!"

Sidney Fowler jogged toward him in a gray polyester tracksuit.

Watching people run amused Drayden. Some people appeared normal in daily life, but looked supremely goofy when they ran. Sidney wasn't one of them; she was an athlete. She was a star basketball player, and was girl-next-door cute, with her brown hair and brown eyes.

"Hey, Sidney."

"Oh good, I wasn't sure if you knew who I was." She sat beside him, so close their legs touched.

"What? Of course I do." There were two hundred sixty kids in their class and they'd never been friends, so her uncertainty wasn't crazy. While Drayden knew her as one of the flirtier and most popular girls in school, he wasn't personally the recipient of

anyone's flirting. He was an observer, always on the outside. It was shocking Sidney knew *him*. "We were in English together last year. How's it going?" Butterflies formed in his belly. Sidney was so pretty up close.

"Okay. Hey, I heard about your mom, I just wanted to say I'm sorry."

A lump formed in Drayden's throat. *Don't cry.* "Thanks." He looked down, picking at a loose thread on his sweater.

"Hey, I love that sweater," Sidney said. "What is that, wool?" She reached over and touched his arm.

"Oh. What, this old thing?" Drayden smoothed out the undyed cable knit sweater. "Yeah, it's wool, nice and warm."

Wool *was* something special, given New America's meager thirty sheep. The sweater was a gift from his parents for his fourteenth birthday. Lacking cotton, the Bureau made most clothing out of rayon, polyester, or more rarely, linen. The actual manufacturing, one of the least desirable occupations, occurred in the Dorms, employing many residents. Some clothing was dyed, usually red or green, using berries or plant extracts. Much of it remained undyed, just grays and tans, and none of it fit well. Kids often joked that if the school had a mascot, it would be a guy in a bland, ill-fitting outfit.

"I don't know if you heard," Sidney said, "both of my parents were exiled two months ago. Me and my little sister live with my grandparents now. So I understand what you're going through."

Drayden cringed. "I...I heard, I'm really sorry. Listen, um, I'm sorry I didn't say anything to you, you know, when it happened."

She waved him off. "No, it's totally fine."

"Is it okay if I ask why?"

She shook her head. "They were accused of dealing drugs. They had issues, and they weren't the best parents, at all. There's no way they were dealing drugs, though. I filed a complaint."

"That's insane. My mom was accused of conspiring against the Bureau, which is ridiculous. I don't believe it for a second. I'm going to figure out the real reason, if there was one. Yeah, it sucks. I can't even imagine losing both parents."

"It's been rough, but my grandparents are great. My sister is pretty happy there. They baby her." She bit down on her lower lip. "I need to think about getting married now, with no parents left." She scooted even closer and locked her arm inside his.

What is this?

"You know, we both had parents exiled. I'm just sayin'," Sidney said, with a playful laugh.

Drayden stared straight ahead. "Uh, yeah."

"I'm joking." She slid her arm out and they both fell silent.

Drayden tried to fill the awkward void. "It is kind of getting to be that age for us, marriage and everything, isn't it?"

In addition to not technically dating, at the age of eighteen—the earliest permitted by the Bureau—most got married. It was simple economics. Once married, a new couple would receive their own apartment, weekly paycheck, and food allocation.

"Sure is." Sidney stood. "Well, hang in there, Dray. I'll see ya." She bounded away and into the school.

He watched Sidney go, thinking how kind it was of her to talk to him, especially since he hadn't said anything when her parents were exiled. What would he have said anyway? *Hey, you don't know me but I'm sorry your life just got wrecked.* That would have sounded dumb. Only it hadn't sounded dumb, not when she'd basically said the same. Maybe he'd misjudged her.

Drayden got up and wandered to the sidewalk, unsure of what to do. Given the incident with the Guardian, he'd probably have to spend the rest of the day in school and visit Wesley after. He surveyed the streets, ensuring the bald Guardian wasn't lurking nearby.

A dark-skinned boy wearing a familiar red bandana, like a pirate, approached with his head down.

Drayden deflated. Alex. Besides the Guardian stalking him, he couldn't think of anyone he wanted to see less. Drayden faced the other way. Hopefully Alex wouldn't see him.

As Alex passed by, he snatched the hat off Drayden's head and tried to put it on. Finding it too small, he plopped it on top of his bandana.

Stupid flunk and his giant hooked nose.

Alex feigned anguish, mocking Drayden's displeasure.

Drayden stepped forward. "Gimme my hat back, Alex." He did not need this right now.

"Come and get it, *wetchop*," Alex taunted, every inch of his wiry frame angling for a fight.

Adrenaline coursed through Drayden's body. His peripheral vision blurred, leaving Alex the sole focus. "I'm not fooling around. My mom gave that to me."

"Aww, your mommy? The one who went bye-bye? Quit your crying, at least you had a mom the past sixteen years. I never had a mom to give me a hat. I think I'll take this one. I think you owe me this."

Damn the rumor mill. "Don't be a shkat. It's not my fault you decided to become a flunk."

"Oh, that's rich, Dray." Alex couldn't hide his outrage. "Whatever makes you sleep better at night."

Other kids gathered around now. Charlie Arnold, Alex's best friend, lumbered through the crowd behind Alex, grinning ear to ear. His bulky, muscular body all but knocked kids over until he reached the front.

Drayden should have known Charlie would be close behind. He followed Alex around like a huge, dumb puppy.

"Whoop whoop!" Charlie danced around behind Alex. "Fight, fight, fight, fight!" He pumped his fist, desperate to incite the crowd. He failed to spark a chant. "Man, this crowd's deader than a fish in the East River."

Drayden could easily go jiu-jitsu on Alex and tackle him to the ground, although that might be excessive if Alex was just being Alex—a jerk. Not to mention Alex was tough. Then Drayden might have to deal with Charlie too, and it wasn't worth the risk of suffering a cut from a punch or the sidewalk. His jiu-jitsu was solid, but book-taught. He didn't have much real-life fighting experience, so victory wasn't guaranteed, especially two on one. He darted his eyes around. *Where are you, Tim?* "Alex, I'm not fighting. This is stupid. Just give me my hat back."

Alex stepped forward, flexing, his hands balled into fists. "You're not fighting because you're a wuss, like you always were."

Drayden knew he should scram ASAP, except he couldn't leave without his hat. "Alex, we have one day of school left and job placements on Monday. It's stupid to screw that up. Think about it."

Alex inched even closer. He pulled the hat off his head and tossed it in the air, over and over. He caught it and swung it at Drayden's face.

Drayden stutter stepped back, the swing missing his nose by inches.

Alex pointed at him, and cracked up.

"Just gimme the hat," Drayden said. Why couldn't Alex leave him alone? Today of all days.

Alex frowned. "We could've been brothers, me and you. Should've been. You want your hat? Fine." He dangled the hat up high in the air with his left hand.

Drayden never even saw the punch.

It connected flush to his left eye.

A bolt of pain shot down to his jaw. He fell backward, and smacked his left elbow on the concrete. He reflexively raised his arms to defend himself.

Alex walked away.

Drayden sat up and touched his eye.

Warm gooey wetness. *Blood.*

Though it wasn't deep, the punch had cut him. Panic set in. *Breathe, relax. You can clean it.*

His hat lay limply on the sidewalk, frosted with dust and sand. Alex had dropped it.

Drayden lowered his head in shame. That hat embodied some tiny piece of his mom, so brave herself.

Charlie strode over and paused above the hat. He picked it up, tossed it to Drayden, and hurried after Alex.

Drayden picked up the cap and dusted it off. He pulled it on tight, rounding the brim. The whole left side of his face throbbed. He couldn't resist touching his eye again, examining the blood on his fingertips.

With the fun over, the crowd thinned.

Oh no.

Over by the doors, clutching her books against her chest, Catrice watched him. Her wispy golden hair blew in the light breeze, dancing like it was alive. She scurried back into the school.

Damn.

CHAPTER 4

'm a loser.

After school, Drayden stood in the bathroom at Tim's jiu-jitsu studio. He cleaned the cut above his eye again with soap and water. It was lush purple, and had swelled like a balloon.

While his father generally lived in his own world, he had taught Drayden all about bacteria, flexing the medical muscles he no longer used. Any cut needed to be cleaned often, but not too often. When you played with it, you risked infection, which meant you risked death.

During the early 21st century, despite all the warnings, doctors had overprescribed antibiotics. Through natural selection, only bacteria resistant to antibiotics would survive, which led to far deadlier strains. They became drug-resistant. Killer strains of salmonella, MRSA, and *E. coli* emerged. As a result, routine infections, food poisoning, and even simple cuts were potentially fatal. They were called superbugs. Ultimately, all bacteria grew fully drug-resistant. Every one became a superbug. Viruses like Ebola had gotten all the attention when bacteria should have been the focus. Antibiotics, arguably the greatest medical achievement of all time, became obsolete. Eventually a strain emerged that rocked civilization.

Enter Pseudomonas Aeruginosa. People referred to it as "Aeru," because once you became a superstar bacteria, you needed a cool name. It was never one of the big-name bacteria, just a bit player in the old days. In humans, it often caused a respiratory infection and could attack the digestive tract or open wounds.

Yet Aeru had two unique properties. One, it could exist in nature without a host; you could unknowingly touch or inhale it. Two, it infected both humans *and* plants. Though not all plants, it wiped out sweeping swaths of crops, destroying the food supply for both people and animals. It affected some animals as well. Once it mutated and grew more virulent, like the plague, it was game over.

Aeru comprised one of the four components of the Confluence. Independently, none of the four would have destroyed the world. Driven to their worst-case scenarios, however, the *confluence* of these events ultimately did. Some people contended only three catastrophic events comprised the Confluence, lumping Aeru in with overpopulation. They argued overpopulation only became a deadly problem once Aeru gutted the world's food supply. Everyone agreed that inequality and cyberterrorism made up the other two distinct causes.

Drayden walked into the main room of the jiu-jitsu studio, which was just a spacious area with a soft mat on the floor. He slumped against the wall. He wasn't here to "roll" today, as they called it; he needed Tim's company. Despite Tim's frequent invitations to train here, Drayden didn't come much. He preferred the privacy of his room where, if he messed up, no big deal. He could perfect techniques, visualizing his opponent. There'd be time for more full-contact grappling later. That's how he'd usually rationalized it. Wincing from the cut on his face, he wasn't so sure now.

Without Mom around, Tim was basically all Drayden had. He loved his big brother, but they were brothers, who fought like

brothers do. Seeing Dad and Wes would only remind him that they weren't Mom, which made him angry at them.

A few other students were warming up on the mat. Tim hadn't arrived yet. Unless Tim had fallen into a coma, he'd heard about the fight. While Drayden had been bullied for years, it rarely escalated to physical violence. Tim would give him grief about it, and Drayden wasn't in the mood today. He knew he shouldn't let Alex bully him. Obviously he shouldn't get beaten up, given his self-defense training. Still, Alex wasn't just any bully.

Tim walked in and marched right up to Drayden. He cast his disapproving eyes downward, and took an audible deep breath.

Drayden averted his eyes. "Don't say it."

Tim sat, facing him. "I'm sorry I wasn't there."

"I could've tackled him to the ground. I just, I hesitated. I always overthink these things. I didn't want to overreact. If someone gives you a wet willy, you don't shoot them with a gun. I thought he was messing around. I never dreamed he would throw a punch."

Tim punched his fist into his palm. "I'll kill that shkat flunk. But dude, you could destroy Alex. I'm sure you were worried about that meathead Charlie too. Honestly, I think you could take him as well."

Drayden half-watched two girls grappling behind Tim. He'd spent his whole life avoiding confrontation, never getting in trouble. He lived under the radar, because it was safe. He began learning jiu-jitsu to defend himself from bullies. If he was being honest, he knew equipping himself with self-defense skills only served to provide a toolkit he was still too afraid to use. It wasn't enough to know the techniques. It took confidence to use them. Confidence he lacked. When the time came, he either feared his skills wouldn't work in a real fight, or he'd go overboard and break someone's arm over harmless teasing. In both cases, he froze up.

Alex presented a special case because of their history. One time, Alex and his winooze friends had chased him all the way

home from middle school, pelting him with little pebbles. He'd made it inside his apartment, severely winded, and Mom was there. She didn't even need to ask him what happened. She bolted down the stairs, out the door, and chased Alex and his friends down the block. And man, did they run, Drayden recalled, missing his mom so much. They wanted no part of that crazy little lady. Once school wrapped up tomorrow and they received their job placements on Monday, he probably wouldn't see much of Alex anymore. If he did, he'd never let Alex beat him up again.

Drayden stood. "Hey, I need to head over to the FDC, talk to Wes about Mom. Dad said something weird this morning. Can you come?"

Tim got up and slapped him on the back. "Of course, bud. Let me just take a quick look at that eye." He raised his hands to Drayden's head and tilted it at various angles.

"Tim, it's fine," Drayden said. "We really have to do this?"

Despite lacking medical training, Tim had become the resident "doctor" at jiu-jitsu class. He insisted on tending to the injuries that inevitably arose.

"Yeah, just a bruise," Tim said.

Drayden and Tim exited the jiu-jitsu studio on Thirty-First Street and Second Avenue, and both stopped in their tracks. Adults often reminisced about how loud Manhattan used to be, buzzing with different sounds. In contrast, New America was always quiet. There were no cars, no sirens, no trains, no airplanes overhead, no birds. Only the howling wind and random conversations occasionally broke the silence. Electric buses, the only form of transportation, were infrequent and silent.

Crowd noise up Second Avenue roared as if it was right on top of them. Several hundred people were gathered a few blocks north.

Tim pointed his thumb up the street. "You know we have to go check that out. Looks like a protest or something."

"Keep a lookout for a sweaty, fat, bald Guardian," Drayden said.

They walked four blocks and immersed themselves in the crowd centered on the steps of a historic church, one of the only houses of worship still maintained. Originally an Armenian Apostolic church, it now served as the primary place of worship for Roman Catholics. They represented the dominant religious group of New America. Although the world grew increasingly religious after the Conflu-ence, Drayden's family didn't practice it. They followed Mom's lead, and she preferred spirituality, as she called it, rather than formal religion.

A sprawling plaza in front of the church sat ten feet above street level. People crowded the plaza, its staircase, and the sidewalk below. A few Guardians hovered around the fringes of the crowd. On a raised podium in the plaza's center stood Lily Haddad.

While the Bureau was the only official body of government in New America, Lily was considered the mayor of the Dorms. Though not an actual title, Lily had served as the primary Dorm advocate for ages. The Bureau maintained an office in the Dorms a few blocks south, called the Council on Dorm Relations. Bureau member Thomas Cox headed it, and Lily represented the Dorms on the council. She was one of the few people Drayden's mother admired. Mom even went through a phase where she dressed like Lily, wearing flowing, full-length dresses.

No sign of the bald Guardian so far. Drayden and Tim pushed closer to hear better. Some good news would be nice. Dorm residents desperately awaited the day the scientists would announce they'd contacted another civilization, or the Bureau was tearing down the walls separating the zones. If the zones were truly equal, why divide them?

The Bureau insisted living conditions were the same in all zones, since equality was the underlying premise for their autonomous society. Yet, nobody truly believed it, certainly nobody who lived in the Dorms. You couldn't see for yourself because of the travel restriction. In addition, the Bureau prohibited anyone with knowledge of life outside their home zone from discussing it. You couldn't even talk about it! To do so would break the law. Hidden surveillance cameras and microphones recorded activity across New America to capture crimes. Some people did work outside their home zone. All doctors lived in the Lab, but many worked in the Dorm hospitals, and some janitors who lived in the Dorms worked in the Precinct.

Lily appeared to be taking questions from the crowd. She spoke through an old-fashioned megaphone, her gray-streaked hair blowing in the breeze. "Yes, I've raised the issue with the Bureau. In the past month we've had a record ten power outages, each lasting longer than average. They've been brownouts, not blackouts. While power is off in the Dorms, we can all observe lights on downtown. So I'm pressing the Bureau to ensure that power is being distributed fairly amongst all zones. We—"

"What about our food?" someone yelled.

"I was getting to that. Many of you have complained that your food allocations have shrunk, which we've confirmed with our own study. The Bureau assures me it's just random variability in food production. If a group of crops is infected or unsuccessful, it's normal to experience a small decline in delivery. They can only dole out what they produce. But we'll be monitoring this closely. My final point is regarding exiles. There were nineteen ex—"

"The Bureau sucks!"

"Yeah!"

"—exiles in April, also a record. I've received many complaints that these were unjust."

Drayden broke out in goosebumps. His mother's wasn't the only exile that seemed unusual. The total number of exiles had spiked as well. It wasn't his imagination; something was up with the power and the food lately.

Lily paused, scanning the crowd. "In isolation, each of these trends is troubling, yet explainable. Together, however, they form a disturbing pattern of decreased livability here in the Dorms, and we won't tolerate it. Equality is one of the basic tenets of New America and we intend to ensure the Bureau is honoring it. I've requested a special meeting with the Bureau councilman on Saturday. If anyone has any complaints outside of the issues we've discussed here today, please log it with my office. Be safe, and be well. Thank you."

The crowd roared. People yelled indistinguishable complaints, derogatory comments, all manner of vile at Lily and her handlers. Being the only defender of the Dorms, Lily was usually popular. Clearly people were angry.

"I've never seen everyone so worked up," Tim said. "I did notice the power outages. My apartment's freezing. You file a complaint about your mom?"

Drayden bit down on his lip and shook his head. "No. Believe me, I'm gonna do something about it. But I don't see the point of the complaints. They're useless. They can't reverse exiles." What was happening in the Dorms?

A siren wailed, and not the wake-up one. It was the broadcast siren. It signaled the Bureau would deliver a broadcast in thirty minutes. The Bureau needed to allow people time to reach a screen, several of which were scattered throughout the Dorms. This was an unscheduled broadcast, which gave it additional significance.

Drayden groaned. "Oh man, what now?"

Tim nodded toward Second Avenue. "Let's go to Madison Square Park."

The late afternoon sun cast elongated shadows across the streets. The trek to the park stretched approximately twenty blocks, just over a mile.

Drayden needed to speak to Wesley, but he couldn't skip this broadcast. It was possible the Bureau had called it to explain what was happening to New America.

At Twenty-Eighth Street, he and Tim passed a group of street vendors and performers. Since the Bureau paid identical low salaries to every family in the Dorms regardless of occupation, some people sought ways to earn extra money. Housing, essential food, healthcare, and most other services were provided for free by the Bureau. Even haircuts were free. Non-food goods, like furniture and clothing, were manufactured by the Bureau, and offered for sale in the Retail Centers. You were free to save or spend your weekly pay as you wished. People spent it on essentials such as these, or on elective foods, like salt, butter, and alcohol, which weren't included in the weekly food allocation.

While the Bureau's self-contained economy worked, it neglected things like art, music, and theater. Drayden's parents, particularly his mother, often recalled how culturally rich the city was before the Confluence.

A teenage girl in a draping green dress played the violin. Her bow glided across the strings with ease, the beautiful melody swaddling the air like a warm blanket. A rusty bucket sat beside her for tips. Though few could afford to spare money, music was such an unusual delight she'd collected a few bills of appreciation.

Three Guardians huddled around a vendor's stall spun around and eyed Drayden and Tim.

Drayden's heart skipped a beat. The bald guy wasn't among them, but what if he'd alerted the others to look out for a tall, skinny

kid? He wondered what he should do if they approached. Run for it, maybe. He tried not to look suspicious, which in turn probably made him appear highly suspicious.

Thankfully they returned their attention to the vendor and Drayden breathed a sigh of relief.

The vendors fared a little better than the performers. Most offered homemade art such as paintings, sculptures, and wood carvings. A few sold practical household items such as end tables or lamps, which the Bureau also sold in the Retail Centers. It was legal, as long as the goods weren't stolen.

In New America's early days, people broke into abandoned apartments and pilfered everything they could to sell on the street. At their discretion, the Guardians confiscated any goods they determined were stolen. Except these days, some corrupt Guardians procured the stolen goods themselves, seeking to generate extra cash. The three Guardians they passed were probably dumping some fleeced stuff. They had access to all the untouched apartments uptown in the Meadow. Mr. Kale said capitalism was inherent in human nature. As such, it would always find a way to poke its head out despite the Bureau's efforts to quash it.

"What job are you gonna take on Monday?" Tim asked.

"I dunno. I wish I could be a scientist, rather than one of these crappy Dorm jobs. I guess I'll go with lab tech, like my dad."

"You're number one in the school. At least you have your pick. I don't think my choices will be too good. I might end up as a seamstress."

"There aren't any good choices," Drayden said.

Drayden and Tim turned right on Twenty-Sixth Street. Everywhere he looked, he saw his mother. From the petite vendor packing up her trinkets for the day, to the swaying ponytail a block ahead. Drayden couldn't shake the idea that getting into the Palace would give him the best chance of finding out what happened to her, and

who was responsible. But her words echoed in his mind. *Promise me you won't do that.* He'd sworn he wouldn't enter the Initiation. Still, new information was emerging. Based on Lily's impromptu gathering and the reaction of the crowd, perhaps Mom's exile formed part of a pattern of deteriorating conditions. Hearing Lily lay out the stats drove it home. Something was definitely up.

They reached Madison Avenue, the northeast corner of the park. Just ahead, a massive video screen towered over the lawn. A few of the bigger parks maintained similar screens. On rare occasions the Bureau played movies, which was just about the biggest treat ever.

The Bureau made routine broadcasts every Monday at 6:00 p.m., though people mostly ignored them. There was never anything exciting to report. A lower ranking Bureau member often gave the address. If the news was meaningful, the Premier, Eli Holst, did it himself. These unscheduled broadcasts attracted attention since the Premier might deliver them.

A siren blared, intermittently beeping, which indicated the broadcast would commence in five minutes. Hundreds of people showed up, many of them the same angry protestors from Lily's address. A hot energy simmered through the crowd.

Drayden and Tim searched for a spot with a good view. The setting sun painted the sky a brilliant canvas of orange, pink, and purple. While not large, Madison Square Park's green grass soothed the mind. When the cherry blossoms bloomed, it turned downright magical. Drayden had come here often with his mom. They'd pretended the buildings surrounding the park didn't exist, and they were in the forest. The concrete jungle of his existence made it unfathomable that grass, trees, and other vegetation covered most of the planet. Or it used to. Who knew what the world looked like now?

They found a narrow patch of available grass and sat. Drayden lay flat on his back and admired the sky through the trees. He held

his hands like blinders next to his face to block out the view of the buildings lining the park.

The screen burst to life, suffused with white noise, emitting a deep buzz. Any moment now the broadcast would begin.

Drayden sat up.

The unruly crowd fell silent. The screen flickered a few times and then glowed crystal clear.

Eli Holst appeared.

CHAPTER 5

Eli Holst had ruled as the Premier since the Confluence. He was the leader of New America, its highest-ranking Bureau member. In his late sixties, his vision on screen was a giant, overly tanned head with big glasses. He often spoke as if he were addressing a group of children, overcompensating to seem courteous and friendly.

Today, as always, he addressed the populace while sitting at a desk in a barren office. It looked like a warehouse, surrounded by dull wood floors and cabinets. He wore his usual drab gray linen suit, the only contrast being the red Bureau pin on his chest.

The pin itself, the size of a dime, was a red square, representing all sides being equal. Against the red background was a yellow balanced scale, with a lion on one side and an owl on the other. The lion represented bravery, while the owl represented intelligence.

At home in private, Drayden's mom would eviscerate Holst for the conditions in the Dorms. She particularly loathed the Bureau's treatment of the less fortunate, like the mentally ill. They were at best forgotten, at worst, exiled.

One night after closing at the FDC, a crazed older man broke in to steal food. Rather than report him to the Guardians, who would have exiled him, Drayden's mother had talked to him. His

name was Toby, and until two weeks prior, he'd been under the care of his mother, who had passed away. Toby was slow, and had no idea how to collect his own food. Mom granted him a full meal allocation and escorted him home. She knocked on all his neighbors' doors and ensured they would care for him. Occasionally, she checked in on Toby. That's just how she was. If she hadn't done that, Toby would be dead. The Bureau didn't care. She held Holst accountable, as its leader.

And now Drayden held Holst responsible for his mother's exile. Even if it wasn't his personal order, it was his policies and his empowerment of the Chancellors to exile as they pleased, even in error.

"Citizens of New America, good evening," Holst said from the screen. "I want to begin today's broadcast with the motto of New America: Bravery. Intelligence. Equality. As you all know, we learned the lessons of the dangers of inequality earlier this century, the greedy pursuit of money at the expense our fellow brothers and sisters. Fortunately, and unfortunately, in New America there is no wealth. It is fortunate because in our world everyone is equal, from the Palace to the Dorms."

The crowd in the park rumbled with murmurs and snickers.

"It is unfortunate because in a world with no wealth, there is no way to advance, no way to improve your lot in life through hard work and ingenuity. The zone system has proved an unquestioned success, quite literally saving civilization. Yet its intent is not to discourage hard work or suppress advancement. To be a fair structure, you must be able to earn your way into greater responsibility. This is why the Bureau created the Initiation many years ago."

A chill ran through Drayden's body. *The Initiation.*

"This Monday, across all zones, approximately 1,200 sixteen-year-olds will graduate and receive job placements. It is a time of great pride and cause for celebration. These fine young people will

join our workforce and contribute to the future success of New America in their respective zones. As an alternative, I strongly encourage all the graduates listening to consider the Initiation. It's only available to graduating seniors, and offers the chance to move to the Palace, join the Bureau, and participate in the governance of New America."

Holst paused, letting that sink in. "For the Bureau, the Initiation is the ideal way for us to identify the future leaders of New America currently living outside the Palace. Sadly, in past years, very few people have taken advantage of this incredible opportunity. When our former world was destroyed and this new one created, two human traits above all others saved humanity from the brink of extinction: bravery and intelligence, as exemplified by our residents of the Precinct and the Lab. As such, the Initiation is a test of bravery and intelligence. If you display these characteristics, you prove you deserve to join the leadership of New America. Monetary wealth is not the only way to move up in life. Holding a position that profoundly affects the future of New America is extremely rewarding itself."

Beads of sweat broke out on Drayden's forehead. It was as if the Premier were speaking directly to him.

"As usual, the Initiation commences this Sunday, the day before job placements. The test itself does not require any special skills, and you need not study or prepare for it in any way. Entrants are termed 'pledges' and take the test together in groups. Pledges will work as a team, but be judged individually. Assuming you pass, at least one pledge in each group is guaranteed a spot in the Palace. The others who pass will be placed in the zones that best match their skills. If you show exceptional courage, you may join the Precinct. If you demonstrate brilliance, perhaps you will move to the Lab. Those decisions will be made by the Initiation Council and

approved by me." Holst smiled. "You have the option of bringing your immediate family with you."

Dad and Wes.

Holst paused again for effect, his smile fading. "However, one of the other lessons of the Confluence, gleaned from the Inequality Riots, is that nothing in life is free. It must be earned. You cannot have reward without tireless effort, achievements, or without taking risks. Therefore, the consequence of failing the Initiation is exile."

And there it was. The great big, fat problem with the Initiation. The reason hardly anyone entered.

The crowd once again came alive with whispers and chatter.

It was the worst kept secret in the Dorms. The Initiation wasn't just about joining the Bureau, or the "consolation prize" of securing a better-fitting job in a different zone. It was about moving to a better *zone*. That was the true carrot being dangled. The Bureau could never admit that, because it would contradict their claims of equality. Nevertheless, everyone got the joke. The Lab and Precinct jobs were superior to the Dorm jobs, yes, but everyone assumed living conditions were better there too.

Still, nobody believed the other zones were *that* much nicer than the Dorms. A resource constraint hamstrung New America. They were an isolated island, cut off from the rest of the world, which was probably a desolate wasteland. While the implicit inequality was troublesome, the Bureau couldn't be living like kings. The Lab and Precinct couldn't be overflowing with eggs. The Dorms were crappy enough to question the Bureau's claims of equality, yet not so crappy that those claims were absurd. It wasn't enough to spur the citizens to revolt, or to persuade sixteen-year-olds to risk exile by entering the Initiation.

The Initiation made perfect sense for the Bureau. The Palace was small. They needed access to the best and brightest in New America who weren't only the children of existing Bureau members.

The Premier paused again, as if he knew the word "exile" would induce the viewers to stir. "Fear not, my fellow New Americans. We have achieved nothing less than the preservation of the human race with our bravery and intelligence. To this year's graduates, I implore you to conquer your fear as the prior generation did, saving the world after the Confluence. If you wish to join the Initiation, you need to register in your zone's Bureau office by 2:00 p.m. Saturday. I hope to see many of you in the Palace on Sunday night as new Bureau members. Remember—Bravery. Intelligence. Equality. Goodnight."

The screen flickered a few times and shut off, releasing a wheeze.

"I wanna see Holst complete the Initiation," Tim said sarcastically.

Drayden remained silent, his eyes locked on the screen.

"You all right, buddy?" Tim asked.

Drayden snapped out of his trance. "Yeah, yeah, I'm fine."

"You're not...considering...?" Tim chewed a nail.

"No. I'll take the shkatty Dorms over exile. It's getting late, we gotta get back. I still need to hit up the FDC to see Wes."

Tim fumbled with the zipper on his sweatshirt. "It is late. I'm supposed to be home. My jerkoff stepdad warned me. 'Better do what I say, or else.' *Or else.* What a flunk that guy is."

"I'm sorry, man." And here Drayden was dragging him around like a selfish jerk. "Things still not going well with him?"

Tim shrugged. "Ah, nothing I can't handle, right? Know what else I can handle? Talking to that cute girl over there." He pointed into the crowd. "Brown hair in braids. You know her?"

"Do I...are you serious? No, I don't know her."

Tim finger-brushed his hair. "She's super cute. I want to go introduce myself real quick."

Tim had almost let him in this time, before he fought it off with macho-Tim. "What about Clara?" Drayden asked.

"Who?"

"Never mind. Good luck."

Tim walked away and Drayden started toward Twenty-Sixth Street. He hadn't even made it one block when the power shut off with an audible click, shrouding the Dorms in darkness.

People shouted in anger and confusion.

The crowd from the broadcast had abruptly halted. A tiny amount of the sky's light remained, now dark purple. Downtown New America emitted a faint glow, which meant a southern zone still retained power.

Drayden pulled over to the edge of the sidewalk, allowing his eyes to adjust to the darkness. Lily was undeniably onto something. Before her speech, Drayden hadn't noticed the Dorms alone lost power.

He headed up Park Avenue. Navigating the crumbling sidewalks and cracked streets was no simple task in the dark. He took tiny, cautious steps to avoid rolling an ankle or tripping. He needed to reach the Food Distribution Center at Thirtieth Street and Second Avenue, a half block from his family's apartment.

Drayden's thoughts swirled, twisting from his mother's exile, to his father's comment, to the Guardian hunting him, to his fight with Alex, impossible to forget, thanks to the throbbing above his eye. And now the Initiation. Despite his promise, maybe it *was* a chance to make something greater out of his life, a way to take care of his family, honoring his mother's final request. He could move them all out of the Dorms and secure a better career for himself. If fortunate enough to earn his way to the Palace, he could hopefully learn the truth about his mother's exile.

Drayden certainly wouldn't struggle with the intelligence portion of the test. That wasn't the problem. It was the other part, the bravery one. Nobody knew the specifics of the test, even the intelligence section. Was it a written test? He didn't even want to

speculate about what a bravery test entailed. The whole thing was a closely guarded secret, since only the Initiation Council got to see it. And there was the whopper: He didn't want to die.

A gigantic rat scurried across the sidewalk, barely missing his feet.

Drayden jerked back and stumbled. He leapt onto a fence in front of an apartment building. "Crud!" Where did it go? He waited, gripping the fence. If he saw a rat in one spot, he would avoid it for a week, even crossing the street.

Rats and cockroaches, the only other living creatures in any meaningful number in New America, were everywhere. It seemed appropriate, since the people of New America were rats and cockroaches too. Hideous creatures that would exile a child's mother for no reason. Scientists estimated the rat population to be ten times the size of the human one. Nobody had dared to contemplate the number of cockroaches. While no one even knew the exact human population, most guessed around 100,000 people. Mr. Kale said the zone breakout was roughly 75,000 in the Dorms, 9,000 in the Lab, 15,000 in the Precinct, and 1,000 in the Palace.

Given the lack of meat in their diet, some people had allegedly eaten rats and subsequently died horrible, disease-ridden deaths. That may have been an old wives' tale. People did kill rats and use their pelts to produce clothing, however. One of those people just happened to be their upstairs neighbor, Dayla Krajewski. She was an eccentric elderly lady whose apartment reeked of, unsurprisingly, rat. She explained that rats contained an oil in their skin called buck grease, which gave the clothing a rodenty smell. She called it a "warm tortilla" smell.

Drayden had never eaten a warm tortilla and was positive he never wanted one. He climbed off the fence and dashed to the next block. Picking up the pace, he turned right when he reached Thirtieth Street.

It was three avenue-blocks to the FDC. Wesley had worked there since he graduated two years ago. His flunky grades limited his choice of occupations, so he selected the loosely-defined "worker" position, because Mom was the manager. He basically moved heavy crates of food all day.

All the available Dorm positions were working-class by definition. In Drayden's opinion, a hierarchy did exist, despite the fact that all jobs paid the same. Tech jobs in the science labs or hospitals were the best, but the list of options was endless: barbers, mechanics, plumbers, electricians, bus drivers, garbage men, janitors, secretaries, construction workers, seamstresses, you name it.

Drayden didn't desire any of those jobs. Even being a lab tech would grow boring.

A half block away now, the FDC came into view, in a former grocery store on the corner. Wesley worked late tonight, so he would have missed the broadcast.

Drayden had too much on his mind to think about the Initiation. He needed answers about his mother.

"Wes? You in here? It's Dray!"

Because the FDC had closed an hour earlier and the power was out, it was silent and pitch black inside. Chilly, moist air permeated the room with the fresh smell of wet vegetables. Late every night, one worker locked up the food to ensure some hungry soul didn't break in and steal it.

Drayden remained by the door, afraid he'd accidentally knock over a barrel of cantaloupes in the dark. It was impossible to be there without thinking of Mom. While he didn't typically visit Wesley at work, he'd come to see Mom often. Drayden would beg her to sneak some extra food home since she oversaw distribution. Nobody would know. Not crates of food, but an extra banana or something. He and

his mom both loved bananas. She always refused and pointed out they would be taking food from someone else.

"Boo!"

Drayden jumped, his heart pounding. "Dammit, Wes! Not cool."

Wesley laughed so hard he cried.

"Oh my God," Drayden said, bent over with his hands on his knees. "You shkat flunk. What the heck is the matter with you?"

Wesley giggled. "Sorry, bro. I couldn't resist. What are you doin' here?"

"Did you forget that whole thing from last night? There was an exile, it was in our apartment, you—"

"Shut up, chotch. I just didn't know if something else was wrong. Whoa, what happened to your eye?"

Drayden wished it was even darker inside. For his tough brother, the black eye would be a badge of shame. "Alex," he said.

"Oh man. I swear, that kid. You want me to give him a beating?"

"No. I should've...I...never mind. It's fine, I got it." Drayden considered telling Wesley about the incident with the Guardian, before stopping himself. He was probably blowing it out of proportion already, and the Guardian had most likely forgotten about him by now.

"Can you give me a hand stacking the oranges?" Wesley asked. "I don't have that much left to do, but it's brutal in the dark. Follow me, carefully."

Drayden clutched the back of Wesley's shirt as they headed down an aisle. They passed through two doors that swung open into a back stockroom and stopped. A window provided enough moonlight to turn objects into silhouettes.

Wesley hoisted a box of oranges up on a shelf. "Hey, I heard the siren earlier. What was the broadcast?"

"Nothing," Drayden said. "It was Holst, actually. He was just talking about the Initiation because it's on Sunday."

"Was there anything new about it?"

"No. The same. The only thing that matters about it didn't change." Drayden passed Wes a box of oranges with a grunt. "Failure equals exile."

Wesley paused and faced Drayden.

"What?" Drayden asked.

"I think you should enter."

"Come again? You think I should *enter*? Enter what, the next room? That box on the floor? Our apartment?"

"I'm serious," Wesley said

"Yeah, easy for you to say. Did I forget you entering two years ago or something?"

"I wouldn't have had a chance in hell. You know that. And we still had Mom back then. What's gonna happen now with Mom gone? She was the glue, man. Dad gave up a long time ago. You really want to be a lab tech the rest of your life? You'll be bored on your first day. You could totally do this. There isn't a question they could ask that you couldn't answer."

"It's not just an intelligence test, Wes. It's a bravery test too, whatever in God's name that means. Let's be honest; that's not exactly my strong suit."

"That's the easy part."

Drayden choked on his spit, retching for a second. "I'm sorry. Have we met? I'm Drayden, your brother. The kid who got beat up today by a flunk I could outgrapple with no hands. Instead I was scared and froze up."

"Listen. I've been thinking about this for a while, even before the exile." Wesley sat on a crate. "The Bureau says every year that the test doesn't require any special skills. No unusual talent, or strength, or agility. Just the guts to give it a shot. It's normal to be scared, but the point is, anybody *can* do the bravery part. The difficult portion

for almost everyone would be the intelligence one. Most kids just aren't smart enough. You are."

Drayden tugged on his left earlobe. His brother was making some sense. Besides, he had been thinking about it himself. Still, thinking and doing were very different things.

"Look, this is the hand we were dealt," he said. "The Dorms suck, but we're safe. Living in the Lab would have been nice if Dad hadn't screwed up. It's not like the Lab, Precinct, or even the Palace could be *that* much better. There literally aren't enough resources in the city for that to be possible. And the entire point of New America is specifically that the zones are all equal. I'm not risking my life just to score a cool job."

"It's not just a cool job for you," Wesley said, his voice cracking. "If we even made it to the Lab, Dad could be a doctor again. I could get out of this hellhole post that I only tolerated because Mom was here. Our family might not fall apart." He paused. "Just think about it. You have two more days to decide."

Typical Wes. This was exactly why he and Dad were not his mother and could never be his mother. Wes was thinking about himself, not Drayden.

"You know, I came here to talk about Mom, not the stupid Initiation. What the heck did Dad mean when he said there were things I didn't know about Mom?"

Wesley returned to stacking boxes. "I'm not sure exactly what he meant, but there *were* some things you didn't know about Mom. I'm not sure if they had anything to do with her exile, or if they're what Dad was talking about. Because…I wasn't sure if he knew."

"Knew what?" Drayden threw his hands in the air. "What the hell are you talking about?"

"Mom was having an affair. With Nathan Locke, the Bureau guy who runs the FDCs."

Speechless, Drayden plopped down on a crate.

Wesley shrugged. "She didn't know I knew. At least, I think she didn't."

"No, she wasn't. Mom? *Our* mom?"

"Dray, I saw it with my own eyes, right here in the FDC. Either Dad knew, or she had other stuff going on too that he knew about. Maybe she *was* involved in some conspiracy against the Bureau. She had been spending a lot of time with Lily Haddad lately. Mom had secrets."

Drayden was floored. Apparently, he didn't know his mother as well as he believed. Having an affair could be a logical reaction to being married to a slacker like Dad for twenty years. Conspiring against the Bureau, however, was illogical and foolish.

"Mom was too smart to get involved in some plot against the Bureau," Drayden stated emphatically. "She would never risk being taken away from us. Wes, did it ever occur to you that this Locke guy could have ordered her exile? What if she broke it off and he got pissed, like in that *Fatal Attraction* movie the Bureau played a few months ago? Should we ask Dad about it?"

Wesley shook his head. "No, man. Mom's gone. I realize you don't respect Dad, but he's not a bad guy. If he didn't know, why crush him? And if he did, why embarrass him by letting him know that we know? You could find out what happened to Mom if you moved into the Palace and joined the Bureau. Now there's a reason to enter the Initiation."

"Of course I want to know what happened. In fact, I need to understand the reason, because otherwise nothing makes sense anymore. Finding out won't bring her back. Mom made me promise I wouldn't enter. Hell, it was her last wish before they dragged her away." Drayden stood, feeling lightheaded. He was used to thinking out every side of an issue, but when *his mom* was the problem, it was just too much. "I'm sorry, Wes. I gotta go home. I can't handle all this."

Wesley wrapped his arms around Drayden. "We'll be fine, bro. We'll make it through this. Think about what I said about the Initiation. You can do this. I know you can. I love you, little bro."

"Love you too."

Drayden left. He needed advice, and he knew just where to turn.

CHAPTER 6

The following morning, Drayden couldn't bear to look his father in the eyes. His heart ached at the deception, embarrassment, and sorrow that must have existed between his parents.

He woke up early, chugged his shot of milk, and wolfed down a pitiful chunk of bread and a banana. The sweet fruit reminded him of Mom again. They wouldn't receive their weekly food allocation for another two days, but the prior one had only lasted five. There wasn't enough food. Although hungry, thankfully he could shower this morning.

Tim was waiting at Lexington Avenue, a block from school, which was unusual. As soon as Drayden got close enough, he knew something was wrong.

Tim's face was twisted in dismay. "Dude, don't freak out. Your Guardian is waiting by the door to school with another Guardian. They're eyeballing everyone going in."

Drayden's face flushed with nervous heat. "Oh shkat. This guy won't let it go, apparently. I hoped it was no big deal. The thing is, I didn't just get caught cutting school. I saw him selling hay to a guy."

Tim's eyes widened. "No way! A Guardian selling drugs? No wonder why he's trying to find you. Why don't you just ditch again? Go home."

"I can't, I have to talk to Mr. Kale. I shouldn't push my luck cutting again either."

Tim peered down the street toward the school. "Yeah. Plus, it's the field trip."

With everything going on, Drayden had totally forgotten. For years, the seniors eagerly anticipated the traditional field trip to the Meadow. It represented not just the grand finale of their academic lives, but the only field trip they'd ever take. It was the one time in their lives most of them would be allowed outside the Dorms.

Tim gripped Drayden by the shoulders. "I have an idea. I'll distract them. I'll jog around the back of the school over to Park Avenue. I'll yell and scream about...someone being hurt. I can find another kid to fake an injury. Lemme take care of it. You gotta be close, just out of view. As soon as they leave their post, get in."

"Won't you get in trouble when they realize there's no emergency?"

Tim tilted his head and gave Drayden a look. "I can smooth talk a few Guardians. Don't worry about me."

"Tim...thank you. I owe you one."

Tim winked. "No you don't. Just wait for my signal. Trust me; you won't miss it." He jogged up Lexington Avenue a block and turned left on Thirty-Fourth Street, disappearing around a corner.

Drayden shuffled toward school, hugging the buildings to remain out of sight. When he reached the wall that bordered the school, he ducked behind it, less than fifty feet from the doors. He peeked over the top.

The bald Guardian and his buddy flanked the doors, inspecting all the kids strolling into the school.

Drayden crouched and waited for Tim's diversion. Tim was so damn loyal. Without exception, he had Drayden's back. Years ago, when bullies tormented Tim over his scar, Drayden befriended him, and Tim never forgot it. It was a simple thing for Drayden, who

didn't have any friends anyway. Even years later, Tim seemed to believe he owed him. While Drayden hadn't used his own jiu-jitsu in fights, Tim had. He could always count on Tim to defuse a situation or fight to protect him.

A scream pierced the morning silence. "Help! Oh my God, help me!"

Drayden peered over the wall. *Jeez, Tim.*

Tim frantically jumped up and down in front of the school, shouting at the Guardians. Everyone stared. The Guardians exchanged a confused glance.

Tim pointed in the direction of Park Avenue. "Help, please! Someone's hurt bad! Hurry!" He dashed toward Park Avenue. The Guardians abandoned their posts and followed.

Drayden sprung up and strode to the door, trying to appear casual. As soon as he stepped into the lobby, he abruptly stopped.

Mr. Kale stood there, a stern look on his face. He grabbed Drayden by the arm. "Come with me," he whispered urgently, leading Drayden up the stairs one floor and into the hallway.

"Mr. Kale, what's going on?"

Mr. Kale held a finger to his lips. "Shhh."

Drayden's pulse quickened. Maybe he was in serious trouble.

They entered Mr. Kale's austere, windowless office. It contained a junky wooden desk, three chairs, and bookshelves stuffed floor-to-ceiling. The whole room smelled dusty. Mr. Kale motioned for Drayden to have a seat while he sat behind the desk. He took a piece of paper off the desk and handed it to Drayden.

It was a grainy photograph printed on recycled paper. It looked like one frame of a video from a surveillance camera.

Goosebumps spread down his arms. The shot was from behind, and showed someone running down the sidewalk. Obviously, they both knew who it was. His heart beating in his ears, Drayden looked up at Mr. Kale.

"That Guardian by the door passed this out to the teachers today. They're looking for you."

Drayden whimpered in fear. "What should I do?"

"You want to tell my why you were running from them?"

Drayden recounted the episode for Mr. Kale.

Mr. Kale let out a deep breath. "Besides me, I doubt anyone can identify you from this video, and no teacher would turn you in anyway. The drug-dealing Guardian can't exactly tell his superiors why he's truly after you. The only thing they can officially cite you for is skipping school. The Chancellors probably wouldn't approve an exile for a first-time offender who happens to be our top student. So I wouldn't worry too much."

Mr. Kale leaned forward, his eyebrows raised. "However...you can't avoid that Guardian forever. That was a nifty stunt Tim pulled to get you in today. If that Guardian catches you in person though..." He shrugged. "I don't need to tell you the Guardians sometimes don't play by the rules. But there's another option, and I intended on calling you to my office today to discuss it even before this incident. Drayden, I think you should enter the Initiation."

Drayden couldn't decide how he felt about yet another person being so free with his life, even Mr. Kale, who had always treated him well. "Wesley said the same thing."

"There are good reasons, Drayden," Mr. Kale whispered. "Early New America was fairly equal. These days I believe the quality of life separation between the zones has exploded. Don't forget, I live in the Lab, so I know. At the very least, whether you move to the Palace or the Lab, you would guarantee a much better life for yourself and your family. A more fulfilling career as well. If you join the Bureau, over time you might even be able to influence policy, advocate for the Dorms. In the ultimate scenario, you could even promote tearing down the walls. Who knows what's possible once

you're there?" Mr. Kale looked hungry, like he was dreaming about the best meal he could ever want.

Drayden crossed his arms and frowned.

Mr. Kale's face relaxed. "I believe you'll pass, Drayden. I really do."

Drayden scoffed. "Nobody knows what the test is like or if anyone has ever passed. The few kids who entered were either exiled or live in another zone now. The Bureau doesn't announce the results, and the pledges can't return to tell everyone what happened, even if they join the Bureau. Supposedly families have moved from the Dorms, but the Bureau could have just exiled them to create this myth that kids pass the Initiation." Drayden stood and paced.

Mr. Kale smiled. "Right there, that's why I believe you'll pass. How can someone with your brain not pass?"

Because it's not just about intelligence.

"No, there's no way to know for sure," Mr. Kale continued. "However, the Bureau is vastly outnumbered by the populace. If the entire premise of the Initiation was revealed as a hoax, they would risk a revolt. They don't want that. They wish to hold onto power."

Drayden leaned on the desk. "Mr. Kale, I'm scared. Okay? I *hope* I could pass the intelligence portion, but who knows? And the so-called bravery part...what if it's, like, fighting a lion or something?"

Mr. Kale stifled a laugh. "Well, there are no lions in New America. In my opinion, the intelligence section won't be a calculus test. It'll be like brainteasers or riddles. The Bureau encourages all sixteen-year-olds to enter, and says the test doesn't require any special skills or studying. So logically, it can't use any complex math, because some kids haven't learned it. It must demand only basic arithmetic. The only way to make arithmetic difficult is by burying it in a brainteaser. Remember, there's always a trick. The answer is never the obvious thing. It's some gimmick, something outside the box."

Mr. Kale's expression softened. "My advice on bravery is that when people need it, they'll be surprised to find out it's there. People don't necessarily feel fearless or brave on a daily basis. When thrust into an extreme situation, you'd be shocked at what you're capable of. I think you would be fine."

Drayden rested his hands on his hips, and cocked his head. "Oh, gee, thanks. Basically, 'Don't worry about it' is your advice? Easy for you to say. Why does everyone want me to enter, anyway?" He plopped down in the chair, turning his hat backward.

"You're the best student I've ever had, Drayden. I believe in you. You're the only one who's ever become my friend. As your friend, I want you to enter because I crave something better for you. You're like a son to me. But I have an even greater personal interest beyond just your future."

Mr. Kale looked directly into his eyes. "This isn't right, Drayden. None of this is. History has taught us that you can't divide humanity. You can't play God, which the Bureau is doing. With the state of the world, that's courting extinction of the species. If you can make it to the Palace and join the Bureau, you can change things. One day you might even help overturn the whole system. Do this for all of us."

In a sick, ironic twist, the only one who could help Drayden sort all this out was his mother. He was confused, frightened, and a dozen other things at the same time.

A few buses had parked in front of the school. Thankfully the Guardians weren't there. Still, to avoid arousing any suspicion that he was the boy in the video, he needed to go on the field trip, although it was the furthest thing from his mind.

Tim snagged his arm. "C'mon, man. We get to go on a bus. A freaking *bus!*"

Electric buses only served people who traveled great distances for work. They included teachers coming to Dorm schools from the Lab, or plumbers leaving the Dorms to work in the Precinct. The students had never ridden on a bus before. While most of their excitement involved seeing the Meadow, the bus itself provided a thrill. Drayden and the other seniors pushed and shoved their way onto them, jockeying for window seats. Drayden scored one near the back of the first bus, and Tim sat beside him.

"This is so awesome," Tim said, rubbing his hands together. The bus buzzed with energy. They pulled out, headed up Park Avenue, and everyone cheered.

While a few kids immediately looked sick from the motion, Drayden found it exhilarating to go so fast. Once they passed Fiftieth Street, he absorbed the fresh sights. Though still in the Dorms, he wasn't familiar with these city blocks. His life encompassed so little of the city. He wanted to enjoy the trip, to soak in the different world. Unfortunately, his mind wandered.

Although Mr. Kale was only trying to help, encouraging Drayden to enter the Initiation for the future of New America muddled his message. Not that it wasn't a good reason; it was. But Mr. Kale wanted to satisfy his *own* desire to fix this broken system. It inadvertently weakened his plea for Drayden to enter, because it called into question the sincerity of his belief in Drayden's ability to pass. Yet... doing it to evade the overzealous Guardian did make some sense.

The bus turned left on Fifty-Seventh Street, passing some towering skyscrapers. The Bureau restricted access to this segment of the Dorms, leaving the streets deserted. They turned right on Sixth Avenue and approached the concrete wall separating the Dorms from the Meadow. The bus stopped at Fifty-Ninth Street before two giant steel doors in the twenty-five-foot-high wall. Heavily armed Guardians swarmed the area. One draped in guns approached the bus, surveyed it, and spoke to the driver.

It was bizarre the gate was so well guarded, since this part of the Dorms was restricted. It seemed like overkill. Why did they need so much security?

Mrs. Cartwright, the school's vice principal and today's chaperone, appeared frazzled at the front of the bus. Another woman fidgeted beside her. She wore glasses, a white lab coat, her red hair in a ponytail.

"Alright, everyone, quiet down! Take your seats!" Mrs. Cartwright yelled. "We're about to enter the Meadow, and I know you're all excited to see it. To help us understand what we're observing, we've asked Lucy Ravenna to be our guide. She's a scientist in the food production facilities. Please give her your undivided attention. Thank you. Lucy?"

"Thank you, Akari. Hello, everyone. If anyone has any questions on the tour, please raise your hand. We're pulling through the gate now, and if you look to your right, you'll see the park. Immediately you'll notice the wind turbines."

The whole bus "oohed" and "ahhed," marveling at the size of the windmills. They rose above the treetops, dominating the skyline.

Drayden had researched wind power on his own. He could build a wind turbine himself if he had the equipment. For all the Bureau's restrictions on every aspect of their lives, ironically, they didn't want to come off as controlling. The Bureau gave the illusion of choice, by allowing kids to do things like go to the library and learn skills such as martial arts. Yet it was freedom within a secure bubble. It was all a facade, which made Drayden wonder what else about the Bureau was an illusion.

"New America has forty-four wind turbines, each standing three hundred fifty feet tall," Lucy continued. "As impressive as the turbines are in size, the most amazing part is that we have them at all."

She looked embarrassed. "The Bureau insists we stress this point about the wind turbines. There's only one reason we have them and

have the power to run this city. We can all thank the disaster planning of the former New York Office of Emergency Management. In particular, its director at the time, our very own Premier, Eli Holst.

"When the Aeru bug started ravaging the world, the former leaders planned for a sustained quarantine contingency. They imported most of the materials for the wind turbines. The OEM stockpiled batteries, solar panels, medicine, farm animals, plants—you name it, they thought of it." Lucy smirked. "But as you all well know, and can see from my unfortunate outfit today, the one thing the OEM forgot was cotton plants."

The whole bus erupted in laughter.

A slight boy with a long neck raised his hand. "Why are some of the windmills not running?"

"Good question. Sometimes we have to shut down the turbines for maintenance," Lucy replied.

While Lucy droned on about hydroponic farming and the monstrous agriculture tents, Drayden digested the foreign scenery. The deserted Meadow was vast and eerie.

The long-necked boy raised his hand again. "Can we see inside the tents?"

"No," Lucy said sharply, and the boy flinched. She blushed. "Sorry. We're not allowed to show that."

While Drayden was no expert on human behavior, even he could see Lucy was a terrible poker player. There was definitely something inside the tents she didn't want them to see.

Lucy pointed to the left of the bus, changing the subject. "Now, way over there you can see a massive concrete structure. That's where all of our clean water comes from, and our salt. The Hudson is actually a two-way river. Fresh water comes down from the mountains and saltwater flows in from the ocean. At this point here, the water is salty. We take it in and desalinate it, and put it through other processes to purify it enough to drink."

The cows appeared when they neared the northwest corner of Central Park. "These are some of New America's most famous residents, providing your milk supply." Two men in gray overalls and red shirts were sprawled out on benches near the barn, fast asleep.

The long-necked boy raised his hand once again, easily winning the championship for most questions asked. "Who are those guys, and why are they asleep?"

"Huh. They feed the cows. They clearly should not be sleeping. I'll report it when I get back to work. Thanks for pointing that out!"

Drayden wondered whether those men would get into trouble or worse, be exiled. Herein lay the precise problem with all Dorm jobs, and what Drayden feared about his own future. If he worked as a lab tech and would always be one, would he not fall asleep on the job a few times? Besides physically showing up at work to prevent exile, exerting real effort seemed pointless since working hard would never earn you more money or a promotion.

He sometimes fantasized if he demonstrated exceptional ability as a lab tech, the Bureau would circumvent the rules and promote him to a full-fledged scientist. They could keep it secret and he'd remain in the Dorms. It *was* only a fantasy, because that would be unprecedented. If he entered the Initiation, he'd have a chance to become a real one.

First he needed to find out everything he could about his mother's exile from the Dorms, since he'd never be able to return. One stone remained unturned. Lily Haddad. Wes had said Mom was spending time with her, which was odd. Although they were both senior Dorm members, Drayden didn't recall them ever socializing.

The bus headed back down Fifth Avenue, the former Upper East Side. The solar farm on the building tops to the left glistened in the sun. When Lucy announced the end of the tour, the bus broke out in applause.

This signified their final moment of school, the event they'd anticipated since they were five.

Drayden's thoughts circled right back to his mom. She'd been there watching when he left for his first day of school all those years ago. He never imagined she wouldn't be there to witness his last.

CHAPTER 7

Drayden woke up early for a Saturday, threw on his beige track-suit, and headed around the corner to wait outside Lily Haddad's office, constantly scanning the area for Guardians.

The one lingering outside the FDC didn't look twice at Drayden.

Lily's office was in the same plaza as the FDC, two doors up on Second Avenue. The Bureau's office was adjacent to Lily's, in an antiquated movie theater. 2:00 p.m. today was the cutoff for entering the Initiation, Drayden noted from the marquee.

He checked the doorknob to Lily's office. Finding it locked and dark inside, he sat on the curb. Drayden was laser-focused on the Initiation now. There were so many reasons to enter, although he still wondered if it was a scam, despite Mr. Kale's assurances. Nobody knew what happened to kids who entered since they were never seen again. Maybe they were all exiled. The risk of the Initiation was not only its content, but the true reason for its existence. It might be a test to determine one's worthiness to move to the Palace as advertised, or it could be a forced exile in disguise. It didn't only require bravery to pass; it required bravery to enter. Drayden was not brave.

A line of people clutching cloth bags began to form at the FDC, which would open any minute.

Lily's unmistakable form walked down Second Avenue. Her long, curly hair blew in the breeze, as did her flowing green dress. A young Asian woman accompanying Lily spoke as they walked.

Drayden sprung up and darted in her direction. He intended on catching her before she reached the office so she wouldn't have any reason not to speak to him. He cut off her path to the door too abruptly.

Startled, she stepped back.

"Oh, sorry." Drayden raised his hands. "I didn't mean to scare you. Hello, Ms. Haddad. My name is Drayden Coulson. I believe you knew my mother Maya?"

"Yes, of course. Hello, Drayden." She turned to the other woman. "Celeste, please go on ahead and unlock the door. Be a sweetheart and stop by the FDC and pick up some tea, please? Thank you."

Celeste unlocked the door and slid by the line to enter the FDC.

"I'm so terribly sorry about your mother, dear," Lily said. "It's a dreadful thing and unfortunately growing more common. How are you doing?" She tilted her head and touched his shoulder, her warm eyes showing genuine concern.

"I'm hanging in there. Still in shock. That's actually what I wanted to ask you about. Do you have any idea why she was exiled? I thought you might have some insight."

"Unfortunately, I don't. Your mother was a saint, serving so many people in the community. We're all just living our lives here in the Dorms, trying to survive. Unfortunately, the Bureau keeps sticking its nose where it doesn't belong. Lately the Chancellors keep popping in and exiling people with no proof of wrongdoing."

Drayden lowered his eyes.

"You were hoping for more?" Lily asked. "Dear, even if I knew more, or if the allegation were true, nothing can be done. I've

started intense discussions with the Bureau to put a stop to the exiles. For now, that is the best we can do. And speak of the devil, there is Thomas right now. Thomas!" she called. "Drayden, I'm so very sorry about your mother. I must run now. You hang in there, and if you need anything else please stop by anytime." She touched his shoulder again and walked past him.

"But—"

Lily hurried over to Thomas Cox, a tall, regal man, who was in charge of the Council on Dorm Relations. PreCon, he purportedly owned a computer company.

Drayden clenched his jaw. He needed answers. Lily wasn't telling him everything, he was sure of it. She'd done it pleasantly, but she'd brushed him off. He needed to stop being such a pushover. He wasn't going to be denied this time. He decided to wait in her office. She had said to stop by anytime. When she entered, he would be waiting and demand the truth, refusing to leave until she told him everything. What was the worst that could happen?

Drayden inched backward toward her door. He peered left and right, doing his best not to appear sketchy. When his hand touched the door behind him, he spun and opened it, bounded through, and eased it shut. He strolled straight past the unoccupied receptionist's desk into a dark corridor.

Though the building appeared quaint from outside, it stretched back quite far. He walked, reading the nameplates on the doors, until he saw it the plate reading Lily Haddad. He turned the knob and opened the door, revealing an expansive office.

Paintings of landscapes adorned the freshly painted white walls. A bulky wooden desk sat in the back of the office, with two black leather chairs facing it.

Drayden plopped into one of them and waited, studying each painting. After a short time, the click-clack of footsteps echoed in the hallway, growing louder.

Drayden rose, his nerves flaring. What should he say when she walked in and discovered him in her private office, uninvited? He should have planned a speech.

Don't panic. Think.

Two voices spoke, Lily's and a man's.

It must be Thomas Cox. What was Drayden thinking? This was a terrible idea. He made a dash for the door, but it was too late. They were almost in the room. Panicking, he ran around the desk and dove underneath it.

Why the hell did I do that? Please don't sit down at the desk.

If she did, or even leaned down, she would bust him.

The door opened and the footsteps entered the room. Someone walked around behind her desk.

Drayden hugged his legs to his chest as tight as he could. On top of everything else, he hated cramped spaces. He'd accidentally locked himself in his bedroom closet as a child, and he'd been claustrophobic ever since.

"That's a load of crap, Thomas," Lily said from behind her desk.

"Watch it, Lily. I'm on your side here. You know that," Cox said, anger in his voice. "I don't know what's happening. I told you: Only the guys at the very top do, and they're keeping it hush hush."

Lily stepped around in front of her desk.

Drayden exhaled slowly, closing his eyes.

"People in the Dorms are angry. They're even turning on me," Lily said. "I gave a speech two days ago and I thought I was going be killed. You have to give me something. Don't feed me this baloney about food-growth variability, blah blah blah. What about the power outages? Does the Bureau realize you can see the damn lights of the Palace from up here? Only the Dorms are dark, and everyone knows it."

"I told you: I don't know what's happened. What I *can* tell you is that it's real, not random. There is a problem with power. The

wind turbines might be failing. I'm not sure exactly. The Dorms will always lose power first. If there's only enough electricity to light one zone, it'll be the Palace. From what I can tell, this is permanent and may even be getting worse."

Cox exhaled. "The power outages have grave consequences beyond not having light. We can't produce enough food or clean water. That's why the food allocations have shrunk. Holst won't tell anyone except his top deputies what's changed. My guy inside tells me they're having non-stop meetings now. I think if we're going to do something about Holst, we need to move quickly. He needs to be removed from power."

Holy shkat!

Drayden couldn't believe his ears. If they found him under the desk, he was done, exiled for sure. Jesus, maybe his mom *was* part of a conspiracy. His head was spinning.

Lily walked behind her desk and pulled the chair out.

Drayden closed his eyes again. He sucked in a breath, held it, and prayed, for the first time ever.

She slammed the chair back in, nearly smashing Drayden's feet.

He flinched, squeezing his legs even tighter to his chest.

"Goddammit, Thomas, we're not ready for that yet! We need a lot more pieces in place. You're going to get us both exiled, for heaven's sake."

"Nobody knows about our plans except our friends. Relax."

Drayden focused on Lily's feet, mere inches away. Her worn out shoes were black with pointy toes.

"You're changing the subject," she snapped. "We'll take care of Holst in due time. This power problem and the food shortages. Why the spike in exiles?"

Cox sighed. "The exiles are a calculated strategy by the Bureau," he said calmly. "Whatever's causing the power shortfall, it's resulting in food shortages. Between the death rate and the exiles

due to crime, the food supply has been in equilibrium with the population size for years. That's no longer the case, so the Bureau launched a new initiative, Project China. Its purpose is to shrink the population down to a size that matches the recent level of food production. Normally the Bureau exiles people because they broke the law, right? That applies to all zones. Under Project China they're exiling people at random. Only in the Dorms. For now, anyway."

Cox wandered around the office as he spoke. "However, as this power problem gets worse, and it will, the rate of exiles will need to increase. Like, a lot. You think nineteen exiles in April was bad? It could skyrocket. I'm sorry to say this, but nobody is safe in the Dorms. Well, you are. You're untouchable. The Bureau knows that. They don't want to spark a revolt."

Drayden sat paralyzed. His face flushed red hot. Was that what happened to his mother? Totally random, thrown away like a piece of trash? He wanted to scream, to cry, to protest, to charge. He ached to grab Cox around the throat. *Nobody* was safe in the Dorms? He struggled to control his breathing. He had to remain silent.

Breathe.

Lily walked back around in front of the desk. "My God, Holst," she spat. "That *snake*. People in the Dorms are always treated like second-class citizens. The Bureau may get a revolt whether they want one or not. Despite what they believe, people in the Dorms are not stupid. If exiles skyrocket, they're going to figure out what the Bureau is doing."

"Careful, Lily. Only the Dorms are suffering right now. The Precinct is fine. The Guardians are totally loyal to the Bureau. The Bureau would accomplish their goal much swifter by crushing a revolt with firepower, and they wouldn't hesitate. You need to keep people calm. I need protection too. I'm risking my own neck here."

"I know that," Lily said. "What am I supposed to tell people? They're looking to me for answers."

"Hell, I don't know," Cox said. "Let's take a walk. Let people see us talking. At a minimum they'll know you're working on it."

"Fine."

The door clicked open and shut, and their footsteps drifted away down the hall.

Drayden let out a huge breath and wiped the sweat from his brow. He eased his way out, spun around and peeked over the desk.

The room was empty.

Monsters. Monsters! Drayden snatched a quill off Lily's desk and hurled it across the room. *Get a hold of yourself.* He needed to ensure they weren't in the lobby. He tiptoed to the door and opened it a crack.

Nobody.

He stepped into the hall and took baby steps back toward the front of the office. The front door was only fifteen feet away now. He reached the lobby.

"Hey! Who are you?"

Oh shkat.

The receptionist gawked, her mouth agape in shock.

Drayden bolted for the door and thrust it open.

"Get back here!" the receptionist yelled.

He sprinted north up Second Avenue.

Drayden ran three blocks before looking back.

No one was following him.

He stopped at Thirty-Fourth Street, bent over with his hands on his knees, huffing and puffing. He jogged east on Thirty-Fourth and slumped down on a stoop, buried his face in his hands, and burst into tears. His mother, his everything, whimsically cast off to her death by the Bureau. Maybe it was this new policy, or Lily's

overthrow plot. It might relate to her affair, or even just have been a mistake. But why her? Why his mother?

He *had* sought the truth, and instead had discovered even more possibilities, and a reality far darker than he could have imagined. It had nothing to do with his mother at all. The world he knew was falling apart. Nobody was safe in the Dorms. Exiles were about to skyrocket. Drayden thought of Wesley and his father. He couldn't bear to lose either of them to exile. How could he allow it when he had an opportunity to do something about it? If he entered the Initiation and won, he could get them all moved to the Palace where they'd be safe. Who was he kidding? He could never truly figure out what happened to his mother from the Dorms. Joining the Bureau was the only way.

Drayden wiped his tears away. Everything became crystal clear. He knew exactly what he needed to do.

He marched down Second Avenue. He didn't care anymore if someone from Lily's office was looking for him, or if the bald Guardian was prowling. After crossing Thirty-First Street, he entered the Bureau's office.

The sprawling lobby revealed no traces of its movie theater past—no old ticket booth or skeleton of a concession stand. A desk sat in the middle of the room, lit with a single lamp. Otherwise the room was empty and completely dark. The lamp illuminated only the face of the man sitting there. A repetitive, wheezy buzzing reverberated around the vast space.

Drayden approached the desk.

The man cradled his head in his hands, fast asleep, snoring. He was a squirrelly fellow with puffy cheeks, glasses, and a receding hairline.

Drayden cleared his throat loudly. "Ahem! Excuse me. Hello, sir?"

The man awoke with a shudder. He thrust his legs out, kicking the desk. "Oh, oh...hello, young man. How can I help you?" he asked, rubbing his eyes.

"I'd like to enter the Initiation," Drayden stated bluntly.

The man scratched his chin. "The Initiation, huh?"

"Am I in the wrong place?"

"No, no, this is the right place. It's just...you're the first person to enter this year."

Drayden swallowed hard, contemplating doing this alone. "Seriously? Nobody else has entered?"

"Sometimes people come in at the last second. Son, are you sure you want to do this?"

Drayden hesitated. "Yes. I think so. Yes, I do."

"I have to tell you, nobody has entered in two years."

Drayden's jaw dropped. *Two years?* He pictured his mom being shoved outside the wall in tears. There was no turning back. "I guess someone has to be the first."

The man handed him a paper form, a quill, and an ink well.

Drayden sat in the chair facing the desk. He filled in his name, age, address, and family members' names. He handed the form back.

"Congratulations. You're officially a pledge now. You need to be back here tomorrow at six o'clock in the morning, sharp."

"What should I wear? Should I bring anything?"

"You don't need to bring anything. Wear whatever you would normally wear. Something comfortable, and shoes you can run in."

Drayden gulped. "Is this where the test takes place?"

The man grinned. "You'll find out tomorrow."

CHAPTER 8

What have I done?

Drayden squinted in the glaring sun. It was just sinking in. He'd entered the Initiation, alone. Alone again. It was only fitting after Mom's exile. He was adrift at sea by himself in this world without her. Tomorrow, he'd literally be alone.

It was possible he'd overreacted to the news from Lily's conversation with Cox. Cox implied staying in the Dorms was suicide, given how much the random exiles would pick up. What if Cox was wrong? He should have considered that before he rushed to enter. Now it was too late.

A nervous heat enveloped Drayden, his mouth choked with cotton. He could be exiled tomorrow in the Initiation. Today might be the last day of his life. And damn the Dorms, there wasn't even a fun way to spend his last day here.

How could he tell his father? What if he didn't approve? Drayden could wait until his father was asleep tonight, sneak in, and sneak back out early. He needed to eat, though, and sleep so he'd be well rested for the Initiation. Plus, however his family felt about it, he should say goodbye.

Dad and Wes would both be home right now. Should he tell them what he overheard from Cox about the power outages and

exiles? He needed to think logically, like a scientist, not a frazzled kid. If he failed in the Initiation and was exiled, his family would remain in the Dorms. They'd be powerless to stop the exiles yet would live in constant fear of the inevitable. It might be better for them not to know.

The sprawling plaza in front of the Bureau office and FDC brimmed with people. Drayden surveyed the crowd, searching for the bald Guardian. His eyes landed on Sidney from school.

A mere thirty feet away, she slumped on a bench facing the Bureau office, her arms cradling her stomach as if she felt sick. She stared at him, but didn't smile or wave.

She must have noticed him come out. Perhaps she was considering the Initiation too and wanted to see if anyone entered. Holst said pledges worked as a team during the test. Being a super athlete, she would be a major help on the bravery section. She'd be company, rather than him doing it solo.

Yet Drayden didn't want her to enter just because she saw him do it. Maybe all she needed to make the leap was knowing someone else would be there. Drayden wasn't just someone; kids at school knew he was smart. Sidney was probably aware the intelligence portion would be her weakness, just like he knew the bravery part would be his. The last thing he needed was liability for another person on the intelligence tests, someone else depending on him to carry them through. It was way too much responsibility, and he was terrified enough already. He felt even more pressure now, considering what he learned from Thomas Cox. Just doing well enough to reach the Lab or Precinct wouldn't cut it. Those zones might be at risk too as power generation deteriorated further. He needed to move to the Palace, and merely passing the Initiation wouldn't suffice. He needed to ace it.

Drayden would love to say hello to Sidney. It wasn't every day that a cute, popular girl randomly talked to him. Still, he didn't

want to tell her he entered, so he turned away and headed for his apartment.

After the two-minute trek, he stopped in front of their brownstone. 328 East Thirtieth Street, second floor. His home for sixteen years. This was the last day he'd ever see it. He'd either pass the Initiation and move zones, or he'd be exiled.

It was now or never.

Tim and Wesley were slouched on the sofa.

In the corner, Dad played chess with Alfie Quintero, his best friend. A scruffy guy, Alfie's graying hair exploded in wild curls. Dad and Alfie played chess every day, and Alfie had still never won a game.

The savory smell of fried potatoes saturated the room. "Drayden, there are some hash browns in the kitchen if you're hungry," Dad said, his eyes fixed on the board.

Drayden's stomach growled. He hadn't eaten yet today. He dashed into the kitchen, grabbed a fork, and stuffed his face right out of the frying pan. He relished the warm, salty, fried potatoes melting in his mouth.

"Get a plate, ya animal!" Wesley yelled.

Drayden dumped the rest of the hash browns on a plate and sat on a chair in the living room.

Tim and Wesley faced each other on the couch, engaged in some deep conversation.

Wesley released an exasperated sigh. "I don't know, man. It sounds creepy. Especially since I work there."

"I'm telling you. The FDC is a gold mine," Tim said. "Everybody has to go there. When you see a cute girl, just go introduce yourself."

Drayden smirked. "You trying to find Wes a wife? Good luck with that."

"Laugh it up, bro." Wesley scowled. "I don't see too many girls waiting outside your door."

"They don't have to," Drayden said through a mouthful of potatoes. "I'm going to marry Catrice."

Tim threw his head back in shock. "I'm sure you're aware she's rejected everyone who's asked her to hang out. Have you told her this yet?"

"No, not yet." He drew in a quick breath. *Catrice.* It hit him like a hammer. He would never lay eyes on her again. Oh God, no. Her last memory of him would be his beating from Alex.

Drayden slumped in his chair and set his empty plate on the coffee table. He observed the room, gauging the mood. There was no way he could bring up the Initiation. Everything in here was so...normal. Routine. Like any other Saturday. Part of him even felt guilty for spoiling their pleasant morning. Drayden stood and cleared his throat. "Everybody? Can I have your attention?"

Tim tossed a crumpled-up ball of paper at him. "I didn't mean tell *us* you plan to marry Catrice. No need for some grand announcement. Go tell her, ya flunk."

Wesley cracked up.

"Knock it off, you guys. This is serious," Drayden said.

Dad and Alfie tabled their chess game and gave Drayden their attention.

"I signed up for the Initiation."

Silence.

Stunned faces gawked at him. While Wesley beamed, Dad turned beet red. Wesley sprung up, arms outstretched inviting a hug. "That's my b—"

"You did *what*?" Dad shouted. He jumped up from the chess table. "Absolutely not! What were you thinking, Drayden? I just lost my wife. I'm not losing my son too. I'm going to march you right

back down to that office, young man, and we're scratching your name off the list."

"It's too late, Dad," Drayden said, shaking his head.

Dad stuffed his feet into his shoes. "Like hell it is."

"Dad, it's too late to change my mind. I had a long talk with Mr. Kale, and he's sure I'll pass. I'm doing this. Not just for me, for all of us. Mom wanted me to take care of this famil—"

"I'm your father, and I'm not allowing you to do this!" His face twitched, the corners of his mouth turned down. "You're just a child. You don't know how cruel the world can be. I'm protecting you, which is my job."

Like you protected Mom?

Angry tears welled up. "Dad, what happened to Mom? You said there were things I didn't know about her. What didn't I know?"

"I don't know what happened! I don't." He took a deep breath, gathering himself. "Gavin Kale is not your father. I am. I'm the only one that has your best interests in mind. Nobody else. Everyone else wants something from you. The Initiation is a trap. Do you hear me? It's not real. Nobody passes. I'll bet you that. Now...go to your room."

Wesley stepped up to their father. "Dad, let him go. He needs to do this. He *can* do this. He'll pass. He's going to get us out of here. We can all have better jobs, more food. You can be a doctor again."

Tim stood tall. "I'm going with him."

Everyone's heads snapped in Tim's direction.

"Tim, no," Drayden said. "I can't let you enter because of me. I mean, I'd love to have you there, believe me. But please don't enter just because of me." He paused. "Would you enter if I didn't?"

"Hells no, I wouldn't! You crazy? I wouldn't have a chance in hell on the intelligence section. That's what I have you for. You'll have me for the other stuff. We'll get through this together."

Perhaps he wasn't alone after all. Drayden rushed Tim and bear hugged him. An enormous weight lifted from his shoulders. "Thank you, buddy."

"Tim, go home," Dad said, jabbing his finger in the air. "Are you two insane? You boys have no clue what you're doing. The Initiation's not meant to be passed, I'm telling you. It's just there to exile more people. God only knows how impossible they've made it these days." He rushed toward Drayden.

Wesley gripped their father in a clumsy hug around the chest, restraining him. "No, Dad. He's going. Drayden, go get your things and stay at Tim's house. Go!"

Drayden hustled to his room. He collected a change of clothes and comfortable shoes.

When he returned, Dad was sitting on the couch in defeat, his shoulders slumped. Wesley stood over him. Alfie still lingered awkwardly by the chess board, his hands in his pockets.

Drayden set his things down and approached Wesley, first ensuring his father wasn't going to spring up and surprise him. He hugged his big brother. "I love you, Wes. If I don't make it, I don't want you to feel bad, okay? This is my decision. I own it. Thanks for believing in me."

Wesley pursed his lips and averted his teary eyes before composing himself. "I'm going to see you soon, in the Palace, when me and Dad move there. I'm going to be the proudest big brother in New America. You're going to make it, little bro. I know it." He gripped Drayden by the shoulders and squeezed hard. "You be strong. Be *tough*."

Drayden looked at his father. "Dad?"

His father didn't move, not even a glance.

Drayden hovered over him. "I'm sorry, Dad. But I know what I'm doing. I'm gonna get us out of here. I love you."

His father remained silent.

"Tim, let's go," Drayden said. He motioned toward the door.

They left the apartment. Drayden had displayed confidence just to make his father and Wes feel better. He was bubbling over with fear and doubt about what lay ahead.

"Tim, we could be exiled. Probably will be. You need to talk to your mom and stepdad about this."

Tim stared straight ahead. "No, I don't. They don't care. Screw him. You're the only family that matters."

They rounded the corner and headed for the Bureau office one block north to sign Tim up. As they neared it, Drayden couldn't help but steal a glance back at that bench where Sidney had sat. She was gone.

CHAPTER 9

The boys left Tim's apartment on Thirty-Fifth Street at 5:45am after a breakfast of milk and cantaloupe. Both wore gray imitation-denim jeans, beige t-shirts, and gray sweatshirts.

A hint of smoke from someone's fire made the morning air smell like winter. A few buses had passed, ferrying workers downtown, from the Dorms to the Lab and Precinct. Tim strolled ahead, hands in his pockets, whistling, as if they were headed to a movie.

In contrast, Drayden's hollow stomach burned with acid and his hands shook.

The only building lit in the darkness, the Bureau office glowed like a beacon even from three blocks away.

Tim stopped suddenly and Drayden crashed into his back.

"What the hell?" Drayden asked.

"Don't shoot," Tim said, his hands in the air.

The bald Guardian blocked their path. He pointed his pistol at the boys, a grin stretched across his face. "Looks like it's your unlucky day, kid. I need to have a chat with your friend, but I guess you'll be coming along with him. You deserve it anyway after your little stunt at school the other day."

Drayden's heart thumped.

Tim peeked back at Drayden with wide eyes, before glancing behind him.

The Guardian waved his gun. "Let's go, both of you. Right now."

Drayden entered full panic mode. They would miss the Initiation. Plus, who knew what the Guardian would do to them?

Tim turned back to the Guardian. "You sure just the two of us, officer?"

The Guardian looked confused. "Yeah. Now move it."

"Let me just round up a few more people."

The Guardian lowered his weapon. "Huh?"

Tim darted into the middle of the Second Avenue, right into the path of an oncoming bus. He waved his arms and jumped up and down. "Help! Stop!" he screamed.

The bus slowed and stopped, its headlights illuminating Tim.

"We need help! Everyone please!" He pointed at Drayden and the Guardian on the sidewalk.

Everyone on the bus turned to see. Some got out of their seats to peer out the windows.

This was his chance. Drayden bolted into the street and joined his friend.

The Guardian holstered his weapon, turning his face away from the prying eyes of the passengers. He cursed and ran off down Thirty-Fourth Street.

Drayden was paralyzed, speechless, his mouth hanging open.

The bus driver opened the door. "Get in."

They hurried on and thanked the driver, who deposited them in front of the Bureau office.

Tim reached the door first. "That was scary, but hopefully it'll be the worst part of the day. You ready?"

"No." Drayden was still shaken by the close call with the Guardian. The whole thing had happened so fast. Tim had saved their lives and carried on as if it were nothing.

"It's me and you, bro," Tim said. "All the way. The Bureau should be scared of the two of us right now. Let's do this."

Tim opened the door, and they stepped inside. They both gasped.

Six chairs formed a circle in the center of the room. Four of them were occupied. In them sat Sidney, Alex, Charlie...and Catrice. They all stared at Drayden and Tim in the doorway. Sidney didn't look surprised.

A squat older man in a gray linen suit with a red Bureau pin approached. A ring of short gray hair framed his otherwise bald head, the white lights overhead gleaming off his extra shiny scalp. "Gentleman, please take those seats."

Tim shrugged. As they sat down, Alex whispered to Charlie, and the two broke out in quiet laughter. Sidney eyed Drayden with a wry smile. Catrice picked at her fingernails, avoiding eye contact with anyone.

Drayden couldn't believe his eyes. With only a few hours left, he and Tim had been the only entrants. Somehow, in that narrow window, four additional kids had entered, among them both his nemesis *and* his crush. As challenging as the Initiation might be, Alex would undoubtedly make it tougher. Out of 1,200 graduates, it *had* to be Alex. Yet why would Catrice enter? Talk about irony. After all the years of longing to get closer to her, he finally scored a chance, under life or death circumstances. Not exactly the hookup house. Drayden's stomach turned at the sight of Sidney. He liked her. He just hoped she hadn't entered only because he had.

Like at school, the lack of clothing variety in the Dorms became glaring. Catrice and Sidney both wore gray leggings, gray t-shirts, and beige sweatshirts. Alex and Charlie exactly mirrored Tim and Drayden. Only Drayden's green hat and Alex's red bandana stood out.

Alex waved his hand to get Drayden's attention. He pretended to punch his own eye, simulated his head snapping back in slow motion, and fake cried. To conclude the performance, he cackled in delight.

Drayden ignored him. He refused to give Alex the satisfaction of a reaction. Alex was not going to ruin this for him.

The shiny-headed Bureau representative addressed the group. "Good morning, pledges. My name is Bruce Tyson. I'm the Chairman of the Initiation Council. The six of you are the only entrants of this year's Initiation. Now that you're all here, it's time to get started."

Drayden tapped his foot, distracting himself from the tension by speculating about how Bruce Tyson made his scalp so shiny. Had he polished it? Oiled it?

Tyson pointed at the door. "There's a bus outside. Everybody on it, please."

Drayden sat up front with Tim, Alex sat with Charlie two rows behind, and Sidney sat with Catrice across the aisle.

"I'm so glad there's another girl here," Sidney said to her.

Catrice smiled.

As soon as Tyson took a seat in the front, the bus sped off, heading north. They entered the Meadow through the same gate from the tour. Drayden wondered for a moment if the Initiation was a sham, and the bus would drive them directly up to the Henry Hudson Bridge to face exile.

It stopped at Seventy-Third Street and Broadway, in front of a massive stone building. Tyson escorted them inside. The towering lobby stretched several stories, with a gorgeous dome and soaring stone archways. Rays of early morning light streaked through titanic windows, making dust in the air sparkle. It appeared to be an old bank. Tyson led them downstairs to the basement, passing them off

to another Bureau member, identifiable by the red Bureau pin on her beige dress.

"Good luck," Bruce Tyson said as he left.

The Bureau woman was tall and elegant, her brown hair held back by a red headband. She glided before them, leading the way down a narrow corridor. They entered a dim, windowless room with exposed pipes on the ceiling. Chairs surrounded a round table, which held six red backpacks.

"Welcome to the Initiation," she said. "My name is Eris Page. I want to express my admiration for your drive and courage. I'm on the Initiation Council, and I'm going to help you prepare. Please, have a seat. The backpacks have your names on them."

The pledges exchanged nervous glances and sat next to their respective backpacks.

"Inside you will find all the items you need for the Initiation."

Drayden and the others unzipped the packs and rifled through them.

"You'll find bottles of water, mixed nuts, fruit, a flashlight, paper, a mechanical pencil, a map, antiseptic wipes, gauze, medical tape, and painkillers."

Drayden shuddered at those last four items.

"Whoa!" Charlie yelled, his head buried in the pack. "A mechanical pencil? And a flashlight? Can we keep these?"

Page looked annoyed. "No, you cannot. Now, the map is not just any map. It's a subway map. As you know, the subways have not run since the Confluence. The Initiation takes place in the abandoned tunnels. The stations have been...modified. You see, the Initiation is not just a test. It's a journey that will usher you from here, underground through the tunnels, all the way into the heart of the Palace." She looked around at them in turn. "Should you succeed."

Jeez, Drayden thought. *The subway tunnels?*

"Challenges along the way will test your intelligence, bravery, or both. We test your intelligence in a variety of ways, while your bravery will be judged through physical tests. On most challenges, failure to complete them will result in exile. On a few, failure won't initiate exile but it may prevent you from getting something that would assist in the following challenge. In those few instances, we will let you know that beforehand."

"So generous of you," Charlie mumbled.

Page slowly walked around the table as she spoke. "Although you will travel through the Initiation as a group, we evaluate you individually. On all challenges, it's up to you to decide how much you want to work collectively, leveraging your different skills. The intelligence challenges compel you to work together. You submit one answer, so it's a group pass or fail. On the bravery challenges, success is more individual. Some of you could pass while others are exiled." She scanned their faces. "There are cameras all throu—"

"Aahhhh!" Sidney screamed. A rat had dropped from the ceiling onto the table.

Drayden shoved himself away, nearly falling from his chair as the creature scampered around. "Crud!" He jumped back and cowered in the corner.

The rat ran laps on the table. Charlie stood, laughing, and Sidney jumped onto his back. Catrice pulled her legs up onto her chair, hugging them tight. Tim backed away, chortling.

Alex scooped up the terrified rat, hugged it to his chest, and caressed it. "Don't worry, little buddy." He glared at the others. "You wetchops. This poor little guy is more scared than you are!"

He carried the rat outside the room, where he gently placed it on the ground.

Drayden was mesmerized. Finally, something Alex cared about. It *would* be a nasty old rat.

Everyone watched with bemusement. Alex returned to his seat, noticing the roomful of eyes on him. "What?"

Charlie was cracking up. "Drayden, you were scareder than a long-tailed cat in a room full of rocking chairs!"

Drayden slammed his chair back into place. "Shut up, Charlie."

Eris Page raised her hands in the air. "Everyone, calm down. I'm sorry about that. Thank you, Alex. Please retake your seats.

"As I was saying, there are cameras and microphones throughout the tunnels, particularly around the challenges. Those will occur in the subway stations. You will be constantly monitored by the Initiation Council. Not all the stations will have challenges. Stations that are brightly lit contain challenges, while those that are dark and abandoned do not. Unless the instructions explicitly state that no exile is involved, you must complete the challenges. Attempting to skip them will result in exile for everyone. I would also recommend completing those challenges that don't result in exile. On those, you'll definitely want the items the Bureau is offering for the subsequent challenge."

She leaned her hands on the table. "This next detail is crucial to understand. Should you complete the Initiation, the Council will need to determine in which zone to place you. If one or more of you finishes, at least one of you will be selected to join the Bureau in the Palace. It could be more than one, although that's not likely. In a sense, you are in competition with each other to earn that spot in the Palace, if that is your goal. The Bureau will choose whoever has shown themselves to be the worthiest of joining it, because it wants the very best. The others who finish will be placed in the Lab or Precinct, based on your demonstrated skills."

Drayden cringed. He'd selfishly accepted his best friend's help without fully comprehending the consequences. Even if they escaped exile, they'd probably be separated at the end. Tim had

sacrificed himself to protect Drayden. He needed to find a way to get them both into the Palace.

"You'll begin here, at the Seventy-Second Street station. The subway lines are numbered, and here we have the Two-Three Line, as well as the One Line. You'll remain on one of those tracks, ending at either Wall Street or South Ferry, both final stations in the Palace. We've marked them on the maps. Which route you take is your choice, though you'll be under a time constraint. You have eight hours to finish the Initiation, so you must use your judgment. There are clocks throughout the journey, displaying the time remaining. You will receive written or verbal instructions for each challenge. If anyone attempts to escape a subway station, everyone will be exiled. Are we clear on the rules?"

Drayden swallowed hard, his throat like sandpaper. This was not at all what he'd expected. He assumed it would be a test, in a room, not a journey in some creepy abandoned world beneath the city.

Page waved to someone outside the door. "We'll start in thirty minutes. You can use this time to study the map, strategize, relax, visit the bathroom, or eat."

Within seconds, a worker set a mountain of scrambled eggs on the table, along with a towering pitcher of milk.

Drayden's mouth watered to the point that some drool may have slipped out. It had to be twenty eggs' worth, and a whole gallon of milk. Not only did the Bureau have working pencils and flashlights, they also had enough eggs to share twenty or so with kids from the Dorms?

The pledges attacked the eggs and milk like a pack of rabid rats, decimating it in minutes. They each spent the leftover time privately, in silence. Drayden studied the map, as did Catrice. Alex retied his red bandana around his head. The others milled around. Everybody took their turn in the bathroom.

Eris Page entered. "It's time."

A hole underground. That was where he would die.

No. Drayden pushed the negative thoughts from his brain. This was just another test, like all the ones he'd spent years acing at school. He wasn't sure he believed that.

Eris Page had left them at the old subway station entrance a block south, the Seventy-Second Street station on the Upper West Side, where they could join the One Line or Two-Three Line.

Drayden trembled. It had taken mere minutes to go from normal life to...this. Whatever *this* was.

The entrance itself consisted of a modest brick structure resembling a house. Page had told them to follow the signs to the downtown track. "God bless you, children," she'd muttered before hurrying off.

Tim opened the door. "Well, what are we waiting for? Let's do this."

They stepped inside the foyer and entered a different world. It was frigid, dark, and damp, with a musty smell like wet vegetation, or a decades-old leak. Dust shrouded antique subway card machines. Dried mud and leaves matted the cracked tile floor.

Tim hopped the rusty turnstiles, leading the way. A crooked sign dangled, pointing them down the stairs to the right for the downtown track. At the top of the staircase, white light from the platform below illuminated their faces.

Drayden stayed glued to Tim as they descended, the others falling in behind. They emerged onto a clean, gray-tiled platform. It was twenty feet wide, with train tracks on both sides sunk five feet below. A second platform sat across the station on the right, sandwiched between its own pair of sunken tracks. Spotless white tiles covered the walls, reflecting the bright lights of the station. Compared to the street-level entryway, the platform was

immaculate, and Drayden thought this must have been exactly how it looked back when the subways ran. It took a moment to orient himself. They were facing the wrong way—uptown, to the north of the city. He spun around, looking downtown, and drew in a quick breath.

Fifty yards down the station, the tracks ran straight into a giant white wall. It stretched floor-to-ceiling, cutting off the tracks and the platform, across the total width of the station. A cloaked man stood on the platform in front of a shiny silver door in the wall. A computer screen and a keyboard sat on a long table beside him.

The pledges hustled in his direction. He was an intimidating figure. He remained poker-faced, with smoldering dark eyes, slicked black hair, and a black goatee. A red Bureau pin adorned his flowing black robe. His expression softened when they reached him.

"Hello, pledges," he said, his voice deep. "My name is Owen Payne. This is your first test. You must pass it to gain entry into the tunnel. Provided you do, the clock will start running. If you fail it, you will be exiled before your Initiation even begins."

He paused, as if letting them digest his threat. "I must warn you, the Initiation is very difficult. You will be tested in ways you cannot possibly imagine. Some places in the Initiation may result in exile, others in immediate death. The Initiation is not for the faint of heart. I hope you have chosen wisely. Are we ready to begin?"

Immediate death? Drayden shuddered. Maybe this was a terrible idea.

"Very well," said Payne. He stepped up to the blank computer screen and keyboard. It rested on a lengthy wooden planked table, like a picnic table without the benches. "Presumably, none of you have used a computer before. It's quite simple. When I press this key, a riddle will appear on the screen, as well as a ticking clock. You have five minutes to solve the riddle and type the solution on

the keyboard, hitting Enter, here. You may answer only once. If you are successful, the clock will stop and I will open the door behind me. You will start your journey. If you are not, this Initiation is over. Understood?"

Drayden nodded. *Remain calm, just think clearly.*

Payne hit the Enter key and stepped off to the side.

The screen read:

"YOU FORCE HEAVEN TO BE EMPTY"
"_ _ _ _ _ _"

A timer appeared: *05:00, 04:59, 04:58...*

Charlie scratched his head. "You force heaven to be empty. What the hell does that mean?"

"There are seven spaces," Sidney spoke up. "The answer has seven letters."

Drayden's face flushed with heat. He didn't know the answer.

Alex grabbed Drayden's arm. "Well?"

Drayden shook him off. "I don't know. Let me think."

"Well, think fast!" Alex yelled.

"I need a minute!" Drayden snapped. He stepped away and tugged on his left ear. *Think, dammit!* He stole a glance at the clock. *04:35, 04:34...*

Catrice squatted. She chewed her nails, staring into space.

Drayden grimaced. Was everyone counting on him to solve this?

Tim corralled Charlie, Alex, and Sidney, and raised his hands. "What forces Heaven to be empty? What would empty out Heaven?"

"God? Or no, the devil?" Sidney asked.

Tim's face lit up. "Good! The devil. That makes sense, right? The devil would empty out Heaven. Nice, Sid!"

"Devil only has five letters," Alex said, examining his outstretched fingers.

Drayden couldn't concentrate with everyone yelling. His mind was blank. The devil was a logical thought, but it was a real answer, not a trick. Mr. Kale had said to search for a gimmick.

Charlie bumped his fists together. "What's another name for the devil?"

"Satan?" Tim asked. "No, five letters."

"Antichrist?" Sidney asked, counting the letters on her fingers.

"Lucifer?" Tim asked. "Lucifer. Lucifer!" he screamed, jumping up and down. "Seven letters!"

Drayden checked the clock again.

03:40, 03:39...

He started to hyperventilate. *Breathe, relax.* He rubbed his temples.

Tim ran over. "Dray, Lucifer? What do you think?"

Drayden shook his head.

"You sure? Okay."

Sidney pressed both hands into the sides of her head. "Three minutes left!"

Tim ran back to Charlie, Alex, and Sidney, huddled around the computer. Catrice sat on the ground in her own world and ran both hands through her hair. She whipped open her backpack and took out her paper and pencil.

"I think we should type Lucifer," Alex said.

Tim grabbed Alex by the arm. "No, Drayden said it's wrong."

"So? What is he, the boss? I don't hear any answers out of mister smarty-pants over there. I'm typing it." Alex shoved Tim away and leaned over the computer.

From behind, Tim jammed his arm under Alex's chin. He yanked him backward and tossed him to the ground on his back. He jabbed his finger at Alex. "It's the wrong answer, Alex! We only get one guess. If we fail this, we're dead!"

Alex shot back up, daggers in his eyes. Tim blocked his path to the computer.

"Two minutes left!" Sidney screamed, on the verge of tears.

Drayden crouched. He removed his cap and wiped sweat from his forehead. *Think! What's the trick?* Nothing came to him.

Charlie stepped forward. "You force heaven to be empty. You force heaven to be empty. You force heaven to be empty." He kept repeating it.

Tim turned to him, his eyes fiery. "Shut up, Charlie."

Charlie continued. "You force heaven to be empty. You force heaven to be empty."

"Oh my God, one minute!" Sidney shrieked, tears streaking her cheeks.

Charlie bellowed. "You force heaven to be empty! You force heaven to be empty!"

Tim rushed Charlie, got right in his face, and punched his finger into Charlie's chest. "For the love of God, please shut the hell up!"

Wait...Something...

"No!" Drayden shouted. "Keep going, Charlie!"

Sidney and Alex gawked at him, their mouths open.

Tim looked flummoxed. "You got something, Dray?"

Drayden held up his hand to Tim, grimacing. There was something there.

"You force heaven to be empty! You force heaven to be empty!"

"Drayden, thirty seconds!" Tim hollered, both hands behind his head.

Drayden tried to block everything else out. He closed his eyes. In his head now. *You force heaven to be empty. You force heaven to be empty. You force heaven to be empty.*

Sidney sobbed. "Fifteen seconds!"

You force heaven to be empty.

You force heaven to be empty.

Something clicked in Drayden's mind.

You force heaven to be empty.

Seven characters.

You four seven two be em ty.

U 4 7 2 B M T.

"Drayden!" Sidney screamed.

Drayden sprinted to the keyboard. Where were the keys? With one shaky finger, scrambling to find each one, he typed "U 4 7 2 B M T" and hit Enter. The clock stopped. Time remaining: *00:02.*

He exhaled, his knees buckling.

Everyone waited a moment, as if making sure they'd really solved it. Finally, Tim whooped and embraced Drayden. "You did it!"

"Yeah!" Charlie shouted and slapped Drayden on the back. "All right!"

Sidney rushed him and hugged him tight. "Thank you, thank you!" she cried, her tears soaking his shirt, her body warm against his.

Alex walked away without a word. The others celebrated, patting Drayden on the head, high-fiving and laughing.

Drayden watched Catrice.

She knelt and placed her things back in her backpack, without looking up even once.

Owen Payne rejoined them, his arms crossed. "Your journey commences. Good luck." He pushed a black button beside the shiny door. The door creaked open, revealing a staircase down into darkness.

CHAPTER 10

*O**ne step closer, Mom.*

Charlie buried his head in his backpack, making exaggerated happy faces. "It's like Christmas in this bag!"

"Guess we'll need our flashlights," Tim said.

Everyone dug them out before heading down the stairs. Nobody had ever used one before. They all sat for a moment, flipping them on and off.

Drayden unscrewed his to check out the battery. He removed it, rotating it in his fingers, feeling the cool, smooth metal of the tiny cylinder. This was like out of his history books. It was shocking that the Bureau had batteries. Supposedly they'd expired decades ago. He made a mental note of the superior technology the Bureau had already showcased: mechanical pencils, computers, flashlights, plenty of eggs, and now batteries.

Tim led the way down the stairs, his flashlight's yellow beam guiding the way. At the bottom they flashed the lights around. They stood on the train tracks in the tunnel, which extended quite wide, with a flat ceiling. It housed tracks for four trains, two downtown and two uptown. Vertical black steel beams every five feet separated the tracks, creating the effect of walls between them. Besides

the steel rails and wooden ties of the track, the ground was mostly dirt and gravel. Everything was damp and reeked of mold.

The tracks themselves didn't look like the ones from books or movies. Six feet separated the railroad ties in most places, with deep ditches between them. It would be near impossible to walk on the tracks. Luckily, a foot of flat space existed on the outside of each rail that would suffice.

"I studied the map already," Drayden said. "Memorized it. The easiest way is just staying on this track for the Two-Three Line, straight down to the Wall Street Station."

"What are all these other tracks?" Tim asked.

"This one on the right is for the One Line train; the 'local' it was called in a footnote," Drayden said. "It runs beside the Two-Three Line. I guess it's local because it stops at more stations along the way, but branches off further down and ends at South Ferry. The Two-Three Line doesn't have that many stops. The other tracks on our left were for the uptown trains that went north. As long as we stay on either the uptown or downtown Two-Three Line tracks, we're good."

Tim hooked his thumb south. "Shall we?"

They hiked in silence. Everyone except Sidney shined their flashlights on the ground to avoid tripping on the ends of the rail ties. She aimed hers at the walls, exposing archaic graffiti. Apart from their flashlights, the tunnel was pitch black. Periodically, grates to the street above cast rays of sunlight onto the tracks.

Drayden's nerves finally settled down, although he remained shaken by his struggle to crack that riddle. Before the Initiation, he mostly feared the bravery tests. After that first intelligence one, both challenge types scared him. If he hadn't solved it, they'd be on a bus to exile right now. Two seconds, two beats of a heart, defined the difference between life and death.

Nobody else was any help either, thrusting all the weight of solving it on his shoulders. He knew Catrice was brilliant from school, yet she hadn't helped at all. If she'd been on the verge of solving it on paper, she kept it to herself. He wondered why she and the others had entered the Initiation. Given the long journey ahead, it would probably come up.

Charlie broke the silence. "Dray, man, thank God you solved that riddle. We were such flunks." He held his hand like a gun, pressed it to his temple, and pretended to fire it. "Were you just playing with us, making it come down to the wire? That was tighter than a cockroach on a crumb." He play-punched Drayden in the shoulder.

Drayden had always hated Charlie because he was Alex's goon. Yet, at times in the past, he could tell Charlie wasn't a totally bad kid. Even a few days ago when Alex sucker punched him, Charlie had tossed him his hat.

"Charlie!" Alex yelled from up ahead, glowering at both of them.

Charlie hustled to catch up to Alex. Alex whispered to him, and Charlie glanced back at Drayden. They continued ahead, separate from the pack.

An amused smile grew on Drayden's face. He hated to admit how much he welcomed the praise, and loved being the hero for once. Catrice's indifference still bugged him. She never thanked him, or even looked him in the eyes. Fear may have paralyzed her, or failing to solve the riddle disappointed her. Perhaps he should approach her to collaborate on the next challenge. But did that make sense either? Completing the Initiation was the goal, and it was too critical to worry about impressing a girl. He had to stay focused.

"What the...?" Tim said, startling Drayden.

He squinted, then saw it, a red glow in the darkness. A black digital clock with a red display hung from the ceiling. It read *07:51:22* and counted down.

"How long is it going to take us anyway?" Tim asked. "Is eight hours enough time? Should we be running?"

Drayden scratched his chin as he walked. There were twenty north-south blocks per mile. They started at Seventy-Second Street. To reach the Lab, at Fourteenth Street, was fifty-eight blocks, roughly three miles. Ignoring the challenges, if they walked three miles per hour, or a block per minute, they'd reach Fourteenth Street in an hour. Fourteenth Street was greater than halfway to Wall Street. Even with some time-consuming challenges ahead, eight hours seemed like way too much time. "I don't think we should stop and nap, but eight hours is plenty, in my opinion."

"If there were no challenges," Catrice said, "the walk to Wall Street would only take two hours or so." She glanced at Drayden.

"Thanks, Catrice," Tim said. "So maybe we can take some breaks along the way."

"Light up ahead!" Charlie yelled.

Drayden gritted his teeth. Hopefully it was a clock and not a station.

The dim light ahead appeared to come from the right side of the tunnel.

Charlie hustled ahead and hollered again from about thirty yards away. "Sixty-Sixth Street station! Nothing here!"

Drayden exhaled, recalling that Eris Page had said only brightly lit stations contained challenges. Many challenges remained, but it was a relief to pass an empty station. If all the small stations on the One Line were empty, there wouldn't be many challenges at all.

As they passed, sunlight canvassed the platform from the street above. Even though the stations were open to the world, this section of the Dorms was off limits. The streets would be deserted. Eris Page

had said if they dared to escape for some reason, they would be exiled. The creepy station sat untouched from its last use a generation ago. The platform, set off to the right, lay covered in dust and garbage.

Sidney strolled up beside Drayden, shining the flashlight on her face. She gazed at him with puffy, red eyes. "Hey." She wrapped her arm around his waist. "Thanks again. Sorry I got all crazy back there."

"You doing better now?"

She pulled her arm away. "Yeah. I was just so nervous. I couldn't stop thinking about my sister and her being all alone if we failed. I'm sure I'll be fine now that we got that first one out of the way. What's up with her, though?" She motioned toward Catrice. "Did she even go to our school? I'm not sure that girl actually has a pulse." She snickered, or maybe sniffled.

Drayden didn't want to make Sidney feel crappy for saying that, but he wasn't going to laugh at Catrice's expense. He had a special appreciation for not being noticed by the popular kids. He shrugged, and decided Sidney had sniffled. "Yeah, she went to our school. She was quiet. I guess we all just deal with things our own way."

Tim slowed and let them catch up. "Hey, Sid. Even though it wasn't the right answer, I dug your devil idea. Sounded right to me. How'd you come up with that?"

Drayden knew Tim too well. He either liked Sidney, he simply couldn't resist hitting on any girl nearby, or he wanted to prove to Drayden that even the Initiation couldn't muzzle his bravado.

"Oh, I dunno." She waved her hand through the air. "I'm Catholic, and my family is pretty religious. It was stupid anyway. Thank God Dray was here to fix it."

"I didn't think it was stupid," Drayden said. "It was smart, very logical."

Tim shined his flashlight on his own face and poked Drayden behind Sidney's back. When Drayden looked, Tim closed his eyes, puckered his lips, and made overly dramatic kissing motions in the air behind her.

Drayden shook his head. He appreciated Tim's attempt to lighten the mood, but the upcoming challenge had to be close. His stomach was already twisted in knots.

Tim quickly pointed his flashlight at the ground before Sidney noticed.

"Can we talk about this death thing for a second?" Sidney asked. "Did anyone know we'd be facing immediate death?"

"No," Drayden said, picturing his head being lopped off by some blade.

"We knew exile was a risk coming in," Tim said. "It's pretty much the same thing."

"Yeah, but there's some hope with exile!" Charlie called from up ahead. "Like you become some crazy person who finds a way to survive in the woods or something. With death, well, there's not much hope."

"Well said, Charlie," Drayden said. "With death, there isn't much hope. I'm not looking forward to the first death challenge."

Tim pulled Drayden back and let Sidney walk ahead. He whispered in Drayden's ear. "Dude, Sid likes you. She's super hot. What are you waiting for?"

After making sure no one else was listening, Drayden said, "I know. I like her too, but you know I'm into Catrice."

"Dray, no offense, but you gotta let that go. She doesn't like anyone. Sid is a real live girl who's interested. I'm just saying."

"We're in the middle of the damn Initiation, chotch," Drayden whispered back. "I'm worried about surviving, not finding a girlfriend. Besides, even if we pass, we'll probably end up in different zones."

"Maybe you can score that elusive first kiss in the tunnel."

"Lights up ahead!" Charlie shouted. "Station!"

The Fifty-Ninth Street station crushed Drayden's spirit. Another stop on the One Line, it dashed any hope the challenges would only occur at the less-frequent stations on the Two-Three Line.

Tim led the way up the steps to the platform. The brilliant white lights revealed another spotless station. On One Line stops, the platform was flush with the far-right wall of the station. All four sets of tracks ran through the center, and the uptown platform sat on the station's left side.

The pledges walked down the platform to a spot brightened by sunlight from the street above. Here, steel supporting pillars with peeling green paint broke up the otherwise circular space. A large table holding a few glass objects stood in the center, with a steel box beside it on the floor. A clock hung above the table, displaying the remaining time: *07:39:48, 07:39:47...*

Drayden's heart pounded. He scanned the area for Owen Payne, or anyone else.

The station was empty. The pledges approached the table which was, as in the first challenge, unnecessarily expansive. Two hourglasses, one taller than the other, sat on the table, a note lay beside them.

Charlie picked up the note and read. *"Logic can show the way, even without the light of day. It is a skill highly prized by the Bureau. Prove your understanding of logic by solving this brainteaser. Doing so will earn you the contents of the metal box, which will greatly assist you in the next challenge. Failing this challenge will not result in exile. The larger hourglass measures eleven minutes, while the smaller measures seven minutes. You must measure exactly fifteen minutes*

using only the two hourglasses. After precisely fifteen minutes, push
the button on the metal box to open it. It will not open one second
before or after the fifteen minutes, and you may only push the button
once. You will have five minutes to prepare, counted down by the
clock above. When it strikes zero, the challenge will begin. Good luck."

Charlie handed Drayden the note and knocked on the wood
table like it was a door. "Are we supposed to solve the puzzle or have
a picnic? The Bureau doesn't have any smaller tables?" He dropped
his backpack on the ground and kicked it. "I know *I'm* not going to
be much help. Score another one for the smart kids."

The clock began counting down from five minutes. Everyone
except Catrice stared at Drayden.

He clenched his jaw. "You know, it's not just me here! You guys
can help too!" he shouted, louder than he intended. He shoved the
note into Tim's hand.

Tim rested his hand on Drayden's shoulder. "Take it easy,
buddy. We're all going to work on this." He nodded. "You seem to
work best by yourself, so why don't you go over there and think
about it, and we'll work on it here. Charlie, get over here. You too,
Alex. Let's see what we can come up with." Both boys joined Tim
and Sidney beside the table. Catrice worked off to the side of the
table on the ground.

Drayden ran over to one of the steel pillars. He whipped off
his backpack, dug out the pencil and paper, and sat with his back
against the pillar. *Breathe, concentrate.* How could he not know this
one either? He played around with the numbers. Flip the eleven-
minute hourglass, then the seven-minute one, that was eighteen
minutes. Nope. Estimate when one was half done? No, it had to be
exact, down to the second. If he were in math class, this would be a
cakewalk. Being timed in an abandoned subway station with everyone's lives on the line, it wasn't so simple.

Tim paced alone in front of the table, apparently giving up on Charlie and Alex. "Hey, Catrice!"

She snatched up her pencil and paper and hustled over.

"Let's talk through this together," he said.

"Okay."

"Any ideas?" Tim asked, tapping his foot.

"You're going to ask the mute?" Alex cracked. "Even if she knows, she won't say. I vote for skipping this stupid one. There's no exile involved this time. We can just advance to the next challenge. I think it's more important to keep moving."

"We're not skipping it, you flunk," Tim snapped. "We need what's in that box. Go ahead, Catrice."

"I was thinking we need to start them both at the same time. When the seven-minute one finishes, there will be four-minutes left in the bigger one. That's as far as I got." She checked her notes.

Drayden bit down on his pencil. She was right. He noted the time: *03:45, 03:44...*

The situation consumed him. Eight hours' worth of life or death tests, and everyone depending on him to carry them through. The pressure hardened his back and neck into stone. He tried his best to refocus.

So, start them at the same time. When the seven-minute hourglass finished, there would be four-minutes left in the larger hourglass. If you immediately flipped the smaller one back over, what then? When the larger one finished, four more minutes would have gone by. That would be eleven minutes elapsed, with three minutes left in the smaller one. Eleven plus three was fourteen, not fifteen. He scratched out his notes and slammed his pencil down. His eyes were drawn to Catrice.

She leaned over the table, buried in her notes. Her blonde hair splashed over her shoulders.

02:55, 02:54...

She was just so beautiful.

Catrice lit up. "I got it!" She cracked her first smile of the Initiation.

Drayden ran over. Everyone huddled around her.

She held up her notes for the others to view. "We flip both over. When the smaller one is done, seven minutes will have gone by, with four minutes left in the bigger one. We flip the smaller one back over, starting it again the other way. When the bigger one is done, four additional minutes will have elapsed. That's eleven minutes total now. There will be three minutes left in the smaller one, which means four minutes' worth of sand will be in the *bottom* of it, because it's a seven-minute hourglass. We flip the smaller one once more, reversing it again. When those four minutes have run out, we'll have our fifteen minutes. Seven plus four plus four. Everybody get it?"

Charlie grunted. "I'm as confused as a fart in a fan factory."

"The only tricky part is the actual flipping," Catrice said. "There's no wiggle room. It has to be exact to the second, and there are three flips. Each one has to be instantaneous, otherwise we'll be off by more than a second at the end."

Tim took charge. "This is going to start in a minute. The moment that clock strikes zero, we have to flip both hourglasses, fast. And then we'll have seven minutes to get ready for the next turn. I'll flip one, and Charlie, you flip the other. I'll say 'turn' when its time and you have to flip it instantly. Got it?"

Alex shoved his way to the table. "There's no way you'll do it simultaneously, or fast enough."

00:44, 00:43...

Tim and Charlie stood side-by-side, their hands on the hourglasses. "Thirty-five seconds," Tim said, his eyes glued to the clock.

Drayden made his way over to Catrice, who stared at her feet. "Hey," he said. "Nicely done. I couldn't get it. I froze up."

She raised her head. The corners of her mouth turned up a tad, not quite a smile, and she tucked a strand of hair behind her ear. "Thanks."

Dripping in sweat, Tim and Charlie clenched the hourglasses. "Charlie," Tim said, "remember, fast! Ready? Five, four, three, two, one, turn!"

They flipped. Everyone exhaled at the same time.

Sidney clapped. "Looked good."

"Only the small one needs turning now, I'll do it," said Tim. "Seven minutes. Anyone got a deck of cards?" He wiped his forehead. "Who wants to hit the button on the box when it's time?"

Sidney shot her hand in the air, like she was in class. "I'll do it!"

Drayden examined the box without touching it. It resembled a safe, but with the door on top and a black button in its center. The note said it contained something to assist them in the subsequent challenge. What if it was some sort of trap? They probably shouldn't stand over the box when it opened. He returned to Tim's side.

The smaller hourglass neared completion. "I gotta do this really quick," Tim said. "No delay, not even a fraction of a second."

Drayden put his face near the hourglass. "The grains are so tiny it's tough to tell exactly when it's going to finish."

Tim studied the hourglass, flexing his fingers in the air around it. "Damn, my hands are sweaty." He wiped them on his pants.

Drayden watched carefully as the last grains of sand dropped. "And...turn!"

Tim flipped it back the other way, releasing a deep breath.

Alex flopped down beside Charlie. "Aaannnd turn!" Alex said, mocking Drayden. He fixed his bandana. "You smart guys think

you're all so awesome. Just wait till we face a challenge that isn't some stupid brainteaser. We'll see how awesome you are then."

Sidney scowled at Alex, her hands on her hips. "You could try and help us, you chotch."

"Oh, like *you're* such a big help. At least you're not crying like a baby this time."

Sidney flushed red. She stormed over to the box, glaring at Alex. "Someone tell me when it's time to push the button."

Drayden glued his eyes on the large hourglass, which was almost done. "Tim, get ready to flip the little one. This is the last time."

Tim's hand hovered over it, his fingers twirling. As the final grain of sand cascaded from the large hourglass, he flipped the small one once more. "Whew! That's it. Four minutes left."

"I don't think you could've turned them any faster," Catrice said. "Let's hope we're on schedule."

Drayden knelt next to Sidney. "Sid, we have no idea what's going to come out of that box. When you hit the button, keep your head out of the way."

She tilted her head, like she appreciated his concern. "Thanks, Dray."

Drayden rejoined Tim at the table. Both were fixated on the small hourglass, hypnotized by the dripping line of sand.

"Sid, it's close," Tim said. "Put your finger on the button, and I'll say—this is just a test; don't do it—I'll say 'now' when it's time."

"Got it," she said.

"Get ready. Finger on the button," Tim said.

Charlie and Alex joined Sidney beside the box, with Catrice right behind them. Drayden stayed with Tim. This was it. Almost there...almost...

"Now!" Tim yelled.

Sidney pushed the button, and jumped away.

Everyone held their breath.

Silence.

Nothing.

Shkat. Guess we were too slow, Drayden thought.

The box's lid slowly creaked open.

CHAPTER 11

Charlie frowned. "Gloves?"

The pledges crowded in to check. Gloves, indeed. Nothing else.

"I hope they're not one-size-fits-all," Charlie said, examining his own banana-like fingers. "Well, that's great," he said sarcastically. "I was just thinking how cold my hands are right now, and I could totally use a good pair of gloves. Thanks, Bureau!"

"Knock it off, Charlie," Tim said. He picked up a pair. "They have our names on them. Oh man, and they're super sticky on the palm side." He smelled one of the gloves, making a sour face. "Smells like ack. I'll pass them out and then we need to get going."

Drayden tried on his gloves, as did the others. What would they need sticky gloves for? To catch something? To hold onto each other? More notably, needing sticky gloves for *anything* terrified him. Even though he'd struggled with the challenges so far, they'd been brainy tests, not physical ones. Sticky gloves pointed to a bravery test.

With Tim leading the way, the pledges marched to the end of the platform and down a second set of stairs, returning to the blackness of the tracks.

Tim had already established himself as the leader of the pack. It didn't surprise Drayden at all. While Tim may not have been the smartest or strongest among them, he excelled at decision-making,

directing, and motivating. He had no fear. When Drayden mentally curled up in the fetal position at the hint of a challenge, Tim was unflappable.

Charlie and Alex hurried ahead to separate themselves from everyone else. Catrice followed behind them by herself. Drayden, Tim, and Sidney formed a group in the rear.

"Man, these gloves are tighter than a baby on a boob," Charlie called back to no one in particular.

Tim leaned into Drayden. "What is it with Charlie and the one-liners anyway?"

"I don't know. He's a nerf, always making jokes," Drayden said. "He seems to have an endless supply of them."

Dim light brightened the tunnel up ahead, more expansive than from a grate to the street above.

Sweet mercy. Another challenge already?

They reached the Fiftieth Street station and found it abandoned like Sixty-Sixth Street. Though sunlight shone down from the street above, it too was mostly dark. Grime smudged the tiled walls, and ancient plastic bottles littered the platform. Everyone stopped to shine their flashlights around. No challenge. Another clock, however, displayed the remaining time: *06:58:22, 06:58:21...*

Drayden's muscles relaxed, a wave of relief washing over him. They were an hour into the Initiation, however, and had only reached Fiftieth Street. That last challenge took a while.

As the group continued past the station, Charlie stopped abruptly and shined his flashlight on the wall. "Bureau sucks. Huh." His expression morphed from curious to concerned. He looked up at the ceiling. "Oh no! I'm not saying the Bureau sucks! Cameras and microphones, I'm just reading from the wall. I love you guys!"

The other pledges noted the graffiti. It was written in red ink that appeared fresh, just past the Fiftieth Street station.

"Wonder who wrote that," Tim said.

"Probably some kids who snuck down into the subway, not that much of a mystery," Alex said.

"Yeah, but this part of the Dorms is off-limits," Tim said.

"Wait," Charlie said. "You mean you guys have never snuck into off-limits areas?" He and Alex looked at each other and burst into laughter.

Tim and Drayden exchanged a glance. "No," Tim said. "Let's get moving."

After a few minutes of cautious walking by flashlight, Tim broke the silence. "So, Sid, why'd you enter the Initiation? Because your parents were exiled?"

She sighed. "Yeah." She flicked her flashlight on and off while she spoke. "My grandparents are pretty old, and if anything happened to them, me and my sister would be all out of family. We haven't had the best life at home, and I just want something better for my sister."

Sidney shined her flashlight in Drayden's eyes. "Now, if I got married to someone in two years, that could have worked." She grinned. "Honestly, if I hadn't seen Drayden enter the Initiation, I never would have. Since he's doing it, I know we have a chance."

Drayden closed his eyes, his heart sinking into his belly. So that *was* why she'd entered. He already bore responsibility for Tim entering, and now Sidney as well.

"What about you?" Sidney asked Tim.

"Great minds think alike!" He gently punched her in the arm. "I entered because of Dray too, so I could protect my boy, make sure he gets through this." He winked at Drayden.

Charlie slowed ahead. "You guys want to know why I entered?"

Tim made a funny face at Drayden. "Sure, Charlie," Tim said. "Why'd you enter?"

"For the hell of it! For the adventure. How boring are the Dorms? It sucks there. Charlie's destined for much bigger things. Hey, you

guys remember that time I jumped out of the second-floor window at school?"

Drayden snickered. Who could forget that? It was equal parts stupid and fascinating.

"This is like that, only, uh, a lot bigger," Charlie said. "I know everybody else wants to be picked for the Palace. But I'm just hoping to get moved into the Precinct so I can be a Guardian. There's nothing Charlie can't do, or is it *can* do...no I was right, can't do, if he wants to."

Drayden whispered to Tim, "Apparently that includes referring to himself in the third person."

Charlie let Catrice catch up to him. His tall, stocky frame dwarfed her in the darkness. Not too many Dorm boys grew big and muscular because of the insufficient nutrition. A few did after they graduated and worked in physical labor, like Wesley. Charlie proved a rare exception, and would make an ideal Guardian. "Hey there, Catrice. Charlie wants—I mean, *I* want to know...why did you enter?"

Drayden stiffened. What made Charlie think he could talk to Catrice?

Catrice walked past Charlie, her eyes locked straight down the tunnel. "Catrice doesn't want to talk about it."

Drayden and Tim both laughed. "Nice one, Catrice!" Tim said.

Charlie scowled at Tim before catching up to Catrice. "Gotcha. I don't like to talk much either. Maybe you'll wanna talk about it later."

Sidney shined her flashlight on Charlie. "Charlie, leave her alone. She obviously doesn't like talking."

"What about you, Alex?" Tim asked. "Wanted to make some new enemies in a different zone?"

"As if I'd ever tell you wetchops," Alex retorted. "I have my reasons."

"Like making my life more difficult," Drayden mumbled under his breath.

"Light up ahead!" Charlie yelled.

His announcement was unnecessary. As the tracks rounded a bend, the light shone brightly, blinding, much greater than in the other stations. It was so glaring the tracks appeared to lead outdoors.

Alex and Charlie jogged ahead to check it out. Alex spun around, his arms crossed, a wide grin spread across his face. "Looks like you smart guys are out of luck."

Drayden's eyes bulged, his hand over his mouth in pure terror. His eyes weren't fixed straight ahead at the station, or rather where it used to be, but up in the air.

The pledges stood in a silent line, looking up to the sky. The Forty-Second Street station was also known as the Times Square station. It had served as a major hub in the former Manhattan, according to the map. Except, no station remained—no tracks, no platform, no ceiling.

They were in the base of a hollowed-out building, a skyscraping one. It rose directly above the missing subway tracks. The Bureau had scooped out the guts of the building, leaving only the outer shell of glass and steel. What sat in the center of the building rendered everyone speechless.

A giant rock wall towered before them. It stretched over a hundred feet tall by Drayden's estimate. Blazing sunlight reflected off the smooth brown monolith. The Bureau left no instructional note on a table for this challenge. It was obvious. The only route to the tracks past this station was traveling over that wall. If they didn't attempt it, they would be exiled. Failing while doing it would most likely mean death, or severe injury, which would also lead to exile.

"Guess we know what the sticky gloves are for," Charlie said.

Drayden's fear overwhelmed him. He teetered, rocked by dizziness. He bent over and dropped his head between his knees. He needed to increase the blood flow to his brain before he fainted, as his mother had taught him.

His baseball hat fell off, landing upright between his feet in a small pile of gravel, like it jumped off his head to taunt him. Or was it a message from Mom?

His mother would be strong right now. She would be brave and selfless, realizing others depended on her, like the time she saved a woman at the FDC. A shelf full of food had crushed the woman, drenching her in blood. People generally avoided touching anyone else's blood for fear of contracting a disease. His mom had used an apron to slow the bleeding and shuttled her to the hospital, the woman's blood soaking her in the process. Drayden had asked her later if she was afraid she would get sick. She said she was, but this woman would have died otherwise.

That was when his mother taught him about karma. She said if she did the right thing and saved this woman, the "karma gods" would protect her. If she acted selfishly and allowed her to die, karma would come back to bite her in return. It was as close as Mom ever came to religion.

Tim and Sidney were counting on him to solve the remaining brainteasers. They needed him to overcome his fear and stay in this thing. If he was exiled, they were toast. He snatched the hat, pulling it on tight, and stood up.

The glass building was effectively a giant greenhouse. Drayden's back dripped with fresh sweat from the sweltering heat.

"Tim, I don't know if I can do this," he said.

"Yes, you can," he said, his voice firm. "Look, none of us have ever climbed something like this before. Check it out, though. It's *designed* to be climbed. There are little notches and ledges all the way up. I bet this is a training facility for the Guardians. Of course,

they probably have harnesses, but whatever. You're going to move one hand and then one foot at a time, and not look down."

Drayden nodded. He could do that.

Alex and Charlie were bickering at the base of the wall. Charlie pointed skyward, explaining something. Off to the side, Sidney stretched and sipped water from her bottle.

Halfway between Drayden and the wall, Catrice sat cross-legged, her face buried in her hands. Charlie noticed her at the same time. He stopped mid-sentence and headed for her.

Drayden hustled her way too. He beat Charlie, and knelt beside Catrice. "Hey, you all right?"

She looked up and whispered, "I can't do this."

"You can, Catrice. I'm gonna help you. So is Charlie. I think he'll be the best at this. He'll climb above you and show you where to go next, and I'll climb behind you to make sure you don't fall. We'll go slow."

Her eyes were red and moist, tears streaking her porcelain cheeks. She wiped them with her palms.

Even as a weepy mess, she was still stunning. Her light eyes glowed, reflecting the sunlight, which highlighted her delicate features. She could really use a tissue, though. Drayden choked back a laugh. He actually *did* love the way the sunlight reflected off the angles of her head.

She nodded. "I'll try. Hopefully I won't fall and kill one of you guys." She forced an unhappy smile.

Drayden ran back to Tim and filled him in on the plan.

"Wait, what?" Tim asked. "A minute ago, I thought I was gonna have to carry you on my back crying like a baby, and now you're helping Catrice climb? Man, you *do* like her."

Drayden pressed his lips together to keep himself from blubbering about Catrice. He knew he needed to focus. As he stuffed his hat in his backpack, he had a thought. "Tim," he whispered, "we

might not all pass this test. Remember what Eris Page said. It's not the same as the brainteasers where we give one answer and all pass or fail. Some could make it, and others could fail and be exiled. Or fall and die. We don't necessarily have to work together. Do you think we need to worry about Alex, like, pushing someone off the wall? That someone would be me."

"Nah. Those two idiots need you around for the intelligence challenges. I wouldn't worry about it."

The pledges gathered beneath the wall. Everyone wore their gloves, and their backpacks were strapped on tight. Charlie called them to attention. "I'm going to go first and figure out the best path up. Catrice is going to follow me, and—"

"Whoa," Alex said. "Why? I don't think so. I'm following you. She can follow me."

Tim rolled his eyes. "Alex, she's scared, just let her follow Charlie. Let's all help each other, okay? We're all going to work together." He glanced at Drayden.

Alex's cheeks turned red. "Well I'm going to take the same steps Charlie does, she can just follow me. What's the difference?" he whined like a bratty kid.

"It's fine," Catrice said. "He can go after Charlie."

Charlie looked at Alex to protest, before lowering his eyes.

"I'll be right behind you, Catrice," Drayden said.

She forced a smile.

Sidney stepped forward, stretching her quads. "I don't need to follow anyone. I can climb next to you guys, in case you have any trouble. Catrice, I may not be all brainy, but I can definitely help on this one."

"Thanks," Catrice said hesitantly.

"You the man, Sid," Tim said, earning a fist-bump back.

"I'm friends with some Guardians who taught me about climbing," Charlie said. "The gloves are sticky; they'll make it easier,

but climb with your legs, not your hands, making sure to keep your waist above your feet. Don't ever lean to the side, you'll fall. And you don't want to look at the ground and get scared. Only watch your feet to find the footholds."

Drayden's hands shook so much it looked as if he were trying to do jazz hands. Standing at the base of the wall, it seemed a mile high.

Charlie began climbing and within seconds reached six feet off the ground. He peered down. "Alex, you start up. Get used to how it feels on the wall while we're still low. The gloves are awesome."

Alex started to climb, copying Charlie's movements.

"Catrice, you start now!" Charlie hollered down as he moved higher.

Catrice took a minute just to mount the wall with all four limbs. She followed Alex's path exactly after that. One foot up, one hand up, the next foot up, the next hand up, zigzagging up the wall. She appeared shaky, but she progressed.

"C'mon, Catrice!" Tim yelled. He clapped a few times in encouragement.

Sidney started a few feet to her left. She jumped on the wall and spidered up several feet within seconds.

"All right, Dray," Tim said. "You're up. Don't worry about Catrice. It's good enough that she thinks you're watching out for her. If she falls there's nothing you can do anyway. Focus on what you're doing. One movement at a time."

Drayden placed each hand in a notch. He lifted his left foot into a low notch, and swung his right foot onto another. His face and body were pressed up so close to the wall that he smelled the dusty scent of the stone. Supporting his weight was tougher than it looked. He employed too much arm and not enough leg.

"Move your foot up a level," Tim said.

Drayden peered down, located a notch, and set his left foot there. He pushed himself up on that foot and secured notches with his left hand and then his right. Now his right foot dangled. He found a notch for it. His fingers, arms, and legs were already fatigued, and he'd only climbed five feet. He looked up to follow Catrice's path.

She continued fifteen feet directly above him now. Sidney was ten feet above him to his left, scaling the wall with ease.

Drayden resumed his ascent, slowly. One foot, one hand, the other hand, the other foot. *Don't look at the ground.* Over and over. He resisted the powerful temptation to glance down. His limbs and fingers throbbed, his abdominal muscles burned, and his back ached. "You doing alright up there, Catrice?"

"Yeah!" she shouted back, about twenty-five feet above him. She neared the top.

Tim grunted. "Man, my arms are on fire. You're doing great, bud, keep going."

"I'm at the top!" Charlie yelled, his voice echoing for seconds. "It's wide, you can rest up here. I know everyone's burning. Just make it to the top and you can take a break!"

Sidney finished next, then Alex. A few moments later, cheers erupted. Catrice had reached the top.

Sweat dripped into Drayden's eyes, stinging them, and he had no free hand to wipe it away. His hands were weakened, so each shaky movement took twice as long now. "Tim, it feels like my hands are going to slip off! I can't grip anything. What do I do?"

"Push, Drayden!"

Drayden stepped up with his left foot.

It slipped.

He held on tight with both hands, flailing his left foot around. He screamed, his heart racing. His foot found the notch. He closed his eyes, breathing heavily. Without the gloves, he would have died right there.

"Five more feet, Drayden!" Sidney shouted.

Drayden forced himself. His fingers touched the top of the wall.

Charlie's strong hands gripped him around the wrists, pulling him up to safety.

Drayden collapsed, panting, soaked in sweat. "I did it," he whispered.

"Almost there, Tim! You got this," Sidney said.

"That sucked," Tim grumbled as he rolled on top of the wall onto his back, his chest heaving.

Drayden sat up, the hot sun on his face, and absorbed his unfamiliar surroundings. The view mesmerized him.

They were perched ten stories in the air on a thick rock, peering through the glass into what was once Times Square. Though technically part of the Dorms, everything west of Fifth Avenue was off-limits. Everyone had viewed PreCon photos of Times Square, with its glittering lights and colossal billboards, brimming with energy. This was the zombie version. Generations-old dark screens, faded billboards, broken windows, crumbling buildings, and jagged roads all painted a grim picture. It was utterly silent.

Drayden's sweaty t-shirt was glued to his back. He swallowed deep, refreshing gulps from his water bottle.

The pledges sat in silence, huffing and puffing, wet hair matted to their heads. Charlie stood and shook out his hands. "Man, it's hotter than two rats making love in a wool sock." He wiped sweat from his forehead. "I might do that again just for fun." He guffawed. "You guys ready to go?"

Drayden nudged Catrice. "I should've had you follow *me*."

She playfully splashed him with some water from her bottle.

Charlie clapped his hands together a few times. "On the way down, it's a lot easier. Piece of cake." He leaned his head back and shouted, "I own you, Bureau! Woohoo!" the sound echoing off the walls.

Charlie lay down on his belly and lowered himself over the cliff, legs first. "It's not that hard. You just have to find those first footholds slowly, and then you can move your hands. Like this." He edged lower, only his arms on top of the wall now. "No!" He'd slipped, and was dangling by his hands. "Help!"

Tim rushed over and seized Charlie's forearms. "Hold me, Dray!"

Drayden clutched Tim around the waist, pulling with all his strength.

"Get your feet in, Charlie," Tim grunted.

"I got it, I got it!" he yelled. "I'm good."

Tim released Charlie and crashed back into Drayden. Charlie started his descent.

Drayden's heart pounded. "Jeez. That was close. I think we should help each person start down."

"Good idea," Tim said. "Alex, you're up. If you still insist on going before Catrice." He smirked.

Alex glared at him. He lay belly down, with Tim and Drayden gripping his arms, and climbed down. They supported Catrice the same way, then Sidney parallel to her.

"You're up," Tim said to Drayden.

"How are you going to start? There's nobody to hold you."

"Someone has to go last. I got this. You just worry about getting down." He peered over the cliff. "Unless I do fall and take everyone out."

Drayden found that starting down wasn't quite as difficult as Charlie made it appear. Descending was easier than climbing, with gravity to assist. One hand and foot at a time.

A scream rippled through the cavernous space from below, the echo magnifying its terror.

Drayden's body jerked. His eyes darted down, the height dizzying him.

Catrice was dangling by her hands, her feet swaying below her. "Drayden!" she screamed.

"Hang on! Don't let go. I'm coming."

"Careful, Dray!" Tim yelled. "Don't go too fast!"

Drayden searched frantically for a foothold then stopped, startled by what he saw.

From beneath her, Alex wordlessly placed each of Catrice's feet into a notch.

"Oh my God, thank you, Alex. I'm all right!"

Drayden exhaled a huge breath. "You sure?"

"Yes. Thank you, Drayden." Their eyes met.

It struck Drayden in that moment, that his concern for Catrice had made him ignore his own fear for a few seconds. He almost felt brave.

They resumed their descent, Drayden following Catrice's path.

The sun singed the skin on the right side of his face. Sweat dripped down his nose and coated his lips, making his mouth salty.

"I made it!" Charlie shouted from what sounded like miles below.

Drayden continued on, deliberate with each movement. His fingers burned. Between notches they were so fatigued he could barely wiggle them. He neared the bottom and couldn't resist a peek.

Twenty feet to go. Charlie and Alex stood safely on the ground, and Catrice was nearly down.

Take your time. Hand, foot, foot, hand. *Almost there.* But the burning! His movements stiffened, slowed. He had to get down pronto. He couldn't hold on much longer. Hand, foot, foot, hand.

His hand missed a notch, slipping past it.

He quickly stabbed his hand out to grab it again, then lost his foothold. His limbs flailed. *No!*

He was falling.

CHAPTER 12

Drayden smashed to the ground, pain exploding in his ankle. He crumpled, rolling onto his back, screaming out in agony.

"Drayden! No!" Tim yelled from up the wall.

Drayden rolled around clutching his left ankle. Hot daggers stabbed into it. He writhed on the floor, moaning.

Both girls hovered over him. Catrice held her hand over her mouth, her forehead wrinkled in concern. Sidney rested her hand on his arm.

"Let me in there!" Tim shouted. He shouldered through the girls and cradled Drayden's head. "What's hurt?"

Drayden grunted. "My ankle." The embarrassment from his fall was almost as godawful as the pain. "Let me sit up."

Tim pulled him up to a sitting position.

Drayden avoided eye contact with the girls. He spotted Alex and Charlie sitting by the entrance to the tunnel.

Charlie watched them, while Alex rifled through his backpack.

Drayden's ankle throbbed, but thankfully the pain had plateaued. "You guys ready to go?" He grunted again.

"Let me see your ankle," Tim said. "Move your hands, dude. This might hurt a bit. I have to see how bad it is." He pulled the sock down and pressed on the ankle.

Pain jolted up Drayden's leg, nauseating him.

He winced and jerked his ankle away. "Watch it, man!"

"It looks okay, bro," Tim said. "Just a little swollen. No bones sticking out or anything, I think it's just a sprain."

"Thanks, Doctor Zade," Drayden said sarcastically.

Sidney rested her hand on his thigh, caressing it. "Hey, you're gonna be fine, Dray. We gotta keep moving. You can do it."

"How am I supposed to walk?" Drayden asked.

"You have to," Tim said. "That's how. You have to suck it up. It'll ache at first, but walking on it might loosen it up. Let's get you standing, and then we'll prop you up. You can walk between me and Sidney with your arms around our shoulders." Tim winked at him.

Sidney pushed by Catrice, bumping her out of the way.

Drayden gave Tim a look. "Thanks." He reminded himself of his goal. He had to focus on completing the Initiation, not on Catrice or Sidney. The hope of finishing had just taken a crushing blow.

Catrice plodded off toward the tunnel. Tim and Sidney hoisted Drayden up.

He didn't dare put any weight down yet. He shuddered pondering that first step, and hopped on his good ankle instead.

"Dude, that's not gonna cut it," Tim said. "Try stepping on it lightly."

Drayden gingerly set his foot down.

On a scale of one to ten, the pain level registered a two. Manageable. He added some more weight and it increased to a three. When he added a tad more, it spiked to a nine, triggering a wave of nausea. Tendons and ligaments popped and crackled.

Drayden grimaced. It was definitely messed up. He'd never been injured like this before, and it couldn't have come at a worse time. Like Tim had said, however, he simply had to suck it up. He tried limping, bearing weight on the left foot for a second before switching, resulting in uncomfortable, yet bearable pain.

Drayden paused to dig out his water and painkillers. The bottle contained four pills. He knew he should probably save them since he might need them even more at some point, but if he was going to survive another bravery challenge, he'd have to walk. He swallowed one pill.

The three of them reached Charlie, Alex, and Catrice, sitting at the entrance to the tunnel where the tracks began.

Alex stood and eyed Drayden up and down. "Look, it's a wetchop sandwich! Two wetchops on both sides, and the king of the wetchops in the middle. You're supposed to *climb* down the wall, not take a swan dive off. What, they didn't teach you that in math class?"

Drayden's face flushed red hot.

"Shut up, you useless shkat flunk," Tim hissed. "It's a miracle he didn't land on your nose, with its gravitational pull."

"Ooh, good one." Alex rolled his eyes and walked off.

They began the trek again, Tim and Sidney partially carrying Drayden. Charlie and Alex surged ahead of the group. Alex kept whispering to Charlie, and they both repeatedly turned around to look at him.

How could Charlie be so helpful one minute, even pulling him to safety on the wall, only to revert to Alex's evil sidekick a minute later? Drayden hated them both.

His ankle throbbed, but the pain began to dull, thanks to the painkiller. Perhaps he had simply sprained it. Years of medical lectures from Dad were finally coming in handy. He was fortunate it wasn't a compound fracture as forcefully as he landed. That spelled a death sentence, with the guaranteed infection that would follow.

Even just sprained though, the next bravery challenge would be a problem. Drayden could barely walk. With some luck, the Bureau would serve up riddles the rest of the way. Or for the upcoming challenge anyway. He would have to focus on those, adding his value

there, and lean on everyone else for the physical tests. He'd known coming into the Initiation the bravery tests would be his weakness. Technically he'd passed the first one, though it didn't exactly go well. And to think, for a moment on that wall he'd felt brave.

Yeah, right.

He thought about Dad and Wes, and what they were doing right now. He bet his father was angry with Wes for defying him, allowing Drayden to enter the Initiation. It must feel empty in the apartment with both him and Mom gone.

Sidney rubbed Drayden's back in a circular motion. "Drayden, why did you enter the Initiation anyway?"

He didn't know what to say. He could tell them what he'd over-heard from Thomas Cox, that random exiles in the Dorms were about to surge. That while they all held their own personal reasons for entering, they truly had no choice at all. They just didn't know it. Would it relieve them, realizing they'd inadvertently made the right decision? Or would grasping the danger facing the families they left behind crush them? The risk of exile might exist even if the pledges *passed* the Initiation. The Lab and Precinct might not be safe if the power situation deteriorated enough. Only the Palace was safe, but not all of them could make it.

There was no urgent reason to tell them right now. The Bureau was supposedly watching and listening to their conversations by camera and microphone. He absolutely could not let the govern-ment discover he possessed this information by blabbing it out loud.

"My brother and Mr. Kale talked me into it," Drayden said. "I was hoping for a better job than the Dorms offered. And once my mom was exiled, I knew it would never be the same at home." He decided to stop there and omit his other reason: finding out what had happened to his mother. He didn't want the Bureau knowing

about that either. If he did make it to the Palace, investigating the exile would be a clandestine operation.

"I prayed that you would enter so I could too." Sidney continued rubbing his back.

Those words cut into Drayden's heart like a hot knife. "I think I want to try walking by myself, you guys."

"Attaboy," Tim said.

With a significant limp and moderate pain, Drayden slogged on his own, slowing their progress. How much time remained? The Bureau hadn't left a clock at the Times Square station, and the rock wall challenge ate up a hefty chunk of time. The tracks curved to the right here, limiting their visibility down the tunnel. According to the map, they were nearing the Thirty-Fourth Street station. It was a major station, certain to contain a challenge.

As if on cue, Charlie yelled, "Light up ahead!"

Thirty-Fourth Street was as close to Drayden's apartment as they would come. Although the pledges journeyed much further west, it wasn't *that* far to his home on East Thirtieth Street. He wished he could pop out and see Wes. He was missing that shkatty couch right about now too.

Not surprisingly, the Thirty-Fourth Street station glowed bright, indicating a challenge.

Drayden shivered. From the end of the platform, no obvious modifications jumped out. It was an encouraging sign that an intellectual challenge awaited them.

Tim led the way. He stopped short, and everyone bunched up behind him.

Three steel boxes the size of washing machines hung from the ceiling. Thick steel cables suspended them several feet in the air. A

long table sat a few feet in front of the boxes. As they approached, further details became clear.

Multiple buttons, lit up in different colors, adorned the front of the boxes, as well as levers and large labels. A quiet humming disturbed the silence of the station, as if the boxes were electrified. A clock displayed the time remaining: *06:00:42, 06:00:41...*

A note sat on the picnic table.

"Man, that rock wall took, like, forty minutes," Tim said.

Drayden frowned. The hanging boxes were a puzzle, and everybody would expect him to solve it. The pressure tensed his back and neck. He reached up to touch his hat, to feel his mother's presence, but he'd forgotten to put it back on after his accident. After retrieving it from his backpack, he held it in his hands for a moment before pulling it on.

Something clicked and all the lights shut off. The glowing buttons on the boxes dimmed and then died. The buzzing sound dissipated and vanished. The pledges could barely see each other in the darkness.

"Um, who touched something?" Charlie asked.

"Is this part of the challenge?" Sidney asked.

There was the sound of a zipper opening, and some rustling ensued. Tim flicked on his flashlight and shined it around. "You gotta be kidding me. A power outage? *During* the Initiation?"

Drayden recounted Thomas Cox's revelation. Even with the power problems, one would expect the Bureau to ensure Dorm electricity stayed on during the Initiation. Was that how dire the situation had become? Perhaps the Bureau couldn't even control it.

"We can't tackle this problem until the power comes back," Catrice said. "Those boxes were electrified. I don't know what we have to do, but it involved pushing buttons on the boxes."

The lights returned, flooding the station, momentarily blinding the group. They shielded their eyes. The boxes powered up. A

buzzing began low in pitch and zoomed higher until it was barely audible. The multicolored buttons lit up once again.

Tim packed away his flashlight. "Let's do this before we lose power again." He snatched the note off the table and read: *"After a problem is read, look several steps ahead. Solve this brainteaser to prove your ability to visualize solutions not obvious at first glance. Doing so will earn you the contents of the boxes, which will greatly assist you in the subsequent challenge. Failing will not result in exile. The boxes contain rubber boots and blowtorches."* Tim looked up at everyone for a second. *"One box contains only boots, one contains only blowtorches, and one contains both. The three boxes are labeled with their contents. However, they are all labeled incorrectly. You must pull the lever on one box to release a single item from that box. From that one item, you must determine the contents of all three boxes. If you do so correctly, the three boxes will release all the boots and blowtorches, which you may take with you. You have five minutes to complete this challenge. The clock above will begin shortly. Good luck."*

Sidney scratched her head. "What's a blowtorch?"

"It's a device that shoots out a hot flame," Charlie said. "Never seen one, but I learned about 'em from the Guardians."

Drayden's eyes shot up to the clock.

It flickered and began counting down: *00:05:00, 00:04:59, 00:04:58...*

"Do you know this one?" Tim asked Drayden.

He shook his head. Blowtorches?

The top of each box displayed the label. The left box read BOTH, the middle read BOOTS, and the right one read BLOWTORCHES. Below the label on each box was a lever, and below that each box offered three colored buttons, also lit up. The blue left button read BOOTS, the red middle button read BLOWTORCHES, and the green right button read BOTH.

Concentrate. Understand the problem.

They had to first choose from which box to sample an item and pull its lever. Then push the appropriate button on all three boxes, correctly guessing their contents. How?

Tim turned to Catrice. "Do you know it?"

"No," she said. "But we can figure it out."

Tim ran both hands through his hair. "It's pretty clear you two are going to solve this. Why don't you guys work together? The rest of us will huddle up and see what we can come up with."

Drayden and Catrice's eyes met. Not only was it logical to join forces, it relieved some of the pressure on Drayden. He flung off his backpack and knelt in front of her, whipping out the paper and pencil.

Catrice followed suit, sitting cross-legged in front of him and tucking her hair behind her ears.

Just pretend you're in class.

Mr. Kale would instruct him to write out everything he knew and search for a trick solution.

"Let's go over what we know," he said. "All the boxes have the wrong labels on them. So that means what? It means the box on the right labeled BLOWTORCHES has either boots or both things, right?"

"Yes," Catrice said. She tapped the pencil against the side of her head. Her eyes brightened, her eyebrows raised. "That means the box labeled BOTH is special! It's the only one we know *doesn't* have both items. So..."

"That's the box that we need to sample the one item from," Drayden said, his excitement building. "One of the other boxes has both items. We aren't sure which one. If we dropped a sample out of the box labeled BLOWTORCHES and we got a boot, we'd have no way of figuring out if that box was all boots or both things. All we

know is it's not *just* blowtorches since we know it's labeled wrong. Nice job!"

Sidney lingered beneath the clock and called out. "Three minutes!"

Tim stayed close by, bouncing ideas off her. Alex and Charlie stood off to the side, engaged in a heated debate. Though they spoke too quietly to overhear, Alex was right in Charlie's face. He bared his teeth and punched his index finger into Charlie's chest.

Focus, Drayden thought. Only three minutes left. They would sample the one item from the one box labeled BOTH. Then what?

"Talk to us, Drayden!" Tim said. "We got zippo here. You guys getting anywhere?"

"Yes! We need to drop the one item out of the box labeled BOTH. We're figuring out what to do after that."

Tim rushed to that box. "You sure? Should I do it? Two minutes left. C'mon you guys, we need you!"

Drayden and Catrice locked eyes. Drayden shrugged.

Catrice nodded. "Yes, you can pull the lever."

Tim pulled the lever down on the box labeled BOTH. A tall gray rubber boot dropped out of the bottom, bouncing once and landing on its side. "What does that mean?" he asked.

"It means that box only contains boots," Catrice answered. "It's labeled as having both, and we know the label is wrong, so it can only have one of the things. Since a boot fell out, it only has boots."

Tim glanced at Sidney, and back to Catrice. "Should I hit the blue BOOTS button?"

"Yes," Catrice said.

Tim pushed it. It changed hues to a lighter shade of blue, and its two other colored buttons went dark.

"Ninety seconds left!" Sidney shrieked, growing increasingly frantic.

Alex and Charlie hunched up on the right of the other two boxes whispering to each other. Charlie nodded.

What the hell are they up to? Drayden rose to his feet and hobbled over to the other two boxes, with Catrice right behind him. "Catrice, we gotta think. We have two boxes, one labeled BOOTS, and one labeled BLOWTORCHES. We know those labels are wrong. We also know neither contains just boots. So one contains blowtorches, and the other contains both."

Catrice took over. "And the one labeled BLOWTORCHES can't contain blowtorches since the labels are wrong. So that one has both! The one labeled BOOTS *must* have blowtorches!" Her blue eyes glowed from the lights overhead.

Sidney ran over. "Please, Drayden. Hurry!"

"Don't worry. We have it," Drayden said. He wiped sweat from his forehead with the back of his hand and stole a cursory peek at the clock.

Forty-five seconds.

Done with time to spare. Drayden's neck relaxed a bit. He spun around to push the buttons.

Charlie blocked his path. He stood between Drayden and the boxes, his arms folded across his chest, a menacing look on his face.

Drayden stepped back. "Charlie, what are you doing? We got it. Get out of the way!"

Charlie shoved him in the chest with both hands, throwing all his weight behind it.

Drayden flew backward. He landed on his back and rolled over completely, ending up in a sitting position. His ankle exploded in pain.

He clutched it with both hands, grimacing.

Tim rushed Charlie and stopped inches from his face. "What the hell is wrong with you?" he raged. "He's got it! Move!"

"Thirty seconds!" Sidney screamed, crying hysterically.

Alex slid behind Charlie. "We're doing this one," he said over Charlie's shoulder, his eyes crazed. "We have the answer. If you wetchops solve all the puzzles, I'm not getting picked for the Palace. And I'm *going* to the Palace."

Tim grabbed Charlie around the waist and fought to wrestle him away, but Charlie was too strong, and tossed Tim aside like a rag doll. Tim stopped himself before falling off the platform. Alex faced the boxes and walked up to the one labeled BOOTS.

"Hit blowtorches, Alex!" Drayden yelled. "Hit it, you shkat!"

Alex reached for the BOTH button, his index finger outstretched.

"No!" Drayden screamed.

Alex pushed BOTH.

CHAPTER 13

All three boxes shut off. The life faded out of the formerly glowing buttons, and the humming noise died with a sad wheeze.

Drayden sat in stunned silence. What happened? They'd solved it, in plenty of time, no less, and Charlie and Alex blew it. They were screwed now.

Sidney dropped to her knees, crying, her hands over her face. Charlie turned sheepishly toward Alex, who cast his eyes down at the ground. Tim's face flushed red. He leapt up off the ground and charged Charlie. He grasped Charlie's shirt with both hands and shoved him hard. Charlie didn't resist.

"You flunks!" Tim screamed. "You two shkat *flunks*! What have you done? You're too stupid to even realize how lucky you are. You have two people with you who can actually solve stuff, who can get you through the Initiation. You're too stupid to just stay out of the way and let it get done for you!" He stormed off, back toward the station entrance.

Catrice methodically placed her things back inside her backpack. Tim returned, still red-faced. He snatched up his backpack and marched toward the far end of the platform.

The pain in Drayden's ankle diminished. After he gathered his paper and pencil, he slung on the backpack and limped over to Alex and Charlie.

They hadn't moved from the site of their epic failure.

With a jutting jaw, Drayden paused before them, staring at them hard. Neither met his gaze.

Drayden called back to Catrice and Sidney, "Let's go." He headed down the platform, with the girls close behind. Alex and Charlie trailed them. Drayden shuffled down the stairs to begin the trek to the next station. He shined his flashlight down the tunnel.

Tim was walking alone thirty yards ahead.

Amidst the pressure of the last challenge, Drayden hadn't considered what hellish test would require boots and blowtorches. Blowtorches? Whatever nightmare awaited, now they would have to face it without them. On the rock wall, the sticky gloves they'd earned had proved invaluable. They probably would have fallen and died without them.

Boots implied they'd have to walk through something wet. But blowtorches...they'd have to burn something. How could they even burn anything if they walked through water or mud? Everything would be wet.

Stupid Alex. Although Drayden had expected Alex to cause problems for *him* in the Initiation, he'd never imagined Alex would ruin it for everyone.

Tim slowed ahead and waited for them to catch up.

"Hey, great job you guys," Tim said, rubbing his temples. "Even though Alex and Charlie botched it, you guys totally had that one. Awesome teamwork. Our superstars combining their brainpower."

Sidney inched closer to Drayden. "I don't know how you do it, Dray. I wish I was as smart as you."

Catrice clenched her jaw.

"Well, that one was mostly Catrice," Drayden said. "In fact, the last two challenges were."

Sidney turned away. Alex and Charlie caught up to them.

"I'm sorry, you guys," Charlie said, his lips pursed. "Dray, I apologize for shoving you like that. Tim, you too."

"Everybody needs to chill," Alex said. "It's not like we got exiled. I don't know what you guys are getting all mad about."

Tim shined his flashlight in Alex's eyes. "Are you serious? Alex, you totally blew it. What about the next challenge? That's when we could be exiled. You're a flunk, a loser. Drayden and Catrice are smart, and you're not. You don't even have to do anything other than ride their coattails right to the finish. Nobody's asking anything of you. Just don't screw everything up."

"I have a right to move to the Palace," Alex said. "How is it fair that they were born smarter than me? So they get to join the Bureau and I don't? We should all have an equal shot at the Palace."

"We all *start* with an equal shot!" Drayden yelled. "You don't get to make it by me and Catrice doing all the work and solving all the problems for you. How is that fair? The purpose of the Initiation is to determine who's worthy of the Palace. If you're not, you're not. Sorry."

"That's why I was trying to solve that last puzzle!" Alex shot back. "I thought that was the right answer."

Tim looked incredulous. "But you can't do what they do!" He stepped closer to Alex. "You can't. I can't either. We have to accept who we are. Did you really think you had any shot at being the one invited into the Palace? Who are you kidding, Alex?"

Charlie stepped between Tim and Alex. "You guys need to lay off Alex. He was just doing his best." He turned to Drayden. "You think he's stupid, Dray, but you never actually look. You don't want to see what's going on, the shkat he's had to deal with. You just think you're smarter than everyone else and you leave it at that."

Tim stood his ground. "He *is* smarter than everyone else."

Alex shined his flashlight in Tim's face. "I'm making it to the Bureau."

"No you're not," Tim said. "They said one, maybe two of us. It *won't* be you."

Alex went to speak but stopped, his expression like he held a secret. He glanced at Charlie, then at Drayden. "We'll see about that." Alex and Charlie hurried ahead of the pack again.

The nerve of that guy. Both of them. Drayden just thought he was smarter than everyone else? They'd be exiled already if it weren't for him!

He didn't mind doing the lion's share of the work. Helping Tim and Sidney was obvious. It wasn't just that he bore responsibility for them entering. They were friends, they appreciated it, and they carried him on the physical challenges.

Catrice intrigued him so much, in part, because she didn't need any help on the intellectual challenges. If anything, Drayden needed hers. Even helping Charlie wasn't crazy; Charlie was invaluable on the rock wall. He taught everyone how to climb, and pulled Drayden to safety at the top.

But Alex? Sure, he did save Catrice on the wall and he deserved credit for that. Yet this wasn't the time for participation medals. He barely exerted any effort, while Drayden and Catrice solved all the problems, and he expected the same benefits. The Palace spot. Even worse, he complained about it! Like the kids in class who goofed off and failed without trying, and whined when they received crappy job assignments. What did they expect? At a minimum you had to exert yourself, to put in the work.

Drayden wasn't going to take it from Alex anymore. That was the last time. If he had to carry his weight, fine. Letting Alex bully him on another challenge, possibly getting them killed in the process? Never again.

The pledges passed a dark, abandoned station at Twenty-Eighth Street. Per the map, Twenty-Third Street followed it, then Eighteenth Street, and Fourteenth Street. Of those, only Fourteenth

Street served as a major hub on the Two-Three Line. The others were small stations on the One Line. With any luck, they would breeze by those.

Regardless of where the next challenge was, they approached it ill equipped by their failure at Thirty-Fourth Street. So far the challenges had alternated between intellectual and bravery ones. That, plus the need for boots and blowtorches, indicated the upcoming one would be a bravery challenge. They should call them physical challenges. Hell, even the brainteasers required courage.

The frigid air in the tunnel chilled Drayden's skin, and his ankle throbbed with each step. He had to maintain a positive attitude about the rest of the Initiation, because a lot of it remained. It wasn't easy. His ankle alone would be a problem on the rest of the physical tests, including the one coming up. He dug the water out of his backpack and sipped it, then wolfed down an apple. He'd planned to conserve food, but his stomach was growling.

None of the pledges spoke. Charlie and Alex walked thirty yards ahead of the pack. Though the tracks ran in a straightaway here, they couldn't see far, as if something ahead blocked the tracks.

Charlie turned around and shined his flashlight at the others. "Um, guys?" he yelled. "We have a problem."

An uneasy rumbling settled deep into Drayden's belly. He had a bad feeling about this.

A solid steel wall blocked the tracks at the Twenty-Third Street station. The wall extended across both downtown and uptown tracks. Their Two-Three Line track ended at a steel door in the wall.

Tim gestured at the door with his thumb. "What's the problem? Looks like we go through that door."

"Do you hear that?" Charlie asked. He cupped his hand around his ear and pressed it against the door.

They all fell silent and listened.

What was that? Drayden strained to hear. It was activity, movement. Chattering? Or...buzzing? It sounded like the school cafeteria at lunchtime from afar.

Sidney touched her ear to the door. "Whatever's in there, we needed boots and blow-thingies to get through it." She clasped her hands together in prayer. "I don't like this."

Drayden took short, rapid breaths. Tim would guide them through this. Whatever it was, Drayden would lean on his friend as he had when kids picked fights back in school.

"Oh hell, you wetchops," Alex said. "I'll peek inside and see what it is."

Everyone else stepped back. Alex cracked the door open, and immediately slammed it shut, throwing his back against it. "Holy shkat!" His eyes bulged. "Man, you guys are screwed. Especially you, Dray."

A chill ran down Drayden's spine.

Alex shined his flashlight in Tim's face. "Who's not making it to the Palace again, Tim?"

"What the hell is it?" Tim asked.

"What is it? Lemme show you." Alex faced the door, kneeling, with his right hand on the handle. He lowered it, pulled the door open a crack, and reached his left arm inside. He yanked it out and slammed the door shut. The others trained their flashlights on him. He spun around, cradling a massive rat. "Take a closer look, wetchop!" He tossed the rat at Drayden.

Drayden flinched back, tripped on the tracks, and fell onto his back. Pain shot through his ankle like a bolt of lightning. He slapped at his face. "Get it off me! Get it off!"

Alex and Charlie cracked up. "You went down faster than a turd in an outhouse!" Charlie said.

Tim shoved past Charlie to get to Drayden.

"What?" Charlie said. "It was funny. You gotta admit."

"Shut up, idiot." Tim pulled Drayden to his feet. "It's gone, buddy, don't worry."

Drayden dusted himself off. "You're a total shkat, Alex. How many are in there?"

"Let's see..." Alex pressed his index finger to his chin. "Anyone else notice we haven't seen a single rat yet in the tunnel? Nobody else thought that was weird? Apparently that's because they're all in there. Looks like the entire length of the station. How long is the station, smart guy?" Alex asked Drayden.

"I don't know. Five-hundred feet or so?"

"Well it's wall-to-wall rats. Must be a hundred thousand in there. They're a foot deep on the ground, and they're all over the walls, crawling over each other, fighting, biting, screeching. Oh, and that's not all! I'd say every cockroach in the world is in there along with them."

If there was something scarier, Drayden couldn't think of it. He dropped to his knees and rested his forehead on the ground.

"Dude, it's not that bad," Tim said. "It's gross, but we'll just run through, right on top of them. Let's go, stand up." He pulled Drayden up again.

Why the heck did it have to be rats? Drayden's well-documented fear of rats dated back to one of his earliest memories. He must have been four or five, in bed at night, when a rat squeaking around his bedroom woke him up. It scampered under his bed. He screamed and cried, afraid it would climb under the sheets. His mother had burst in and trapped the rat in a box.

Catrice squatted, covering her face with her hands. Sidney said a quiet prayer to herself with her eyes closed.

"Hey, Catrice," Charlie said, approaching her, "if you're scared you can ride on my back. I can carry you."

Drayden had a moment there with Catrice on the rock wall when she almost fell. It was brief, but she'd cried out for him. In her time of need, it was Drayden she sought. Charlie was being quite opportunistic. He was the only one strong enough to carry Catrice through the rats.

Catrice stood and wiped her eyes. "No, I'm fine, thanks anyway."

Alex chuckled. "Maybe you should carry Drayden."

Drayden pulled his hat down tight. He wasn't going to be bullied by Alex. He marched up to the door.

Tim rubbed his chin. "Alex, how likely are we to get bitten? You're the rat specialist."

"They only bite when they're agitated. They don't want anything to do with people. Same with cockroaches. Unfortunately, all piled up on top of each other like that, they're probably pretty pissy. When you step on them, they'll absolutely try and bite, and their nails will scratch you. Cockroaches can bite too, by the way."

"Now we know what the antiseptic wipes and bandages are for," Drayden said. "Rats carry tons of diseases, and those bites could get infected. We could all finish the Initiation and die anyway."

Tim waved a hand through the air. "We have no choice. If we don't do it, we're exiled. You know what would have been a big help, Alex? Tall rubber boots. And blowtorches, to scatter them. You shkat flunk."

"Quit your whining," Alex said. "I could move into that room. I'd rather live with them than you guys."

"That would work for us too," Drayden grumbled under his breath.

Alex bore his eyes into Drayden. "That *would* work for you wouldn't it, Dray? You've never had a problem leaving me behind."

Drayden shook his head. It was hard to believe they'd once been best friends.

Charlie pulled out his sticky gloves from the rock wall challenge. "What about these? They might help."

"I don't think so," Sidney said. "They'll be covered with cockroaches and rats stuck to them."

"Hmmm. Yeah." Charlie stuffed them back into his backpack.

Drayden ambled over to Catrice. "Hey, you want me to follow you?"

She stared at her feet. "No, I'm fine. I'll just run as fast as I can."

"Oh, okay." Drayden returned to the door, disappointed. She'd seemed so thankful to have him follow her on the rock wall. Her rejection reminded Drayden that this challenge, like the rock wall, didn't require the pledges to work together. Some of them could pass it, and others not. If some didn't survive, it would increase the others' odds of capturing the coveted Palace spot.

Tim tucked his pants into his socks. "You guys might want to do the same. Keep the cockroaches from running inside your pants. Less exposed skin to get bit."

Everyone followed his lead. "Well, don't we look cool?" Tim said, effectively wearing knickers. "It's time. If you fall, yell out for help. Let's not leave anyone behind. Except Alex, of course."

Alex snickered. "It's not a big door, but as soon as I open it, they'll come pouring out. No time to sit and pee your pants. Just go."

"Wait," Drayden said. "Catrice, should we have a strategy? Can you think of any clever way through this?"

She hugged her arms around her body, as if already protecting herself from the critters. "I can't think of one, other than getting through as fast as possible."

They formed a line. Alex first, then Charlie, followed by Catrice, Drayden, Sidney, and Tim.

This was it. Drayden couldn't conceive of any method other than brute force. He shook so violently it hurt his ankle. Tim was right—not even trying would result in exile. Yet attempting and

failing would mean getting eaten alive by rats. A whimper escaped his lips. Not wanting to lose his hat, he stuffed it into his backpack. He glanced back at Tim.

Tim gave him a thumbs-up.

"Five seconds!" Alex shouted. *"Five, four, three, two, one..."* He swung the door open.

Drayden's jaw dropped.

Dozens of rats and hundreds of cockroaches that had been smushed up against the door spilled into the tunnel. After that initial bunch, hundreds of the repulsive creatures rushed out the door. That was nothing compared to the view into the station, which ignited raw terror.

The Bureau had created one humongous room. They'd removed the platforms and tracks, leaving only the supporting pillars. Rather than the usual brightness, a reddish glow illuminated the station, creating the illusion of everything covered in blood. As far as the eye could see, the ground undulated like a single beast, an ocean, made of hundreds of thousands of rats. Possibly millions. To Drayden, it was Hell on Earth.

"Drayden, go!" Tim screamed.

Alex and Charlie had already advanced twenty yards ahead, but struggled, repeatedly falling. Charlie slapped frantically at his legs. Catrice stood still in the doorway, crying.

Drayden forced his feet to move. He sidestepped her, moving in front. He stepped up on a lumpy pile of rats, which made him a foot taller. He reached back and caught Catrice's hand, pulling her forward, up onto the rats. His stomach turned and he bent over to dry heave, affording a close-up view of them.

Most were a grayish brown, though a few were black. Both varieties had slithery, hairless tails.

Drayden readjusted his feet.

Rats crunched underneath them, screeching and squealing.

It was like standing on a deflated basketball. One with diseased teeth trying to bite you. Holding Catrice's hand helped maintain Drayden's balance.

Catrice clutched his hand tight. Her teary, terrified eyes met his.

"Drayden!" Tim said. "Start walking, we gotta move."

Drayden's heartbeat pulsed in his ears. He lurched forward, legs wobbling. Each wobble ignited a fireball of pain in his ankle. Each step produced squishing, squeaking, and crunching beneath his feet.

He peered down to take another step.

Cockroaches blanketed his legs, zigzagging in every direction.

He swatted at them with his free hand, but his attempts to clear them proved futile. My God, how were they going to forge through? The critters were overwhelming them already.

A sharp pain erupted in Drayden's calf. The first rat bite.

He cried out and lost his balance. He fell to his side, dragging Catrice down with him, landing on a warm, jittery pile of fur and bones.

Catrice screamed and lost her grip on Drayden's hand. Another rat bit into his wrist, blasting a wave of pain up his forearm.

Drayden wailed again, hyperventilating, and slapped at his wrist. He battled to push himself back to his feet, but the pile of rats wasn't solid. The soft mass simply absorbed the pressure from his hands.

Get up! Now!

He scrambled back to standing and spun around to rescue Catrice.

Sidney wrapped her arms around Catrice's waist to stand her up.

Drayden offered his hand and she took it. Enough of this! Gingerly tiptoeing over the rats wasn't working. He stepped forward with authority, and stomped down as forcefully as he could with his

good foot. He did it again. In place, he thrust his right foot down, stunning or killing some of them. "You like that?"

"Drayden, move goddammit!" Tim yelled from behind. Sidney was right on Catrice's heels, Tim right behind her.

Drayden staggered forward, taking one unstable step after another. He dragged Catrice along with him and picked up the pace, aiming to reach the halfway mark. His intense focus on balance distracted him, so he hadn't noticed the tickling on his stomach. With his free hand, he untucked his shirt.

More than a dozen cockroaches fell out.

Drayden retched again. Eventually they got into a rhythm, one step, then another, stop, repeat. He began to regard the rats not as individual little monsters, but as a singular, heaving floor. He then pretended the rats were fake robotic creatures created by the Bureau. It made them seem less scary. He succeeded until rats bit him again, making him cry out each time. He swatted at them with his hands, which bled profusely with bites. If cockroaches penetrated Drayden's clothes or traversed his face, he frantically scraped them away. Otherwise he ignored them. He checked on Catrice.

She maniacally pulled and shook her hair, struggling to dislodge a cockroach. Her long hair proved a major liability when a cockroach invaded it, tangling its hairy legs in her wispy strands.

Drayden released her hand and seized the tiny creature, its grotesque wiggling body and legs making him shiver. He untangled as many strands as he could and yanked, pulling a few of her hairs out with it.

She screeched. "Thank you!" She grabbed his hand again before he even offered.

They trudged along. Alex and Charlie walked fifty yards ahead and were nearing the end.

Drayden stepped with his left foot and rolled his gimpy ankle on a pile of rats, shooting daggers up his leg. He lost his balance

and fell face first into the chomping, wriggling ocean of rats. As he tried to pop back up, a cockroach scampered into his mouth. He spit it out, gagging and retching. He shot back to his feet, spitting over and over. He keeled over, braced on his knees, about to vomit, but fought it off. When he reached back, Catrice caught his hand.

As they staggered further, Drayden yanked up his shirt and brushed the cockroaches off his chest. Catrice scraped the ones off his back. Finally, the end was in sight. A steel wall with a door like the entrance marked the exit, now about thirty yards away. The door was closed.

Alex and Charlie must have already gone through. Would they attempt to lock them in? As foolish as they were, they knew they had no chance to finish the Initiation without Drayden or Catrice to solve the brainteasers. At least one of them. Alex and Charlie must have closed the door to keep the vermin from escaping into the tunnel.

"Fifty feet!" Tim shouted.

Drayden's legs burned from the exertion. He panted, his ankle throbbed, he was pouring sweat, and he'd been bitten more times than he could count. But he was going to pull through to the end. He would beat this challenge. Ten yards.

A sharp pain cut into Drayden's thigh right above the knee. He swatted down reflexively, and knocked the angry black rat off his leg. "Crud!" he cried out. He soccer kicked the rats in front of him, sending them flying, then stomped his way to the door. He pushed down on the handle and shoved. He fell through, pulling Catrice with him. He released her hand and spun around.

She ran right into him, hugged him tight, and buried her face in his chest.

CHAPTER 14

Drayden held Catrice tight, savoring the moment. It felt so good to hold someone, and to be held.

Catrice released first.

Sidney, and then Tim, tumbled through the door. He slammed it shut.

The rats and cockroaches that escaped into the tunnel disappeared into the darkness.

Alex and Charlie sat on the tracks, having already removed their shirts, shoes, and socks. They'd propped their flashlights up, bathing the tunnel in light. Bloody bites dotted both boys, mostly around their ankles and calves, and also on their hands. They cleaned the bites with the antiseptic wipes.

Drayden, Catrice, Sidney, and Tim slumped over with their hands on their knees, their chests heaving.

Tim rested his hand on Drayden's shoulder. "I admit that was horrendous," he said, "but we made it. Better get these cuts cleaned right away. Hey, Alex, you still like rats?"

"More than I like you," Alex said without looking up.

The surge of adrenaline dissipated in Drayden's body. For the first time, he really felt all of the stinging bites. His ankles and calves throbbed, and the cuts on his hands stung as he removed his

backpack. The pain wasn't the problem, it was the potential infection. Even a cut from something clean could kill you if it became infected. If a filthy rat's mouth, teeming with diseases, produced the wounds, how could they possibly survive? They might all be dead in a week.

"I can't believe the Bureau would expose us to rat bites," Drayden said to Tim. "What sort of challenge is that? Test how strong our immune systems are? What does that have to do with bravery or intelligence? It's total shkat."

Tim shook out his hands. "Yeah, that wasn't cool at all." He searched for a hidden camera or microphone. "Hey Bureau, not cool!" he bellowed.

How could the Initiation Council be watching a bunch of kids suffer like this? These were adults, some of whom probably had their own children.

"I don't think the Watchers care." Drayden shook his head.

"Try the wipes," Charlie said. He sniffed one. "We don't have anything like this in the Dorms. They smell funny, I think they're medicated or something. The bites feel better right away."

Drayden flung off his shoes and bloody socks, and tore off his sweaty shirt. He counted eight bites on his legs, and five on his hands and wrist. Two red spots on his stomach the size of dimes puffed out like the king and queen of pimples. "What the hell are these?"

"Cockroach bites," Alex said.

"Man," Drayden said. "One time when I fell back there I got a cockroach right in my mouth." He spat again. "I almost puked, like that time we ate the rotten egg at your house. I gagged a few times."

"Ha, I remember," Alex said. "You shoulda' chomped down and ate it. Lot of protein in those buggers."

"Dude," Tim said with a grimace, "you're disgusting."

Drayden scrubbed his ankles with the first wipe, which formed lathery foam on each cut. Charlie was right. The pain dissipated instantly, and the bleeding stopped. He closed his eyes and released a slow breath.

He'd known the Palace would offer a better lifestyle. It was one of the reasons he'd entered the Initiation. But he'd always maintained that the Palace couldn't be that much better than the Dorms. Resources were limited in all of New America. That position was becoming untenable. The Bureau continued to reveal superior technology and luxury—computers, batteries, flashlights, working pencils, and now these miraculous wipes.

Drayden wrapped gauze bandages tightly around his legs and hands, covering every cut, then secured them with tape. With the urgency of the situation over, he became acutely aware that he was shirtless in front of the girls. He blushed. His long, skinny limbs and bony chest drew a tough comparison with Charlie, who was all chiseled muscle. Even Tim and Alex were more muscular than he was. Drayden dressed as speedily as he could.

"Charlie, how'd you get so big on the Dorm diet?" Drayden asked. "You sneaking an extra food allocation or something?"

"Ah, mostly from lifting weights. I'm also an only child, and my parents spoiled me. They let me eat whatever I wanted, even if it meant they didn't have enough. Your parents starve you or something? You're so skinny if you turned sideways and stuck your tongue out, you'd look like a zipper."

Drayden cracked up. "Where do you get all these one-liners from anyway?"

"My old man. He's got a zillion of 'em."

"Hey, you guys?" Sidney asked. "You mind walking down the tunnel a bit so Catrice and I can take off our shirts and treat our bites?"

"No, I think we're good here." Charlie howled and high-fived Alex.

Sidney glared at him, her hands on her hips. "Beat it, Charlie."

"Let's go, you flunks," Tim said. He strapped on his backpack. "Time for a bathroom break for me anyway."

"Me too," Drayden said. "We haven't seen a clock in a while. Wonder how we're doing on time."

The boys headed down the tunnel. Charlie draped his arm around Tim's shoulders. "Tim, let's not do that again with the rats. That sucked."

Drayden grew hot in the face. Was Charlie just messing with his head? He'd long been best friends with Alex, Drayden's former friend. He seemed to like Catrice, and now he was buddying up to Tim?

After fifty yards, they reached the red glow of a clock: *04:47:16, 04:47:15...*

"Approaching halfway through," Tim said. He walked over to the darkness of the uptown tracks to relieve himself.

Drayden headed for the One Line track, brightened by a grating to the street above, to do the same. When he returned, something caught his eye on the tracks.

It was a playing card.

Someone on the street must have dropped it through the grate. He picked up the card and flipped it over.

The queen of hearts.

A lump formed in Drayden's throat, the card reminding him of his mom. He'd never played cards with anyone else. That time at age eleven when he fought for his life with an infection, Mom had occupied him with endless games of gin rummy, pinochle, and blackjack. He wiped his watery eyes with the back of his hand, thankful for the darkness of the tunnel. He didn't want anyone to notice his tears. He slid the card in his back pocket.

Sidney and Catrice caught up and the pledges continued walking the dark tracks, guided by their flashlights.

"Eighteenth Street is the next station on the One Line," Drayden said. "Hopefully the Bureau will give us a break there. After that is Fourteenth Street, a major station on the Two-Three Line. Since they're alternating, we should expect an intelligence challenge."

"I thought about locking you all in the rat room," Alex said, "but I needed you for the intelligence tests. It's not like Charlie's gonna be solving them. He's dumber than a...dumber than..."

"Dumber than a bag of hammers," Charlie offered. "Dumber than fried rice. About as sharp as a marble. Dumber than a—"

"We got it, Charlie," Drayden said. "Wow, Alex. Admitting you need us for the intelligence challenges is about as close as you get to a compliment."

Charlie sighed. "I don't know, you guys. The challenges are getting tougher. I can't imagine what could be harder than that rat and cockroach pit we went through. The Initiation was exciting at first, but now it just sucks, you know? Charlie kind of wants to go home."

"I know," Sidney said. "I'm kind of jealous of the kids who didn't enter. They get to graduate tomorrow and receive their jobs, even though the assignments stink."

Home did sound pretty sweet right now to Drayden.

Alex and Charlie sped up, marching ahead of everyone else again. Tim and Sidney walked a few yards ahead of Drayden, chatting. Sidney laughed and punched Tim in the shoulder. Tim made a goofy face back.

Drayden watched them, feeling warm inside. Tim was his most charming when he was just himself, rather than angling to impress girls by being "macho" Tim. Drayden was thankful now that Sidney had entered. She was a tad emotional during the challenges, but it

was gratifying to have someone else around who appreciated and believed in him.

A hand touched Drayden's shoulder. Catrice shined her flashlight up under her face so he could see her.

Even covered in tunnel dirt, sweat, and rat bites, she still managed to look pretty. Though aiming the flashlight under her chin made her resemble a demon goddess. He chuckled to himself, acknowledging his own dorkiness. He bit his lip so he wouldn't laugh out loud.

"Hey," she said. "Thanks for helping me back there. I wouldn't have made it otherwise. I couldn't move, I froze."

Drayden held his flashlight the same way, under his chin. "You're welcome. I was really scared. Holding your hand helped me too."

"And thanks for pulling that cockroach out of my hair." She flipped her hair to the other side of her head. "That was going to be my final moment. The first person to ever die by cockroach."

Drayden yearned to tell her how beautiful she was, and how he felt about her. Butterflies flitted in his stomach. He stared too long without saying anything. "Yeah, well, it's a good thing it was just that one. Two cockroaches, and you were on your own."

Catrice feigned shock and slapped Drayden on the arm.

They walked side by side. Though his body was banged up, the Bureau hadn't defeated him yet. He'd confronted one of his worst fears with the rats, and survived. Something else happened in that challenge. He'd already decided to focus on passing the Initiation rather than worrying about impressing Catrice. But in the rat pit, he hadn't been trying to win her over. He'd legitimately tried to help her. And worrying about her safety allowed him to ignore his own fear.

That last thought struck him as both fascinating and satisfying. Maybe that's how Tim was always so brave, since he constantly

looked out for Drayden. Caring about someone to that degree and protecting them refreshed Drayden's soul. Perhaps he didn't need to be so afraid anymore.

On the surface, it didn't make sense that Catrice had entered the Initiation. She seemed to have everything. Brilliant, beautiful, both parents. Back in the Dorms, she certainly could have married anyone she wished. She may have longed for a chance at a decent career and a better life, but most people didn't risk the Initiation for that. She'd rebuffed Charlie when he'd asked. Either she didn't want to tell Charlie, or didn't want everybody else to hear. Drayden turned to ask her about it.

"Catrice, why did—"

"Station!" Charlie yelled.

"I thought you said there wouldn't be a challenge at Eighteenth Street?" Charlie said to Drayden. They approached a staircase straight ahead, rather than off to the right where the platform should have been.

"I said I *hoped* there wouldn't be. They're getting closer together now, I guess."

Charlie sulked. "Awesome."

"Catrice?" Drayden asked. "Can we team up again on this next test?"

"Of course," she replied.

Tim ascended the stairs into the light with everyone else in tow. They stopped to scan the heavily modified space.

It was a narrow, elongated room, barely resembling a subway station. Only two rows of steel pillars supporting the ceiling remained. Even the ceiling itself was white. In other stations it was open, exposing pipes and vents. The floor covered the tracks, and the room ended with a back wall, way down the station. Normally,

tiles covered the walls and platform floor. Here, however, the walls were painted white, and the floor was cement.

"Hmmm," Charlie said, scratching his head. "It's a room. Looks like it ends about halfway up the station."

"Let's go then," Tim said, lacking his usual enthusiasm, "get this over with."

Fifty yards away, something sat in the back of the room, before the wall.

Charlie took the lead. Ten yards away from the wall he stopped, his muscular arms extended. "I don't like the looks of that."

A few objects rested atop a picnic table, all of them small. One stood out—a shiny black box.

What was that? Another computer? Drayden couldn't tell.

A deafening, metallic, screeching noise erupted behind them.

Drayden covered his head with his arms, and spun around in alarm.

A steel wall crashed down from the ceiling, slamming onto the cement floor with an epic boom and a billowing cloud of dust.

Drayden covered his ears, though only the echo reverberated throughout the chamber now.

The steel wall had trapped them in the room, now roughly forty feet long by twenty feet wide.

"What the hell is going on?" Sidney asked, her voice quivering. "Is that part of the challenge? Was that supposed to happen?"

"I'm sure there's instructions." Tim stormed impatiently toward the table with the others trailing him.

"Hey look, there's a door behind the table," Charlie said. "It's white so it doesn't stand out, but it's there. Guess that's our way out."

Alex flicked him on the arm. "I'm pretty sure it's locked, chotch. I think the idea was to trap us in here."

"Yeah, I know. I'm just saying, assuming we pass the test."

Drayden examined the table, which contained a strange assortment of items: two short, thick strings held up by clamps; four boxes of matches; and the shiny box-like device. A miniature silver box sat atop the larger black object's base, and the same string jutted out from the silver box.

Drayden didn't dig the sight of that shiny box either.

A clock above the table ticked down: *04:39:21, 04:39:20...*

Tim picked up a note on the table and read. *"Search your heart and mind when death is on the line. Prove your ability to manage situations with life or death consequences. To advance, you must survive this challenge."* He paused, and raised his eyes to the others.

Drayden shuddered. *Survive.*

Tim continued. *"On the table are two loose wicks held up by clamps, each taking exactly one minute to burn. They do not burn evenly, but they take precisely one minute. A third wick, also one minute in length, is attached to a silver detonator, which is attached to a bomb. You must light the wick attached to the bomb. In exactly forty-five seconds, you can pull out the detonator, disarming the bomb. You must measure exactly forty-five seconds using the two loose wicks. If the detonator is pulled before forty-five seconds, the bomb will detonate. After forty-five seconds, the detonator will lock in, and cannot be pulled out. In that event, the bomb will detonate fifteen seconds later. If you successfully disarm the bomb, the door before you will open. If you do not, you must seek cover. Whoever survives may continue the Initiation. You will have five minutes to prepare, at which point the wick to the bomb must be lit. If it is not, you will all be exiled. The clock will begin counting down momentarily. Good luck."*

"Oh my God." Sidney covered her mouth with both hands.

The clock began counting down from five minutes.

Tim, Sidney, Charlie, and Alex stared at Drayden with pleading eyes.

He shook his head and looked down.

Tim clapped his hands. "Drayden and Catrice, get to work!"

Drayden pulled out his paper and pencil, as did Catrice. They knelt, facing each other.

"Catrice, I have no idea."

Her lip trembled. "Me either."

There's a trick. What would Mr. Kale say? State what you know. Two wicks. Each takes a minute. Nope, that's two minutes. Light both? Guess when they're three-quarters done? No, it has to be exact to the second.

Catrice perked up. "Light one wick at both ends."

"Yes!" Drayden said. "Good. They don't burn evenly but that won't matter. They'll meet in the middle at exactly thirty seconds."

"Four minutes left!" Tim yelled.

The others had pretty much abandoned participating on the brainteasers, Drayden noted.

"Lighting the other one when it's done doesn't help," Catrice said. "That would just give you a minute and a half."

Drayden's shirt soaked through with fresh sweat. "What happens if we light wick two at the same time as we light both ends of wick one?"

"I don't know, it'll be done in a minute, that doesn't get us anywhere," Catrice said.

Tim gently tugged on the wicks and Sidney tested the matches. Charlie touched the bomb.

"Get away from that, you flunk!" Alex snapped. "It might explode."

"Three minutes!" Sidney screeched, both hands in her hair.

"Dray," Tim said, wringing his hands. "Dray, I know you guys are doing your best, but we're going to need a minute to set up for this one. Deciding who's lighting each wick, all that. You got this, bro!"

Drayden balled his fists. They were running out of time. *Think, dammit!* They had thirty seconds done. How could they add that last fifteen?

"Catrice, anything?"

She bit down on her lower lip. "I...I don't know. It's too much pressure. Something with that second wick? We relight it, or pause it, I'm not sure."

Drayden pictured the burning wicks in his mind. "What if..." He dropped his pencil. Wait. Was that it? "Catrice! That second wick."

She inched closer and tucked her hair behind her ears.

"Two minutes, Drayden! Hurry!" Sidney screamed.

"That second wick." Drayden bounced up and down. "We start it at the same time as we light both ends of wick one. When wick one is done, thirty seconds will have gone by, right? Wick two will be half done. We light the other end of wick two, and—"

"Yes! That's it. You got it! If you light the other end of wick two when it's half done and it's burning from both ends, it'll finish in fifteen seconds!" She leaned forward and hugged Drayden.

They both jumped up.

"Tim! Tim!" Drayden said. "We got it!"

"Nice job, bud. Everyone gather around!" he called out. The pledges gathered around Drayden. "What do we need to do?" Tim asked.

Drayden scanned their faces. "We need, how many, four people to light wicks at the same time. Who wants to be a lighter?"

"I'm in," Tim said.

"Me too," Sidney said.

Charlie slapped himself. "Hell yeah."

Nobody else volunteered. They needed one more. All eyes shifted to Alex, as he slowly backed away.

"Screw that," Alex said. "Sorry, guys. I'll be in the back row." He jogged back to the furthest steel pillar in the room and crouched behind it.

"Freaking shkat flunk," Tim said. "He's probably hoping some of us don't survive. One minute left."

Catrice and Drayden faced each other, their eyes locked. One of them needed to absorb the greater risk of death as a lighter.

Tim wrinkled his forehead. "Dray, maybe...maybe I can light two at once. You and Catrice go take cover. We can do it."

Drayden needed to do this. He was going to protect Catrice. He wasn't going to be scared anymore.

"No," Drayden stated. He stood tall. "I'll do it."

"Drayden, no," Catrice protested.

"It has to be exact," Drayden said, "and we need to ensure it's done right. One of us needs to be up here to direct. If something goes wrong..." he gulped, "either me or you need to survive to handle the rest of the brainteasers. You go take cover. I got this."

Tim patted Drayden on the back. "That's my boy!"

Catrice hugged Drayden tight. She pulled back and gazed into his eyes with her hands on his cheeks.

Sidney scowled at Catrice, unable to hide her disgust. "If you're gonna hide, then do it!"

Catrice snatched up her backpack and bolted. She crouched behind the other pillar in the back across from Alex.

Drayden checked the clock.

Thirty seconds left.

"Everybody get a pack of matches," he said. "Practice lighting them once right now."

Everyone struck a match. They all burst into flame on the first attempt.

"Good, blow them out. Get another match ready for the real thing." Drayden wiped sweat from his forehead with the back of his hand. "Crud! Almost out of time. Um, Tim and Sidney, you're on that wick closest to the wall, we'll call that wick one. Each light an end when I say so. Charlie, you're on this wick nearest to us, we'll call it wick two, and just light one end. I'll light the bomb. I'll count down from three. I'll say—this is just practice!—I'll say three, two, one, light. Have your match already lit, ready to go."

00:08, 00:07...

"Light your match!" Drayden held his breath.

He exhaled as they all lit, his hands shaking. *Please don't mess this up. Don't miss the wick. Don't drop the match.* "Get in position near the wick." He eyed the clock. "Three, two, one, *light!*" He touched the flame to the wick on the bomb.

Everyone executed. The wicks ignited simultaneously, fizzing, crackling, and burning. The miniature fireballs crawled along the length of the wicks in uneven bursts. The flames lurched on a collision course on Tim and Sidney's wick.

"Sid and Charlie, take cover!" Drayden shouted. "Tim, stay with me."

Sidney and Charlie ran for the pillars.

Tim jumped up and down. "Dray, what do I do now?"

Drayden wiped sweat out of his eyes. He was drenched. He couldn't remember. Oh God. What was next?

"Drayden!" Tim screamed, contorting his face.

"Okay, okay!" he said. "Uh, right, when your wick is done, when the two flames meet, you light the other end of Charlie's wick. Get ready."

Tim teed up his match. "What are you going to do?"

"When that second wick is done, the one you're about to light, I'm pulling out the detonator. As soon as you light the other end of that wick, go hide."

"No way. I'll do it, you go."

"Tim, we're almost out of time!" Drayden screamed.

"Dammit, Drayden!"

"It's very close, Tim, light your match." Drayden virtually touched his nose to wick one's moving fireballs to capture the exact moment they converged. "Ready...*light!*"

Tim lit the end of wick two. Fifteen seconds left.

The blinding fizzle of the burning wick hypnotized them both. Drayden checked the wick on the bomb, which was about two-thirds done.

"Tim, go! Run!" Drayden yelled.

Tim stood fast. "I'm staying."

"Come on, you guys! You can do it!" Sidney shouted from the back of the room.

This is it. Drayden shuddered. If he pulled out the detonator even a second early they were both dead for sure, and the others might die too. He wiped his clammy palms on his jeans. How hard was it to dislodge the detonator? Should he just tug it straight up? Rotate it? He couldn't test it, or practice, it might go off. He wiped his hands on his jeans once again.

Tim looked crazed. "Almost there, Drayden!"

"Say 'now' when it's done, Tim, I'm focusing on the detonator."

Please don't explode.

"Ready...now!" Tim yelled.

Drayden gripped the detonator and yanked up.

His fingers slipped off.

He stopped breathing. *No!*

He seized it again and pulled up.

It didn't budge. He tried again. It was locked.

Oh no.

He looked at Tim.

Tim gawked at the bomb in horror.

"Tim, run!" Drayden screamed. He turned to bolt.

Tim grabbed the bomb, jerked the detonator, but failed to dislodge it. "C'mon!" He pulled with all his strength, turning red in the face.

"Tim, leave it! Run!" Drayden spun and bolted.

"*Tim!*" Sidney shrieked.

As swiftly as Drayden ran, time slowed down. His movements occurred in slow motion. His mind went blank.

The others crouched behind the furthest pillars, hands over their ears and their eyes closed.

Drayden sprinted for the nearest one. He planned on diving behind it.

That was the last thing he remembered.

CHAPTER 15

*P*ain.

A sharp throbbing in the back of Drayden's head, and his back. *Ringing. Something was ringing.*

He was lying face down. What the hell was going on? And what was ringing?

When he opened his eyes, they immediately burned and watered. It was so smoky in here. The smoke burned his nostrils with each breath, made difficult by his runny nose. His face was an inch from a cement floor.

Bright red ink covered it.

Or was that blood?

Drayden started to prop himself up on his elbows.

Pain exploded in his back.

He cried out and dropped his head back down.

Wait. The bomb.

Tim.

"Tim!" His throat burned like acid, sound barely escaping his lips. He touched his nose.

His fingers came away dripping with blood.

He managed to rest his chin on the cement so he could see in front of him. Lifting his head at all aggravated the stabbing pain in his back. Where was everybody else?

Catrice.

"Catrice!" he tried to yell, only managing a whisper. He squinted to glimpse through the smoky white haze.

Bodies lay on the ground.

They're dead. No, there's movement!

Hands clutched heads. Someone got on their hands and knees. Another stood up shakily and stumbled toward him.

"Who is that?" Drayden rasped.

The figure was ten feet away...five.

Drayden drew in a quick breath. *Oh my God.*

It was Sidney. Blood dripped down her face from the top of her head. She wiped it out of her eyes. "Drayden! You're alive! Thank God. Don't move."

He could barely hear her. The ringing. His eardrums must have been damaged.

Kneeling by his head, she stroked his hair, smearing it with blood from her hands. "Can you get up? What's hurt?"

"My back, my head. Mostly my back," he groaned. "Tim. Where's Tim?"

Sidney looked beyond Drayden. "Oh no. Dray, sit tight." She rose and stumbled behind him.

Drayden couldn't turn his head. "Sid!" he struggled to yell. "Is he okay? Tim!"

Sidney returned and slumped on the ground, facing away from Drayden.

"Sid, where's Tim? Where's Tim!"

She faced him, her hands clasped over her mouth, her eyes red. She whimpered, tears forming streaks of exposed pale skin on her bloody cheeks.

"No, Sid. No! Tim!" he cried.

"He's dead, Drayden," she whispered.

"No, he's not. Tim!" Drayden burst into tears. "Sid, go check him again. Please, go check again."

"He's dead! He's gone. He's not breathing, he has no heartbeat, he's got...terrible injuries." She buried her face in her hands and sobbed, blood and tears dripping all over her hands.

Drayden forgot everything. His pain, the Initiation, Catrice. He wailed, crying raw, savage tears. He shook uncontrollably, moaning. Tim *couldn't* be gone. He was just there. And it was Drayden's fault. It was his fault Tim entered at all. His fault Tim died. Drayden had screwed up. He didn't deserve to live. He should be dead, not Tim.

He bawled unashamedly.

"Drayden?"

The ringing dissipated. He peered through his fingers.

Catrice's hair had turned totally pink from blood, which also splotched her face.

"Catrice, you're injured," Drayden whispered. He wiped blood and tears from his eyes.

"It's a cut on my head, that's all. Probably looks worse than it is." She knelt beside him.

"Catrice...Tim," he wailed.

"I know," she said, tearing up. "I'm so sorry. Tim was a great friend, and very brave. Drayden, what's hurt?"

"My back." He sniffled. "I can't move. It hurts too much when I try."

Catrice craned her neck up to check out his back and gasped. She jumped back down, shielding her eyes.

Drayden began to hyperventilate. "What? What is it?"

Catrice kept her eyes covered. "Sidney, can you look at his back?"

Drayden's eyes darted between the two of them. Panic set in, nervous heat enveloping his face.

Sidney rolled up onto her knees and peered over his shoulder at his back. She sat back on her feet and brushed the hair out of Drayden's eyes. "It's no big deal," she said in an extra calm voice. "Don't freak out. We can fix it. You have a piece of metal sticking out of your back. I'm going to pull it out."

Drayden stretched to reach Sidney. "No! Don't touch it. Please!"

"Shhhh. I'm just going to take a closer look right now. Don't worry. I'm not going to touch it yet. I just want to see how deep it is." She stood and walked behind him.

"Don't touch it, Sid, please," Drayden whimpered. "How does it look? Is it bad?"

A volcano of pain erupted in his back and his vision blurred. He cried out in agony, writhing. The pain radiated throughout his entire body in waves, unbearable at their crest.

"Got it," Sid said. She knelt in front of him, caressing Drayden's hair again, her face mere inches from his. "I'm sorry, but that was the best way. It had to come out. You would have died here otherwise."

Drayden cried. From the pain in his back and his head, though mostly because of Tim.

"I'm going to use your wipes and gauze to treat that wound," Sidney said. "Then I'm going to clean the cut on the back of your head, which is pretty serious."

Drayden didn't respond, only continued to sob.

Sidney dressed Drayden's wounds, delicately tending to him. Whatever astonishing substance existed in those wipes decreased his pain in seconds. Catrice sat in front of him, using her wipes to clean her own face and the cut on her head. Charlie and Alex hobbled over, their heads bandaged, blood spattering their necks and shirts. Alex had tied his red bandana over the head dressing.

"Just like new," Sidney said to Drayden. "Time to try and get up."

He propped up on his elbows. So far so good. He tucked his knees forward.

Searing daggers shot into his back and he gasped in pain.

Sidney supported him under the arms to assist. "Power through it, Drayden. You can do it."

He forced himself up, his body screaming in agony. The room spun, the dark spots coming again.

Arms braced him.

His eyes closed, he reached for Sidney and Catrice, who both hovered nearby. "I'm all right," Drayden said. He opened his eyes and found Sidney inches away.

Blood, now caked into a dark crimson, still covered her face and stained her shirt.

"You took care of me before yourself," Drayden said, his eyes moistening again. "Thank you, Sidney." He hugged her and held her close for a moment, resting his head on her shoulder.

She hugged back gently and pulled away. She smiled. Not a flirty smile, but a genuine, warm smile.

"Can I help you clean up that cut?" Drayden asked her.

"Thanks. I'd appreciate that."

Catrice watched them. She'd wrapped the bandages on her own head like a headband. Her flowing pink locks cascaded down her shoulders.

Drayden gently scrubbed the deep gash in Sidney's head first, then cleaned her face. He secured her wound with gauze and tape, then wiped his own face clean. He didn't dare look at Tim's body just yet.

"Thank you, Drayden," Sidney said, gazing into his eyes.

"You guys?" Charlie said. "Dray, I'm sorry about Tim. It's time to get going."

Drayden faced Tim's body.

Tim lay on his stomach, his arms splayed out to the sides. One leg was scrunched forward, the other extended back. His cheek rested in a wide pool of dark red blood, his blank eyes open.

A wave of nausea overcame Drayden.

"Don't look," Sidney said. "It'll only make it harder."

Drayden gingerly bent down and pulled the water and pain-killers from his backpack. He swallowed another pill. Two left now. He loosened the back of his hat and carefully pulled it down over the bandaging. No longer able to wear his backpack, he carried it in his hand.

Alex and Charlie passed the body without stopping. They rounded the smoldering pile of wood that used to be the table and walked through the open door.

Drayden lumbered for the door flanked by Sidney and Catrice. He stopped in front of the body and knelt in front of Tim, ignoring the stabbing pain in his back.

Tim's vacant eyes stared into space. Blood soaked his hair, matting it to his head. The severe and clearly fatal wound was to the back of his head.

Drayden stroked Tim's hair, tears running down his cheeks. "I'm so sorry, Tim. You're the best friend anyone ever had. It's all my fault. I'm sorry. I love you." He wiped his tears and took Tim's lifeless hand in his own. "Goodbye," he whispered.

Sidney and Catrice both wrapped their arms around his shoulders as he stood. They rounded the burning rubble and exited through the door, back into the tunnel.

Nobody spoke. Only four blocks away, Fourteenth Street all but guaranteed another challenge. The tracks ran in an extended straightaway here. Light from the approaching station already glowed in the distance.

Drayden eventually stopped crying, internalizing his pain. Tim had been there so many times to protect him over the years. Fighting so Drayden didn't have to, turning the tables on bullies. He didn't deserve Tim as a best friend. Why was Tim so wonderful to him?

That's what friendship was, he guessed. They were each other's only real friends. Tim wasn't even close to his own family. Drayden was all he'd had. In a way, Tim was like a second brother to Drayden, only without all the sibling fighting, and only the good stuff.

Now, because of Drayden, he was dead. He had been alive thirty minutes ago, and now he wasn't. He was murdered by the Bureau, and by Drayden's carelessness. First the Bureau took away his mom, and now his best friend. How could a government allow this to happen to its citizens? Its children? The Watchers had just witnessed a child get blown up on camera. They were monsters. Screw the Bureau and their stupid Initiation.

Drayden should have let Tim pull out the damn detonator. Why did he insist on doing it himself? To prove to himself and everyone else he wasn't a coward? Look how that turned out. He didn't pay the price for his failure—Tim did. Although Drayden's family wasn't religious, if Heaven existed, or wherever the soul floated after death, he might just let himself be exiled. He could die and join Tim and his mother.

Except...

What would Tim want him to do? He would never wish for Drayden to fail, to wilt away and die. Tim wouldn't have been the slightest bit upset with him. Tim would insist it could have happened to anyone, or the same thing would have happened if he'd pulled the detonator. Tim would expect him to collaborate with Catrice to advance Sidney through the intelligence challenges. He'd compel Drayden to team up with Sidney to carry Catrice through the bravery ones. And he wouldn't give a damn about Charlie or Alex, demanding Drayden stand up to them. Tim never feared those guys.

Charlie was misguided, but he displayed basic morality outside of Alex's influence. Alex presented a real problem, though. While Drayden could defeat him in a fight, the strongest or most skilled

person didn't always win fights. Sometimes it was the person who was willing to do what the other person wasn't. If the stronger threw punches while the weaker attacked with a knife, the weaker would win. That was Alex.

What was Alex up to anyway? He'd sabotaged the three boxes challenge, though it could have been an honest mistake. He generally didn't help, particularly on the intelligence ones. Nevertheless, he swore he would move into the Palace. He couldn't possibly believe he'd be the one selected, yet he seemed sure of it.

Instead of battling against Charlie and Alex, should Drayden befriend them? He didn't have Tim on his side anymore. They outnumbered him. And he might need their help on the remaining bravery challenges, especially with his busted ankle and various bomb injuries.

Charlie and Alex plodded along up front, with Catrice alone behind them. Sidney walked beside Drayden.

"Sid," Drayden said, "how did you guys all get those cuts on your heads? Weren't you behind the pillars?"

"We were, and assumed we were safe. When the bomb exploded, we got sucked forward somehow, like hard and fast. We all smashed our heads against the steel pillars."

Charlie turned his head back. "It's called blast wind. The blast wave blows out, and the blast wind pulls you back. I braced myself for it. I was working harder than a one-legged man in a butt kicking contest. Unfortunately, the blast wind was too strong."

Drayden hurried to catch up with Charlie and Alex. "That's interesting, Charlie. Where'd you learn that?"

"My Guardian buddies. Being in an explosion turned out to be not so fun, but I still wanna join the Guardians."

"You guys get banged up pretty bad?" Drayden asked.

"Looks like someone needs a friend," Alex said. "Isn't that right? Not so tough without Tim around." He sneered at Drayden. "Sucks

when you need a friend and they're not there for you, doesn't it, Dray?"

Alex may not have been book smart, but he was certainly street smart. It had taken him all of two seconds to see through Drayden's disingenuous attempt to buddy up to them. Drayden slowed down to let Catrice catch up.

She continued straight ahead, stone faced. She refused his eye contact and passed by without a word.

The brightly lit Fourteenth Street station marked the beginning of the Lab. It meant they'd finally left the Dorms.

Drayden felt a tinge of sadness as he bid farewell to the only home he'd ever known. Whatever happened, he would never see it again.

The bomb was both a bravery *and* intelligence challenge. The impending challenge could be either. Thankfully, that last painkiller had kicked in. It dulled the pain from Drayden's injuries, and even soothed his mind. He'd never taken one before the Initiation since they didn't exist in the Dorms. He mentally added painkillers to the growing list of luxuries the Bureau had that the Dorms didn't.

He slogged up the stairs behind Sidney.

She turned back and offered her hand.

"Thanks," he said, accepting her assistance. Sidney had shown her true colors since the bomb. She cared for and comforted him, even putting his needs before her own, the same way Tim had done. While he hadn't seriously considered Sidney in a girlfriend way, despite her obvious attempts to draw his attention, he couldn't ignore her any longer. Maybe Tim was right about her.

Drayden actually snorted out loud at the thought. What did he know about girlfriends? What did he know about *friends*? It had just been he and Tim, and now Tim was gone. Just like after the exile,

once again he was alone, except this time it was real. He was fresh out of people. Sure, there was Dad and Wes, but they didn't get him as Mom and Tim did. Nobody could know him as they did.

Down the platform, a white wall cut off the station again.

"Are those...people down there?" asked Charlie.

The pledges approached. Two men draped in black robes displaying red Bureau pins stood on opposite sides of two black doors in the wall. Both men were tall, and older. The one on the left was pale and bald; the other was dark, with bushy gray hair. Neither moved, said anything, or even made eye contact with them. A long table bearing a note sat in front of them. A hanging clock displayed the time remaining: *03:59:52, 03:59:51...*

Charlie walked up to the bald guy. "Hi," he said.

The Bureau man didn't react, merely gazed straight ahead.

Charlie shrugged and strolled to the picnic table. He picked up the note and read in a comical voice like he was impersonating Premier Holst. *"Think before you ask, or this will be your last task. Deductive reasoning skills are paramount to success in the Bureau. Prove you have them by solving this riddle. Standing before you are two doors. One leads back into the tunnel. The other leads to exile. These men are the guards to the doors. One always tells the truth. The other always lies. You do not know which is which. You may ask one question to one of the guards, and then you must choose which door to walk through. You have five minutes. The clock above will begin counting down momentarily. Good luck."* Charlie shook his head and shoved the note into Drayden's hand.

Drayden glanced at the note. "Catrice, can we work together again?" The weight of this challenge fell on his and Catrice's shoulders, and the consequence of failure was exile.

Her eyes downcast, she plopped down with her paper and pencil. "I'm going to work on this one alone."

Drayden was unable to hide his disappointment. Witnessing Tim's death must have shaken her.

"I'll work on it with you Drayden," Sidney said, flashing Catrice a dirty look. "If I can help at all."

"Thanks." After sitting, he touched his fingers to the brim of his hat. He and Catrice had made a stellar team on the brainteasers, and she'd seemed to enjoy working with him. Now he'd just have to focus on his own, like on the first challenge. So what did he know? Two guards. One tells the truth, the other lies.

"Why don't we just ask which door we take?" Charlie asked.

"Because," Drayden said, irritated, "we can't tell which guard lies and which tells the truth. If we ask one and he points at a door, we don't know if he's lying or not."

"The bald guy is the liar," Charlie said. "Bald guys always lie."

"Shut up, Charlie," Drayden snapped. "Stop being such a nerf. I need to focus here."

Sidney knelt beside Drayden. "Four minutes left, Dray. How can I help?"

She could let him concentrate; that's how. "Um, if you can keep telling me the time, that would be huge. Thanks." He'd heard this problem before, possibly in school? But he didn't remember the solution. What was the trick? You could never know which guard was which. If you wasted your one question ferreting out the liar, you wouldn't have any questions left to decide which door to choose. So the question must result in them pointing to one of the doors.

Alex flopped down, wrapped his arms around his head, and started rocking.

"Three minutes," Sidney called out, growing increasingly frenzied.

"It's all over!" Charlie cried out, his arms in the air. "We're dead. The Bureau's gonna kill us all. Don't you see? It doesn't matter anymore."

"Will you guys please be quiet?" Drayden asked. What was going on with Charlie and Alex? Alex had gone catatonic and Charlie had lost his mind.

Catrice wrote furiously, pausing every so often to tap her pencil on the side of her head.

Charlie hovered over her shoulder. "Man, she's busier than a one-armed paper hanger. Hey, how mad would you guys be if I asked the bald guard what his favorite color is?"

Drayden groaned, and squeezed his pencil with all his force. This was impossible. The team chemistry soured without Tim here to direct, or at least keep Charlie and Alex in line. Sidney tried to help, but got in the way. Catrice seemed upset. Exile awaited them in minutes, and he couldn't solve this.

Focus!

Sidney cupped her mouth with her hands. "Two minutes, Drayden! Hurry!"

The one question you ask must point to the right door, regardless of which guard you ask. One question must lead to the liar pointing to the same door as the truth-teller. That's it.

What question would do that? Drayden bit down on his pencil.

Charlie danced around in front of one of the guards. He made faces and googly eyes. Unable to elicit any reaction, he strolled over to Drayden. "Ask the guards one question. Ask the guards one question. Ask the guards one question. Ask the—"

"Chotch!" Drayden barked. "I'm begging you. Please shut the hell up!" The pressure of the Initiation, and seeing Tim die, had clearly gotten to Charlie.

"Oh, I thought you liked that. You were lovin' it the first time."

Drayden buried his face in his hands. They were screwed.

"I've got it," Catrice whispered.

Drayden released a breathy sigh and closed his eyes.

Catrice stood and headed toward the bald guard, her paper and pencil in hand.

"Catrice, wait!" Drayden shouted. "We have ninety seconds left, don't you want to talk it over? Have another set of eyes check it?"

She turned back, looking annoyed, like he'd just called her a flunk. "Fine."

Drayden and the others crowded around her.

Catrice checked her notes. "We can only ask one question, and that question must result in them pointing at a door. We don't know which guard will tell the truth, so the question also must result in either of them pointing at the *same* door, regardless of who we ask. Everyone with me?"

"You lost me when you said door," Charlie said.

Sidney whacked him on the arm. "Why are you joking around? Let her finish!"

Catrice continued. "So we pick either guard, and the question is, 'If I ask the *other* guard which door leads to the tunnel, which one will he point to?' In this case, both guards will point to the wrong door. We'll go through the other one. Get it?"

"Yes!" Drayden said. "Nicely done, Catrice."

She met his eyes, looking pained.

Sidney scratched her head. "I don't get it."

"Let's say the guard we ask is the one who always tells the truth," Drayden explained. "Since he always tells the truth, he'll actually tell us what the other guard would say. The other guard is the liar. The liar would point us to the wrong door, the one that leads to exile. So the guard we asked will point to the wrong door too, and then we take the other door. Make sense?"

"I think so," Sidney said doubtfully.

Catrice slammed her notes into her legs and made a face at Drayden. "We don't have time to explain it to her!"

Sidney scoffed. "Screw you!"

"Everyone calm down," Drayden said. "We still have time. Sid, let's say the guard we ask is the one who always lies. Since he always lies, he'll lie about what the other guard would say. The other guard is truthful. He would point to the correct door, the tunnel door. So the liar will point to the wrong door, to exile. Either way, both guards will point to the wrong door. That's brilliant, Catrice. Why don't you do the honors?" Drayden peeked at the clock.

Ten seconds left.

Catrice rushed to the bald guard, glancing back at the others. "If I ask the other guard which door leads to the tunnel, which one will he point to?"

He started to move his arm, and paused. He pointed to the door nearest to him, the one on the left.

The pledges all looked at each other. Catrice walked to the other door, on the right. She lowered the handle and pushed the door open.

CHAPTER 16

The pledges descended a dark staircase which led right onto the tracks.

"Woohoo!" Charlie yelled. "Way to go, Catrice!" He picked her up by the waist and thrust her high in the air. "This cat's sharper than a two-edged sword!" Charlie couldn't contain his joy over the pun. "Get it? Cat? Cat-rice?"

She pretended to hate the attention.

Heat flowed into Drayden's cheeks. For someone who wasn't too clever, Charlie had a knack for wedging himself between Drayden and the few people he liked.

Sidney nudged him and whispered in his ear, "You would've totally gotten it in another minute. You're way smarter than she is."

Charlie set Catrice down.

She straightened her gray t-shirt and pulled her backpack straps tighter. Her eyes met Drayden's.

Drayden stormed ahead of everyone else down the tunnel.

He set a brisk pace, despite his limp. Leaning on Catrice for the intelligence challenges made some sense. It relieved the pressure. With Tim no longer around to hold his hand, he'd have to step up on the bravery challenges. Catrice would need him on

those, while Sidney would be an asset. Essentially, he needed to be more like Tim.

The frequency and difficulty of the challenges had increased. The next one would presumably be at Christopher Street, the following One Line stop, only a few blocks south. It would almost certainly be a physical test. Drayden decided he wasn't going to back down, or be afraid. He would take charge, just like Tim.

There was one tiny problem. He wasn't Tim. You couldn't fake being a leader, being strong and confident. You might be able to fool others, but never yourself. Everyone tasted dynamite the last time he assumed command. With the rats, his concern for Catrice propelled him through the challenge. It made him forget, or ignore, his own fear. That was real.

"Hi," a soft voice behind him said.

Drayden glanced back at Catrice. He continued to walk without responding. Now she was talking to him?

She caught up, and walked beside him. They carried on for a minute without speaking.

Drayden still wouldn't look at her. "How come you didn't want to work with me on that last riddle?"

She paused before answering. "Sometimes I just prefer to work alone. That's how I've always done it."

"I thought we worked well together on the three boxes and the wicks problem. We made a great team, no? That is, before I bungled it and killed Tim and almost everybody else, including myself."

One step, then two. "I think the Bureau intended for the bomb to go off," she said.

He stumbled a bit. "What?"

"I mean, what if the detonator wasn't enabled to be pulled out? I think the challenge was surviving the blast." They picked up the pace again. "Maybe we were supposed to die."

Drayden's mind spun back to those terrifying minutes under the desk in Lily's office, when he'd overheard the Bureau's mass exile plan. People who would do that could easily murder a bunch of kids. At best, they were indifferent about the pledges dying, and at worst they were trying to kill them. Perhaps he should tell Catrice what he'd heard. She might believe him. The other pledges wouldn't. How could they? It was too horrible to believe. Then again, so was the idea of blowing up six teenagers.

It could cause her to worry about her family though. Too much. Distraction in these tunnels meant certain death. He knew that now. No, telling her wouldn't do her or anyone any good.

"That might be true," Drayden said. "But if the Bureau intended on killing us, we should be scared about the challenges coming up."

Catrice shivered. "I am scared. Actually, I'm terrified."

"It's all in your head," he said, adopting Tim's bravado. He waved his hand casually. "You just push out the negative thoughts and imagine success. Poof. Gone."

She side-eyed him. "That's what you do?"

"It's what I *try* to do," he allowed. He wasn't Tim, not by a long shot. "I'm not very good at it."

"You're probably better at it than you think."

"I don't know." They walked for another minute or two, then Drayden turned to her. "You know, you never answered my question. About us making a great team."

"I thought we made a great team too, but..."

"But what?"

She gazed into his eyes before looking away. "Nothing." She deflated a bit. "I guess I'm just different from you. Tim died, Drayden. This is life and death, and we're all, like, in competition with each other. I'm just not used to working with other people. Before the Initiation, I barely worked with anyone on anything. You have. With Tim, and Sidney."

"I don't know," he said. "I think you've connected with everyone. I saw Sidney helping you in the rat challenge, Alex saved you on the rock wall. And you seem to have clicked with Charlie."

She tilted her head and gave him a look. "Seriously?"

They walked for a few minutes without speaking. The silence in the tunnel, except for their footsteps and breaths, was so unnatural. Drayden felt like his senses were numb. Maybe the explosion had done something to his brain. Or he just didn't feel human anymore.

"Hey, Catrice? Can I ask you something?"

"Sure."

"Why did you enter the Initiation?"

"Why are you asking?"

"This thing is crazy dangerous. Kids don't usually enter the Initiation. I heard nobody had entered in two years. You're really smart, and I can understand wanting a chance at a better life. Except most people don't risk death for a better life. Both of Sidney's parents were exiled, and she feels like she has nothing to lose. Charlie's crazy; that's why he entered. Tim did because he hoped to protect me."

Drayden leaned in and whispered, to avoid the Watchers. "My mom was exiled and something was fishy about it. If I make it to the Palace, I'm going to find out what happened. Alex's dad is a drug dealer. Probably has something to do with him entering." He was so close to her neck. He pulled back, speaking normally again. "But you, you're so smart, and beautiful, you have both your parents. I just...I was interested to know."

Catrice watched her feet while she walked. "I'd seen your mom at the FDC. She seemed nice. She was always helping old people with their groceries, and smiling. She must have been a good mom."

"She was." Drayden beamed. "She was amazing. I loved her more than anyone in the world." Picturing her running the FDC, something struck Drayden. Mom was important, and senior in the

Dorms. It was highly unlikely she would have been randomly exiled. Though horrid to think, since all exiles were awful, the Bureau would probably exile seamstresses or janitors first. There were hundreds of them. That would imply her exile was not random. Someone had ordered it.

"What's your dad like?" Catrice asked.

"Very smart. To his credit, he's been trying his best with my mom gone. For most of my life though, he's been totally detached. There, but not present, if you know what I mean."

"Mine too," she said. "He's a genius, in his own world. I guess our fathers are similar. My mom isn't like yours, though. Just because you have both parents doesn't mean everything is good."

"Oh, I didn't mean to imply...yeah, I know. What's your mom like?"

"She...I don't really want to talk about it." Catrice bowed her head. "You know how if we pass the Initiation we have the option of bringing our families along? Well, let's just say not only would I not bring mine, I entered the Initiation to get away from...her." She paused. "So I could be safe," she added quietly.

"I'm sorry." Drayden had been avoiding the fact that only one of them would likely be picked to move to the Palace. While Catrice wasn't concerned about moving her family, the others undoubtedly were, as was he. He wondered if the Bureau had exiled anyone else from the Dorms this morning. What were the odds people that cruel would pick more than one? "I hope you make it to the Palace."

"Thanks. I hope you make it too."

"Hey, you want to hear a joke?" Drayden asked, lightening the mood. "It's math humor, so you're the only one who would appreciate it."

She raised her eyebrows and nodded.

"What did the zero say to the eight?"

"What?"

"Nice belt."

Catrice cringed. "Got any better ones?"

"Uh...you remember Mr. Kale used to have that plant in math class? Do you know why it died?"

"No, why?" she asked, her expression suspicious.

"Because it grew square roots."

She chuckled. "I think you should just stick to doing math."

The tracks rounded a turn and the familiar white glow came into view.

Those few moments of peace and normal conversation came to an abrupt halt at the Christopher Street station. Drayden was starting to cherish the brief interludes of quiet and safety that fell between the terror of the subway stations.

Once again, the pledges stood in a giant room. This time it stretched the entire width of the station. The Bureau had covered all the tracks with the platform floor. Again, a white wall cut the station short in the distance. It also blocked them.

Drayden led everyone down the platform in the direction of the wall. A long table came into view, sitting well in front of the wall. Otherwise, the station was empty.

Drayden slowed.

The ground shimmered in front of the wall.

"Anyone else see that?" Charlie asked.

"It's water," Sidney said.

As they reached it, Drayden's pulse quickened.

Right before the wall there was a gap in the floor filled with water. It was only about fifteen feet of water to the wall, but the water stretched from the left edge of the station all the way to the right, like a river through the middle of the platform they had to

traverse. Simply crossing it would accomplish nothing, since a wall blocked everything past it.

Yet this was no ordinary river. It was crystal clear, like a swimming pool, and so deep the bottom wasn't visible. The water appeared to continue underneath the rest of the platform, past the wall. Though the station lights illuminated the water in front of them, it turned dark beneath the platform. The wall blocked the view further down the station, so it was unclear how far under the platform the water extended. No airspace existed between the surface of the water and the underside of the platform.

Without even reading the note, Drayden knew what this challenge was about. They had to swim, underwater, beneath the platform. In the darkness, with no idea where, or how far, to go.

"Man, that water gets darker than the Dorms on a Tuesday night," Charlie said. He lay down on his stomach, peering over the surface of the water. "What are the chances we only have to swim under the wall and can come right up on the other side?"

"About one in a million," Drayden mumbled.

Charlie pointed at him. "So you're saying there's a chance."

Sidney snatched the note from the table and read out loud, *"Control your breath, and you might prevent death. Prove you can overcome your fear of the unknown. You must swim under the platform and find the exit further down the station. You may leave your backpacks here, and they will be waiting for you a hundred yards down the tracks. Your flashlights will work underwater. Good luck."*

Drayden bent over, his hands on his knees. He wasn't an adept swimmer, and had no idea how long he could hold his breath underwater. Swimming underwater triggered his claustrophobia, something about the inability to breathe. Thus, he'd never spent much time submerged.

A clock hung over the table, ticking down: *03:38:02, 03:38:01...*

"Any chance that water is warm?" Alex asked.

Charlie dipped in his hand, and quickly jerked it back out. "It's colder than a polar bear's toes."

Drayden needed to lead and ignore his fear. Tim's voice spoke in his head. All he had to do was emulate it. "You guys, let's leave our backpacks here like they said. Most of this stuff needs to stay dry. I know the air is cool and the water is freezing, but we might want to take our clothes off and stuff them in our backpacks so they'll be dry when we come out."

"Who put you in charge, wetchop?" Alex asked.

Drayden had thought it himself. You couldn't fake being a leader. Leave it to Alex to immediately seize upon his insecurity.

"You can do whatever you want, Alex. I don't care," Drayden said. "I'm talking to Sidney and Catrice, and Charlie if he wants my opinion. You want to get your clothes and backpack wet, be my guest."

After Alex made a face at him, he shut up and joined Charlie by the pool.

Sidney pumped her fist and high-fived Drayden.

Charlie approached. "I think it's genius. Everybody should totally take their clothes off." He eyed both girls up and down.

"Don't be a creep, Charlie," Sidney said, looking disgusted.

Charlie raised his hands, proclaiming innocence. "Who? Me? I'm just very worried about your clothes staying dry."

A sniffle behind Drayden caught his attention. He spun around.

Catrice was leaning against one of the steel pillars, her arms crossed over her chest.

Drayden ran to her. "Catrice? What's wrong?"

She just shook her head.

She had reacted the same way at the start of the other bravery challenges, Drayden noted. She probably just needed a minute to get over her fear. He leaned down to look in her eyes.

"Hey. What is it? Are you scared of water or something?"

Catrice looked at him, tears streaming down her cheeks. "I can't swim."

Drayden stared, his mouth agape. *Oh no.* Who couldn't swim? Then again, Dorm kids didn't exactly spend their summers by a lake in the woods. While the school basement housed a pool, swimming wasn't required. Life was so dull in the Dorms, most kids went berserk for two things: swimming and riding bikes. Catrice, on the other hand, avoided anything athletic. Recalling the rat challenge, Catrice initially refused help. The moment the doors opened, she had taken his hand and never let go. His concern for her propelled him through the challenge then. Why not simply do that again?

Because Drayden wasn't a strong swimmer himself; that was why. Struggling to drag her along underwater might not help either of them. Furthermore, his injuries limited his strength and mobility. He shuddered, imagining the deep puncture wound in his back touching the water.

"You can ride on my back," Charlie said, walking over. "I'm an expert swimmer. You don't need to know how to swim. You just need to hold your breath and hang onto me. You can even close your eyes."

It did make sense for her to go with him, and this certainly wasn't the time for petty jealousy. Charlie could save her life.

"He's right, Catrice. Most people can hold their breath for a while, even under stress. You'll get in the water with Charlie and practice going underwater with him."

She wiped her eyes with her palms. "Thanks, you guys," she said, her voice quivering.

"Thanks, Charlie," Drayden said.

Charlie patted Drayden on the shoulder. "No, thank *you.*" He winked and walked away.

Drayden felt weak, inadequate, and embarrassed. "Hey, I would've offered to do it. It's just, I'm not a great swimmer myself. I don't think I'd be doing us any favors."

Catrice dried her cheeks with her shirt. "It's all right, Drayden. You don't have to be the hero. Being brave is enough."

Maybe. How would he feel when he saw her wrapped around Charlie's back, both in their underwear?

"Hey, you guys!" Sidney shouted.

Everyone gathered around her. She blew warm breath into her hands and rubbed them together. "Being awesome at riddles won't save us this time, but being a great swimmer will. And I'm really good." She glanced at Catrice. "What if I swim as far as I can and come back and tell you what I find? It might be a maze under there."

"That's a brilliant idea," Drayden said. "Just please, don't get lost. Thanks, Sid."

She gave him a thumbs-up.

"Charlie," Drayden said, "you and Catrice should practice swimming underwater right here while Sidney explores."

"Roger that," Charlie said. "As soon as I watch Sidney and Catrice undress." He fist-bumped Alex. "Look. We gotta do it. You said so yourself." He pulled off his t-shirt and stuffed it into his backpack, his shoulder muscles rippling. "Oh, like you're not gonna sneak a peek?" he asked Drayden. "I know Alex will."

Drayden blushed and avoided eye contact with Sidney or Catrice. He hated Charlie more than ever. He hated even more that Charlie was right, as brazenly slimy as he was about it. Drayden had spied girls in bulky, ill-fitted Dorm bathing suits at the pool, but never one in her underwear. He'd never dreamed he'd get to see Catrice like that, though he'd often fantasized about it. He trembled with excitement, and hated himself for that too.

The pledges exchanged apprehensive looks and undressed.

Drayden consciously focused on the ground beneath him, refusing to raise his eyes. He stuffed his clothes and hat into his backpack. Standing there in his underwear, he became awkwardly aware of his arms. He fidgeted, unsure what to do with them. The brief embarrassment about his skinny body after the rat challenge returned tenfold.

Charlie's muscular legs stretched his underwear tight, whereas Drayden's baggy underwear sagged. With his stick legs, he just didn't have enough body to fill them up. Charlie was so much more damn manly than he was. He couldn't help but wonder: Considering how much girls claimed they desired boys who were smart and interesting, why did they always seem to go for moronic Adonises like Charlie?

Drayden couldn't resist any longer, and looked at Sidney and Catrice. He sought not to react in any visible way, but he stopped breathing.

They both wore gray underwear, and Sidney had on a red bra, while Catrice sported a green one. Sidney stood with her shoulders back and her ample chest out. She seemed not the slightest bit embarrassed.

Had she been semi-naked in front of boys before?

Catrice, on the other hand, swaddled both arms around her body, doing everything she could to cover up.

She was exquisite. Her skin was flawless, and while skinny, she appeared soft, not bony.

Sidney cocked her head. "Can you guys not stare?"

Drayden snapped out of his spell and glanced at the other boys.

Both were doing the same thing he was. Staring.

Drayden blushed again. He couldn't help ogling Sidney as she bounced up to the water's edge.

Charlie followed her and they both dipped in their toes. "Holy shkatnuts!" Charlie bellowed. "Man, that's chillier than a tin toilet seat in an igloo."

Sidney swished her foot around. "Crap. I've never swum in water that freezing."

Drayden tiptoed up to the edge and stuck in his foot.

The water wasn't just cold. It was icy. Within seconds, his foot ached.

He jerked it out, his whole body shivering. How could he pass this challenge? It was impossible. He couldn't even touch the water, let alone swim through it, submerged, in the dark, with no clue how far it would be. He flopped down on the platform and wrapped his arms around his legs. He wished Tim was here.

He visualized Tim's face looking down on him from somewhere above. Smiling. What would Tim say? He'd say, *"We're doing this no matter what, since we have no choice. Be cold, or be exiled. Like the rat challenge, just get through it."* Drayden rose, his chin up. He had to push. He had to do this. He *could* do this.

He recalled a moment with his mother, after he'd suffered through a cold bath during a power outage. She'd told him about this PreCon thing called the Polar Bear Club. People would willingly swim in frigid water during winter, sometimes even beneath ice. It sounded totally stupid. Mom said people did it to refresh the soul or something. Dad had chimed in from a medical angle, saying it increased bloodflow and could boost your immune system, though it also carried a lot of danger.

"Sidney," he said, "I think the water is too frosty for a test run. You'll be in the water too long. You might get hypothermia. Catrice, it's too cold for you and Charlie to practice. Usually in a chilly pool, the best way to get in is to close your eyes and jump, right? I think it's too cold for that, our bodies might go into shock. We need to

ease our way in. Besides just freezing, we're going to hyperventilate at first. As soon as it passes, we have to go."

Drayden knelt and eyed the surface of the water. "We should probably shine our flashlights up at the ceiling, the platform's underside, when we're underwater. There's no space between the water and the ceiling, but if we're lucky they left some air pockets, caves basically, where we can catch our breath. If you don't see a ceiling above your head, go up for air."

"I don't know what all you wetchops are crying about," Alex said. "I take a beating from my five older brothers every week. I can swim in a cold pool."

"Good," Drayden said. "You can help everyone else get through this then."

The pledges retrieved their flashlights and sat on the edge of the platform. They dipped their feet in.

Pain snaked through Drayden's toes and ankles. He fought the powerful urge to jerk them out. He lowered further, down to his knees, his teeth chattering.

"Jumping Jesus on a pogo stick!" Charlie cried out, now submerged down to his chest. "Wait till you guys get to the...waist area." His voice trembled.

Catrice lay on her stomach, her legs underwater up to her knees. Already shaking, her eyes were closed and her lips pursed.

Drayden's eyes wandered down her arched back to her butt. *Stop it,* he thought, turning away. She was terrified and suffering, they all faced death or exile, and he was leering like a peeping Tom. *Focus on the task at hand.* He looked again.

"I'm in," Sidney squeaked. She treaded water away from the edge.

Drayden lowered down to his thighs, expanding the pain surface area. Thankfully the ice water had already numbed his feet and ankles. The next part, the plunge, terrified him. Five more

seconds. It had to be done. He flipped over, his stomach on the ledge. He held the ledge, and dropped in.

He gasped, sucking in a deep, audible breath.

So cold!

The hyperventilation began. The breaths came faster and faster. His body screamed in pain, and his legs turned to cement.

Think about Catrice! She needs you.

Drayden sucked in a breath, attempted to hold it, but failed. He closed his eyes and thought about how much Mom must have suffered when she was exiled. The pain she experienced. Terrified, alone, no food or water, facing the unknown. Icy water paled in comparison. Drayden's breathing slowed. He breathed through his nose, which helped. He opened his eyes. He was through it.

Charlie treaded water in the center of the pool. Alex hung on the ledge, like Drayden, breathing hard. Catrice had made the plunge, though she clutched the platform with her arms fully out. Her whole body quivered. Where was Sidney?

Drayden crab-crawled along the platform to Catrice. "Catrice... I'm here. Your...breathing will...slow...down...in a minute." He placed his hand on her shoulder.

She gawked at him with wild, frightful eyes. Her chest expanded and contracted at an alarming pace, her frantic breaths escaping through blue lips and chattering teeth. She nodded.

The pool splashed behind them. Sidney popped up from under the water and swam to the platform ledge, out of breath. "I did... the test run anyway. There...are...three passageways. The...middle one...is blocked. We...take...the right...one. About...twenty-five feet in, you can...go up...for air. There's...a small...air pocket. That's as far...as I could go." Her lips had turned blue, and the color was drained from her face.

"Thanks, Sid," Drayden said.

Catrice gripped the platform so tight her fingertips turned white.

In between his teeth chattering, Drayden said, "Catrice, you need to...feel what...it's like...going under water. As long as...your mouth...stays...closed, and you...don't breathe in...you're fine. D-Don't...panic."

After closing her eyes, Catrice submerged down to her neck, still clutching the platform. She inhaled a deep breath and dunked her head. A second later, she shot back up, frantically wiping the water from her face. A pink cloud expanded in the water from the dried blood in her hair.

"That's it," Drayden said encouragingly. Frozen or not, she needed to practice once with Charlie. "Charlie! Come...get... Catrice. Quick test run."

Charlie swam over. He treaded water with his back to Catrice. "Okay, sweetheart, you're...going to wrap your...legs...around my waist, locking...them...together. And your arms...around...my chest. I'll tell you...when I'm going to go...under. We'll do it...for just a few seconds."

"Catrice," Drayden said, "take...a big breath in...before you go under. Whatever...you do...resist the urge...to breathe...under-water. You...have to...stay relaxed."

Weeping, Catrice nodded. She climbed on Charlie's back, wrapping herself around him like a baby monkey on its mother. She pressed her cheek against his back and closed her eyes. Charlie swam a few feet into the pool, wearing Catrice like a backpack.

"Okay, Catrice," Charlie said, panting. "On three. One...two... three...now!" They dunked, swam underwater for five seconds, and zoomed up beside the platform edge. Catrice gasped for air, pawing at her eyes.

"That's it," Drayden said, forcing a smile. "You...did it! Nice job."

"You all right, Catrice?" Charlie asked.

"Yeah," she whispered.

Charlie's going to save her life. Shaking his head, Drayden pushed aside his stupid jealousy. Who cared if he looked like freaking Poseidon in the water? She wouldn't survive this challenge without Charlie.

"You guys," Sidney said, "we have...to go. Now. It's...so cold. I can't...take it. You can...follow me. But I can't...wait anymore."

Even in the dead of winter with no jacket, Drayden hadn't experienced cold like this. It penetrated his internal organs, freezing him to the core. This test wasn't quite as obviously designed to kill like the bomb was, but it was just as deadly. They could easily drown. He was sure now the Bureau was out to kill them. The real question was, why had they left even a sliver of chance for survival?

Drayden groaned, in frustration, in anger, in pain. He was too cold to think straight. Deadened and numb, his limbs refused to move on command. Shivering uncontrollably, he switched on his flashlight after a few attempts. He would go last, as Tim would, following Catrice in case she needed him.

"Ready?" Sidney asked. She sucked in a deep breath and dunked under, rocketed off the near wall underwater, and disappeared under the darkness of the platform. Alex followed. Charlie and Catrice inhaled deeply and dove under after him.

Drayden took three short breaths in rapid succession, followed by one enormous breath. He submerged and launched off the platform underwater to gain some momentum, shining his flashlight ahead.

The frigid water shot knives into his eyes. It felt as if someone were pounding a nail into his back wound. The blurry figure of Charlie and Catrice kicked in front of him before the water turned pitch black. His flashlight beam provided the only light. Thankfully, the ceiling—the underside of the platform—was white, making it easily visible when he pointed his flashlight up. He was still beneath

it. He kicked and pumped with his free hand, blowing some air out of his lungs.

How much farther to the air pocket? His oxygen already running low, he started to panic. He needed to breathe! His chest began to ache. He swam with urgency, using both arms to propel him.

I need to take a breath! Fight it!

He kicked harder with heavy legs, aiming his flashlight forward. Legs dangled five feet ahead.

Push!

He pointed his flashlight up.

No ceiling!

Drayden shot up and thrust his head out of the water. He sucked in a loud breath, gasping for air. Each chilly breath diminished the pain in his lungs.

The flashlights illuminated the confined space enough to reveal everyone's pale faces, blue lips, chattering teeth, and frightened eyes. Breathing heavily, they bobbed up and down in a tiny underwater room. It was like a cave, the ceiling a mere foot above their heads. Catrice quaked on Charlie's back, but she'd survived.

"I don't know...where to...go next," Sidney said, her voice echoing in the restricted chamber. "You can...follow me, but we're kind of...on our own now."

She took two deep breaths and disappeared below. Alex eyed Drayden, then Charlie. "I'm not ready yet. You go."

"Catrice, you ready?" Charlie asked. "On three. One, two, three." She closed her eyes and squeezed Charlie tight. Her cheeks puffed out and they submerged.

Alex followed them.

You can do this, Drayden encouraged himself. His mother had probably suffered much worse. He had to reach the Palace. He breathed in as much as he could, held it, and dove under.

Darkness.

His flashlight revealed legs kicking ten feet in front of him. Within a second he was tangled in those legs.

What the hell?

Whoever it was kicked him in the head as they swam away. It didn't hurt, but it disrupted his breath-holding. He checked up.

Ceiling.

He pointed the flashlight straight ahead. His lungs began to ache. Already? His stinging eyes bulged at the sight ahead.

A wall divided the pool, forcing them right or left. Whoever swam in front of him chose left, though other legs kicked right.

Which way? Panic set in. He was going to run out of air! Left. After veering left, Drayden shined the flashlight ahead.

The kicking legs, formerly in front of him, were now out of sight, but the water became lighter. The exit must be near.

Drayden's oxygen was running low, and the urge to take a breath grew exponentially. How much longer could he hold on? It was too far to return to the air pocket now. He kicked frantically with his legs.

A wall, directly in front of him, blocked his path. Could it be the exit?

He pointed his flashlight up.

Ceiling!

Drayden was trapped. He looked right.

Light! Twenty feet away. The water glowed much brighter.

He pumped and kicked, his wooden limbs resisting. *Don't breathe. Don't breathe!*

Ten feet.

A hand! Reaching down into the water. No ceiling there!

Fire burned in his lungs. Black spots swarmed his vision. His numb arms and legs became concrete, barely working now.

Swim dammit!

He couldn't move.

Five feet. He wasn't going to make it. He couldn't hold out any longer. His consciousness faded.

No! Don't!

Drayden's reflexes took over. He inhaled.

Pain exploded in his chest. A pain he'd never experienced—a burning like a hundred red-hot irons shoved down his throat.

The world turned black.

CHAPTER 17

Drayden was hanging over someone's lap, on his stomach, coughing up water. He thought he might cough up a lung, but he couldn't stop. Could you cough to death?

Someone pounded on his back. "There you go. Get all that out." It was Sidney's voice.

I'm alive.

Drayden continued to hack. A small puddle of water on the ground beneath him reflected his sickly face. And was that...bile? He must have thrown up. His mind began to clear. "I'm...I'm f-freezing."

Catrice knelt beside him. Still in her underwear, dripping wet, she wrapped her arms around her shivering body. "Thank God you're okay," she said through blue lips. "We thought we lost you."

Drayden rolled off Sidney's lap. "What happened?"

"You were the last one in the water," Sidney said. "You'd almost made it, and then you just stopped swimming. You passed out. I guess you took a breath underwater. Charlie and I dove in and dragged you out."

He knelt next to Sidney and gazed into her warm eyes. "Sid, thank you. I don't even know what to say." Without thinking, he

kissed her on the cheek and hugged her. Again, she was there for him.

Sidney held him close. "You're welcome. If it wasn't for you, we'd be exiled already." She pulled back and rested her hand on his cheek.

Her affectionate touch made Drayden think of Catrice and he turned to her. "Catrice, thank God *you* made it. You'd never been in the water before, and you made it. That's incredible. Congratulations."

Congratulating her sounded stupid, but it just came out.

She nodded. "Thanks. That was terrifying. I was about a second away from taking a breath. Charlie saved my life. So did you." She scooted closer. "Thank you for watching out for me."

"You're welcome," Drayden said, wondering if caring was enough, because he wasn't strong enough to actually save her. "Speaking of Charlie, where are those two flunks? I suppose I can't call Charlie a flunk anymore, considering he saved my life, and yours, in the span of a few minutes. I need to thank him."

"They went to collect the backpacks." Sidney craned her neck and squinted to glimpse down the platform. "Should be back by now."

Charlie and Alex emerged at the end of the platform, fully dressed, and headed toward them. Charlie wore one backpack and carried three, while Alex wore one. His own, of course.

Charlie set Sidney's backpack in front of her. "How you feeling, chief?" he asked Drayden. "You were deader than a baby gazelle in a lion's mouth."

Drayden stood. "Charlie, thank you for saving my life. I can't imagine you and Sid jumping back into that freezing water once you were out."

"Don't go getting all sentimental there, Dorothy," Alex interjected. "We need you to finish the Initiation. I don't think you and Charlie are gonna be roommates anytime soon."

Charlie cracked up. "Ah, you're welcome, Dray. You've saved us a few times too. Charlie doesn't forget that." Charlie set Catrice's backpack down, pulled his sweatshirt out of his, and draped it over her shoulders. It was so big it looked like a dress.

She snuggled inside it. "You're the best, Charlie."

Charlie dropped Drayden's backpack in front of him and patted him on the shoulder as he passed by.

Between the time it took to regain consciousness, cough up a lung, throw up, and lay on Sidney's lap, Drayden had mostly air dried. Still chilled, he itched to get dressed, but he needed fresh bandages on his various wounds. Thankfully, the pool had washed most of the blood off everyone, and they no longer resembled murder victims. While he treated his rat wounds himself, he needed a hand with his back and head. Sidney read his mind. "Can I help you with your other cuts?"

"Yes, please. Thanks, Sid."

As she applied his bandages, she whispered in his ear, "Your nerdy girlfriend over there seems to be getting pretty close to Charlie, by the way."

"Really?" Drayden asked, his temperature rising. "She's not my girlfriend, though. And yes, she is nerdy."

"She totally is. She's a total dork." Sidney snortled. "But yeah, you should have seen them when they got out of the water."

Drayden's heart sank. "I mean, Charlie had just saved her life and all. She was probably pretty happy."

"Yeah, well. Whatever," Sidney said.

He didn't want to hear any more. As soon as Sidney wrapped up, he dressed as expeditiously as he could. The coldness penetrated his core, to his bones, and it was tough to warm up again. The

clothes helped, even with wet underwear. He was the last to dress. "Everyone ready?"

"We've *been* ready," Alex said.

"Well," Drayden said, "you did get a head start when you got dressed and had a snack before returning everyone else's backpacks."

"Well," Alex said, mocking him, "not all of us were busy dying on the platform."

"Shut up, Alex," Sidney said. "If you drowned nobody would have rescued you."

"Thanks for your expert opinion, Sidney. Good thing you're here. But you're forgetting someone." He pointed at Charlie.

Drayden shook his head. He led the group across the platform and down the stairs to the tracks. He had the urge to make obscene gestures at the hidden cameras. They'd survived another deadly challenge. Were the Watchers getting nervous?

The tracks ran straight for an extended stretch. Houston Street, the upcoming stop on the One Line, shined in the distance.

Though Drayden had completed over half the Initiation, he wasn't sure how much more of this could he endure. While the physical exhaustion and damage showed all over his body, the mental exhaustion had taken its toll as well.

Even so, he'd absorbed the best the Bureau could throw at him. Maybe Mr. Kale was right. People didn't normally feel brave, and Drayden definitely didn't. When you needed it though, you would find it was there. What did he have left to fear? He'd nearly died twice. Yet he survived. His body screamed in pain, from his ankle to his head. But he was still moving, still advancing. It was almost enough to be convincing.

Except, he was Drayden, full of self-doubt by nature. Hadn't he simply been lucky? Despite the fact that Tim was far braver, he'd died. Since the difficulty level of the challenges had steadily

increased, what would be coming up? He didn't want to think about it. He hated the Bureau for their depravity, and was devastated about Tim. He was also purely worn out. He needed to savor these few minutes of peace.

Drayden thought about the girls. While he knew he should be concentrating on the Initiation, he couldn't erase the image now burned into his retinas of Catrice and Sidney in their underwear. Like when you looked at the sun too long, whenever he closed his eyes, he saw their bodies. But they'd seen his too. So what if he wasn't manly like Charlie, or even Tim? Strength was more than the size of his muscles. Why should he have to worry about impressing them anyway? Who were they? He stopped himself and pushed the negativity away. That kind of attitude would get him nowhere, with them, or in this godawful test. He did allow himself a moment to acknowledge that two girls seemed to like him. It was exciting and new. A small spark had ignited between him and Catrice after the rat challenge.

Still, he might have been focused on the wrong girl. Sidney consistently showed obvious interest and genuine concern for him. Following any injury, she cared for him, even before herself. She always defended him. She had saved his life even. What if the truth had been staring him in the face all along, but his stubborn crush on Catrice had blinded him? Wasn't his crush somewhat superficial? Before today, all he knew about Catrice was she was beautiful and smart.

Maybe since he'd decided ages ago that he desired Catrice before he honestly knew her, he'd grown complacent. He'd assumed he knew what he wanted. It was like a little kid who decided to become an electrician when he grew up because he thought it sounded cool. He navigated all his schooling with his career objective in mind. But during his first week on the job, he discovered he didn't like wires so much. He never put much thought into the original goal, and was too naive to make such a decision anyway.

Knowing what he wanted offered a sense of comfort though, rather than the uncertain reality of life. He clung to it, despite mounting evidence to the contrary, until it was no longer tenable. Was he not at that point with Sidney and Catrice?

The elephant in the room, however, loomed large. Catrice probably had a shot to be selected for the Palace, and Sidney most likely didn't. Catrice was incredible on the intellectual challenges while Sidney was weak. The opposite was true on the bravery challenges. Sidney was so strong, and skilled. Which trait did the Bureau weigh more? Value more?

Wesley might have captured the essence of that question when he'd encouraged Drayden to enter the Initiation. He said anyone *could* do the bravery challenges. Completing them at all signified a person displayed the requisite bravery. Everyone had technically passed them, including Catrice. Performing well on them was more about physical ability than bravery. But on the intelligence challenges, some kids simply couldn't do them. The Bureau was scrutinizing them and knew who solved the brainteasers and who didn't.

Assuming Drayden himself was invited to move to the Palace, Catrice was more likely to join him than Sidney. Then again, did he even still have a shot at the Palace? He'd been weak in the bravery challenges, cowering in fear at each one. Sidney and Charlie weren't just more physically skilled, they'd been braver, another reason he needed to step up on the upcoming challenges. The Bureau might select only one person.

"Station ahead," Charlie said from behind without his usual gusto. "For the love of God."

Drayden had almost died on two of the last three challenges. He tried to push the phrase "third time's the charm" from his mind.

How many times could you *almost* die before it finally happened? He needed to get to the Palace. For Mom.

Lights blared. A clock, usually found in the middle of the station, hung at the platform entrance. It continued its countdown: *02:55:32, 02:55:31....* Nothing else appeared out of the ordinary. The Houston Street station seemed otherwise untouched.

Drayden led the way down the platform, everyone crowded behind him.

A figure emerged in the distance.

Sidney pointed. "You guys, look!"

Drayden's body kicked into challenge mode. His heart rate picked up, and nervous sweat coated his body. He marched toward the person.

At fifty yards away, the black robe identified him as a likely Bureau member.

At twenty-five yards, Drayden stopped in his tracks, recognizing him.

Owen Payne.

"Isn't that the guy from the first challenge?" Sidney asked. "The heaven riddle?"

"Yup," Charlie said. "Charlie never forgets a face."

Owen Payne's mouth spread into a wide, creepy grin. This time, he stood alone—no computer, no table.

Sidney looked overjoyed. "Do you think this is the end?" she whispered. "Did we make it?"

"It can't be," Drayden whispered back. "At Houston Street we're leaving the Lab and entering the Precinct. We're not in the Palace yet."

"Maybe we've done well enough," Charlie said. "I have a feeling this could be it." Charlie and Sidney locked arms and giggled like little kids.

The pledges stopped in front of Owen Payne. He spread his arms out as if offering a hug. With his black robe, dark skin, and evil smile, he brought to mind the grim reaper. "Well done, pledges. Well done, indeed. The Bureau sends its congratulations for succeeding thus far."

Sidney and Charlie shared a giddy look.

"As a reward for performing so admirably, the Bureau would like to offer you a choice," Payne continued. "This is highly unusual, but the choice is the following. You may continue the Initiation, in which case the clock will be adjusted. You will have only ninety minutes to finish, rather than the roughly three hours left on the clock. As formidable as you may believe the Initiation has been thus far, you have yet to encounter the most difficult challenges. It is your option to continue."

Drayden broke out in goosebumps. *You have yet to encounter the most difficult challenges.*

Payne scanned their faces. "Or you may quit now, without exile. You may return to your lives in Zone D without any repercussions. You'll receive your job assignments tomorrow with the rest of the graduates. This is a group decision. Either you all continue or none of you do. Since there are five of you now, a majority decision will rule. You have five minutes to make your choice. Good luck." He stepped back and stood with his hands clasped.

Drayden was really starting to hate this Payne guy. This was not a "reward" from the Bureau. It was a dilemma.

The pledges gathered in a circle, each of them studying the others' faces.

"I want to quit," Sidney said. "I don't want to do this anymore." She covered her mouth with both hands, on the verge of tears. "I want to go home."

Drayden wasn't surprised. She'd rushed to enter the Initiation without thoroughly considering it. Although she'd believed

Drayden could carry her through, he could only do so much. A lot of what the Initiation demanded you had to do yourself, particularly on the bravery challenges, which had been brutal.

"Me too," Charlie said. "I'm sorry guys, I just...I wanted some adventure. Who could stop Charlie, right? But this sucks. I don't need to be a Guardian that bad. I don't think I care to see the next few challenges. Charlie, out."

Alex flicked Charlie on the arm. "What the hell, chotch? We're doing this. I'm still in. So is Charlie."

"Alex, I'm out," Charlie insisted. "I'm sorry, bro. I know you'll have a situation with your dad if we quit, and he's meaner than a sack of rattlesnakes, but I'm not dying for it."

"Charlie!" Alex snapped.

Charlie stepped up to Alex, puffed his chest out, and balled his hands into fists. "I *said* I'm *out*."

Alex shrunk away from him. "Well I'm in, all the way."

Sidney, Charlie, and Alex turned to Catrice and Drayden.

Two out and one in, Drayden thought. Just him and Catrice left.

She looked deep into his eyes, tucking her hair behind her ears. "I'm in," she said softly.

"Thank you!" Alex said, scowling. "Charlie, this tiny girl here is tougher than you are."

Charlie showed no reaction. He fixed his eyes on Drayden. "Looks like you get to decide," he said.

Alex hooked his thumb at Drayden. "This wetchop gets to decide for me? No way."

Oh God. How did this happen?

Whatever Drayden decided, two people would hate him. He didn't care about Charlie or Alex, so his decision represented a choice between Sidney and Catrice. But an even bigger question loomed. What did *he* want to do?

Sidney slinked up to him. "Drayden..."

Catrice stiffened, her arms crossed. She glowered at Sidney.

Sidney took Drayden's hand and led him back toward the platform entrance. "I just want to talk to you alone for a minute," she said. "Let's quit the Initiation. This is crazy. You almost died, and the Bureau guy said we haven't even seen the worst challenges yet. What if you haggled with the Bureau to score a better job in the Dorms? And...we could be together, me and you. I'm not saying we have to get married or anything. I was obviously joking, but it might be nice if we had each other, you know? I could take care of you like I have been, and you could take care of me. I could make you very happy."

Sidney bore her pretty brown eyes into him, stepping closer. She pushed her chest against his, and placed her hands on his hips. "Please, Drayden?"

Drayden trembled with excitement at what she appeared to be offering. If he had someone he loved, who loved him back, couldn't life in the Dorms be tolerable? Even pleasant? Also, her idea about negotiating his career wasn't crazy.

But, no. That was shkat and he knew it. He needed to move to the Palace to find out the truth about his mother. The Dorms would never be livable, not given what he knew. Something was destroying their world, and the Palace offered the only refuge. Not just for him—for his father and brother as well.

Unless Thomas Cox was wrong about the surging exiles. Drayden was confused.

"Sidney..." He wrinkled his nose. "I need a minute to myself, if you don't mind. I need to think."

"All right." She chewed on her lower lip. "Remember what I said." She smiled wryly and sashayed away.

The other pledges were watching. They'd seen everything. Alex and Charlie leered at Sidney. Catrice fixed her eyes on Drayden.

He eased down, leaning his back against a steel pillar, facing away from the group.

Quitting did tempt him. His whole body was screaming in pain. If the upcoming challenges were harder, he'd be attempting tougher tests in his weakest state. Any hope the Bureau would be merciful was extinguished when the bomb exploded and killed Tim. Rat bites covered his body, begging to become infected. He had lost consciousness twice in the last hour, for crying out loud.

While he'd entered the Initiation for multiple reasons, what had nudged him over the hump were Thomas Cox's claims. Who knew how reliable Cox was? He wasn't even a senior Bureau member. Maybe he was a fool, and that's why he held the lowly Dorm rep role. Cox might be known as that guy who said crazy, provocative stuff all the time, none of it true.

And, dammit...Drayden was scared. He was terrified of even worse injury, exile, or death.

He pulled off his hat and rubbed the Yankees logo. He thought of his mother. Her exile was undeniable. She was gone. Wasn't that reason enough to go on? She epitomized bravery and strength.

Drayden reminisced about the oft-told story of how she and his father met. Seventeen-years-old, she was walking down Second Avenue on a Friday afternoon. She passed some little kids playing with a ball. It rolled into the street, which was usually deserted and safe. A young girl sprang out to retrieve it, right into the path of an oncoming bus. Mom didn't hesitate. She dove into the street and shoved the girl out of harm's way. The bumper clipped Mom's leg, badly breaking it. She met Dad at the hospital where he worked, and the rest was history. There was no question his mother would continue if she were him.

He closed his eyes and imagined himself with Mr. Kale and Tim in Mr. Kale's office. Drayden warmed at the image. *Drayden, there's no decision to make,"* Tim said in his vision. *"You have to continue.*

You have to see this through. There's no turning back. You can do this. Only you. Be strong. Don't be afraid. You've seen what you can do when you ignore your fear. I believe in you.

In his visualization, Mr. Kale held up his hand to cut Tim off. *Drayden, what you heard from Thomas Cox is true. Even if it wasn't, you need to move to the Palace. You'll never be content in the Dorms. We all need you in the Palace.*

Tim winked at him. *C'mon, kid. You know what to do.*

Drayden pushed himself up, growing used to the pain everywhere. He pulled his hat down tight and returned to the group, avoiding eye contact with everyone.

All eyes were on him. Owen Payne stepped forward. "You've reached your decision?"

Drayden stood tall, his shoulders back. "We're going to continue."

Sidney drew in a quick breath, unable to hide her shock. Her teary eyes burned like fireballs of fury. She shoved Drayden out of the way, snatched up her backpack, and stormed down the platform.

CHAPTER 18

Alone once again.

The others stared at Drayden.

Catrice wrapped her thin arms around his waist and nuzzled her head into his neck. "Thank you," she whispered.

Drayden peered over her head at Charlie. He looked pissed.

Was it the show of affection from Catrice, or his deciding vote on the Initiation? Either way, they needed Charlie's strength to conquer the rest of the challenges.

Drayden cleared his throat. "Charlie, I'm sorry. I know you wanted to quit. But I promise you I'm going to get us through this. I know I can't do it alone, and we can't do it without you. I won't let us down on any more intelligence challenges. I'll solve them, or Catrice will. We can do this. We can win."

Charlie turned away and kicked his backpack. He exhaled, looked back at Drayden, and nodded.

Owen Payne took a step forward. "The clock has begun. I suggest you move along."

Drayden scanned the platform. Sidney must already be on the tracks. "Ninety minutes? We need to run. Now."

The pledges grabbed their backpacks and darted down the platform. His ankle throbbing with each step, Drayden led the group

down to the tracks and into the darkness. He caught up to Sidney, who moped along with her head down. After her blow up, couldn't someone else be the one to tell her they needed to run? Everyone flew by her without a word.

"Hey, you guys!" Drayden shouted. "Slow down for a minute." He walked beside Sidney.

She sniffled, and wiped her eyes.

"Sid, I'm sorry. The decision to continue had nothing to do with you." He remembered they were being observed and recorded, and knew he had to be careful what he said. "It's just, we can't go back to the Dorms. You have to trust me. We need to make it the whole way. I'm scared too. If we all work toge—"

"Leave me alone!" she yelled and sped up.

"Sidney, listen," he said, after catching up to her. "You hate me now, fine, but I like you, and if you don't start running, you're going to be exiled. We're in it now, whether you wanted to continue or not."

She turned her head away from Drayden and held her hand up to his face. "We're done," she murmured.

The others waited further down the tracks.

"Sid!" Drayden said, lacking any trace of tenderness. "We have to run, dammit. Let's go! Now!"

"Fine!" she yelled. She broke into a jog, distancing herself from him.

Drayden ran behind the others. He'd taken Sidney for granted. Her attention and support meant a lot to him. He'd enjoyed it. Now she hated him. No girl had even acknowledged his existence before Sidney. He'd focused so much on Catrice that he'd failed to recognize what he had until it was too late.

He should be so lucky to snag someone like Sidney. Brave, strong, and caring, she was a catch. Without her support, who did he truly have? He'd won Catrice over a bit, though she wouldn't

gush with praise anytime soon. The only other people who boosted his self-esteem were Tim and his mother, both now gone. He hated to admit how much those words of encouragement helped.

Drayden ran in the narrow lane outside the rails. Even that contained the ends of the railroad ties. Spacing his strides correctly without tripping proved nerve-wracking. Throwing in a bum ankle that could be rolled at any time with the utter darkness, and running demanded constant attention.

Drayden hopped onto the actual tracks and sprinted by the others. He ignored the pain in his ankle and back so he could reach the front of the group. He needed to lead. He'd forced Sidney and Charlie to continue the Initiation. He needed to get them through it.

As much as he yearned to fix things with Sidney, finishing the Initiation needed to be the focus. Wesley and Dad needed him to rescue them from the Dorms. Mom deserved answers. He felt a tinge of excitement, a renewed sense of purpose.

The choice presented at Houston Street wasn't an actual challenge. Was it? Something bugged him about that choice. It didn't make sense. Why would the unmerciful Bureau suddenly show mercy? He couldn't put his finger on it.

Either way, it was unclear what would be waiting for them at Canal Street. Even if the Bureau threw a deadly bravery challenge at them, he would lead the charge. Drayden couldn't sort out the paradox of the Bureau seemingly trying to kill them while also allowing them to advance. If the Bureau truly wanted to kill them, they could storm the tunnels at any time with guns and open fire. Nobody was watching. They didn't have to go through the trouble of the Initiation just to kill a few teenagers. That must mean the test was legitimate, existing for its stated purpose, right? He wasn't sure. Maybe they were sadists and wanted to see how much the pledges could endure.

The faint lights of Canal Street shone up ahead. Catrice followed right behind him, with Sidney behind her. Alex and Charlie ran

together in the rear. Alex was muttering to Charlie, soft enough not to be heard, pointing at Drayden.

What were they up to? The last time Alex and Charlie schemed, bad things happened. Not only was Tim not around to help fight them off, but for the moment, he couldn't count on Sidney either.

Charlie remained an enigma. He showed flashes of decency, like pulling him to safety on the rock wall, and saving his life in the pool. He'd helped Catrice too, though with ulterior motives. Yet he was so easily controlled by Alex.

Alex steadfastly insisted he would be the one chosen to join the Bureau in the Palace. And Charlie mentioned dealing with Alex's dad if they quit the Initiation. Alex's father must have forced him to enter, possibly to expand his drug-dealing business. Whatever the reason, Alex's combination of desperation and craziness spelled danger.

The light from the station grew bright as they arrived at Canal Street. The station's glaring lights revealed heavy modifications. The Bureau had extended the platform across all four tracks to the platform on the other side. They'd created one giant room, once again.

Drayden took charge. He held his chin up and advanced down the platform. He stopped in his tracks.

"I'm sorry, guys," he said. "I messed up. We should have quit. I can't do this one."

A white wall with three circular holes carved into it cut off the room a quarter of the way into the station. The holes began a few feet off the ground, each spread about fifteen feet apart. A clock dangled above a long table in front of the right hole.

Drayden doubled over. And to think, he'd considered the underground pool a test of his claustrophobia, which he was overjoyed to move past. He should have known better.

"What's wrong?" Charlie asked. "What the hell is that? What are those holes?"

"They're tunnels," Drayden said.

"For what?" Charlie asked. "To where?"

Drayden felt nauseated now. "I don't know. But even from here you can see they're the only way through the station."

Charlie pointed. "Wait, we have to shimmy through those little pipes? Man, I don't think they're wider than my shoulders."

The others groaned. No one liked the idea of being trapped in a constricting tube, for God knew how long. Even Alex didn't look pleased.

"Let's go then," Charlie finally said. "We gotta do it. Dray, is ninety minutes not enough time?"

Dizziness rocked Drayden when he stood. He pictured the Watchers mocking him right now. He had to try. He needed to reach the Palace.

"I don't know for sure, but ninety minutes sounds tight to me. We have no idea how long the challenges will take. I think we need to hurry, yes."

They dashed to the table. The clock displayed the time remaining: *01:24:43, 01:24:42...*

Drayden picked up the note. *"See the light if you manage your fright. Prove you can solve problems under uncomfortable conditions. To advance, you must find your way through the tunnel maze. While there is only one exit, several paths exist to reach it. You may leave your backpacks here and they will be waiting for you a hundred yards down the tracks. Good luck."*

The pledges all dropped their backpacks. Charlie knelt in front of the nearest hole. "Man, that looks tight. How am I going to fit in there?"

Drayden averted his eyes from the tunnels. He could easily get stuck inside. What if they all got stuck behind Charlie?

"How do you do a maze without seeing it?" Alex asked. "Mazes on paper are tough enough, and you can see those."

Charlie crossed his arms. "Yeah, how do you do that?"

Drayden closed his eyes for a moment. *Don't look at the tunnels yet.* "There's a trick to mazes." He rubbed his hand on his forehead. "It's called the right-hand method. Basically, imagine going through any maze. If you touch your right hand to the wall when you begin, and never pick it up, eventually you'll find your way out."

Catrice sat on the ground, scribbling on her paper. "If you never pick up your hand, you'll automatically walk through every passageway," she said. "At a dead end, you'll turn around. Or think about, it's like if you blew the whole maze out into a big circle, it's like walking around the circle once."

"It guarantees you'll get out," Drayden said. "Unfortunately, it's not the fastest or most efficient way."

Alex and Charlie's faces went blank. Both held their right hands out to simulate touching a wall. Sidney stood alone off to the side, her shoulders slumped, looking uninterested.

"Finding our way through is only part of the problem," Drayden said. "One, we have to do it fast. Two, there are three choices of where to start. And three, the biggest problem is those tunnels look extremely tight. It's gonna be suffocating in there. No room to turn around. I'm not even sure we'll be able to back up if we pick the wrong way."

Drayden had no clue how to do this. They could go individually, each testing the different openings, or as a group. "Catrice, I need your help."

She hustled over. "I'm trying to brainstorm the different ways we can get through," she said. "I'm assuming we can back up, but not turn around."

Drayden pulled off his hat and ran his fingers through his hair. "I don't know how I can do this at all. My claustrophobia."

"You'll get through this the same way I got through the pool," she said firmly. "We'll all help each other, help you."

Drayden contemplated the fear she overcame in the water. "You're right." He stuffed his hat in his backpack. "So, we can't do the maze individually, like every person for themselves. We'll probably bump into each other, with people having to back up. We risk losing somebody in there for an hour. The problem with going as a group, single file, is winding up in a dead end. Everyone would have to back up together."

Charlie knelt in front of the middle tunnel opening. "I gotta check this out for a sec." He tried squeezing inside. His shoulders barely cleared the tube's width. He shoved his upper body inside.

A wave of nausea crested over Drayden. He could almost feel the tight tube squeezing his body until he couldn't move, or breathe.

Catrice tapped her pencil on the side of her head. "What if we go in a line but with one person as a scout, way ahead? The scout plots out the right course using the right-hand method. Everybody else waits until the scout says it's not a dead end."

Drayden's eyes widened. "Great idea. Or have one person do the whole maze and then come back and show everyone the way. Wait, that might take too long. Plus, that person could forget the way. I think you're right, a scout using the right-hand method. Let's do that."

"The other question," she said, "is where do we start? There are three choices."

Drayden eyed the tunnels. On all the challenges, the pledges reacted to whatever the Bureau threw at them. Presented with a problem, they solved it the best they could. They played defense; each problem had a solution. Picking the starting tunnel was a problem with no definitive solution. You couldn't know you picked right until after you were inside.

He reflected on school, and how he always managed to excel on tests. It wasn't that he knew all the answers. He didn't. Nobody

could have every answer. Still, he could make educated guesses. The best way to do that was to get inside the head of the test maker. To Drayden, that represented going on offense. It was about identifying which answers the test designer *wanted* you to pick.

"Why would they give us three choices?" Drayden asked. "Or, how about, what would you think if there were only two tunnel openings?"

"Probably one is the right way and the other is wrong."

"Exactly. The other factor at play is the time. We only have an hour and a half to finish the Initiation, with, like, five challenges after this. The Bureau wouldn't give us an hour and a half total if it took an hour to do the maze. I think the addition of a third choice was to make it easier, not harder. In other words, either two of the openings lead to the exit and one is a dead end, or they might all work. Maybe one of the ways is the fastest, like a straight shot."

Catrice raised her eyebrows. "So...which one do we pick?"

Drayden tugged on his left earlobe. "If you designed this, which one would you expect the pledges to pick?"

"The middle one."

"Yes. It's too obvious. That might be the dead end, if there is one. Let's not pick that one. After that, it's pretty much a guess. Far one or near one. If I'm the Bureau, and I believe the pledges are smart enough to avoid the middle tunnel, I would expect their next choice to be the far one. Because they wouldn't think the direct-shot tunnel would be right in front of them. In my opinion, we should pick the near opening, the one on the right. Again, it's just a guess."

"There's no way to know for sure, and that's certainly logical," Catrice said. She stuffed her paper and pencil in her backpack and stood. "We need to move."

"Wait," Drayden said. "Who's going to be the scout? I think I should do it. I'm responsible for us continuing, and I want to prove I can do this."

Catrice cocked her head. "Drayden, the goal is to get through it, not prove something. I'll be the scout, I'm the smallest, I can scoot backward the easiest. You're way too big."

She was right. "Everyone gather around!" Drayden shouted.

Charlie and Alex faced Drayden and Catrice, while Sidney lingered in the back.

Drayden explained how Catrice would go ahead as a scout using the right-hand method. "There's still a chance that we run into a dead end. If we do, we'll all have to back up. It'll be dark in there, so let's have our flashlights out. We're not sure which entrance will be the correct one but we've decided to use this one." He pointed to the nearest hole.

Alex glanced at the tunnels. "I think we should start in the middle one."

Charlie chortled. "X in the center square!"

Drayden flashed a sly smile at Catrice. "I'm not surprised you do, Alex. You can do whatever you want, but if you're stuck in the maze, we're not waiting for you."

Alex scoffed. "I've already learned you won't wait for me, Dray."

Drayden shook his head. How many times could Alex say that in one day? Alex hadn't left him any other choice, all those years ago.

Charlie raised his hand. "Should I go last? In case I get stuck."

"No," Drayden said. "Even if you're last, we may have to back up. We could all get stuck in front of you. Someone should go behind you in case they need to pull. This is the order: Catrice, me, Sidney, Charlie, and Alex."

"I'm not going last," Alex said. "Why do you get to go second?"

Drayden grunted in frustration. "I might need to communicate with Catrice, who's the scout, and we need someone behind Charlie who's strong enough to pull him."

Alex grumbled but didn't push it. They formed a line at the entrance to the right-most tunnel. Catrice touched Drayden on the arm, and then snaked into the hole. She flipped on her flashlight.

Drayden knelt to peer inside the tunnel for the first time. He trembled.

Though it looked more "pipe" than "tunnel", Catrice's petite body left some space around her.

He aimed his flashlight past her.

It revealed a junction approximately fifteen feet further down, with options of going right, left, or straight.

Drayden shouted. "Remember, Catrice. Right-hand method! Yell when we should start following!"

"I got it!" she yelled back, her voiced muffled. She turned right at the junction and disappeared.

"What are you waiting for?" Alex asked Drayden. "Scared?"

God, he hated Alex. "I'm waiting for Catrice to tell us to follow, you flunk. I don't feel like hanging out in the tunnel any more than I have to." He glanced at the clock.

01:19:33, 01:19:32...

Catrice needed to hurry. He shined his flashlight in again.

At that junction, her feet appeared. They edged back into view from the right, in short bursts. She slinked back until her face was visible. Her cheeks glowed red, glistening with streaks of sweat. "That's a dead end to the right! Right-hand method implies we need to go straight. It looks like it goes far, so you guys should start!"

Drayden's tongue transformed into a dry sock. "It's time," he said to the others. "Everyone follow me, in order. I'll be following Catrice." He closed his eyes. What would Tim say? *Just do it. Get it over with. Don't think.* He flipped on his flashlight and jammed his arms and head into the tube. His shoulders touched both rounded walls. He started to hyperventilate, each breath echoing off the

walls. It was so tight, so enclosed. His chin touched the bottom, and if he lifted his head at all, it touched the top.

Someone kicked him in the butt.

He flinched and banged his head on the top of the tunnel. He snapped his head back as much as he could.

"Move it, chickenboy," Alex taunted.

"Leave him alone, Alex," Sidney said from somewhere behind. "And get in the back of the line, where you're supposed to be."

"Alex, don't make me come out there and choke you unconscious," Drayden said, standing up to him, like Tim would.

Sliding inside the tunnel proved challenging. He used his elbows to propel his body while lifting with his hips. On the first try, he advanced a few inches. After three further attempts, his entire body was inside. His back wound throbbed from the exertion. He looked up, down, left, and right. Panic set in.

I'm trapped.

"Let me out! Let me out of here!" He fought to slither backward.

"Drayden," Sidney said, just behind him in the tunnel. "I'm here. Just keep talking to me. You're not going to get stuck. It's uncomfortable, but we can move just fine in here."

Tears blurred Drayden's vision. He couldn't even move his hands to wipe them away. Why didn't he quit when he had the chance?

"I'm sorry, Sid. You were right. We should have quit."

"No. *You* were right. I was being weak. We've come too far to quit. I needed to remember that my goal is to get me and my sister into the Palace. I'm sorry I freaked. I just...I lost it for a minute. Push yourself, Dray. Move forward."

He'd picked the right opening, he was sure of it. They could be out in ten minutes. His breathing slowed. He slid forward, and then did it again, and again. After passing that first junction, he continued straight.

Catrice was twenty feet straight ahead. "Drayden?" she called back. "There's a tunnel to the left here, where I am. Straight up ahead of me, I can see it turns right. I'm going straight to see where that goes. You stop when you get to this tunnel to the left in case I find a dead end."

"Okay!" he yelled. He slid forward a few inches, and peeked back. "Guys, we're going to keep going about twenty more feet and then wait for instructions from Catrice."

The other pledges lined up inside the tunnel behind him, their flashlights shining in his eyes. It was scorching hot.

He couldn't slide back out now if he wanted. His heartrate picked up.

"Drayden, you all right?" Sidney asked.

He paused, closing his eyes. *Breathe.* "Yeah, I guess."

"Shkatnuts!" Charlie yelled from behind. "I'd say I was a little scared, but there isn't enough room for any emotions in here."

Drayden stopped when he reached the tunnel to the left and awaited word from Catrice. She was currently out of sight. He shined his flashlight down that tunnel to the left.

It ran about fifteen feet and then turned right. If Catrice's way was a dead end, this would be the next one they would try by the right-hand method.

"Charlie, did you fart?" Alex asked.

Charlie giggled.

"Goddammit, Charlie," Alex said. "It's uncomfortable enough in here. Hey, Dray, thanks again for making me go after Charlie!"

Catrice's feet appeared up ahead. She inched backward, rounding the turn. "Dead end that way!" she yelled through heavy breaths, scooting back toward Drayden. "We need to go left where you are."

"Crud," Drayden said. He hadn't left enough space for Catrice to execute the turn. "You guys! You all need to back up about eight feet!"

Groaning ensued in the back of the tunnel.

Drayden waited until Sidney moved. He propped up on his elbows, lifted his hips, and jerked backward. He did it again, and again. Sweat dripped into his eyes, stinging them. "Good to go, Catrice," he huffed.

Catrice slid back and made the left turn.

Drayden crawled forward to follow her. Turning in here, with his rangy body, was like turning a bus inside the school hallway.

The corner of the intersection dug deep into his side. He got stuck.

He panicked again. "I'm stuck! I'm stuck!" he whimpered, and closed his eyes.

"Curl your knees up a little," Sidney said. "Like you're jumping over a basketball. Then walk on your elbows."

He followed Sidney's instructions, and freed himself. "Oh my God. Thanks, Sid."

Catrice had already made the right turn ahead. "Drayden?" she yelled from out of sight, his name echoing throughout the maze.

"Yeah?"

"After you make the right turn in front of you, we can go left or straight! Wait at that spot. I'm going to go straight, like I'm supposed to, and see if that's a dead end!"

"Got it!" Drayden scooted forward until he reached the right turn. He took a deep breath and made the turn by the Sidney-method, tucking his knees under him. He stopped at the tunnel to the left and shined his flashlight straight ahead.

Catrice slid twenty feet further, about to turn right again. While not conventionally athletic, she maneuvered like a mole inside the tunnels due to her size.

Drayden darted his eyes in every direction. From where he rested, no exit was in sight. The oppressive heat inside the tight tube drenched his body in sweat.

"You doing all right?" Sidney asked.

"Not really, but thanks for asking," Drayden said.

"You know, I was thinking," she said. "You were right. We can't go back to the Dorms. The Dorms suck. I think you and I would be much happier together in the Palace." She laughed. "Relax. I'm just joking."

Drayden breathed a sigh of relief. Sidney was back. "Just so you know, I'm smiling right now," he said.

"Hey, this right-finger thing sucks, smart guy!" Alex yelled. "Good plan."

Charlie cracked up. "Dray, how's that claustrophobia treating you right now?"

"It's—"

Catrice yelled something indecipherable, the sound echoing throughout the tunnels.

"What?" Drayden shouted. "Catrice?"

She didn't answer.

"Sid, stay here, I'm going to head in her direction and see what's going on." Drayden squeezed down the tunnel.

Catrice's feet appeared at the right turn ahead. "Drayden! This is it! This is the way. I found the exit!"

"Oh thank God. Well done, Catrice!" He turned his head back. "Sid! This is it!"

Sidney hollered back to Charlie and Alex.

Drayden waited until Sidney caught up then slithered forward, following Catrice around the turn to the right.

The tunnel turned left fifteen feet ahead.

"It's just after that next left turn!" Catrice yelled back. She surged ahead, disappearing after she turned left.

Drayden rounded the corner, executing the Sidney-turn one last time. His eyes widened. The exit was only ten feet away.

Light!

And Catrice's skinny legs standing outside.

Drayden pulled and pushed harder and harder until he fell out of the hole. He broke the fall with his arms, biting his lip as hot daggers ripped through his back. "Yeah!" He sprung to his feet, shaking off the pain. He pulled Catrice into a warm, sweaty embrace.

She hugged back, squeezing tight before letting go.

Sidney emerged, bracing herself on the ground with her hands. She slid out like she'd practiced it a dozen times. Through reddened cheeks she gasped for breath, but she popped right up. She wrapped her arms around Drayden. "You did it! I never doubted you."

Drayden held her close. "Thank you, Sid. I couldn't have done that without you. I thought I might have a heart attack when I got stuck."

She pulled back, leaving her hands draped on his shoulders. "The Bureau didn't build that tunnel for big guys like you and Charlie."

Charlie, and then Alex, fell out of the tunnel, both red-faced and dripping with sweat. Charlie bum-rushed Catrice and gripped her in a bear hug, hoisting her like a doll. She disappeared in his beefy arms, an embarrassed look on her face.

"Thank you," Charlie said. "Thank you so much for finding the way out. You saved me. Man, I'm happier than a camel on Wednesday."

Catrice burst out laughing. "You're welcome. Your shoulders are so broad I have no clue how you moved at all in there. Finally, for once it was good to be small."

For crying out loud, it's a hug-fest out here, Drayden thought. "We have to hurry."

A clock hung outside the maze exit: *01:08:35, 01:08:34...*

Drayden thought it had gone pretty well. They conquered the maze in sixteen minutes; a decent chunk of time. Still, now that the maze was behind them, he couldn't help but face reality. Unless one or more of the upcoming stations didn't have challenges, which was unlikely, they couldn't finish the Initiation.

CHAPTER 19

Drayden kept his pessimistic evaluation to himself. As long as they were moving as fast as they could, he didn't see the point of letting the others know they didn't have nearly enough time left.

The pledges raced through the dark tunnel.

Alex, who'd fallen behind, called out, "We need to stop. I have to catch my breath."

Drayden replied, out of breath as well, "We'll take a quick breather when we're at the backpacks."

The tunnel maze had sapped everyone's energy. Without time to rest, they'd resumed a full sprint on the dark tracks. Five hours straight of the Initiation was also catching up to them. Everybody wore the exhaustion on their faces.

They stopped at the backpacks and gulped water. Alex plopped down on the third rail, the elevated one that used to carry the electricity.

"Guys, time to go," Drayden said through a mouthful of mixed nuts.

Alex rested his elbows on his knees and hung his head low. "I need another minute."

While Drayden felt the same way, and the others probably did too, it didn't matter. "We don't have a minute," he snapped. "I don't

want to be alarmist, but we may not have enough time to finish. We have to hustle."

"Let's go, Alex," Charlie said.

Alex clenched his jaw. "In a second!"

"Fine, Alex," Drayden said, "we'll just leave without you."

Alex stood. "You like doing that, don't you?"

"Shut up, chotch. I'm getting sick of that leaving-you-behind garbage." Drayden faced him. "You chose your own path. Stop blaming me for not coming along."

Drayden took off running, leading the sprint again toward the Franklin Street Station.

Catrice and Sidney ran behind him, each of them on opposite sides of the track. Charlie and Alex ran well behind them.

He suspected the tracks must turn somewhere ahead. Franklin Street wasn't far, yet the tunnel ahead only revealed further blackness. After the maze challenge, a brainteaser likely awaited next. The pressure would fall on his shoulders. He craved a distraction, before the stress of the impending challenge kicked in.

Drayden turned back to Catrice and Sidney. "Hey, you guys going to miss being in school?"

For a few seconds, neither answered.

"I think we'll miss seeing our friends every day," Sidney said. "Those of us that had friends."

Drayden wondered whether that was a dig at him or Catrice.

Catrice stared straight ahead. "I think we'll find out who our friends really were, now that school's over. People who are friends with everyone usually have no real friends."

"Yeah, it's probably better to hide and not talk to anyone," Sidney said.

Catrice fake-laughed. "I know I'll miss learning. It's amazing how some kids went through eleven years of school and never learned a thing."

"That's true," Sidney said. "Like how to swim."

"Or how to solve even basic problems," Catrice said. "I guess if you're destined to be a seamstress, you don't have to know how."

"Luckily in New America we're all treated the same whether you're a seamstress or a scientist."

Catrice snickered. "Luckily for you, yes."

"Well, luckily for me," Sidney said, mocking Catrice, "I know I'll pass the next bravery challenge, because I'm not a coward. We've got Dray for the intelligence ones. I don't think we need you."

"Oh, for crying out loud," Drayden said, sounding exactly like his father. "I'm sorry I asked."

The station glowed ahead like the noon sun on a July day.

The issue of the remaining time gnawed at Drayden. Given the lights ahead, Franklin Street housed a challenge. They hadn't passed a deserted station since the early stages of the Initiation. Yet one or more of the next few stations simply *had* to be empty. After Franklin Street came Chambers Street, a major station. Then came Park Place, Fulton Street, and finally, Wall Street. That made five stations, with roughly an hour left.

Assuming five minutes to run between stations, that equaled twenty minutes of travel time after Franklin Street. He was being generous about their speed. It could take longer. That, at best, left forty minutes for five challenges. Eight minutes per challenge.

They'd spent more than eight minutes on most of the challenges. Some of the bravery ones burned up to forty minutes, and the upcoming challenges were supposedly tougher. It didn't add up. How could the Bureau only grant them ninety minutes from Houston Street?

Drayden didn't just need to solve the upcoming challenge; he needed to blow it out of the water. Take charge. Be decisive. Determine how each person could be utilized most effectively.

Sure, on the brainteasers that meant everyone besides Catrice in a supporting role. But on the bravery challenges, Charlie had proven to be brave, strong, and skilled. Like on the rock wall, and in the pool. Who knew what else he excelled at? Similarly, Sidney had displayed bravery and skill at everything from the rock wall, to the pool, to the rats. She'd even supported Catrice in the rat challenge, though the girls' brief friendship had gone off the rails.

The only one with no value to add, anywhere, and who expected to be carried on everyone's backs, was Alex. He needed to stay out of the way. Or be kept out of the way.

Drayden's ankle ached, but thankfully they were arriving at Franklin Street. "Station ahead!" he yelled.

<hr />

Damn the Bureau for cutting the time. They had said eight hours. What a bunch of cheaters, changing the rules in the middle of the game. If they'd lied about the time, what else had they lied about?

Drayden breathlessly sprinted down the platform, trailed by the other pledges, and stopped in the middle of the Franklin Street station. Where was the challenge? It was set up for one.

A clock hung here: *01:02:04, 01:02:03....* There was no table with instructions.

The pledges rotated around, devouring every corner of the station with their eyes. They braced themselves for some horrible surprise, like a wall crashing down, or someone jumping out. Anything.

Nothing happened.

Charlie peered down the tunnel. "Um, we missing something?"

"I don't know." Drayden rubbed his eyes. "They lit the station and put up a clock. Something should be here."

Alex stepped forward. "Since you had us running like a pack of cheetahs, they probably didn't have time to set it up. I'm sure it's coming though. Any second now."

Drayden wasn't so sure anymore. He'd done the math. At a minimum one station *had* to be a free pass. Again, he tried to pry inside the heads of the Initiation Council who had designed this challenge. Maybe prepping this station and lighting it as if it contained a challenge was a trick to throw them off. A curveball.

Drayden faced the other pledges. "We can wait a few minutes to be sure, but I don't believe there's a challenge here." He laid out the math. "With five stations left, including this one, that would only give us about eight minutes per challenge. Pretty impossible unless they're stupid easy, and we know they won't be. Even if they skipped this one, it still only leaves us eleven minutes per challenge. Not exactly time to sit and have a snack."

Sidney wrinkled her nose. "Should we just go, then?"

Drayden placed both hands on top of his hat and paced. It was possible the Bureau had planned a challenge here, but realized the pledges couldn't finish in time and changed their mind. Though only a guess, the pledges had been at the station a few minutes and nothing had happened, which supported his theory. He exhaled in relief.

He pulled off his hat and turned it over in his hands. He thought of his mom. He had to change. The people closest to him in his life, Mom and Tim, exemplified bravery. He couldn't be afraid anymore. Tim hadn't been, and Drayden didn't need to be either. Tim *got* it. Drayden had been striving to emulate Tim, but that just made him an actor. His mom and Tim weren't innately any braver than he was, nor did they possess any special skills that he lacked. They simply understood that bravery was a choice. They consciously chose it, conquering their fear. They became free.

Drayden couldn't go on this way, trembling at the prospect of each challenge. He needed to meet them head on. He didn't have weaker fingers than everyone else; it was his fear on the rock wall that had led him to rush and fall. His lungs could retain just as much

air as the other pledges; his fear had led him to panic underwater, sapping his oxygen. He held his hat, picturing both Mom and Tim looking down on him right now, disappointed with his cowardice. Well, no longer. If a challenge waited at the following station, he would lead the charge, without fear.

"Yes, we should go. There's no challenge here," Drayden said. "We need to hurry." He retrieved his backpack and turned to leave.

"Whoa, whoa there, chief!" Alex shouted. "Where you running off to with your tail between your legs?"

Drayden stopped, his cheeks flushing with heat. He walked back to Alex.

"What?" Alex asked. "We're waiting for this challenge. I'm not getting exiled because you were too scared to face a challenge and we skipped it."

Charlie, Catrice, and Sidney stood off to the sides, shifting uncomfortably.

"I'm not scared," Drayden said. "There's just no challenge here."

"You *are* scared, wetchop. You're the biggest coward there is. Just a skinny wuss."

"No, I'm not. What about you, chotch?" Drayden jabbed a finger at him. "You're a shkat flunk with a huge nose. I'm surprised the Bureau didn't give your nose its own backpack."

Alex stared at him. "The only extra backpack we got was Tim's."

Drayden balled his hands into fists. He stepped toward Alex, but stopped. He wasn't worth it. Why waste precious time fighting with him? He turned to go.

"That's right, Dray, do what you do best. Leave," Alex said.

Drayden turned back again. He had to put a stop to this conflict once and for all. He had an idea. "Enough, Alex. You've been crying about this for years. What did you expect me to do? Keep hanging out with you after you started doing drugs *and* dealing them? Pounding ack with the winoozes? Things changed."

"*Things* didn't change. *You* changed!" Alex said, his tone changing from tough guy to eight-year-old kid. "You were a lousy friend. You left me behind."

"Alex, when we started middle school, they put me in the advanced classes, and we didn't see each other much after that. Then you started working for your dad! I couldn't be a part of that. My parents forbade me from hanging out with you." Drayden raised his hands, palms up. "What was I supposed to do?"

Alex stomped his foot. "I had no choice!" he screamed, his voice cracking. "My dad made me! You were the only one who knew that! You were the only one who knew how bad I had it at home. How my dad would be drunk, or high, and hand out beatings like he was an evil Santa Claus at Christmas. If it wasn't from him, it was my older brothers. You just looked the other way!"

"Alex, I'm sorry for how bad it was at home. I was sorry, I *am* sorry. But it wasn't my fault, and there was nothing I could do about it. If you weren't dealing we could have stayed friends. Unfortunately, you went down that rabbit hole, and I couldn't follow you. If you were really my friend, you would have understood that. Instead you've made it your life's goal to make me miserable." He pointed his thumb down the tracks. "Now, if you don't mind, we need to finish the Initiation. We're leaving now." Drayden turned to walk away.

"We're staying. Who made you boss anyway?" Alex asked.

Drayden returned, exasperated. "Alex, I'm just trying to get us through this, like Tim was before the Bureau killed him."

Alex scoffed. "We all saw what happened. The Bureau didn't kill Tim. You did."

Something snapped inside Drayden. Adrenaline surged through his veins. He dove at Alex's legs. He powered through them, and executed the double-leg takedown he'd practiced so many times.

Alex crashed down onto his back.

Drayden landed on top of Alex flawlessly, sitting on his hips, raining down vicious punches to his nose and eyes.

Alex's nose dripped blood. He covered his face and rolled onto his stomach to avoid more blows.

Drayden sat on top of Alex's back now. He leaned forward, swiftly snaked his right arm under Alex's throat, and connected it with his left arm. The perfect rear-naked choke. He squeezed with every ounce of muscle, cutting off Alex's air and the blood to his brain.

Within seconds, Alex went limp.

Drayden was wild, animalistic. He should have let go, but he couldn't. All those years of abuse from Alex, and the bullying from other kids before that, he let it all out on Alex. The jiu-jitsu skill he'd been bottling up finally uncorked and flowed like a barrel of ack. Drayden was a boa constrictor around Alex's neck.

Strong hands gripped Drayden's wrists and separated them, releasing the choke. Charlie yanked Drayden up and tossed him backward.

Drayden fell onto his back, executing a back roll to end up squatting. Powering through the pain, he shot up, in a fighting stance, ready to take on Charlie. For the first time in his life, he had the confidence to use his jiu-jitsu.

Charlie was kneeling over Alex, and rolled him onto his back. He wiped blood from Alex's face with his shirt. Alex moaned. Sidney and Catrice both stood in shock, gawking at Alex's bloody face. Alex's busted left eye was already swelling shut.

Drayden touched his own black eye, courtesy of Alex four days ago.

Charlie dragged Alex to his feet. Alex wobbled, squeezing his nose shut with his shirt. Charlie used his own shirt to slow the bleeding from Alex's eye.

Drayden's moment of triumph over Alex proved short-lived. His heart still racing from the fight, he pitied Alex. Everything Alex

said was true. Drayden didn't have a choice, but he did abandon Alex, in a way. The accusation that he killed Tim hurt the most, because Drayden felt the same way. With Alex's tough guy routine, his constant needling, and the bullying, he didn't make it easy to feel sorry for him. Yet he did have a sad life. He never had a chance, growing up with no mother and a brutal father. Drayden limped over to Catrice and Sidney.

Both stood frozen in place and didn't say anything.

They were probably thinking the same thing. Alex had that coming, but now that it happened, they felt bad. Drayden studied both girls' faces. Would his sudden outburst of violence alter either girl's opinion of him? If anything, it might make Sidney like him more, and Catrice like him less.

Drayden checked the clock.

That stupid fight had wasted five minutes. They had just under an hour left.

"We have to go, right now," he said to Catrice and Sidney. "There's no challenge here. If there was, we would know what it is by now. I think it was a trick by the Bureau, a head fake. We've already wasted enough time." He snatched up his backpack and ran. He no longer cared if Charlie or Alex came along. He didn't need them anymore.

CHAPTER 20

Drayden set a brisk pace on the tracks, between a full sprint and a jog. He still couldn't believe what he'd just done. Despite his own conflicting feelings about it, Tim would be so proud.

Charlie and Alex ran thirty yards behind the girls, only their flashlight beams visible.

Drayden wondered what was going through their heads right now. Charlie must understand. Wouldn't he? He'd watched Alex sucker punch Drayden four days ago. Not to mention, Alex had not helped one bit in the Initiation. Quite the opposite, in fact.

"Drayden," Catrice said, out of breath. "I know what you did back there."

"What do you mean?" he asked. "You mean beating up Alex?"

"No. Before that."

"I don't know what you're talking about."

"Yes, you do. You did something for Alex right before you tackled him and punched him in the face."

Wow. Nothing gets by Catrice. She's so smart.

Drayden winked at her.

"What is psycho girl talking about?" Sidney asked, breathing hard.

Catrice frowned. "Why am I not surprised she doesn't get it?"

Drayden *had* done something for him, but Alex wasn't clever enough to realize it. While not without risk, it was one final act of compassion to try and make amends for everything that had happened between them.

The Watchers had heard every detail of that argument. They'd learned about Alex's father dealing drugs, and forcing Alex to sell them. The Bureau would exile Alex's father before day's end.

If they followed the same protocol they always had, they would pardon Alex. His father had forced him to commit a crime under the threat of violence, and he'd carried out that threat with savage beatings. They couldn't hold Alex, legally a child, responsible.

Alex's father was pure evil. The fact that he hadn't been exiled already suggested he paid off Guardians or Chancellors with drug money. Since the Initiation Council was observing them, and perhaps even Premier Holst himself, they had all heard Alex's confession. There would be no escaping this time.

"I'll tell you later, Sid," Drayden said. He pointed to his eye and then to the ceiling.

Sidney nodded, indicating she understood they were being recorded.

Though not far, the looming station at Chambers Street remained out of view. The tracks probably turned somewhere ahead.

Chambers Street's significance stood out on several levels. It served both the Two-Three Line and the One Line. It was the first major station since Fourteenth Street to do so, and the final one as well. The One Line, which ran parallel to the Two-Three Line they were following, branched off there. More notably, Chambers marked the southern boundary of the Precinct and the beginning of the Palace. If they passed through, they would enter the Palace. Underneath it, but still.

The pledges sped through the tunnel now, making decent time. When they arrived at the station, a little over fifty minutes should remain. The Bureau gave them a gift at Franklin Street with no challenge. That freebie, combined with the significance of the Chambers Street station, guaranteed a brutal challenge.

Voices echoed somewhere up ahead.

Drayden slowed to a walk and pressed his index finger to his lips. "Shhhh," he whispered to Catrice and Sidney.

Sunlight through a grate to the street above brightened the tunnel.

Drayden walked below the grate and stopped to rest. He looked up.

Charlie and Alex reached them, and everyone was huffing and puffing, out of breath.

Two Guardians huddled on the grate above their heads, chatting. One appeared middle-aged and the other much younger, barely older than the pledges.

"You think bigger rocks eat the smaller ones?" the younger one asked.

"What? You're some kind of special, aren't you? No, big rocks don't eat small ones," the older said with food in his mouth.

"How do you know? How do they grow then?"

"Kid, how'd you make it through Guardian training? I need a new partner. How can they eat without *mouths*? The rocks just grow naturally. They don't eat each other. Break's over; let's go." He dropped something through the grate.

The banana peel landed on Charlie's head.

The other pledges laughed in silence. Charlie laughed too, and threw the peel at Drayden. It smacked him in the chest.

He held it, the levity of the moment fading. It reminded him of his mom. Drayden reached up and touched his hat. The Initiation was designed to test for bravery, and indeed it did. He would enter

the upcoming challenge and handle whatever the Bureau threw at him.

They hustled again, Charlie and Alex lingering far behind.

"Dray," Sidney said, "what type of challenge do you think is next?"

"No idea. The last challenge wasn't a challenge, and the one before that was the maze. I think it was a bravery challenge, though it was kinda both. But whatever's waiting, between the three of us, we've got it covered."

"You worried about Alex trying to retaliate?" Sidney asked quietly.

"No," Drayden said. "He was asking for it, and he knows it. He also knows if he comes at me, I'd beat him down again. I should have done that years ago."

Sidney practically swooned, grinning widely.

The tracks curved to the right. As soon as they rounded the turn, they ran into Chambers Street, the gateway to the Palace.

Drayden wished his mother could see him now, on the outskirts of the Palace. He got the sense that she *could* see, that she was with him. It was probably his imagination, or the painkillers at work. Still, he felt her presence, a warmth, watching over him.

Drayden took a deep breath, shook out his hands, and marched down the platform. The others followed.

The Bureau had blocked off the whole uptown side of the station with a wall that ran the length of the platform. They walked on the downtown platform with the Two-Three Line tracks on the left, and the One Line tracks on the right. Not a significant modification, and nothing else jumped out.

Drayden picked up the pace, cognizant of the dwindling time. He reached the middle of the station where they usually faced the challenges, and stopped, digesting the scene.

Nothing.

Would the Bureau cut them a break two stations in a row? It was possible, but unlikely. As he examined his surroundings, he locked eyes with Alex.

Alex's purple left eye puffed out grotesquely, nearly swelling shut. Dried blood crusted the edges. Alex said nothing, dripping rage.

"Could today be our lucky day?" Sidney asked. "That whole thing about the upcoming challenges being harder might have been a bluff to get us to quit."

"I don't think so," Charlie said. He pointed at the far end of the platform. "Look!"

A table.

The pledges sprinted toward it, slowing when they reached the familiar picnic table.

Past it, the Bureau had painted five red circles on the floor in a straight line. They ran parallel to the tracks, spaced a few feet apart, about a foot in diameter each. Each one contained a number, painted in white. Number one started in the back, with number five in the front.

A small metal box with a black button in the center rested on a stand alongside the first circle. Above the circles, a narrow shiny metal box hung down from the ceiling. About eight feet in the air, it began at the first circle and ended at the last. A clock above the table continued its countdown: *00:53:53, 00:53:52...*

Drayden ran to the table and plucked up the note. *"All might be done, but for one. A group's wellbeing supersedes any individual's. Solve this complex puzzle to demonstrate your embrace of this core ideal of the Bureau. Each of you will stand on one of the circles. A hat*

will be lowered from the box onto each of your heads. The hat will be either green or red. You will not know the color of your own hat, or the hat of anyone behind you. You must each correctly guess the color of your own hat, starting from the back, by saying red or green out loud. You will not know if you guessed correctly until the end."

Sweat trickled down Drayden's cheek. He cleared his throat and continued. *"If the person in circle one guesses incorrectly, that person will be exiled. If more than one person guesses incorrectly, everyone will be exiled. If anyone attempts to view their own hat, or a hat behind them, or if any word other than red or green is spoken, everyone will be exiled. After the last person has answered, you are to remain still until you are given a signal of the results. When you are ready to begin, the person in circle one will push the button. Good luck."*

Drayden fell to his knees, the note floating to the ground. Up to this point, the difficulty of the brainteasers was mostly due to the pressure. It came from both the time constraint, and the consequence of answering wrong.

This was something different. This problem was *really* tricky. Even alone in a classroom with nothing on the line, Drayden would struggle to solve it. How could every person possibly know what color hat they wore without looking? It must have a solution. But while not given a defined time limit, they must solve it in less than ten minutes. Otherwise they had no shot of finishing the Initiation, based on how many challenges remained. Some of those would be bravery ones. It couldn't be done. The maze took sixteen minutes, the pool thirty, and the rock wall forty.

Drayden pictured his father getting the news that he'd been exiled. The last time he'd seen his father, the man had been red-faced and yelling. He'd shown more emotion than Drayden had observed in sixteen years. Maybe Dad was right after all. The Initiation was a trap. They were never intended to pass. The Bureau

hadn't underestimated the time required to finish when they gave only ninety minutes. They just handed the pledges an insurmountable task. They'd lied about the time at the start. Perhaps they'd lied about the prize at the end as well. Did the Initiation exist solely to exile kids? Or kill them, after torturing them for a while?

Drayden should have heeded his father's warning. It even fit with Thomas Cox's claims. The Bureau had a sudden need to furtively increase exiles, and the Initiation offered a convenient solution, if anyone was stupid enough to enter. Then why bother hosting an Initiation at all? Why not just exile them from the start? He bet in years past the Initiation accomplished what the Bureau claimed, so most of it was already set up. Much of it could even double as training facilities for the Guardians. They might have held it anyway this year because the twisted Premier had a sick interest in seeing how far they could push people before they'd break. Drayden buried his face in his hands.

"Drayden?"

He raised his head.

Catrice stood in front of him, clutching her paper and pencil. "Let's get to work. We can solve this, but I can't do it without your help."

He gazed into her dazzling eyes. A tiny spark lit in his belly. To hell with it. Trap or not, he wasn't going down without a fight.

"Um, you guys," Charlie said. "If there's anything we can do, let us know. We should probably just stay out of the way. We're here if you need anything." He, Alex, and Sidney wandered over to the circles.

Drayden and Catrice sat facing each other. Drayden stuffed his hat inside his backpack and pulled out his pencil and paper. It felt a bit pointless, given they needed the solution about five minutes ago. They would still have to go through some sort of iterative

problem-solving routine. He should approach it methodically like a real scientist would.

"Let's start basic. We all just guess the color of our own hats. Fifty-fifty chance of being right. Two-and-a-half of us would answer wrong. Two or three people, probably. We could get lucky, but that's a terrible strategy. If even two people are wrong, we're exiled."

Catrice tapped her pencil on the side of her head. "What if... what if we split into pairs? One and two, three and four, and then five, alone. The person in the back of the pair calls out the color of the hat in front of them. That person in the back has a fifty-fifty chance of getting their own right, and the person in front has a hundred percent chance."

Drayden tugged on his left ear. "It's better than everyone guessing. But only a little better, right? Let's think. Person four and person two would answer right. Persons one, three, and five would still be guessing, with a fifty-fifty chance. We would need two of those three to guess right. And let's not forget that person one can be exiled by themselves if they get theirs wrong. Why'd they create that rule, anyway?"

"I don't know," Catrice said. "I guess just to make position one more dangerous? That whole thing they said about the group versus the individual wellbeing. However we do it, who's going to want to go first?"

A chill ran through Drayden's body.

00:51:45, 00:51:44...

He slapped a hand on the floor. "There has to be a better way, Catrice. I refuse to accept that this challenge tests our luck. There's a trick, and we're missing it."

She chewed on her pencil.

Drayden rubbed his chin. "Each person will be wearing either a green or red hat, but we won't know how many of each there are.

You won't know yours, or the ones behind you. You'll know what the people in front of you are wearing."

"Is that all we know?" she asked.

Wait a minute. Drayden's eyes widened. "No, that's not all. You know what each person behind you *said.* That's the key, it has to be."

Catrice closed her eyes, deep in thought.

Drayden ran his fingers through his hair. "What if the person behind you could give a code somehow?"

"They can't," Catrice said. "You can only say 'red' or 'green,' and it has to be a guess about your *own* hat."

She was right. Drayden groaned in frustration. "I don't know... something to do with probability? Like, if the person in the back sees all red hats, he would guess green? Or if the person in front heard all greens, he guesses red?"

"I don't know..." Catrice shifted uncomfortably.

What the person in the back sees.

It hit him at once.

"Catrice," he said softly, "I know how to do it. And why the first person is special."

She bolted to attention. She tucked her hair behind her ears, and stole a peek at the clock. "How?"

"The color you guess *is* the code, and it all starts with what the first person says. He tells everyone else exactly what they need to know. That first person still has a fifty-fifty chance of guessing right. Everybody else is guaranteed to get theirs."

Catrice shook her head. "I don't understand."

"The first person can see everyone else's hats, right? He counts the number of green and red hats. He's going to say a color, but it's not going to be a guess about his own hat, it's going to be a code. If he sees an *odd* number of green hats, he says green. If he sees an *even* number of green hats, he says red. He just has to hope he was right for himself, but he solved it for everybody else."

Drayden scooted closer. "Let's assume he sees an odd number of green hats, like one, with the other three red. He calls out green because one is an odd number. Now it's the second person's turn. He can see three hats in front of him. If he also sees an odd number of green hats—one—it's the same thing the first person saw. Which means his own hat must be red. Because if his hat was green, the person behind him would have seen two green hats, an even number. Then you go to the third person. If he sees an even number of green hats, say zero for example, then he knows he's wearing a green hat. Since the person behind him saw an odd number of green hats—one, and so on. Unfortunately, the first person still only has a fifty-fifty chance of being right."

"I got it! Nice job!" Catrice leaned forward and hugged Drayden. She pulled back, looking into his eyes. "We can't do this one for everyone else. They're going to have to think their way through it. If any of them mess up, we're all screwed."

Drayden frowned. "Yeah. I know. Let's walk them through exactly what they need to do."

"Person one only has a fifty-fifty chance of passing, and can be exiled alone. They can't improve those odds. Someone is going to have to take that first spot."

Indeed, someone was. Who would volunteer? Nobody, of course.

"I know what you're thinking," Catrice said.

"Alex." Drayden deflated a bit from guilt as he said it.

Catrice whispered in his ear, "You could tell him to stand in position one because it's the easiest. He calls out green or red depending on how many green hats he sees. He probably wouldn't even understand that he might be exiled. If he guessed wrong, and we all got ours right, we continue the Initiation and he's gone forever. Kill two birds with one stone. But Drayden...that would be wrong. No matter how evil he is, we can't do that to him."

She was right. As tempting as it was, Drayden could never do that, even to Alex. Despite the years of torment, at one time they were best friends. Alex didn't deserve to be duped, exploiting his lack of intelligence for their own gain, at the cost of his life. It would be a despicable act.

They were so close to the finish line, though. Even if the Bureau expected them to fail, they solved this puzzle and could be on schedule for the following challenge. He was so close to the end he could taste the Palace. He could guarantee a safe and better life for himself as well as his family. Wasn't that why he'd entered the Initiation? Wasn't that more important than Alex, a genuinely bad kid? Three more stations to go, and he achieved the safety he craved.

But at what cost? He might reach the Palace that way and attain its facade of security. He would never truly feel safe, because an act of cowardice would have paved the way. He would never be free, the way Tim and Mom were. He would always find something to fear. Despite its evil, the Initiation had taught him something about bravery. *Bravery isn't the absence fear. It's choosing to overcome it.*

The Drayden of yesterday, the scared and weaker one, would choose the darker path, shafting Alex, just as he had all those years ago when he turned his back on Alex in the first place. He wasn't totally innocent. Alex was right about that, and Drayden had to face it. It *had* been easier not to see what was happening to Alex's life, so he didn't look. He could have been his friend at school or something, just someone to lean on, but he hadn't done that. He had cut him off completely.

Drayden recalled what his mother had taught him about karma, after she saved that woman's life at the FDC. If he tried to screw over Alex now, karma would come back to bite him. Conversely, if he were brave, the karma gods might protect him. He wasn't even sure he believed in all that stuff, but this would be a heck of a time to test it out.

It was as if the Bureau had designed this challenge specifically for him. The challenge wasn't even about red and green hats, it was all about choosing who would go first.

All might be done, but for one.

While the Bureau ostensibly presented this as an intelligence challenge, choosing to go first required more bravery than any of the other challenges thus far. It carried a fifty-fifty chance of exile for only that person. The architects of the Initiation were keenly aware of the dilemma of circle one. The Watchers were watching. He knew deep down what the answer was. He knew who had to be the one.

"You're right, Catrice." Drayden rose and stood tall. "I need to go first."

"What? No! I didn't mean you. Charlie or Sidney might even volunteer for it. Drayden, it can't be you."

"It's okay. I need to go first. For me."

She hugged him. "You don't have to prove anything. And I don't have anyone else."

Drayden held her. Those words revealed the most emotion, and direct affection, Catrice had ever expressed. It moved him. She meant it. Throughout all the years he'd known her, she'd never seemed to need anyone. It only increased his desire to become closer to her. Except she was human too. He pulled her closer.

"Listen. I'm not going to be exiled," Drayden said. "I'm not. The karma gods will reward me for this." He nodded. "Yeah. Everyone else is going to guess right, and we're all going to move on. In a few minutes we'll be inside the Palace. Trust me."

Drayden squeezed her once more before letting go. "Hey, guys! Gather around."

Drayden and Catrice explained how the problem worked and how to solve it. The other pledges listened. Charlie made no jokes, and Alex stopped scowling.

"What if I forget which color is even and odd?" Charlie asked.

Drayden scratched his head. "You gotta associate green with odd. Green would be an odd color for skin, right? Imagine me with green skin. Since we're talking about it, you'll probably remember now. If person one calls out green, there are an odd number of green hats. If they call out red, there's an even number of green hats. That's not all you have to remember though. You have to think after that. This problem doesn't have a timer. We need to hustle, but don't rush, think before you answer. You must remember if there are an odd or even number of green hats to start. You must keep track of how many green hats have been called out. And you must note how many of each you can see in front of you. Don't forget: Zero is an even number."

Sidney's face lit up. "I got it, Drayden! It just clicked. I understand. I'll get mine right." She beamed.

Drayden fist-bumped her. "Now, if we all do this right, there's no chance involved. Everybody will guess correctly."

Sidney furrowed her brow. "But...what about the first person? Won't they be totally guessing? Like *totally*?"

Drayden nodded. She did get it. "Yes. Which means the first person is the only one who has a chance of being wrong. He's calling out green or red based on how many green hats he sees. It's random whether that will be correct for his own hat. Hopefully he'll get lucky."

"Wait," Sidney said. "Who's going first?"

"Not it!" Alex yelled.

Drayden and Catrice exchanged a glance. "Me," Drayden said.

"Brilliant idea," Alex said. "First smart thing you've said all day."

Charlie looked uncomfortable. "Dray, you sure? It's not really fair that you have to do it. We might need you after this too."

"I'm sure," he said. "I feel good about it. Thanks. I wanted to do a practice run, but we don't have time. I have to know, is everyone crystal clear on what they need to do? Is anyone confused at all?"

Catrice gave a thumbs-up, and Sidney and Charlie both said yes. Alex didn't react.

Drayden stepped to him, right in his face. "Alex, this isn't the time for hurt feelings. This is too crucial. Do you understand exactly what you need to do?"

Alex avoided eye contact. "I got it, wetchop. I'm not stupid, you know."

"Let's do it, then. I'm first, then Charlie, then Sidney, then Catrice, and Alex in circle five. Everyone stand in their designated spots. Remember not to look up when the hats come down. It would be a natural reaction. Look straight ahead. We don't want to get exiled for something silly like a flinch."

Moment of truth. Drayden stepped onto circle one. Despite facing his most risky moment of the whole Initiation, a wave of serenity washed over him. He brimmed with confidence in his decision to go first, and would be rewarded for his courage. They'd solved the problem correctly. Now everybody simply needed to execute.

Drayden reached for the button, then hesitated, his heart thumping. Old habits died hard. He pushed the button, and stared straight ahead.

A winding noise overhead pierced the silence, followed by a repetitive clicking noise. Something dropped onto his head. At the same time, in front of him, metal chains with mechanical fingers on the ends dropped boxy baseball hats on everyone else's heads. The chains retracted, the winding noise ensued, and the station fell silent.

Drayden closed his eyes for a moment and breathed deeply. He opened them. In front of him, Charlie wore a red hat, Sidney wore a red hat, Catrice wore a green hat, and Alex wore a red hat. Oh God. Which was odd, which was even? Green, an odd color for skin. Only

Catrice wore a green hat. One, an odd number. An odd number of green hats meant he called out green.

"Green!"

Please let my hat be green.

Charlie could see Sidney's red hat, Catrice's green hat, and Alex's red hat. Charlie knew that Drayden saw an odd number of green hats, and he also saw an odd number—one. Which implied he must be wearing a red hat.

You can do this, Charlie, Drayden silently urged.

If he answered wrong, he'd blow the whole scheme.

Charlie fidgeted. He shifted his weight between legs, taking longer than he should. "Red!" he finally yelled.

Drayden exhaled. *Attaboy, Charlie! Sidney, same thing. Piece of cake.* She could see Catrice's green hat, and Alex's red hat. She saw an odd number of green hats—one. Drayden had started them off with an odd number of green hats. Charlie had said red, so the number of green hats remained odd. She had to be wearing red.

She took a long time too. She scratched her cheek.

Drayden's stomach was in knots. If she messed up and guessed green, Catrice would surely answer red, and that would be two wrong answers. Exile.

"Red?" Sidney yelled, as a question.

Yes! Drayden grinned. Question or not, she guessed right. *Way to go, Sid!* He couldn't wait to give her a giant hug when this was over.

Catrice's turn. Thank God for Catrice's brain. Drayden had not a shred of doubt she would answer correctly. She could only see Alex's red hat. She knew she was wearing the green one.

"Green!" she yelled without hesitation.

She is amazing.

That was a big one, because if Drayden was lucky enough to have guessed his own right, it wouldn't matter if Alex flubbed up.

It was why he had to be last. One wrong guess was fine, as long as it wasn't the person in circle one, and nobody would be exiled. However, if Drayden had guessed wrong, this one was huge for the other pledges. A wrong answer from Alex would then mean exile for everybody.

Alex, for once, don't screw everything up.

He knew there were an odd number of green hats to start, and only one person said green. He was the last one. He had to be wearing red.

Alex remained silent. He shifted his feet, and scratched his leg. He tapped his foot.

Drayden began to sweat profusely. What would the signal be if they were successful? Or if not? He wondered if it would be obvious. If they were safe, perhaps nothing would happen at all, and they could go on their way.

Alex continued to squirm, taking way too much time. Something was wrong.

He doesn't know.

That flunk. He gave Drayden attitude about not being stupid, and he didn't understand how to do it.

Please, just guess right then, Alex. Please say red. Red, Alex, come on.

"Green!"

Oh no.

A massive metal gate crashed down over the tracks with a boom, blocking them.

Wait. What is this? Oh my God.

"No!" Drayden screamed.

CHAPTER 21

Drayden stood in disbelief, his mouth hung open. The reality of what had just occurred, and what it meant, sunk in like acid on his skin. His stunned eyes locked on the thick metal gate blocking the tunnel. There was the sign of the results. Couldn't be any clearer. They'd failed. The Initiation was over.

"What does that mean?" Sidney yelled. She spun around, both hands on her head.

Alex pulled off his red hat and studied it. Without turning around, Catrice whimpered into her hands and squatted on the ground. Charlie yanked off his red hat, flung it onto the tracks, and stormed off.

Drayden collapsed to his knees.

"Oh God," Sidney said. She burst into tears.

It can't be.

Drayden had done what he needed to do. Where were those damn karma gods? He'd chosen to be brave, to lead. Now everyone would be exiled. Any moment a battalion of Guardians would swarm them, drive them in a bus up to the Henry Hudson Bridge, and shove them outside the wall.

He did the right thing! He could have made Alex go first! Everybody else would have answered correctly, and Alex would be facing

exile alone. Why did Drayden have to be the hero? Maybe he forced it, went too far. Tempted fate. Mathematically, he always had a fifty-fifty chance of guessing wrong. The powers of the universe had no obligation to look after him, making sure things were fair. Life was unfair.

Drayden recalled his father once more, and how he had proven to be correct about everything. He'd never see Dad again. Wesley had declared with certainty they would reunite in the Palace when Drayden passed the Initiation. He'd never see his brother again either. The guilt Wes would feel for encouraging Drayden to enter would probably push him over the edge. But he'd be alive. Drayden and the other pledges would not.

At least he would die with dignity. His mother surely beamed with pride over his decision to absorb all the risk himself to spare Alex's life. Even though it resulted in failure, it was an incredibly brave and virtuous act, especially for a kid who started the Initiation afraid of his own shadow.

Now he could shed that blanket of fear, even outside the wall. Why must the strength he discovered within himself vanish because the Initiation ended? He would still protect Catrice, and keep everyone alive as long as possible outside. When the time finally came to die, perhaps he would get to see Mom and Tim again, if Heaven indeed existed. The tears came and he didn't fight this time. He covered his face and sobbed quietly into his hands.

"Drayden," Catrice said, softly. Then she shouted, "Drayden!"

He wiped his tears, trying to compose himself. Their watery eyes met.

"Look at your hat!" she yelled.

"What?"

She pointed at him. "Your hat! Look at it!"

He hadn't even bothered to look. Once the gate dropped, the Initiation ended anyway. He pulled the hat off.

It was green.

Wait. What?

"My hat's green," he said. "My hat's green!"

Catrice scrambled to her feet. "There are no Guardians here."

Sidney sat up and wiped her eyes. "I don't understand. What's going on?"

Drayden stood. "Alex was the only one who answered wrong." There were his karma gods. Or his mom watching over him. Of course his hat was green. He'd been wearing a green hat his mother gave him since her exile. It was only fitting. "That means we're not exiled, because we were allowed one wrong answer, as long as it wasn't me." He cocked his head. "But that gate's blocking the tracks. Is it some sort of trick? Can we lift it?"

Charlie jumped down onto the tracks and sprinted to the gate. He squatted down, his muscular legs stretching his pants. He grunted, struggling to lift it. It didn't budge.

"Drayden!" Catrice yelled. She fanned her arm over the other tracks, the One Line.

"They don't go to Wall Street," Drayden said.

"We don't have to reach Wall Street," Catrice said. "They said we have to finish in the Palace, at *either* Wall Street or South Ferry, where the One Line goes. We were just shooting for Wall Street."

My God. She's right.

He'd set in his mind that they would arrive at the Wall Street station because it was the most direct. They had another option. Blocking the Two-Three Line tracks was a trick, a head fake. The clock even continued counting down: 00:42:24, 00:42:23...

"Holy shkat," Drayden said. He pulled his hat out of his backpack. "We gotta go! Now!"

The pledges jumped down onto the One Line tracks and broke into a full sprint. They dug out their flashlights as they bolted into the dark tunnel.

The constant pain in Drayden's ankle was wearing him down. He was surely doing permanent damage to it.

Up until this point, the tunnel housed four sets of tracks. Although separated by steel columns resembling walls, they created a wide space. Here, where the One Line branched off alone, the pledges ran in a much narrower tunnel. It was two tracks wide, separated by the same regularly-spaced columns. In some places an actual concrete wall separated the two sets of tracks, making the whole tunnel only one track wide. It was enclosed and claustrophobic.

"What's the next station?" Charlie yelled between heavy breaths.

"Uh, I don't know," Drayden said. He'd only memorized the stations to Wall Street, and now they ran on a track he hadn't studied. He dug out the map and shined his flashlight on it. "Cortlandt Street!" He stuffed the unfolded map back into his backpack, taking his eye off the tracks for a split second.

His foot caught a railroad tie. He was airborne.

Drayden crashed down, his right shoulder absorbing the brunt of the fall. His back and ankle screamed out in pain, like a railroad spike had impaled them. He cried out.

"Drayden!" Catrice shrieked.

He clutched his ankle, moaning, rolling around on the tracks in the darkness.

Catrice cradled his head in her hand. "What can I do?"

Sidney rushed over and knelt beside him.

What a flunk I am.

As if the Initiation weren't tough enough already. "Can someone get me a pain pill and the water?" Drayden mumbled through gritted teeth.

Catrice and Sidney both reached for his backpack at the same time. Sidney jerked it away, opened it, and pulled out the pills and the water.

He downed a pill. "Let's go," he grunted. His ankle throbbed, the pain coming in waves.

The girls hauled Drayden up. Two flashlights flitted around thirty yards ahead.

"Can you run?" Sidney asked, still out of breath.

"No, but I have to. We won't make it otherwise."

Each step felt like someone taking a ferocious swing at his ankle with an axe. More than once he nearly vomited from the pain.

Charlie and Alex's flashlights stopped moving up ahead. Drayden, Catrice, and Sidney caught up to them. Both boys were doubled over with their hands on their knees, panting.

"Sweet mother of Jesus," Charlie said. "How much farther is it?"

"Cortlandt is far, according to the map," Drayden said, struggling to catch his own breath. "We have to go."

Alex crossed his arms. "I don't understand what the rush is. Clock said we had forty minutes left. Sounds like plenty of time to me."

"There are three stations left," Drayden said. "Cortlandt, Rector, and South Ferry. They're all far apart. At least twenty minutes of travel time, even running. That only leaves twenty minutes for three challenges. I think we have to assume that last one is gonna be a doozy."

Charlie nodded down the tracks. "Let's go, then."

Drayden pushed forward through the exhaustion. Screw the Bureau. He'd beaten them every time so far, even their absurd red-and-green-hats problem. He endured their pretend exile when they blocked the Two-Three Line tracks. So close to winning, he wasn't about to stop.

What would the upcoming challenges be like? Bravery challenges the rest of the way, he bet. Now he knew how cruel and unmerciful the Bureau could be. The challenges might have immediately fatal consequences, not just exile, on the line.

Charlie and Alex's pace slowed, and the whole group bunched up, with Drayden in the back. Charlie and Alex conversed, gestured, and glanced back at Drayden.

While Drayden no longer feared Alex, that didn't preclude him from doing something stupid or dangerous. Alex was crazy, evil, and dumb. He probably craved revenge for the beatdown Drayden gave him. Luckily, in another forty minutes, he would never see Alex again. No way they'd be put in the same zone.

Charlie and Alex stopped without warning. Catrice and Sidney slammed into them. Drayden stopped just in time, but ignited a raw jolt of pain in his ankle.

"What the hell, chotch?" Drayden asked. "Why'd you stop?"

Charlie held his finger up to his lips. "Listen."

A mechanical sound up ahead, like machinery, broke the silence.

Sidney grimaced. "Sounds like grinding metal."

Catrice wrapped her arms around herself as if she were cold. Charlie shined his flashlight ahead, and thirty yards down, the tracks ended. A steel wall blocked them.

"Let's do this," Drayden said, as Tim would've.

They jogged down to the wall and found a staircase up to the platform on the right. Charlie climbed up first, followed by the others, with Drayden in the back. The mechanical sounds blared. Grating metal. A breeze in the air created a sensation of movement.

As Drayden climbed the stairs, his eye caught a glimpse of gleaming metal through a crack in the wall.

Charlie reached the top and stopped. He stepped back and his jaw dropped. "You have *got* to be kidding me."

Despite Drayden's recent decision to act without fear the rest of the way, he couldn't fight his body's natural defense mechanisms. His

face grew hot and his heart raced. When the Bureau designed this challenge, he bet they named it "The Swinging Blades."

At the Cortlandt Street station, the Bureau had created a tall, narrow room. They'd covered up the tracks, removed the supporting pillars, and raised the ceiling to forty feet or so.

A lengthy steel cylinder, like the axle of a bus, only far longer, ran the length of the soaring ceiling, parallel with the direction of the tracks. Scores of thick steel rods hung down from the axle all the way from front to back. Cruel looking spikes of all sizes emblazoned the rods down their lengths. Some rods reached the floor, while others ended at waist level. It made even the shortest ones thirty feet long. An enormous blade tipped each one at its end, like an upside-down grim reaper's sickle, if he were a giant.

All the blades varied in size and shape, with some molded like the blade of a knife, and others more like an axe. Some sported clean edges and some were serrated, but all blades were sharp on both sides. They looked menacing.

They all swung back and forth at different times and varying speeds, like pendulums. For nearly thirty yards in front of them, this hellzone of heavy blades swung violently, like a malignant playground swing set, creating a battlefield of glistening steel, whirring wind, and the sound of shrieking metal.

The Bureau had narrowed the soaring chamber that housed this monstrosity. When the blades reached the peak of their swing, they just grazed the walls. Those walls were lined with metal spikes that jutted out several feet, and razor-covered barbed wire.

The pledges stood in silence, mesmerized by the powerful blades, hypnotized by their rhythmic repetition. Catrice wrapped her arm around Drayden's.

The simple gesture snapped Drayden out of his trance. He needed to get Catrice through. The Bureau had constructed a challenge, not an execution chamber. He could defeat it. If they failed

attempting it, death would be swift and brutal. Not attempting it would mean exile.

Drayden surveyed the area in front of the blades, yet found no table or note. This challenge was obvious: Reach the other side of the platform by navigating through the gauntlet of swinging blades.

He imagined the Watchers studying them right now, recording their reactions to the horrific scene. He looked up to where he figured the cameras were hidden. "See the blade, but don't be swayed, right? How about that?" He shook his head. "Let's do this."

Drayden jogged down the platform and stopped before the path of the first blade. He inspected it.

As it whizzed by, the wind it generated blew dust in his eyes and whipped his shirt into a flutter. The powerful blade itself stretched five feet long and two feet tall at its widest point. Just standing near it evoked terror. Forget killing a person. One of those blades could slice a bus in half. It roared back down in the other direction.

A clock indicated the time remaining: *00:35:08, 00:35:07...*

"How are we supposed to get across?" Charlie asked, perplexed.

Drayden strutted the width of the platform. He eyeballed all the swinging blades down the station, searching for any sign of a way through.

"Catrice!" he shouted. "Can you join me?"

She hurried over.

He tugged on his left ear. "This problem has a solution, just like the brainteasers. There's a way to do this. I don't know how yet. We need to look for clues. You see those spikes on the walls and the barbed wire? I think that's so we can't scoot along the wall. We need to understand this. Watch the blades. It seems like a chaotic random mess, but it probably isn't. There has to be some pattern, something we can exploit."

"Got it," Catrice said. She hustled back to the beginning of the station to view the blades from afar.

Standing in front of the blades peering through the whole gauntlet, it looked like twenty or so equally-spaced blades in a row. Drayden scurried over to the far-left wall of the station. He viewed the series of blades from a diagonal angle, searching for anything unusual. Then he found it.

A space. A gap, after the first three blades. Not deep, about four feet. It provided enough room to stand and avoid getting sliced by the blades on either side.

"Catrice! I got something!"

She held up her index finger at him. She knelt, holding her hands on both sides of her face to frame the view in front of her. She ran over, grinning. "Me too! It's not random. There's a pattern. I studied the first ten blades. They move the same way every time, and they move in bunches. If we can nail the pattern, the timing, we can figure out when to go."

"Nicely done. If it repeats, we can form a plan. Look at this!" Drayden took her hand and led her to the far wall. "You see that?" He pointed. "There's a space to stand, a gap, behind the third blade. We only have to get the timing on the first three, decide exactly when to go, and we can stop there. If we had to memorize the timing on every blade before we started...that would be impossible. We'd screw up at some point."

"What do we do after the first three?"

"Hopefully the rest of the blades are sectioned off too," Drayden said. "We'll have to take this sideways angle each time in those gaps to see where the next gap is. Then lock down the timing on that section. But..." He rubbed his chin.

"What is it?" Catrice asked.

"The safest lane is down the middle, right? The tunnel's narrow. If we stand five across, the people on the ends have a lot less time to get through because they have to go last after the blade passes

them, and it will reach them first on the way back down. We should probably split up into groups."

"Fine, but I'm going with you."

He nodded, touching her cheek. "We need to hurry. Let's fill everyone in." He and Catrice rejoined the other pledges in the center of the platform.

Drayden explained about the gaps and the blade patterns. "I think we can only be two or three people wide, max. This is how it's going to work. I'll go in the middle, with Catrice and Sidney by my side." If he could have two people beside him, choosing Catrice and Sidney was an obvious decision. "We'll pass the first section and stop in the gap." He addressed Charlie directly. "Then I'll turn back and tell you guys exactly when to go. We'll keep going that way, through each section, assuming there *are* additional sections."

Alex shook his head. "Fat chance, wetchop. If we don't make it through, it gives you a better shot of being chosen for the Palace. You'd only have to beat out two people instead of four. I don't think so. We're all going in a group."

"No we're not," Drayden said, getting in Alex's face. "If we do it this way, we'll all make it. If we go five across, we might all die. Alex, I'm not going to shaft you and Charlie. At this point, we're all in this together. We need to worry about finishing the Initiation at all, not about who's getting picked for the Palace. And we need Charlie, at least, to survive the next two challenges. I'll tell you exactly when to go, as if you were beside me."

"It's cool, Alex," Charlie said. "We'll make it. You think one of those blades could cut you? Who's tougher than you, bro? Blade'd probably bounce right off."

Alex sulked. "Fine."

"What about our backpacks?" Sidney asked. "Won't they get in the way?"

She made a valid point. Fractions of seconds and inches mattered. If a blade caught your backpack, it would knock you over, and then you were screwed. "I don't know," he said. "We could leave them. There's only thirty-five minutes left in the Initiation. Besides the flashlights, and I guess the pain pills, we don't need this stuff anymore."

Catrice pulled a piece of paper and a pencil out of hers and handed it to Drayden. "Can you put these in your pocket? In case we need it for a brainteaser." She rubbed her hands on her leggings. "No pockets."

Drayden stuffed them in his pockets, along with his last pill.

Charlie waved his mechanical pencil in the air, a big grin on his face. "I'm taking this baby. Could probably trade it for a few bucks. Or an egg."

Alex flicked his ear. "The lady said we wouldn't get to keep it, dummy."

"Knock it off, you guys," Drayden said. "Everyone have some water and get your flashlight. Charlie, Alex, stuff your pain pills and some antiseptic wipes in your pockets for everybody to share."

Drayden chugged his water and studied the path of the first blades.

In terms of timing, the first three swung closely together, passing one right after another, about a second apart. The first one passed at knee level; the second passed at waist level, about a foot beyond it; the third passed at ankle level, another foot beyond that.

A foot between their trajectories wasn't enough space to stand between them without risking death. They needed to make it across in one shot. When the third finally cleared center, the first was beginning its descent back down. They would have to bolt as the third blade approached the center, but they must abruptly stop in the gap to avoid plowing into the following section of blades.

Definitely doable, though executing it with the gruesome conse-quence of failing on the line made it terrifying.

Catrice stood on Drayden's right and Sidney on his left.

"I'm going to count the blades out loud as they cross center," he said. "I'll say 'one, two, three,' so we can all feel the timing. I'll say 'three' as blade three crosses center up to the right, and we go right after that. Run as fast as you can, but you have to stop in the gap after the three blades. I'll yell out 'stop' when we get there as a reminder. We probably have a second or two to reach it. Don't think about the blades. Don't look at them. Just focus on the gap. Everyone clear?"

"Yup," Sidney said.

Catrice nodded, though she was shaking. "Maybe...maybe we should let the blades pass a few times, to get the rhythm."

"Good idea." Drayden hoped his ankle held up and didn't roll in the dash across. He snagged Catrice's hand. She squeezed it tight.

Charlie clapped a few times. "C'mon, guys. You got this."

The blades flew by to the right—one, two, three, screaming through the air. They rocketed back down to the left—one, two, three. The air swirled all around them, the rods screeching on the axle. Back over to the right once more.

Drayden locked his eyes on the third blade. "Next cycle we're going. Get ready," he said. "Ready..."

Blade one passed. "One!" Then two. "Two!" Then three.

"Three! Go!"

He bounded across, clutching Catrice's hand. "Stop!" he screamed.

They stopped just as the blade in the upcoming section whizzed by in front of them.

Drayden exhaled the breath he didn't know he had been holding. His ankle pulsed with his fluttering heartbeat.

"We made it," Catrice squeaked, cradling her cheeks in her hands.

Being inside the blade maze amplified the noise of the grinding metal and swooshing blades. The powerful winds rippled their clothes. The gap was about three or four feet deep, and stretched across the whole station widthwise, like a narrow aisle in the FDC.

"Hey, chotch!" Alex shouted from behind. "Remember us?"

Drayden whipped around. Plenty of space existed to move right or left. "You guys step to the sides a bit so they don't run into you," he said to Catrice and Sidney. "Get ready!" he yelled to Charlie and Alex. "I'll count for you guys. You go after three, right after the third blade crosses the center."

Charlie gave him a thumbs-up. He and Alex crouched as if they were about to start a race.

Remember, it's the reverse from this side, Drayden thought. He focused on the third blade, now the closest one.

"Ready...one...two...three! Go!" he shouted, just as the third blade zipped past.

They darted across. Too hastily. Alex tried to stop in the gap, only to find he couldn't fight his momentum. He teetered forward, in the path of the next blade.

Drayden grabbed him by the neckline of his shirt and yanked him back.

The blade zoomed past Alex's stomach, missing it by inches. Silent but panting, his wild eyes bulged.

"You're welcome," Drayden said.

Catrice and Sidney returned to the center. Drayden carefully hurried over to the left side to view the upcoming blades from the sideways angle. As he'd suspected, the remaining blades were grouped into sections, with gaps between them. This challenge was about to intensify, though.

Five blades flew in the subsequent section, followed by another gap in which to stand. Three swung in the same direction, one right after another, like in the first section they cleared. The last two swung in the other direction, one following the other. They flew at various heights, from ankle level up to waist.

Drayden pulled off his hat and ran his hands through his hair. Sweat formed around the edges. No clear path existed through at any given time. While one, two, and three peaked, four and five crossed center. How would they pass through?

"Catrice!"

She tiptoed over, her hair blowing wildly in the blustery wind. Charlie followed her.

Drayden wasn't sure why Charlie came along, but perhaps he could figure it out. Charlie was gifted at all things physical.

"Hey," Drayden said, "can you guys check out this next section of blades? The first three blades are like the section we just finished. The Bureau added two more blades, basically blocking our path through. At no time is there a clear path, it's always blocked. When those last two clear, the first three get in the way."

Both studied the blades. Charlie knelt and dropped his head until his cheek touched the floor. "Can we slide underneath?"

"Great thinking, Charlie," Drayden said. "I believe the Bureau thought of that though. That third blade grazes the floor, and the last one is uncomfortably low."

Catrice picked at her fingernails. "I see a way, but..."

Drayden's eyes widened. "But what?"

She exhaled. "We need to pause in the middle. In the path of blade three." She pointed at the blades as she spoke. "We let one, two, and three pass up to the right. Then we run out into blade three's path and wait until blade four and five have crossed to the right. Blade five is actually ahead of blade four, so we have to wait

for them both to pass. We go before blade three slices us coming back down. It'll be close." She cringed.

Oh God.

Charlie stood. "Jeez."

Drayden blew out a long, slow breath. "Well done, Catrice. Let's fill in Sid and Alex." He walked back to the center of the chamber in the aisle, with Catrice and Charlie in tow, to where Alex and Sidney were chatting.

Was Alex...smiling?

"So yeah," Alex said to Sidney, "I'd like to toss my brother Chad right into those blades."

Sidney looked shocked. "That's nuts."

"Listen up," Drayden said, and explained the strategy to them. "Don't look up at that third blade. You don't want to freeze watching it coming toward you. We'll only have a fraction of a second to clear it. We'll go in groups again. Catrice, Sid, let's get ready."

Drayden took Catrice's hand, interlocking her fingers with his.

"On my mark," he said. "I'll count off the first three blades again, and we go after I say 'three.' I'm going to yell 'stop' when we pause, and 'go' when we start again. Ready..."

The first blade, a four-foot-long smooth blade curved like a sickle, flew by at waist level to the right.

"One!" The second blade blew by. "Two!" The third blade reached the center heading right.

"Three! Go!"

They ran a few steps.

"Stop!"

Sidney screamed. She turned and jumped back to the gap where Charlie and Alex waited.

"Sid!" Drayden yelled. He released Catrice's hand and stepped back, confused. He didn't know what to do.

He was standing right in the path of blade two, now rocketing back down toward him.

Drayden looked up at it. He froze.

It would slice him in half in a microsecond. Blade one was ahead of it, just crossing center, blocking his path back.

"Drayden!" Catrice shrieked.

He dove back toward the gap, as low as he could, attempting to slide beneath blade one.

It sliced the back of his shirt as he tumbled out. Charlie caught him before he rolled into the previous set of blades.

Drayden whipped his head back. "Catrice!"

She'd waited for blades five and four to cross and dashed across a millisecond before blade three would have sliced her. Exactly as planned.

"I'm across!" Catrice shouted, safely in the next gap.

Drayden's heart pounded in his ears. *Holy shkat.* Another fraction of a second or an inch higher, and he'd be in two pieces. He shuddered.

Sidney pulled him up and hugged him. "I'm sorry! Oh my God, I'm so sorry. I don't know what happened. I panicked."

"I'm fine." Drayden wasn't though, he was still shaking. He took a slow breath to regain his composure. "You ready to try again?"

"Yeah," she whimpered.

He grabbed Sidney's hand and they positioned themselves in the center again. Drayden monitored blade three.

It screeched by to the right, up to its peak, and then blew again to the left.

"Ready...one...two..."

Blade three crossed center heading right.

"Three! Go!"

Hand in hand, they sprinted into its path after it shot past, up to the right.

"Stop!"

Blade five screamed by heading right, blade four closely behind it.

Drayden avoided looking at blade three, but unfortunately his peripheral vision was strong enough. It screamed toward them from the right. "Go!"

He launched, yanking Sidney. The wind from the third blade rippled his pants as it shrieked left behind them. They made it.

Drayden closed his eyes, breathing heavy. He bent over.

"I'm sorry, Catrice," Sidney said. "I screwed up and we left you all alone. I panicked. I just...I forgot what to do."

Catrice touched Sidney's shoulder. "Don't worry. That was scary. But we all made it."

"Great job, by the way," Sidney said. "You did it perfectly."

"Oh, hey!" Alex yelled. "I'm sorry to interrupt social hour over there. Can we get a little help?"

"Maybe we *should* leave them behind," Drayden grumbled under his breath. "You make it such a pleasure, Alex!" he shouted back.

Catrice and Sidney stepped to the sides to allow room for Charlie and Alex to land.

"You guys know what to do?" Drayden asked. "Pause right in the path of the third blade, and I'll yell when to continue."

Charlie gave him a thumbs-up. Alex kept his head down.

Drayden zeroed in on the third blade, which was the key. The first three blades were about to begin their descent.

"Ready...one...two...three, go!" he yelled as the third blade zoomed by to the left, from this side.

They bounded across.

"Stop!" he shouted when they reached the path of blade three.

They paused in blade three's lane. Alex locked his eyes on it, cowering. His face contorted in terror as it reached its peak and began its descent.

The fifth blade passed, and the fourth was just zipping by.

"Go now!" Drayden screamed.

Alex was frozen. Charlie jumped forward. He reached back and gripped Alex by the arm, yanking him along.

For a moment, Drayden was sure Alex would be cut in half, but he made it in one piece.

Charlie grasped Alex by the front of his shirt and pulled him close. "Alex, focus, goddammit! You almost died. Don't look at the blades!" Charlie released him, shaking his head.

Alex's pale lips quivered, his vacant eyes staring into space.

Charlie peered over his shoulder at his calves. "I felt that blade. That was about as fun as dinner over at Alex's house."

They were running out of time. This was taking way too long. Drayden turned to stone at the sight of the looming next section. The gap in which they stood offered the first clear view of it, unobstructed by the blades that preceded it. And it was intimidating.

The others fell silent.

Sidney stared in shock. "Seriously?"

"Is it just me, or does that look like a monster?" Charlie asked.

Drayden thought it did. He didn't need to view it from the left side of the station to find the next gap. This was the last section and it represented the grand finale of the blades. It contained ten blades, all various heights and blade types. Some were downright medieval.

But it was the way they moved, like a python would slither. Effectively, each blade swung one after another, creating the effect of a wave. So while blade five was at its peak, blade six tumbled down, while blade four approached its peak. If it wasn't designed to kill them, one might find it quite elegant.

"It's a wave pattern," Drayden said. "Look. There's always one peak, and one trough, and it moves down the line and starts again."

"How do we get through it?" Charlie asked.

Drayden studied the movement. While a simple pattern to understand, visualizing how to traverse it baffled him. "Catrice?"

She focused on it, her expression revealing intense mental gymnastics. She squinted. "We need to move where the wave is at its crest or trough, and pause where it crosses center, then move again. I think."

Catrice seemed much less scared when she was busy solving a problem, Drayden noted. He visualized her suggestion. Start when the first blade crosses to the right. The few that follow will still be near their peak on the right. They could pass some of those blades, but eventually one would be coming down too close to continue. They would have to stop, let it cross, and then jet to avoid being filleted by the one in whose path they waited. This would require some thought, some adjustment, on the fly. It differed from the previous sections, in which they could strategize in advance.

"Yeah, that's it," Drayden said. "We have to go in groups again. Charlie, I'll talk you guys through it after we're through. Okay?"

Charlie's face looked pained, and he pinched his nose. "I guess."

Drayden felt like Charlie looked. His necked tensed contemplating this final section. Yet the clock was ticking and they needed to move. "Catrice, Sid, let's get ready."

They lined up, with Drayden in the middle. "Sid, stay close, right on me. I'll yell out 'stop,' but when we do that, let the blade in front cross and then rocket immediately. Don't look at the blade approaching us. It'll be very close. Just look straight ahead."

"I got it." Sidney closed her eyes and said a quick prayer.

Drayden memorized the pattern. If he hesitated, if he was indecisive in there, they would die. This section required split-second decisions. The stops and starts simply couldn't be determined at the outset. Ten blades were a lot to clear.

"We're going when blade one crosses going right," Drayden said. "One more cycle. Get ready."

Drayden followed blade one, his eyes glued to it. It was a shiny curved blade, five feet long, serrated on the top edge, smooth on the bottom. It blew by to the right with a swoosh. *Wait...what was that?* A tiny red mark dotted the blade on the side. *Was it an imperfection of some sort? No, it was too square, too exact.* As the fearsome blade screamed by to the left, Drayden recognized it. The Bureau insignia.

He clenched his jaw. "Ready..."

Blade one crested on the left, and began its drop. It crossed the center.

"Go!" he yelled.

They took five hurried steps out. Drayden fixed his wide eyes up to the right, at the airborne blades. They passed blades one through three, but blade four plummeted down toward the center. They wouldn't make it.

"Stop!" he yelled, freezing in blade three's path.

Ignoring his own instructions, he glanced up at blade three, rapidly approaching from the right. Blade four crossed the center to the left in front of them.

"Go now!" he screamed.

They bolted, barely making it before blade three impaled them. They took five additional steps. Drayden peered up to the left now, observing the blades at their crest. They passed blades four, five, and six, but blade seven rapidly neared center.

"Stop!" he yelled.

He maintained his gaze straight ahead this time, avoiding the sight of the plummeting blade six. Blade seven screamed by in front to the right.

"Go!"

They passed blades seven, eight, and nine peaking on the right. Blade ten was too close to risk.

"Stop!"

One more to go, he thought.

Sidney screamed. She gawked past him to the right at the axe-like blade nine shrieking toward them.

Blade ten flew by to the left.

"Go!" Drayden yelled, pulling Catrice by the hand.

They crossed the finish.

"We made it!" Sidney cried out.

Catrice doubled over, holding her stomach.

"Yeah!" Drayden screamed. He jumped up and down. "Woohoo!" He'd survived the swinging blades.

What else you got, Bureau? It's going to take more than that.

Thank God he'd never have to do that again. Now he needed to guide the guys through.

"Hey, Charlie!" Drayden yelled, over the grinding metal and swooshing blades. "You guys ready?"

Charlie raised both hands in the air, like he didn't understand. He cupped his hand around his ear.

"I said, are you guys ready!" Drayden screamed at the top of his lungs.

Charlie mouthed something inaudible back.

Oh no.

"They can't hear me," Drayden said. "We're too far away. What should we do?"

"They saw us do it," Sidney said. "Maybe they'll copy us."

Charlie and Alex stood beside each other. Charlie stretched, as if warming up to play football. He clapped his hands, and rubbed them together.

Catrice approached the blades. "Charlie! Can you hear me?" she shrieked.

He didn't respond.

She scrunched her face up, and pressed her lips together. "We have to rescue Charlie. We have to do something."

Drayden studied Catrice, with her worried expression and palpable concern. Did she feel she needed to repay Charlie for saving her life, or was it something more?

Stop being so petty. Drayden shrugged it off and refocused his attention on Charlie and Alex. "My God, are they starting?"

The first blade flew by to their right. Charlie and Alex stepped out three feet, and stopped, in the path of blade one.

What were they doing? They could have made it much further.

Charlie's eyes flashed right, then left. He grabbed Alex and jerked him backward, jumping out of the blades, back to the start. He raised his hands up in the air, as if he were asking a question.

Drayden positioned himself in the center, in front of blade ten, following it closely.

"What are you doing?" Sidney asked. "Are you crazy? We were lucky enough to survive ourselves. You want to push your luck? For Alex?"

"I have to do this," Drayden said. "We can't leave them." Technically, they *could* leave them behind. If Charlie and Alex stayed there, they would be exiled, which would increase the other pledges' chances of being chosen for the Bureau and moving to the Palace. Charlie and Alex were not likely contenders for that Palace spot. Two challenges remained, as well. Though Alex would be useless, they would almost certainly need Charlie.

Yet those weren't the only reasons Drayden couldn't leave them. He needed to save them because it was the right thing to do. It was what Mom would want him to do. They shouldn't be exiled if he could do something to stop it.

"Thank you, Drayden," Catrice said. She pulled him into an embrace. "Please be careful."

When she let go, Sidney took her turn to hug him. "You're so brave, Dray. Good luck."

Their words felt so good. He needed that.

Focus on blade ten. It's the same thing, just in reverse this time.

Up to the right, crossing center, up to the left, coming back down, and crossing the center.

Drayden started. Five steps, and stopped.

Blade seven whizzed by right.

He lunged, four steps, and stopped.

Blade four blew by left.

He sprinted and dove, barely clearing blade one.

Charlie caught him before he hit the ground.

He should have waited for blade one to pass. That was stupid. Reckless. Although his confidence in himself was growing, he shouldn't become cocky.

Charlie pulled Drayden into a bear hug. "Oh man, thank you. We were screwed. I can't believe you came back through that."

Alex turned away.

"Still going to make jokes about leaving you behind, Alex?" Drayden asked. "You ungrateful flunk. You've complained about me leaving you behind so many times that when I save your butt, you don't even appreciate it. You think I owe it to you. I could never do enough. You believe the whole world owes you. What a joke."

"I...I don't...nobody owes me anything," Alex said.

Charlie slapped himself in the face a few times. "I'm ready now."

Drayden knew he shouldn't be cocky, but he owned this blade challenge. He'd done it twice now. He knew how fast to go, and when to pause. He'd even improvised on the trip back, diving when he should have stopped, and *still* survived.

"Follow my lead, Charlie. We'll probably stop three times. When we stop, and the blade in front of us crosses, we have to sprint. Clear?"

"Clearer than Catrice's eyes," he replied. He play-punched Drayden in the shoulder. "It's all good, bud. I know you like her.

I'll stay out of your way. She likes you and not me, anyway." He chuckled.

Drayden eyed the ten deadly blades before them with Catrice waiting at the end, wondering if Charlie had only said that because he needed Drayden's help. Still, it was pretty cool of him.

"Thanks."

Alex stood on the other side of Charlie, probably so Charlie could pull him along. When blade one swung down to the right, they started. They paused at blade four, moved again, paused at blade seven, went again, paused at blade ten, and ran through the finish.

Catrice hugged Charlie after he passed the final blade.

"No time to celebrate," Drayden said. "We have to go. Now."

He sprinted down the platform. The Watchers must be freaking out at their success. He held his chin up as he ran. "That all you got?" he screamed.

Drayden jumped down onto the tracks with the others following him.

CHAPTER 22

Everyone's footsteps and heavy breaths echoed throughout the bleak, narrow tunnel.

Drayden's body was a wreck. He'd never been injured like this before, because he'd always been so cautious.

His ankle wobbled in a mush of tendons and ligaments, his back and head had deep puncture wounds, his arms and legs festered with open rat bites. His whole body ached. For the first time, exhaustion overcame him. He'd never experienced such fatigue. The urge to stop and lie down on the tracks, just for a moment, overwhelmed him.

Although his lungs felt inflamed from the running, they needed to maintain this pace. The clock indicated thirty-five minutes remaining when they *began* the last challenge. How long had it taken to cross the blades? They must have burned ten minutes, perhaps more.

They should reach the next station, Rector Street, in a few minutes. He'd studied the subway map before he'd abandoned it with his backpack. Following Rector Street was the final station— South Ferry. They had approximately twenty minutes to complete the upcoming challenge, the lengthy run to South Ferry, and whatever final challenge waited there. He tried to maintain a positive

attitude, but that was going to be damn near impossible. The run from Rector to South Ferry was probably eight to ten minutes alone. For just once, he wished his mind would stop doing calculations. They weren't quitting, even if the math painted a daunting picture.

What in the world was left for them to face? Drayden recalled his conversation with Mr. Kale, joking about how he'd have to slay a lion. He was kidding then. It wasn't so far-fetched anymore.

He waxed nostalgic, calling to mind Mr. Kale. Drayden had been so naive listening to both him and Wes about entering the Initiation. They had no clue what it entailed. How could they? They were only guilty of believing in him. If they only knew. The rock wall, the bomb, the underground pool, the swinging blades—the Bureau was indeed trying to kill them.

Like they had killed his mother, and that's what this was truly about. Even if Mr. Kale and Wes had known the truth about the Initiation, or Drayden himself had, it didn't matter. The Bureau murdered his mother. Now he needed to save what family he had left. That desire powered him through the burning lungs, and the legs suffused with lactic acid, which was like running with cinderblocks on his feet. Only crossing the finish line would suffice when he was so close to the end.

Mr. Kale was right about bravery. While often dormant, it existed inside everyone. Now that he'd tasted it, there was no going back. Drayden could finally be free of the burden he'd carried since early childhood, when bigger kids bullied him for being skinny or too smart. His and Tim's early lives had followed the same pattern, with the bullying. That formed the foundation of their friendship too. Drayden never figured out the truth about bravery, while Tim had. Even though it cost Tim his life, he was positive Tim wouldn't change a thing about the way he'd lived it.

Drayden pictured Tim and his mom looking down on him now, their arms around each other, both cheering for him. His

eyes watered. That he still advanced in the Initiation, and Tim did not, wasn't fair. He was alive, and Tim was dead. He wasn't sure he could ever forgive himself or get over Tim's death. It would haunt him forever.

Drayden should have let Tim handle the bomb. Defusing a bomb, or other physical acts of bravery, were Tim's strengths, not his. Instead of struggling to do everything himself to prove he could, he should take advantage of everyone's abilities. Bravery had nothing to do with it. In fact, it was intelligence, just a different type. It was common sense, street smarts, but intelligence nonetheless.

If the upcoming challenge required athleticism and physical skill, Sidney and Charlie should shoulder the burden. That provided the highest probability of success. Attempting to lead it himself, to prove his courage to himself and everyone else, would be stupid. The bravery challenges were intelligence challenges as well, as it turned out. It wasn't enough to simply be brave. Drayden needed to be brave *and* smart. This just happened to be what the Initiation was all about.

"How much farther?" Charlie yelled.

"Almost there I think," Drayden said. Though Rector was far, they'd been running for a while.

"If the Bureau wants to kill us," Charlie said, "for the next challenge they should just have us run around the subway station a few times. My legs feel like they're made out of lettuce."

"Only two stations left!" Drayden shouted. "We go in hard. No hesitating. No fear."

"Why don't you tell that to my boiled noodle legs?" Charlie said.

Drayden wanted everybody laser-focused for these last two challenges. "I'm serious, Charlie! We need you."

"Booyah, Dray-man," Charlie said.

"Charlie!" Alex shouted.

Drayden shook his head. Charlie was actually becoming his friend. "What's the matter, Alex? Charlie's not allowed to talk to me? Afraid I'm gonna steal your best friend?"

Alex eyed him for a moment, his face twitching. He carried on in silence.

"I'm with you, Dray," Sidney said.

Drayden pumped his fist at her.

The tracks curved gently to the left. A faint glow emerged ahead. That was it. Rector Street.

Drayden stopped at the staircase to the platform and faced the other pledges. "Second-to-last challenge. Follow my lead. Whatever's up there, we'll get through it. Our biggest challenge right now is time."

A clock hung in the Rector Street station. Time remaining: *00:18:47, 00:18:46...*

But it was dark, unlit. Like a station with no challenge. The dim light was nothing more than sunlight trickling down the staircases to the street above.

The pledges stopped on the platform to scan the station.

"Nothing here," Sidney said.

"Hey, thanks Bureau!" Charlie shouted.

Ancient plastic bottles and other garbage littered the platform floor. A fine layer of dust coated everything.

Drayden remained suspicious. They hadn't passed an empty station in hours, though it did make sense by his calculations. Even with a break here, it was going to be tight. Still, this gave them new life. They had a chance now. If there had been a challenge here, they were doomed.

Catrice checked the clock. "Should we just go?"

Drayden bit down on his lip, his nerves frayed. "Yeah. They said stations that were dark had no challenges. We wouldn't have enough time if there was one. Let's hurry." He led the pledges in a jog down the platform.

Already thinking about the final challenge, Drayden couldn't help but notice their surroundings in the station were changing a bit.

"Is it just me or is it getting cleaner in here?" Sidney asked from behind.

"Thanks again, Bureau!" Charlie called out. "Nice of you to tidy up!"

It *had* gotten cleaner. Gone was the garbage and dust. The tracks were now blocked off too, preventing them from jumping down there until the end of the platform, just thirty feet away. Maybe the pledges were being paranoid, and really, who could blame them? There obviously was no challenge here and they still needed to race to face the final one.

A hissing sound permeated the air.

Drayden stopped and extended his arms for the others to do the same. Everyone bunched up around him.

"Um, what is that?" Sidney asked.

Alex whacked Charlie's arm. "Dude, you touch something?"

White gas billowed into the station from both walls and the ceiling. It formed a cloud, swirling in intricate vortices through the air.

"That can't be good!" Alex yelled.

"Run!" Drayden screamed.

"Hold your breath!" Charlie shouted. "It might have poison in it."

Drayden sucked in a huge breath and held it. He broke into a full sprint to the platform's end.

His eyes burned and watered. The gas made his skin tingle.

Don't take a breath!

He'd nearly reached the end of the platform.

Luckily, the gas remained on the platform or rose to the ceiling, so it wasn't spreading down to the tracks. Someone behind Drayden started coughing, gasping for air.

He turned back before jumping down onto the tracks.

Catrice had taken a breath and stopped. She was doubled over, choking, struggling for air.

Drayden's own oxygen ran low, and his watery eyes clouded his vision. Should he jump down into the tunnel, gulp a breath, and come back for Catrice? No time, she was suffering. He sprinted back for her.

She violently rubbed her bleary, bloodshot eyes. She sucked in hefty, audible breaths.

Drayden scooped her up by the legs, flopping her over his shoulder. He ran back toward the edge of the platform, his ankle throbbing with the extra weight. His lungs screamed for oxygen. Ten more feet. Dark spots dotted his field of vision. He leapt down onto the tracks, making sure to land on his right foot, and stumbled ten feet into the tunnel.

No gas here.

Drayden sucked in a deep breath as he collapsed to his knees with Catrice still on his shoulder. His vision darkened, so he dipped his head to increase the blood flow before he passed out. His eyes burned so intensely he could barely see. Rubbing them only made it worse.

Coughing, Catrice tumbled off his shoulder and fell onto her hands and knees. She gasped a few times and vomited.

The other pledges scattered. They wheezed, clawed at their eyes, blew their noses, and scratched their skin.

After a few seconds, Drayden regained full consciousness, his eyes still burning. He knelt beside Catrice, who was dry heaving. He

pulled her long golden hair behind her head and rubbed her back. Watching someone else puke usually made Drayden want to hurl himself, but he fought through it.

She recovered and leaned back with her eyes closed, sitting on her own feet. "I'm sorry," she squeaked. She wiped her mouth with her shirt. "Yuck. I'd kill for some water right now." She rotated her body so she faced Drayden. "Thank you. I want to hug you, but..." She pointed to her pukey mouth and managed a weak smile.

Drayden leaned forward, pulling her close. "I could use some water too. If we finish this, we can have all the water we want. Fifteen minutes. You think you can start moving again?"

"Yes." She cradled his cheeks in her hands, looking deep into his eyes. "Let's do this," she said, just like Tim would have.

CHAPTER 23

South Ferry was a hike.

Drayden led the pledges down the tunnel at a full sprint to the next, and final, station. Their only option was to run their hearts out and pray enough time remained. They sprinted, powering through the exhaustion and pain.

The Bureau had shown there was no limit to its depravity. There wasn't even a challenge in the previous station, yet they'd hit them with poison gas? It probably wouldn't have killed them, but it sure as hell wasn't pleasant. The Bureau kept changing the rules, which left a lot of questions heading into the Initiation's end. Namely, there was no guarantee they wouldn't renege on their promises of someone joining the Bureau, the others moving to better zones, bringing their families along. The modicum of respect he once had for the Bureau seemed so foolish now.

Drayden peeked back at Catrice and Sidney, who ran directly behind him.

Both were sweating and breathing heavy, their tousled hair in knots.

What was that movie about a horse the Bureau played in Madison Square Park last year? *The Black Stallion*. Sidney ran like the horse, with lengthy, elegant, coordinated strides. Catrice ran

like the old guy, the horse trainer. Drayden snortled. Sidney was so athletic; Catrice was not.

Both girls smiled back, blissfully unaware of his thoughts.

He pushed forward in the Initiation because of his mother, his family, and the deterioration in the Dorms. Yet it was for the girls too. That motivation hadn't existed even a day ago, and now it was just as powerful as the other reasons. The bond they shared, experiencing the struggle and terror of the Initiation together, would last a lifetime. Whether it would be a short one outside the walls, or an enduring one in the Palace remained to be seen.

Except...all three of them couldn't end up in the Palace. He'd tried not to think about it, focusing solely on surviving the Initiation, but it ate away at him beneath the surface like an infection.

The possibility of separation from Catrice in particular made Drayden's heart ache. Her attractiveness multiplied with each passing moment, and her looks had nothing to do with it. She was fascinating, an enigma, and totally genuine. She could outthink him. Concrete walls surrounded her, and when he cracked them, even more beauty revealed itself inside.

Sidney, by contrast, was an open book. She wore her emotions on her sleeve, which was not necessarily a bad thing. She always made you aware of exactly who you were getting. What if Drayden never saw either of them again? If placed in separate zones, they couldn't visit each other, or even correspond in any way. In fifteen minutes, he might never see them again. He'd be alone.

It was so puzzling that he liked them both, and they both liked him, yet they couldn't stand each other. Apparently, the transitive property in math didn't apply to feelings. Maybe it was the popular girl hating on the social outcast, just like in school. Or the smart girl not respecting the athlete. However, if it were competition for his affection, well...that was simply too outrageous to believe. Before yesterday, no girls had even noticed Drayden was alive. His sudden

desirability might have been nothing more than the circumstance of the Initiation. The pledges formed a limited group, confined in an intense setting. The only other boys present, Alex and Charlie, weren't exactly the all-star team of potential boyfriends.

In an alternate reality, where they all stayed together after the Initiation, the girls would probably revert to forgetting he existed. Drayden hadn't even kissed a girl yet, so he was hardly an expert on love, but it seemed so fleeting, so transitory. One moment it was there, and then it was gone, like with his parents. He reminisced about his best friend, who embodied the fragility and transience of love. For weeks at a time, Tim would fall in love with someone new every day. He'd *call* it love anyway, though a more objective observer would term it lust.

Realistically, as the finale neared, Drayden thought he'd earned a decent shot at a Palace spot, assuming they finished. He'd performed pretty well on the intellectual challenges. Though he was terrible on the first half of the bravery ones, he'd done much better on the last few. Catrice probably had a shot too, either with him, or instead of him, if only one made it. They'd both find a home in the Lab if they weren't picked for the Palace. Charlie and Sidney were both strong on the bravery challenges. They might have a shot at the Palace on that basis, though the Precinct was more likely. It was also Charlie's goal.

What would the Bureau do with Alex? He'd displayed weakness everywhere. He lacked both the intelligence for the Lab, and the bravery for the Precinct. Perhaps they would allow him to live in the Palace as a worker rather than joining the Bureau, which would be unprecedented as far as Drayden knew. Whatever they decided, Alex could never return to the Dorms. It would violate the Bureau's guidelines, plus Alex knew far too much about the Initiation.

Then it clicked.

The choice.

Owen Payne's option of quitting or continuing. Something about it had bugged Drayden ever since. The Bureau had shown no mercy throughout the Initiation, so why would they then? Because it wasn't a choice at all. It was just another test. They could never be allowed to quit and return to the Dorms. They knew way too much about the Initiation. It must have been just another challenge to see if they had the resolve to carry on. Thank God he had chosen to continue, because he bet a decision to quit most likely would have meant exile for everyone. Bullet dodged.

"Drayden?" Sidney yelled.

"Yeah?"

"What do you think will be waiting for us at South Ferry?"

He shined his flashlight at Sidney to see her. "No idea. Given it's the last challenge, I think we have to assume it's going to be bad."

He aimed it past her, at Alex and Charlie.

They were engaged in a heated discussion, though spoke too softly to hear.

Again?

"Hey, Charlie!" he called. "You know what kind of poison gas that was?"

Charlie turned his head toward Drayden, looked back at Alex, and didn't answer.

"Okay, then," Drayden said. "Good talk."

Screw them. He'd focus on this grand finale coming up. Whatever awaited, he wouldn't let it intimidate him. There wouldn't be much time. Based on the last few challenges, the Bureau would present something visually shocking, designed to petrify them. If a monster swam in a freezing pool covered in swinging blades, he needed to dive right in.

They'd been running steady for six or seven minutes, on tracks that gently curved left the whole way. It seemed like they'd run in a complete circle at this point. It couldn't be too much farther. The

tunnel narrowed to one track wide, with concrete walls on both sides, running noticeably downhill now.

The tracks rounded sharply to the left, obstructed by a steel wall. A staircase to the left led up to the platform. Everyone bent over, catching their breath.

Drayden was about to address the group, to pump them up for this challenge, but stopped. "Anyone else feel that?"

"Um, yes." Sidney fanned herself. "It just got real hot in here."

Indeed. The wall was radiating heat.

Drayden would not be defeated. Not now. Not after all they'd been through. He needed to finish this for Mom, for Tim. For Dad and Wes, and Catrice and Sidney. And himself.

He clenched his fists and thundered, "Don't be afraid of whatever's up there! We can beat it! We've beaten everything else so far. This is no different. You guys ready?"

The other pledges hooted and hollered, pumping their fists.

He hopped up the steps. When he emerged at the top, the oppressive heat knocked him backward into Catrice. It felt like being inside an oven.

"Holy shkatnuts," Charlie said. "It's so hot you could eat a chili pepper and cool down."

The scene, unusual even before the modifications, blew Drayden away. The station curved sharply right along its length, with only one platform. The Bureau had created a broad floor area by covering the tracks. They'd raised the ceiling throughout the station around thirty feet, and removed the supporting pillars. Unlike the other stations, dim orange, flickering light bathed the cavernous room. Why was it flickering? Was it a power problem? Drayden walked down the platform and froze.

The answer lay fifty yards away. A gap. A chasm. A void existed where the platform should be, like a section was removed. Past that, the platform continued. In that gap, smoke rose and sparks flew, violently strewn about the air by powerful winds. It emitted a red glow that illuminated the station.

"That looks like...Hell," Sidney said.

The scene became clearer as they neared the chasm and the temperature surged. A long table bearing a note sat before the chasm. After the chasm, the platform continued for forty or fifty feet. It ended at an enlarged open doorway cut into a white wall. A massive clock hung above the door. Time remaining: *00:06:49, 00:06:48...*

Drayden gulped. *That doorway must mark the finish line to the entire Initiation.*

The chasm, or gap, stretched about twenty feet across, and thirty feet wide. Monstrous rotating fans surrounded the gap on the sides, and from above. They blew high-pressured air in different directions, creating turbulent winds.

Before picking up the note, Drayden shuffled closer to the edge of the chasm. The hot winds rippled his clothing and the searing heat stung his face.

He inched closer and closer until the bottom came into view. He gasped.

The gap wasn't a gap at all. It was an abyss, dropping at least two-hundred feet. An epic fire raged at the bottom, the only reason the bottom was visible at all. Nasty looking spikes jutted upwards on the walls of the chasm. At platform level the walls were smooth, save for the fans built into them.

Drayden ran back to the table and snatched up the note, which was weighted down with a brick.

The others rushed to surround him.

Drayden read out loud. "*Not won is not done. Prove you can finish the job. You must cross through the door at the end of the platform to complete the Initiation. Good luck.*"

"That's all it says?" Sidney asked.

"Yeah." Drayden flipped the note over to make sure the Bureau hadn't written on the back.

The pledges walked up to the edge of the gorge.

Drayden searched for any kind of clue, his heart racing. Smoke and blustery wind watered his eyes.

A violent screeching, a visceral grinding of metal, erupted way behind them. It came from the station's entrance.

Drayden whipped his head around. "What was that?"

A grinding noise ensued and dust kicked up, as if something were moving.

"Lemme check it out," Charlie said. He sprinted back for the beginning of the platform. He touched the metal wall, and then pushed against it with both arms. His straining was visible from fifty yards away. "It's the wall!" he yelled. "It's the wall!" He raced back. "It's the wall. It's moving. Toward us!"

"Oh my God," Sidney said. "Drayden, what do we do? How do we get across?"

"Holy shkat." Drayden's adrenaline spiked. He ran up to the abyss. Could they jump it? No way, twenty feet across. Climb along the wall somehow? It was totally smooth. "Anyone see anything around? Any tools, a rope?"

Everyone scoured the area, but found nothing. Catrice stood frozen, catatonic even.

Drayden gripped her by the shoulders. "Catrice, I need you. Work with me. Help me think this through. How can we get across?"

She bit her nails. "I don't know."

"Can we form a human chain or something?" Drayden darted his eyes everywhere.

Catrice paced. She stopped and faced Drayden, her eyes wild. "Can we tie a rope with our clothes? Swing across somehow?"

Drayden examined the ceiling.

It was smooth, no exposed pipes or beams.

"Nowhere to hang it," he said. Sweat soaked through his shirt already.

Think, dammit!

He looked back at the wall.

It moved slowly, but at only forty yards away now, it demanded they solve this challenge immediately. A violent death, not exile, was the other alternative. Drayden checked the clock.

00:05:10, 00:05:09...

He couldn't believe it. They'd come this far, and to complete the Initiation they simply had to traverse a hole in the ground. He saw no way to do it. It was as if the Bureau intended on leaving them tools, and they forgot.

Or had they?

Drayden digested the whole scene again. The wind. Why was it there? To create a challenging walk across the chasm. There must be a way to walk across, and the wind existed to make it harder. How?

He ran over and picked up the note again. It was so...basic. This note served no purpose. On other obvious challenges, like the rock wall, the Bureau left no note. So why did they leave this one?

Drayden's eyes widened. One peculiarity had escaped him throughout the Initiation.

I know.

Because it was on a long table. The Bureau gave them the table to cross the chasm.

"Charlie!" Drayden yelled. "Give me a hand with this table."

Charlie ran over. "It's way too short. Can't be more than ten feet long and the gap has gotta be twenty."

"I know, but it's a picnic table, it has planks, maybe we can extend it or something." They each grasped an end to pick it up. "Let's tip it over so we can see the bottom."

As soon as they lifted, the table fell into two long halves.

"What the...?" Charlie muttered. He held one side while the other laid on the ground.

The table featured all sorts of intricate bolts and fasteners on its bottom.

Drayden glanced at the steel wall.

Thirty yards away now.

"Catrice!" Drayden shouted. "Can you help? Charlie, you and Sid play around with that one! See if you can unfold it."

That was why the tables were so big and clunky throughout the Initiation. So this one wouldn't stand out. If the tables had been small all along and this one was huge, it would have been obvious. Drayden loosened a bolt on one of the top pieces of the picnic table. He swung the board all the way around, extending it.

The former half-table top was now twice as long, and half as wide. There was a slight kink to the side where the two pieces met.

Charlie watched, and did the same on his half. Catrice undid one of the legs, and folded it down. They loosened, twisted, swung, and extended legs and pieces until each half of the table transformed into a stretched plank. Each one was jagged, narrow, and uneven, but a walkable plank nonetheless. Fully expanded, each reached about twenty-five feet long, and six inches across. More than long enough to reach across the chasm.

"How do we get them across the gap?" Sidney asked.

Drayden pondered it for a moment, both hands atop his hat. "We need to stand them up on their ends, right at the edge, and tip them across. We'll hold the ends firm so they don't fall into the hole when they slam down on the other side."

While Alex and Catrice hung back, Drayden, Sidney, and Charlie lugged the first plank to the edge. They stood it on its end. The plank swayed and wobbled from the wind. All three of them struggled to stabilize it.

"Charlie," Drayden said, "you and Sid hold the bottom. Don't let it slide into the chasm. I'm going to tip it forward."

Drayden gently shoved the board, and then held it the best he could, though it fell too forcefully to slow. It tipped slowly at first, and then accelerated, crashing toward the far side of the platform, like a tree falling in the park. It slammed down with a loud bang, bouncing a few times. Charlie and Sidney held it firm, and it stayed up on the platform. They took the second plank, started ten feet to the right of the first, and repeated the process. Both lengthy, narrow boards granted a precarious path to the other side, with barely over a foot to spare on each end.

While narrow, the boards were quite thick. They should support a person's weight, even in the center. Dashing across without falling off, given the winds, posed an entirely different problem, however. He peered back at the moving wall.

Twenty yards away. Time remaining: *00:03:45, 00:03:44…*

Drayden clapped his hands. "No time to sit and get scared. We have less than four minutes left. We have to go one at a time on each plank, because I don't think they can support more than one person. It's going to be incredibly hot, even like we're burning, but we have to take it. Between the wind and the rickety boards, it'll be hell to balance. We have no choice. Get across any way you can. Crawl if you have to, as long as you get across fast. As soon as you make it, go through that door. Don't wait. Better that some of us pass than nobody. Catrice and Sidney are going first."

Time might run out, and Drayden cared about the girls more than he did Charlie or Alex. Plus, Alex couldn't be trusted to go first.

It would be simple to push the planks into the chasm, leaving the others to die.

"Whoa, whoa, there, cowboy," Alex said. "You can be a hero if you want, but I'm going first."

Drayden balled his hands into fists and got in Alex's face. "You're going last. You've been useless so far. If it wasn't for Catrice, Sid, me, and Charlie, you'd be outside the walls right now." He grabbed Alex by his shirt. "That's it, Alex. End of story. You want to fight me again over it?" Drayden shoved him.

Alex curled his lip and his face turned red. He grunted in anger.

Catrice approached Drayden, her eyes crazed. "I'm scared, Drayden."

He looked her straight in the eyes, and said firmly, "You can do this. Like you've done everything else so far. Crawl on your hands and knees. It's only twenty feet. It'll be over before you know it. Hang on tight, focus on your balance, don't be surprised by a gust of air, and don't look down past the board at the chasm. You've almost made it, Catrice. Don't give up now. This is what you want. Two minutes and you're there." He placed his hands on her cheeks and kissed her forehead, pulling her into a hug.

Sidney hugged Charlie, and they fist bumped each other. She closed her eyes and made the sign of the cross with her right hand. She and Catrice stepped up to the walkways.

"Charlie," Drayden said. "You hold that one, and I'll hold this one. Just to ensure they don't fall off or something."

Charlie nodded. He knelt and secured Sidney's plank.

Catrice glanced back once more, locking eyes with Drayden. She climbed onto the plank on her knees, gripping it tight with her hands. She crawled forward a foot, then screamed.

"What is it?" Drayden asked.

She looked back, crying, breathing rapidly, her eyes crazed. "It's too hot! I'm burning!" she shrieked.

Drayden felt for her. Unfortunately, there was no time. "Go, Catrice! Go. Make it across!"

Smoke swirled, embers of fire flitting through the air like fireflies. Catrice's wispy blonde locks blew wildly to one side as a gust of wind blasted her. She collapsed onto her chest and hugged the plank. She screamed again, freezing five feet out. Sidney fared better. She walked crouched down, on her feet, but balanced using her hands. Her face glowed bright red, and she struggled to breathe between the smoke and wind. Her eyes tearing, she hit the midpoint.

"Catrice! Get up! Keep moving!" Drayden shouted. His eyes watered. While on the platform he could wipe them. Out there, he couldn't without lifting a hand off the board. He glanced back.

The wall continued to advance toward them, now only fifteen yards away.

Catrice propped back up on her knees and crawled slowly, making one movement at a time. Her hair swirled in the turbulent wind. Sidney reached the three-quarter mark. Both girls erupted in coughing fits.

"Attagirl, Sid!" Charlie hollered.

Drayden checked the time.

00:02:15, 00:02:14...

They weren't all going to make it. There wasn't enough time. He and Charlie still had to climb across, and then Alex. Traversing a narrow board, two hundred feet over a raging inferno, wasn't exactly a situation in which you wanted to be rushed.

Sidney finished first. She mouthed something, like she wanted to yell but she couldn't speak. She waved her hands toward herself, motioning at Charlie. She knelt and held the wood beam. Charlie checked with Drayden, who gave him a thumbs-up.

Charlie stepped up on the plank, crouched low on his feet. He held his hands out to the sides for balance. He looked awfully big on that board.

"Charlie!" Drayden warned. "You might want to crawl!"

He clutched the plank with both hands, walking like a monkey would.

Catrice lay on her belly, straddling the plank, sliding herself across now. A few more feet and she'd reach safety. She scooted forward. A strong gust blew just as she began to advance again. She tilted left, rolling.

Drayden gripped the plank tight to ensure it wouldn't spin. He wished he could run out and rescue her, but it was too risky with his extra weight.

"Drayden!" she screamed.

"Catrice, hold on tight! Use your legs to get back up!"

She stretched her right leg, gripping the plank with it. Slowly, she pulled herself back on top. She scooted forward again. One more foot.

She made it across, crawling on her hands and knees. Charlie lurched a quarter of the way across, struggling. His knees wobbled, and he coughed uncontrollably. He still tried to walk, rather than crawl. Every time a strong gust came along he needed to grab the board.

Time was going to be real tight for the boys. Drayden checked the wall and the time.

The wall inched toward him, only ten yards away. Time remaining: *00:01:35, 00:01:34...*

He wiped his eyes. It all came down to this. No fear. He might fail, but he wouldn't lose to himself. If he fell to his death, it would be by a gust of wind, not his own trembling. He refused to be defeated by the Bureau. He simply had to get across. Catrice and Sidney were guaranteed to finish now. He eyed the other side of the gap.

Catrice had not run through the doorway as Drayden suggested. She was holding the plank for him, like Sidney was for Charlie.

Even though crawling was the safest way across, time was expiring. He'd have to walk. He pulled his hat down tight, stepped out onto the plank, and stuck his arms out for balance, like a tightrope walker.

The heat consumed him. His palms burned like they were touching the flames. His face felt like it was melting, his skin searing. Drayden took a step, watching his feet through watery eyes, peripherally noticing the horrific drop below. It looked like Hell indeed.

The plank wobbled.

He lost his balance, but squatted down to regain it.

Smoky wind battered his face from all directions.

Drayden took two brisk steps and paused. He crouched down and grabbed the board for support as it wobbled dangerously. He let go and took three more hurried steps, gripping it once again. His lungs burned, making him hack over and over.

The plank kinked to the right a bit, where one board of the tabletop ended and another began.

Using his hands to traverse that part, Drayden made progress, reaching a quarter of the way across. He glanced at Charlie, who was halfway across now. He couldn't resist a look up at the clock.

Time remaining: *00:01:05, 00:01:04...*

He had to go for it. He took five impetuous steps standing up, his ankle pain flaring up.

The plank wobbled.

He lost his balance, tipping forward. His knees hit the plank first. When his chest hit it, he wrapped his arms around it with all his strength, smacking his face on the board.

"Get up, Drayden. Hurry!" Catrice screamed.

Get up! Now! He scooted his knees forward and propped up on them. He'd reached halfway. Ten feet to go.

The board wobbled violently, but he wasn't moving yet. It sagged.

Drayden peeked behind him.

Alex was walking on Drayden's plank, approaching fast. The moving wall was five feet away from the chasm.

"Alex! What are you doing? Get off! Go on the other one. Charlie will be done any second."

Alex glared at him with crazed eyes and a menacing grin.

Drayden needed to finish, pronto. The plank might not support them both. He watched in horror as Alex moved with reckless abandon, walking perfectly upright. He would surely fall.

But he didn't, and he was gaining on Drayden. The plank sagged further. Both its ends lifted dangerously off the ground. Either one could easily slide off.

"Drayden! Move!" Catrice screamed at the top of her lungs.

Drayden crawled as speedily as he could. Each blustery gust of wind forced him to pause, to brace himself. He could barely see, and he couldn't stop coughing.

Charlie reached the platform. He hustled over to the end of Drayden's plank.

"Catrice!" Drayden shouted between coughs. "Go! Go through the door. Charlie can hold it!"

Their eyes met once more, her face looking pained. She ran to the doorway and just through it, with Sidney right behind her. Both girls were safe.

Drayden checked behind him again.

Alex teetered only five feet away now.

What the hell was he doing? Drayden faced forward and scooted another two feet. He viewed the end of the plank, expecting to see Charlie kneeling, stabilizing it.

He wasn't. His face twisted, his foot on the plank, he appeared on the verge of climbing out there.

Oh God. No.

He was blocking the way, and Alex was coming from behind. They were going to kill him.

Drayden looked at the clock: *00:00:44, 00:00:43...*

He crawled another three feet, stopping to brace for a furious wind gust. Only five feet to go.

"Alex!" Charlie yelled.

Alex yanked Drayden's left foot hard from behind.

His left knee slid off the plank. Before Drayden tumbled into the chasm, he caught the plank with the crook of his right knee. He held on tight with both hands, spinning to his left. He summoned all his strength to keep from rotating. It was no use. He spun all the way around, losing his grip on the plank with his legs. Drayden wound up underneath it, dangling only by his fingertips, facing away from the finish.

No! Don't let go, dammit!

Alex hovered directly above him, seething with rage. "I don't know who's getting that Palace spot, but I know who's *not* getting it." He raised his foot straight up in the air, directly above Drayden's fingers.

Drayden jerked both hands back a few inches. He let go of the plank just long enough to shimmy them out of the way, before Alex's foot stomped them.

Alex's foot slammed down on the board. He crouched down to brace himself against a gust of wind.

"Alex, please! Don't!"

Alex just mocked him, pretending to cry.

Drayden had to fight back. First, he needed to get his legs up. He swung them back and forth, gaining momentum, his adrenaline pumping. He employed every bit of abdominal muscle to thrust them up and wrap them around the plank behind Alex.

Alex tried to stomp his fingers again.

Drayden slid them out of the way, shifting them further down the plank. It was easier this time with his legs gripping it. He was shaking, but his legs were rangy. If he could grab onto the board

with his hands and only one leg, he could free up his other leg to kick Alex's legs out. Doing so might result in Alex's death. Not doing it would guarantee his own.

He flexed his muscles to pull his body snug to the board so his chest touched its bottom.

Alex raised his right foot again to stomp on Drayden's fingers.

Drayden wound his left leg around the plank, freeing his right. He swung it upward at Alex's left leg, which was planted on the board. It connected.

Alex flew up in the air. He crashed onto his butt on the plank, bounced, and slid backward. He caught the board with his hands before falling off. Now *he* dangled, two hundred feet in the air, hanging by his fingertips.

"Charlie! Charlie! Help!" Alex screamed.

Drayden squeezed both legs and his abs to rotate his body back up to the top of the board. "Get out of my way, Charlie!" he roared.

Charlie stepped aside, both hands in his hair, his worried eyes fixed on Alex. "Alex, I'm coming!"

Drayden rose to his feet and took five powerful steps to the end. He collapsed to his knees on the sweet platform. He lifted his head to the clock: *00:00:21, 00:00:20...*

Charlie dove onto the plank on his stomach, scooting toward Alex. "Give me your hand!" Charlie extended his right hand. Alex grabbed it with his left. He released the plank and grabbed it with his right too. Alex's full weight proved too great to support, since Charlie lay atop the narrow board without wrapping his legs around it. Charlie began sliding off, head first. Alex lowered even further, below the point where he could still reach the plank.

"Help!" Alex shouted.

Charlie was toppling over. As his head went over the side he caught the plank with his left arm. He couldn't hold Alex any longer.

Alex fell.

"Charlie!" he screamed one last time as he plummeted. The sound echoed off the sides of the chasm as he plunged two hundred feet to his grisly death.

Drayden's eyes bulged.

"Drayden!" Catrice shrieked.

He turned to her as a gust of wind blew off his hat. He looked up at the clock.

00:00:10, 00:00:09...

He could still make it.

"Drayden! Help me! Please!" Charlie yelled, dangling from the plank by both hands. He'd used his incredible strength to slither down the plank on his fingertips to the platform edge, but he couldn't get up.

Drayden could finish the Initiation, or he could save Charlie. He could not do both. If he saved Charlie, time would run out. He would be exiled. Charlie, the guy who had collaborated with Alex to try to murder him. Was this even a decision? He swiped his hat and turned to run.

As his fingers touched the hat, a powerful vision of his mother materialized in his mind. What would she do? It wasn't even a question. His mother, so brave, so caring, would save Charlie and deal with the consequences. She could never abandon another person to die like that. Charlie would fall, and die a gruesome death.

Drayden wouldn't complete the Initiation after all. He wouldn't achieve the safety he desired, and he wouldn't get to be with Catrice. He would be exiled.

He ran to Charlie, braced himself, and clutched Charlie around the wrists. Charlie was astonishingly heavy, but Drayden pulled with all his strength. Slowly, he hoisted Charlie up.

Charlie helped, thrusting his feet along the platform wall.

"Swing your legs onto the plank," Drayden grunted.

Charlie wrapped his legs around it. He was up, safe.

Still on his hands and knees, Drayden turned his head. His eyes met Catrice's.

A steel gate with bars crashed down, blocking the doorway. Catrice and Sidney stood on the other side.

Time remaining: *00:00:00.*

CHAPTER 24

"**N**o!" Catrice screamed. She burst into tears.

It was over. Drayden had failed. And this time it wasn't a trick by the Bureau.

He sat cross-legged on the platform, holding the green Yankees hat in his hands, examining it. He hoped Mom would be proud. He'd tried his best. Forced to make a split-second decision, he'd chosen to save his enemy from a cruel death rather than complete the Initiation. Had he made the right call? There was no going back.

For perhaps the first time in the Initiation, Mom and Tim would disagree about what he should have done. Tim would be berating Drayden for not running through the finish. He never would have sacrificed himself to save Charlie. Drayden was certain his mom would have. Ultimately, pleasing her was all he ever wished to do.

Now he and Charlie would face exile together. Catrice and Sidney would move up in life, one of them joining the Bureau. A tear rolled down Drayden's cheek.

Catrice sat with her legs tucked up to her chest, her arms wrapped around them, her face buried. Sidney knelt, grasping the gate's bars. She stared at Drayden and Charlie, her mouth open in disbelief.

"Dray," Charlie panted. He crawled over and wrapped his muscular arms around Drayden, hugging him. Charlie's weight overpowered him and they both toppled over. Charlie landed on top of him. "Oh my God, man. Thank you. Thank you so much. You saved my life. I don't even know what to say. I didn't want to die." Charlie laid on Drayden, weeping.

"Get off me!" Drayden said. He pushed Charlie off and sat up.

Charlie sat back on his feet. He looked like a confused little kid whose feelings were hurt. "What?"

"You tried to kill me! You and Alex! Why the hell did I even save you? We're both dead now anyway. We're getting exiled."

"Drayden, no! I swear." Charlie pressed his hands together as if in prayer. "I was coming to *save* you from Alex. I just couldn't climb out there, because the plank couldn't hold all three of us. He was trying to kill you. *He* was. I wanted to stop it. I yelled his name out, and he looked at me, and I shook my head. I was telling him not to do it. I never thought he'd go through with it. I'm sorry. I'm so sorry. You have to believe me!"

Drayden remained skeptical. "What was Alex thinking anyway? What good would it do to kill me? He wouldn't be picked by the Bureau. Even if I died, one of you guys would be selected before him. Plus, the Bureau might exile him for killing someone."

"He was planning to kill everyone except me. Then I would request the Precinct, and by default he would get the Palace. That was his plan. He assumed if he and I were the last ones standing, the Bureau would have to accept him on a technicality. Their rules, at least one person *has* to join the Bureau in the Palace. That's why he was so confident he'd make the Palace."

Charlie shook his head. "He knew it was a gamble, but he knew he had no chance to win by outperforming everybody else. He was gonna attempt to make the deaths look accidental along the way.

I'd been working my butt off to talk him out of it. Told him I wanted no part of it. Turns out it was a lot trickier than he thought. He never really had a chance to get anyone, which is why I never thought he'd come after you at the end. I guess he still hoped to kill you anyway. Exact some revenge for all the stuff he hated you for, and probably for beating him up earlier."

"What a flunk," Drayden said, his face twisted. "Even after we saved him time and again today, he never appreciated it. He never got it." Alex was crazy, a bad kid, and on the surface they hated each other. But Drayden believed that deep down, Alex remembered their old friendship. That he cherished some of the joyful memories from their childhood. Even further down, a good kid existed inside, the one Drayden used to know. Only he didn't. Alex was too damaged, beyond repair. That innocent kid died long ago.

Charlie walked back to the chasm, muttering Alex's name over and over. He peered down it.

Any minute now, Drayden and Charlie would be separated from the girls, and never see them again. Drayden needed to say goodbye. He rose and limped over to the gate.

"Catrice?"

Her eyes red and moist, she jumped to her feet.

Drayden reached his hands through the gate, taking both of hers. She pressed her body up against the bars, and he did the same, wrapping his arms around her. He bent down so he could press his face up against hers, feeling the soft skin of her cheek.

"I'm sorry, Catrice," Drayden said. "I don't know if I did the right thing."

"You did the heroic thing," she said, sniffling. "I think your karma gods are going to protect you for that."

"It's kind of late to tell you now," Drayden said. "But...I wanted... I guess I always wanted—"

A grinding metal noise screeched from above, like gears turning, cutting him off.

The gate began to rise.

Drayden fully embraced Catrice once the gate rose. He'd never hugged anyone like that before. Every inch of their bodies touched. He pulled away, resting his hands on the arch of her lower back. They gazed at each other in silence.

Charlie lumbered over, wiping his eyes. Sidney leapt into his arms, burying her head in his neck. She climbed off Charlie and ran to Drayden. She wrapped her arms around him and kissed his cheek. "Thank you, Drayden. You saved me. You got me through. I knew you would."

"You're welcome," Drayden whispered. "You saved me too, a bunch of times. So thank *you.*"

Charlie squatted down, his eyes fixed on the platform floor. "Alex is gone. Just like that. I know you guys didn't care for him, but he was just misunderstood. He was a scared kid. I couldn't save him." His head drooped.

Drayden was in no way ready to show sympathy to Charlie, or feel bad for Alex. Even if Charlie was telling the truth about his innocence, he still knew about Alex's plot.

Sidney rested her hand on his shoulder. "We're sorry, Charlie. You were a great friend to Alex. What you did, to try and save him, was incredibly brave. You couldn't have done any more."

He placed his hand atop hers and nodded, his eyes glued to the floor. "What now?"

The door led into a narrow hallway, with faint light in the distance.

"I assume they'll separate us any moment," Drayden said. "Me and you are getting exiled, the girls are not. Let's see where this hallway leads."

Drayden caught Catrice's hand. It was magical for a moment to imagine what it would be like to do that, to take her hand and hold it whenever he wished. He relished the touch of her soft skin against his rough hands as they walked. He cherished every last second, memorizing the feel of it.

The hallway spilled them out into an open area, which was the South Ferry Station entrance. Stairs led up to the street above.

The Palace.

Footsteps rumbled. Two Palace Guardians stormed down the stairs with their rifles drawn. Dressed in gray fatigues, both men were young and muscular, with short-cropped haircuts.

"Follow us," the taller one said.

The pledges exchanged wary looks.

As they ascended the stairs into the sunlight, Drayden shielded his eyes. He needed a moment to adjust to the light, having been underground so long.

The mid-afternoon sun painted their first ever view of the Palace. They stood in an expansive plaza, surrounded by a few tall buildings, a particularly eerie one behind them. The massive structure consisted entirely of green glass panels, many shattered. A decrepit sign on the front of the building in giant letters read "Stat—n Isl—nd Fe—ry." A few people were walking around, but not many. Overall, it appeared similar to the Dorms.

"This is the Palace?" Sidney asked. "Looks like Thirty-Fourth Street."

"Nobody lives or works in this part," one of the Guardians said. "This way." He gestured toward the street, where a miniature bus idled by the curb.

Unlike the electric buses in the Dorms, this one had no windows, and was painted white with a red cross on the side. As they approached, the back doors swung open. Several doctors and nurses

stepped out, sporting their telltale scrubs. Two of them greeted each pledge.

A woman with red hair and freckles greeted Drayden with a warm smile. "Hi, Drayden, my name is Molly. This is Manny," she said, pointing to the chubby, dark-skinned guy next to her. "Come inside, we're going to make you feel better." She guided him inside the bus and laid him down on a stretcher.

Drayden's wrecked body throbbed everywhere. He craned his neck, searching for Catrice, to make sure they were still together.

She, Sidney, and Charlie all lay on stretchers too. The Guardians entered, and the bus started to move.

Drayden latched on to Molly's sleeve. "Why are you taking care of me if I'm being exiled? What's going on? Where are we going?"

"I'm sorry," Molly said, her eyes softening. "We were just told to take care of you. That's all I know. We're taking you to a hospital."

"Where are we going after that?"

One of the Guardians stepped forward. "Stop asking so many questions," he barked. "She doesn't know. You'll find out when you find out."

Molly held up a syringe. "I'm going to give you something that will reduce your pain and relax you," Molly said. "Look at the wall for me."

Drayden turned away. Something pinched his arm, and instantly his entire body sank a few inches lower into the bed. His pain dulled, his body relaxed, and he tingled inside. After that moment, everything was a blur. Molly knew about all his injuries without asking. She iced and wrapped his ankle, and rubbed ointment on wounds to his face, head, back, hands, and legs. Manny gave him a banana and an icy pink drink.

After arriving at the hospital, Molly wheeled Drayden to a room by himself. A woman named Doctor Spencer secured his ankle in a soft cast, treated his wounds further, and gave him medication.

A nurse called Bob gave him a sponge bath and hooked him up with new clothes. Drayden's head was foggy, but not too much to notice the hospital facility and medical care that was vastly superior to what the Dorms offered. He dozed off a few times. Eventually, a Guardian led him back outside onto the sidewalk, which was draped in elongated shadows from the late afternoon sun. The other pledges waited outside already, all dressed the same in red polyester track suits.

Why was the Bureau addressing his medical needs if he was being exiled? It didn't make any sense. He hobbled over to the others.

Catrice and Sidney greeted him with hugs. Charlie spread his arms wide, and before Drayden could refuse, Charlie pulled him into an embrace.

Charlie released Drayden and beheld his outfit. "Well, don't we look cool? What are we, joining the Bureau track team? This thing's redder than a nun's cheeks at a peepshow."

"Drayden, what's going on?" Sidney asked.

"I have no idea," Drayden said. "It's pretty clear you and Catrice made it, and me and Charlie didn't. I don't understand why they bothered to treat us. I thought we'd be gone by now."

A small black bus with darkened windows pulled up. One of the Guardians slid the door open. "Get in."

Drayden marveled at all the different vehicles in the Palace. As they drove, more people packed the streets. Unlike the expansive, precise grid in the Dorms, the narrow streets here zigzagged in odd directions. After a short drive, the bus stopped. A Guardian outside opened the door. "Get out."

Drayden exited the bus first. He faced a massive stone building, built like a fortress, the few windows covered with iron bars. As he surveyed the area, his jaw dropped.

The Palace was immaculate. Some of the buildings showed the same wear and tear as those in the Dorms, but everything was clean. People dressed in better-fitting clothing that varied in color. Vendors sold goods from actual storefronts, not makeshift stands on the sidewalk. Across the way, people sat leisurely at tables, eating, and sipping from tea cups.

"Equality, my butt," Charlie grumbled.

The stone building crawled with Palace Guardians outside. Above the door, etched in the stone, it read, "Federal Reserve Bank of New York."

"Follow me," the Guardian said. They walked up steps and through the doors, which were flanked by other Guardians.

Inside, Guardians patted them down and granted them entry through another set of doors. The building was stunning, like a medieval castle inside. It featured white, tan, and gold stone walls, soaring archways, and polished tile floors, some of them mosaics.

Drayden had never seen anything like it. "Is this the Bureau headquarters?" he asked.

"Yes," the Guardian said. "No more questions." The Guardian led them to an elevator bank and pushed a button, which lit up.

"The elevators *work*?" Charlie asked.

The Guardian didn't answer. No elevators worked in the Dorms. Charlie giggled as the elevator climbed. It deposited them in a seemingly endless hallway, lined with Guardians. Their guide led them down the hallway to a broad, dark wood door, flanked by two enormous Guardians on each side. One of them knocked on the door.

It opened from the inside.

Premier Eli Holst stood before them.

CHAPTER 25

Eli Holst's mouth spread into a terrifying grin. In his broadcasts, he wore a drab gray suit, but today he wore a tailored black one. Sweat beaded on his over-tanned forehead and nose. He eyed the pledges through his trademark round glasses, which made his eyes appear too big for his face.

"Welcome, children!" he said, as if he were greeting his own long-lost family. "Please, come in. Sit down." He led them to four chairs facing a desk in a gigantic office. The burliest of the Guardians joined them in the room, standing against the closed door. The pledges all sat.

Even the grandeur of the lobby didn't prepare Drayden for this office, which was the most spectacular room he'd ever seen. It was the polar opposite of the barren office from which Holst delivered his broadcasts. All the furniture was dark polished wood, the cushions and curtains red velvet. Every instrument, like the pen on Holst's desk, was adorned in gold.

Holst stood facing them, his hands clasped in front of his body. "I want to congratulate you on a superb performance in the Initiation. Truly, superb."

He raised a finger in the air. "Now, I know you're eager to understand what's going on, particularly Drayden and Charlie.

We'll be getting to that. I need to set the context first, and I believe you'll want to hear it." He paused for a moment. "Nobody's finished the Initiation in eight years. And this was the toughest one yet." He stared at Drayden. "Contrary to what your father believes, Drayden, the Initiation is very real, not a trap."

Heat flushed Drayden's cheeks. How could he know what Dad said?

"Having said that, this year's *was* different," Holst continued, addressing everyone again. "Not just because of the increased difficulty. Because we were looking for something special." He paced, his arms crossed. "As you know, we believe the two most critical human characteristics, from a societal view, are intelligence and bravery. We have proof. These traits saved New America after the Confluence, through the brilliance of the scientists and the courage of the Guardians. Therefore, the Initiation tests for those qualities. We have you test in groups because usually those traits are mutually exclusive in individuals. Some of you will be intelligent, some will be brave, but it's rare to find one person who excels in both. Participating as a group, you can lean on each other's strengths, depending on the challenge."

Holst stopped in front of Drayden, peering down at him. "Despite your slow start, Drayden, you displayed an impressive aptitude for both."

Drayden fought off a smile, fixing his eyes on the floor. His mind was a jumbled mess. He hated Holst, and the wicked Bureau. Holst exiled his mother and killed his best friend. He'd just put the pledges through hell, and the reward awaiting Drayden after all this was exile. But damn, he was still a sucker for flattery.

Holst leaned against his desk. "For your Initiation, we were searching for additional characteristics, because we had a specific assignment in mind for whoever finished. We looked for resourcefulness, teamwork, selflessness, creativity, critical thinking, and—

for lack of a better word—clutchness. In addition to the Initiation Council, a team of psychologists analyzed you throughout every second of the Initiation. Every decision, every conflict." He scowled at Charlie. "Every joke." He turned his gaze to the whole group, smiling wryly. "Every sign of affection."

The pledges all shifted uncomfortably in their seats.

Holst straightened and stepped in front of them. His expression grew serious, the corners of his mouth turned down. "So here it is. All four of you will be joining the Bureau."

Drayden sat bolt upright. *What?* His jaw dropped. He wanted to shout out. He snapped his head toward Catrice.

She beamed with joy, smiling ear to ear at him, her eyebrows raised. She wiped fresh tears from her eyes.

"Yeah!" Charlie hollered. He leaned forward and pumped his fist at Drayden.

Sidney bounced up and down in her seat, giggling.

Holst held his hands up at them. "It was Drayden's selfless act to save Charlie at the end that guaranteed it. While finishing the Initiation, or not, is clear cut, our decision on your placement is highly subjective. Had he not done that, only one of you would have joined the Bureau. Except he did, proving the four of you, as a team, are exactly what we're looking for. And so, here you are," he said, spreading his arms out wide. Holst's face twisted into a smile.

Relief smothered Drayden like a warm blanket. He sank down into the chair. The Bureau was cruel and evil, but perhaps the tiniest bit merciful as well. Instead of exiling him as they should, they bent the rules and showed humaneness. As usual, Catrice was right. The karma gods had his back. Having things work out the way they should, like the unwritten rules of the universe remained in order, delivered the ultimate satisfaction. He wasn't going to die. He'd get to be with Catrice *and* Sidney. Wesley and Dad would move to the

Palace. He could find out the truth about Mom. It was the greatest moment of Drayden's life. For just a second, he wanted to savor it.

I did it.

He'd doubted himself, but he came through in the end. So many people had believed in him, and he didn't let them down.

The smile faded from Holst's face, along with any other trace of hospitality. He cocked his head. "There is, however, a catch."

Drayden swallowed hard. He exchanged a nervous glance with the others.

Holst licked his lips. "Your Initiation is not quite over."

Drayden's stomach sank.

Holst stood behind his desk, leaning on the chair. "You see, New America has a problem, and you are going to help us solve it." He paused, letting the news sink in. "Despite my own efforts to plan for the quarantine of New America before the Confluence, even I did not foresee the quarantine would last forever. Even if I had, I don't believe I could have done much more."

"Except maybe bring in some cotton plants," Charlie muttered under his breath.

Holst glowered at him, the cotton a well-known sore spot. He opened his top desk drawer and pulled something out, keeping it hidden in his hand. "The problem is this." He raised his hand. In it, he held a small battery, like the ones in their flashlights. "Power storage."

He paused again, scanning the eyes of the pledges. "The wind turbines and solar cells rely on what's called deep-cycle batteries. They store immense amounts of energy and last decades. Unfortunately, they don't last forever. They've lasted a generation, but they're wearing out, as we always knew they would. The solar cells themselves are wearing out too. New America doesn't have the mineral resources to produce new batteries in any meaningful size. Without power, we can't grow food or produce clean water. Every person in New America will die. This is happening now. Six of the

forty-four wind turbines are no longer usable. We may have a year or two. Or less. It's only a matter of time until they all go down."

Holst dropped the battery back in the drawer and walked back in front of the pledges. He folded his hands in front of him. "The time has come to launch an expedition outside the walls. To attempt to achieve direct contact with another civilization. And you, children, will lead it."

Drayden drew in a quick breath. *No!*

Catrice, Sidney, and Charlie stared at Holst with shocked faces.

What about our families? Drayden thought.

"Everything I said earlier stands," Holst said. "You *are* Bureau members. When you've accomplished your mission, you will return to the Bureau not just as members, but as heroes. The saviors of the world. Your families will still move here as promised. This is not a punishment. You represent New America's best chance of survival."

Drayden shook his head in disgust. What a load of shkat. He seriously doubted a few sixteen-year-olds were civilization's best chance at survival. The Bureau probably didn't care to risk people who truly were valuable to them, like the scientists.

Holst walked behind his desk, pulled his chair out, and sat. "Here is what's going to happen. You will be given lovely new accommodations in the Palace. For the next week, you will rest and heal. You will spend the following week receiving training. You will be trained in weaponry and other survival techniques by the Guardians. You will study with the scientists. They'll teach you everything we know about the world outside the walls, and all our endeavors to contact other civilizations. You'll meet the elite team of Guardians that will accompany you on your journey. Their mission is solely to protect you. Make no mistake. You are in charge. They will be taking orders from you."

Holst used a handkerchief to buff an antique gold telephone on his desk. "You will receive every safeguard we have, including the latest advances in vaccinating against Aeru. We've made excellent

progress. Unlike the freshly exiled who pound at the gates, you will be allowed back into New America. Provided you haven't contracted the illness, of course. In limited quantities, we have the ability to test for its presence. Your families will move to the Palace the day you depart, so you can see them. We will notify them immediately that you have completed the Initiation." He looked up. "I'm sure they're worried."

Drayden's head spun at all the information Holst dumped on them. The Bureau had an Aeru vaccine? He'd have to wait two weeks, but he'd get to see Wesley and Dad. That would give him only two weeks to investigate the exile.

Holst rose and stood before them. "Any questions?"

Catrice raised her hand.

"Yes, Catrice?"

"Can you please not notify my family?" she asked. "And I don't want them to be moved here." She glanced at Drayden before casting her eyes down.

Charlie and Sidney looked stunned.

Drayden recalled what she'd told him. She'd hinted at past abuse.

"As you wish," Holst said. "Anything else?"

Nobody replied.

Holst clapped his hands together. "In the meantime, please enjoy your time in the Palace. A rep from the Initiation Council will set you up in your new apartments, give you money to spend, and arrange for daily nursing visits to treat your injuries. Thank you. And congratulations again." He walked to his desk.

The Guardian opened the door, and the other pledges stood up to leave.

Drayden rubbed the hat in his hands, thinking of his mom. Who knew if he'd ever have a chance to speak directly to the Premier again? He wanted to inquire about her exile, but surely Holst himself wouldn't know anything about it. Drayden needed to start

making connections. He could only think of one place to begin: the Bureau rep for the Dorms.

"Is it possible to meet with Thomas Cox?" Drayden asked.

Holst stopped in his tracks. Before turning around, he motioned for the Guardian to close the door again. He spun around and marched right up to Drayden, standing so close he almost stepped on his feet. "And why would you want to meet with Thomas Cox?"

Sidney, Charlie, and Catrice awkwardly sat back down.

Holst's reaction raised Drayden's heart rate. Cox was plotting to overthrow Holst. Drayden knew about it. He should have assumed that Holst might know something about it as well. "I-I just thought it might be nice for us to see a familiar face. He was our Bureau rep in the Dorms. Maybe he could tell us about how things are back in our former home." Drayden thought it was a reasonable explanation.

Holst remained silent, studying him.

He suspected Holst was a master at reading people. You didn't become Premier and hold onto it for twenty-five years without being able to delve beneath the surface, to read between the lines.

Holst's demeanor softened. "Thomas Cox was executed. This morning, in fact."

Drayden's mouth dried out. "*Executed*? Why?"

"For conspiring to overthrow the Bureau. You wouldn't know anything about that, would you, Drayden?"

Drayden's heart pounded so hard he feared Holst would hear it. "Me? No, not at all."

"I see. Well, we'll have a new Bureau rep for the Dorms this week. Whoever that is, I'm certain you can meet with them. Congratulations again on your performance. Get some well-deserved rest." Holst turned to walk away, motioning for the Guardian to open the door again.

Drayden contemplated everything he'd learned in the Initiation. This moment probably offered his only chance to challenge

Holst. Since he would be sent outside the walls anyway, what did he have to lose?

"Excuse me, Premier Holst? I have another question," Drayden said, his voice firm.

Holst sat in his chair, now clearly irritated. "Yes?"

"We've only been in the Palace a short time," Drayden said. "But from the little I've seen, the Palace offers a high standard of living. Compared to the Dorms, food is more abundant; people appear healthier; they dress in nicer clothes; it's cleaner.... How is that fair? Doesn't that run counter to your claims of equality?"

Catrice and Sidney stared at Drayden with bulging eyes. Charlie made a face and slowly shook his head.

Holst rose, and strolled over to Drayden. "I think I'm beginning to understand your true interest in meeting with Thomas Cox. You know, it's not too late to change my mind about your exile." He looked at Drayden with piercing eyes.

Drayden glared right back, never dropping his gaze. *Don't back down.* "I think you need me to lead that expedition."

Holst smirked.

Drayden was right, and Holst knew it.

"You're just a child, Drayden. You didn't live through the Confluence. I spend every day of my life striving to apply its lessons. You didn't witness the growing cries of inequality that played a major role in destroying the world. We gave the people what they wanted. Equality. A flat societal structure. Quite frankly, we had no other option, because our world offered nothing. Assets, wealth, all suddenly meaningless."

Holst held a finger in the air again. "Then things began to change. A few very smart scientists figured out how to purify water from that swamp in the Hudson River. Other brilliant ones devised a modern sewage system. The Guardians protected everyone from chaos. Should we not have rewarded them? Would it have been fairer *not*

to reward them? We didn't have much to give, but we gave what few perks we had. An extra meal, a better apartment. After all, if a person could solve water purification, what else could they figure out, if properly motivated? Maybe curing the fatal illness caused by Aeru. Or building a solar airplane to establish contact outside our world."

Holst rolled his eyes. "Of course, Dorm residents started protesting all over again about inequality, forcing us to build walls between the zones to protect everyone. They failed to understand that incentives are how civilizations are driven to advance. If we gave what little extra food we had to all the janitors of New America, would that be more fair? Would that propel civilization forward? Why would the brilliant minds in our world bother to apply them if they received nothing for their accomplishments? What if people incapable of advancing civilization received the spoils themselves? Would you call that equality?

"Didn't you, Drayden, believe you deserved to join the Bureau because you solved most of the problems in the Initiation? While Alex, who contributed little, did not? Is that so different?"

Drayden scoffed. That was totally different. Alex didn't...he felt...no, it was just...Drayden exhaled, his eyes downcast. Holst was right. It *was* the same.

Holst continued. "The problem is this. Human beings, in terms of basic human rights, are all created equal, yes. But from the perspective of human *society*, humans are not equal. Some add more value than others. I didn't make it this way; it's just a fact of life. What you call inequality, I call equality. You complain about inequality, and I tell you there are no easy solutions to it. I wish New America overflowed with food so no citizen would ever go to bed hungry. It doesn't, forcing us to divide it in the most beneficial way for New America. I believe we do that, as unfair as you shallowly think it is. Leaving people no chance to earn their way out of their birth zone was indeed unfair, but we've solved that with the Initiation."

Holst veered from logical to delusional. Despite the Bureau's advertised incentive for the Initiation—securing a job in the government—the existence of the Initiation itself implied inequality in New America's zones. In theory, the Initiation addressed that obvious inequity. Except barely anyone entered, and Holst himself said nobody had passed in eight years. In Holst's mind, offering the Initiation was enough. It was irrelevant that people chose not to enter and did not pass.

Holst leaned against the front of his desk. "The Confluence taught us that the population must be commensurately sized with its resource supply. Since you enjoy mathematics, Drayden, consider the following. A world with five people, who each require five eggs per day to survive, but in which only twenty eggs are produced daily. If divided equally, each person would receive four eggs per day and everyone would die. Alternatively, if you exile one person, the remaining four would receive their five daily eggs and survive. If you have a limited food supply, and ours is diminishing due to the failing power storage, the only solution is to shrink the population to the right size, or we risk everybody dying.

"The exiles are a travesty. I have no illusions about that. Once reaching the conclusion that it must be done, whom should we exile? The head scientist working on an alternative approach to fighting bacterial infections? Would that be best for New America? Perhaps it makes more sense to exile those in the Dorms. You think I'm a monster, but I'm trying to save the world. I thought you were intelligent, Drayden. Don't make me change my mind about you."

Drayden lowered his eyes. He couldn't win this debate. Holst had spent his entire life contemplating equality. He offered intelligent, logical arguments, but it didn't feel right. Everyone's lives mattered. There had to be a better way.

"Now, please, if you will, go get some food and some rest," Holst said, returning to his desk.

It was time to go. The Guardian approached them this time, forcing Drayden and the others out of their chairs. He escorted them out of the room.

A cool breeze chilled Drayden's face. The view from the rooftop terrace at Seventy-Five Wall Street astonished him, even at night. With the lights still on, New America glowed, granting a magical view all the way up to the Dorms. The full moon provided enough light to glimpse into the former Brooklyn and even Queens, where Mom grew up.

"How nice are the rooms?" Charlie asked nobody in particular. "Makes my old apartment look like a dump."

Each of them had received adjacent apartments. The rooms were clean, and expansive. Once a hotel, each apartment had been outfitted with kitchens.

"How much of that food did you guys eat when you got inside?" Sidney asked.

"I ate all the eggs right away," Charlie said.

The Bureau had stocked their kitchens with food, of far superior quality and quantity than the weekly Dorm allocation. They'd also included items never seen in the Dorms, like ice cream, pickles, and cookies.

Drayden hadn't reflected much yet on the task before them, and nobody had discussed it. They were being railroaded into doing a job nobody else would do, with no choice in the matter. Anyone else smart or strong enough to undertake such a journey was too valuable to the Bureau to sacrifice. While he didn't trust Holst, the more Drayden mulled it over, his portrayal of the situation was logical. Thomas Cox had been aware of a secret power problem resulting in forced exiles. It fit perfectly with Holst's claims of failing power storage. Even the Palace didn't offer the safety Drayden imagined.

New America would die out unless someone did something about it. Why not them? They could die on the expedition, but they could die staying in the Palace too. At least he would have the opportunity to solve it himself. He wasn't afraid to do so. After surviving the Initiation, it was hard to imagine anything would scare him again.

The real silver lining was Mom. During Drayden's short time in the Palace, he was going to find out who was responsible for her exile. If she was alive outside the walls, he was going to find her. When the Bureau exiled her, they made the critical mistake of underestimating a son's love for his mother.

"You guys ready for this?" Drayden asked.

"Not really," Sidney said. "I wish we could just stay here, like they promised."

"Well," Drayden said, "now we know it's no longer safe, even here." He faced the three of them. "I was upset too when Holst told us, and it's not fair that we have no choice, but I don't think this is the worst thing. Would you rather be sitting here helpless, hoping someone else can figure this out before we run out of food? Wondering when that'll happen? You guys have witnessed what we can do when we work together. We're a great team, like Holst said."

"Yeah, man," Charlie said, "I'm with you. It's like an adventure. We get to see what's outside the walls. I want to shoot some guns too. Maybe we'll even become famous. They'll be writing about us in the history books."

"You spend a lot of time reading those history books, Charlie?" Drayden asked, smirking.

"Oh yeah, all the time," Charlie said. "Me and Alex used to sit around reading about the Revolutionary War to each other." He giggled.

"I'm sorry about Alex," Drayden said somberly. "Even though you guys tried to kill me and all, I know how it feels to lose your best friend."

Charlie made a face. "Is this going to be one of those things where every time you talk to me you're going to remind me of that time I almost murdered you? I swear, Dray, I would never do that, or be a part of that. You're my boy."

"I'm just messing with you, Charlie."

Catrice stood close, grinning at Drayden. She looked absolutely radiant, glowing.

Drayden smiled back. He wouldn't get to test out his theory that the pressure and isolation of the Initiation solely drove both girls' sudden interest in him. That once they returned to normal life, they would forget about him again. There would be no return to normal life. The expedition would force the girls into another similar circumstance with him. This time around, he knew them better, particularly Catrice. He'd seen her at her best, and her worst. He knew what frightened her and what didn't. Inside that quiet, petite, frail body lived a strong, smart, fascinating girl who enthralled him. Her physical beauty was merely a bonus at this point. He didn't want to get his hopes up, but she seemed to care about him too. He wasn't alone after all.

Catrice took Drayden's hand and dragged him away.

Drayden peeked back.

Charlie and Sidney were watching them, looking surprised. Sidney frowned.

Catrice rounded a corner of the deck behind part of the building, hidden from view. She stopped, released his hand, and faced him. She placed her hands on Drayden's hips and pushed him gently back against the wall. She rested her hands on his chest and nestled her cheek between them, closing her eyes.

Drayden's heart raced. Could she feel that? Did she know how nervous he was? He wrapped his arms around her back, pulling her even closer, feeling her body heat against his.

Catrice's silky hair smelled like flowers. She raised her eyes to his, their faces only an inch apart.

Drayden noticed a few freckles he hadn't seen before.

"Drayden, I've been watching you at school for a long time too." She smiled, and tucked her hair behind her ears. "I never followed you around in the hallways, but I always admired how smart you were."

Drayden's jaw dropped. "You knew about me following you?"

"It was hard not to notice, especially that time everything fell out of your backpack."

Drayden chuckled. "Damn. Tim used to tease me about that a lot."

She laughed too and bit her lower lip.

They stared into each other's eyes in the awkward silence after that. Sweat greased Drayden's palms. They were so close he smelled her breath, which was minty and fresh. He panicked.

My God, how is my breath?

Catrice wrapped her arms around his neck and stood on her tippy toes. She leaned in. They both tilted their heads the same way, bumped noses, and laughed. They tried again. Their lips met this time.

An electric current ran through Drayden's whole body. Her lips were so soft, and moist. He placed his hand behind her head, pulling her further into the kiss. Warmth spread through to his limbs. He couldn't get enough. He savored every moment. Eventually they pulled back and held each other.

Drayden looked up to the sky. It was a strange moment to think of Tim. But Tim would always be with him, and Mom too. Even when they're gone, the ones you love never truly leave. Somewhere up there Tim was watching, going crazy cheering for him.

He finally got that first kiss.

Tonight only, Drayden would allow himself to bask in the glory of finishing the Initiation. For tomorrow, another harrowing journey would begin.

ACKNOWLEDGMENTS

I always thought writing a novel would be a solitary effort. But this book would have been impossible without the help of so many people. To everyone who was there to support me along the way: Please know how greatly I appreciate you.

A few deserve special thanks:

Anthony Ziccardi, for believing in me. All the amazing people at Permuted Press: Michael Wilson, Devon Brown, and Maddie Sturgeon, to name just a few. Editors Felicia Sullivan and Ethan Blackbird, without whom my writing would have been far clunkier. My editors Maya Rock and Deborah Halverson, who massaged this story into something worth reading. Christiana Sciaudone, Kristen Holt Browning, and Deneen Howell for all their invaluable editorial input. The team at Simon and Schuster for getting my book out into the world.

The Initiation would still be a .docx file on my computer without Dr. Erika Schwartz and Dr. Karen Kieserman.

A fist-bump to my young adult beta readers: Jack Babu, Samantha Miller, Sydney Miller, Taylor Manett, and Jay Gupta. Much gratitude to attorney Jesseca Salky, photographer Greg Berg, cover designer Ryan Truso, and artist Ivan Zamyslov.

I reserve my greatest thanks for my wife Michelle, daughter Lily, and parents Susan and Suresh. Your support means everything.

One final shout-out to the New York MTA and my fellow strap-hangers, without whom the story of a hellish journey through the subway might never have been conceived.

ABOUT THE AUTHOR

Chris Babu has always had a thing for young adult books. He's also a math and science geek, with a math degree from MIT. For nineteen years, he worked as a bond trader on Wall Street, riding the subway to and from work every day. Now he writes full-time, always with his trusted assistant Buddy, a 130-pound Great Dane who can usually be found on his lap. They split their time between New York City and the east end of Long Island, where their omnipresence at home drives his wife Michelle and daughter Lily crazy. *The Initiation* is Chris's first novel.